There's never been a day when there haven't been stories in **Amalie Berlin**'s head. When she was a child they were called daydreams, and she was supposed to stop having them and pay attention. Now when someone interrupts her daydreams to ask, 'What are you doing?' she delights in answering, 'I'm working!'

Lucy Clark is actually a husband-and-wife writing team. They enjoy taking holidays with their children, during which they discuss and develop new ideas for their books using the fantastic Australian scenery. They use their daily walks to talk over characterisation and fine details of the wonderful stories they produce, and are avid movie buffs. They live on the edge of a popular wine district in South Australia with their two children, and enjoy spending family time together at weekends.

From as soon as **Melanie Milburne** could pick up a pen she knew she wanted to write. It was when she picked up her first Mills & Boon at seventeen that she realised she wanted to write romance. Five submissions later she sold her first book and is now a multi-published, bestselling, award-winning *USA Today* author. In 2008 she won the Australian Readers' Association most popular category/ series romance, and in 2011 she won the prestigious Romance Writers of Australia R*BY award.

Melanie loves to hear from her readers via her website, www. melaniemilburne.com.au, or on Facebook: www.facebook.com/ melanie.milburne

The Doctor Will See You Now

AMALIE BERLIN
LUCY CLARK
MELANIE MILBURNE

MILLS & BOON

First Published in Great Britain 2018
by Mills & Boon, an imprint of HarperCollins*Publishers*
1 London Bridge Street, London, SE1 9GF

THE DOCTOR WILL SEE YOU NOW © 2018 Harlequin Books S. A.

Return of Dr Irresistible © 2014 Amalie Berlin
Dr Perfect on Her Doorstep © 2014 Anne Clark & Peter Clark
Flirting With The Socialite Doc © 2014 Melanie Milburne

ISBN: 978-0-263-26802-7

05-0618

MIX
Paper from
responsible sources
FSC® C007454

This book is produced from independently certified FSC™ paper to ensure responsible forest management.

For more information visit: www.harpercollins.co.uk/green

Printed and bound in Spain
by CPI, Barcelona

RETURN OF DR IRRESISTIBLE

AMALIE BERLIN

To my little brother Seth, a great writer whose name will be on the front of a book before long. He who read my first book (even though it's a romance) and promotes my new releases to the point that my secret identity is no longer secret with my family (doh!).
If I end up on the prayer chain for acts of text-based naughtiness it's all his fault.

To my editor, Laurie Johnson. She's either very brave or she's got a heck of a poker face. This was our first book together and she didn't even hesitate when I emailed to let her know: 'I WANT TO WRITE A MEDICAL ROMANCE SET AT THE CIRCUS! YAY!'
Nerves. Of. Steel.

CHAPTER ONE

FOR TEN YEARS Dr. Reece Keightly had been dreading this night.

He'd known it would come to this. Of course he'd known. It was all on his shoulders—the dynasty, the future of the company and the weight of the past. Two centuries of history all ending with him.

The tenth-generation owner of Keightly Circus was the one who would tear it all down. Nice round number, ten. Like Fate had decreed it. Like he was just filling the role assigned to him. Like it wasn't his fault.

Except it was. That's how they'd see it.

Reece took a step forward, shuffling with the crowded line to the ticket booth. The traditional last annual stop of the circus was always Atlanta due to its proximity to where they summered, but it was also the best crowd. The local, hometown circus returning triumphant from a season on the road, played out the last week near home. Traditional, like so many other things with his family's circus. Keightly's prided themselves on tradition.

Due to the coverage given to the impending closing— local television and radio stations had blared the news for weeks—they were enjoying record crowds for the last performances. For Atlantans, parents had been coming with their children for generations. Another tradition that would be violated after this year.

As excited as he was to see the show—and he never lost that excitement—the prospect of seeing people he cared for putting their lives in danger built in him a kind of extreme awareness of the world around him. It slowed things down, pulled him out of himself, and amplified every ounce of fear until it became a physical sensation, the taste of cold metal on the back of his tongue and he couldn't swallow past it.

Excited terror. He almost longed for ignorance, to be just one of the crowd, another random person in line who only knew the fantasy. But Reece knew the horror too.

All around him children giggled and chattered happily. Ahead, inside the massive blue tent, the band tuned up, readying to start the show, and every note amplified the dread eating at him. The sawdust awaited him. A tradition he could do without.

Dwelling on the unpleasant details wouldn't help him deal with them better. Shut it down. He just needed to see this show. One last time, make certain he was making the right decision. Not that he had any real doubts, but two hundred years deserved one last think. One last chance for them to change his mind.

Two people away from the ticket counter, he heard the first slow whistles of the calliope wheezing through the lot. Soon the ancient steam-powered contraption blanketed the area in sound—cheerful music silenced his chaotic thoughts.

He'd always loved the old calliope, but in the wake of those first warbling notes a surge of homesickness slammed into him. Nostalgia so strong it was like overlapping two realities—belonging and alienation, comfort and terror, peace and anger.

He latched on to the last emotion. Anger was better. He could do this—be angry enough to drown out the rest. But he should at least be honest with himself—he wanted to be there if for no other reason than to see her perform. He wanted to see them all, but the promise of Jolie Bohannon in the spotlight would see him through.

He just needed to see the show one more time. Everything would be fine.

Say goodbye.

Purge the sawdust from his blood, and all the rest of it. One last time.

Then he'd take care of everyone. See them settled. And go back to his safe and orderly life. Find a place to build his practice. Buy a home with a foundation beneath it. He could have people relying on him for their health—it's what he'd been raised to do—but not while he had to stand by and watch them put their lives in jeopardy to make people cheer.

Out of the corner of his eye he caught his first glimpse of the steam-powered calliope rolling across the lot. His mother sat at the back, playing the piano-like keyboard that operated the old steam whistles, while Mack Bohannon drove the carriage.

Jolie's family had traveled with Keightly Circus since before the Civil War. They might as well be family for real, and soon there would be a link when his mother married Mack and left Reece as the last Keightly standing.

Not yet ready to be seen, Reece pulled down the brim of his fedora, hunching his shoulders like that would make him stand out less. Keightly men grew tall. Every one well over six feet. But nobody expected him to be here tonight, and he didn't know how they'd react to his presence. He wanted to just be an observer.

He had a right to be angry. Reece harbored no illusions, though—if this were a movie, he'd be wearing black and twirling a weird mustache in the corner. Only villains closed circuses… Even if he was making the right call for the right reasons, something beloved was dying. Making the death of the circus quick rather than letting it limp along on life support was a kindness.

If he wasn't going to take the reins, if he wasn't going to step up as the last Keightly and lead, he had to take care of laying the show to rest. And he would do that. With the respect and honor it deserved.

But first he'd see one last show and say goodbye on his own.

And maybe somewhere along the way he'd find a way of convincing himself he wasn't a monster.

Jolie Bohannon stood at the back of the tent, holding Gordy's leash. The miniature white stallion always had to be held back until it was absolutely time for him to enter the ring. He lived to perform, a feeling she could once have identified with. It was still there—in theory—but she had other important responsibilities to handle now. Like making sure the full-sized mounts and the Bohannon Trick-riders didn't accidentally trample Gordy because someone let him off his leash too soon. Calm and orderly, that's how everything and everyone stayed safe.

She listened for the change in the music—everyone in the circus learned to gauge where the performance was by the music—and adjusted Gordy's flashy silver bridle and the wee matching and no less flashy saddle. His costume.

At the first trumpet, she unclipped his harness and reached for the tent flap, barely getting her hand in before he barreled through the flap and down the causeway. She stepped through in time to see him enter the ring. Darting between the other horses ridden by the Bohannon Trick-riders, he stopped dead center, reared on his back legs to stretch to his tallest—four feet and some change—and whinnied.

One by one, the other horses in the ring bowed to him,

the little king. The little clown to end the act, the segment of the horse act that reached out to the children and in the audience, drew them in, and got their minds away from the scary excitement of moments before. Jolie smiled. Gordy could still make her smile.

The show was almost over. One more act and then the finale.

She stepped back outside, listening and watching the bustle of the crew getting ready to change the ring for the next act.

Watching the show was a little too much for her right now. She never let her emotions get out of control. Never. But with the circus closing down for good, emotions she'd long ago buried seemed closer to the surface. The last thing she needed was for something to set her off. Watching the show, getting sentimental and weepy over the last performances? Would interfere with her job. Everyone had a job to do and they'd do it with or without her, but she had to hold up her end. That meant right now she had to stand here and wait while Gordy played the fool and the crew changed the set, but she didn't have to watch the well-oiled machine.

The music stopped suddenly, snapping Jolie's attention back to the present. In a well-oiled machine, the music never stopped for no reason.

A cold feeling crept up over the back of her head. That emotion could never be buried or ignored. But fear could be used.

Cries had barely begun rising from the crowd before Jolie was inside the tent, running toward the ring. There she found her family off their mounts, surrounding something.

Where was Gordy?

She burrowed through and found him lying on his side, all playfulness gone. He thrashed about, repeatedly trying and failing to rise. She didn't have to look hard to see that his front left leg was injured. Not again.

Three of her cousins stepped in to try and get him to his feet, but he bit at them.

"Get out of the way. Call a vet. We need a vet." Her order was loud enough to be heard above the din. Gordy was her responsibility. Her job… But more than that, she loved him. He depended on her to take care of him.

Grabbing her phone from her pocket, she thrust it at her uncle as she moved past, holding on to her calm. Gordy needed orderliness and calm from her. "Whoa, Gordy. It's okay. Whoa…"

He was just scared and in pain. She squatted at his side and, despite his thrashing, got the straps circling his belly unbuckled and the spangled saddle off. Freeing him from the extra weight didn't help him rise on his own, and she needed to see him on his feet.

He wouldn't bite her. He'd never bitten her.

Taking a breath, she leaned in, arms surging for his chest and belly to try and help the small stallion to his feet.

"Jolie, his leg is broken." She heard a deep man's voice, winded but loud. Someone who'd been running too, familiar and unfamiliar even if he said her name. Too busy to question it further, she tried again to lift Gordy. So heavy. Jolie adjusted her arms and tried harder, straining to get the tiny stallion off the ground without putting any pressure on that leg.

He got on his knees, but she wasn't strong enough to get him all the way up. The position put pressure put on his leg and her favorite friend peeled his lips back and bit into her forearm. The shock of the bite hit her almost as sharply as the pain radiating up her arm.

She must have hurt him because it wasn't a quick bite. His jaw clenched and ground slightly, like he was holding back something intent on hurting him. He held on, and so did Jolie.

Someone stepped to the other side of the horse and put his arms around Gordy's middle. "On three." She gritted her teeth, counted, and the excessively large man lifted with her.

This time Gordy's back legs came under him and they got him to his feet, or least to the three good ones. She needed to see him standing, assess how bad the break was. It occurred to her that she should be more freaked out about this.

Veterinary medicine had come a long way since the days when a broken leg had been a death sentence for a horse, but Gordy may as well be living in the Wild West. He had a history of leg problems. Jolie remembered what they'd gone through the last time and what Gordy had gone through. Someone would make that terrible suggestion. Someone would say they should put him down… She needed to keep that from happening.

She also really needed him to stop biting. A few deep breaths and she'd be able to control the pain, but it'd be easier if he'd let go. Having her screaming at him would freak the tiny horse out and he was already afraid.

"Let go now," the man said, pulling her attention back to him over Gordy's pristine white back. She expected to see a vet, or maybe someone who had traveled with the circus in the past…

Ten years had changed his face. Broadened it. Made it more angular. But she knew those eyes—the boy she'd known ten years ago. The boy she'd loved.

Reece wasn't supposed to be there yet. And he probably wasn't supposed to be looking like he was about to throw up.

"I can't let go." Jolie grunted. Speaking took effort. Suddenly everything took effort. Controlling the pain.

Controlling her voice. Breathing… "He's got me." And letting go might just mean that he fell again, hurt himself worse, and maybe his teeth would take her flesh with him.

As much as Jolie might normally appreciate the value of distraction to help her control wayward emotions, Reece was the wrong kind of distraction. He just added a new dimension of badness to the waves racing up her arm. She didn't want him there. He wasn't supposed to come until they were all on the farm, where she'd have room to avoid him. He'd stayed gone for ten years so why in the world would he come to see the show now?

Because she didn't want it. But here he was, helping with Gordy and being gigantic. Good lord, he was big.

She could use that to help Gordy.

Get the horse and the show back on their feet.

The throng of people gathered around, children in the audience pressed against the raised outside of the ring, getting as close as they could… The weight of all their emotions pressed into her.

It had to be their emotions she was feeling. She'd mastered her own emotions several years ago, and maintained proper distance from anything hairy, she reminded herself. And she'd regain control of them as soon as she got Gordy out of there and Reece the hell away from her.

First things first. "We have to get him out of here." She needed out of there too.

A single nod and Reece reached for the horse's mouth while she kept him standing. Large, strong hands curled around the snout and lower jaw and he firmly pried the miniature horse's jaws apart, all the while speaking to him gently, making comforting sounds that did nothing to comfort her—but which seemed to do the trick with Gordy.

Or the combination of comfort and brute strength did the trick. Gordy released her bleeding arm and immediately Reece slid his arms under the horse's neck and through his legs to support his chest and hind quarters. Then he did what she'd never seen anyone do before: He picked the horse up.

"Which way?" Strained voice to go with strained muscles, and the look of nausea was still on his face. How had Reece gotten so strong? She thought doctors studied all the time and played golf... Even as small as Gordy was, he was still a horse and weighed a good one hundred and eighty pounds. But Reece carried the miniature horse out of the ring. By himself.

Right. Not the time to think about that. Gordy was hurt. She was hurt. The show had stopped. Children were probably very scared and upset. "This way." She cleared a path and led Reece and his load out the back of the tent, the way she'd come, off toward the stables.

He could carry Gordy to the stable and then go away, let her have her mind back. The stable was Bohannon property, she would just order him out and take care of her horse.

Someone else would step in, get the show moving again, and she didn't care who that task fell to. As long as the vet came soon.

The stable wasn't far, but by the time they reached it, Reece was breathing hard. Maybe harder than she was while desperately trying not to feel nothing—not the pain in her arm, and really not the anger and betrayal bubbling up from that dark place she stuffed all her Reece emotions.

Once in Gordy's stall with the fresh hay she'd put down earlier, Jolie directed, "Lay him in the straw." That was something she could think to say. One step at a time, that's as far ahead as she could make her mind work. It took more effort than it might have otherwise done if she hadn't been bitten and her arm didn't ache to the point she was considering that maybe the bone had fractured...

The rest of her mental capacity was filled to the brim with the echoes of voices reminding her of Gordy's history, the way Mack would undoubtedly react, and all the animals she'd lost over the years. Of everything she'd lost...

Ignoring those voices took effort.

Nothing was going to happen to Gordy. He was practically a sibling. Her first mount when she'd been little more than a toddler herself.

Jolie forced herself to still. Reece gently laid the injured but considerably calmer animal in the bedding. "I think he remembers you," she murmured. Gordy remembered Reece, even if he looked loads different—even if he'd bitten *her*. He remembered Reece enough to go docilely into the straw.

Still not a good enough reason to keep Reece in the stable. She couldn't focus with him there. "Thank you. Go watch the rest of the show." She got in between him and the horse, focusing with all her might on first-aid training for horses.

Reece stood behind her, looking down over her shoulder. "Let me look at your arm."

"It will wait." Gordy might have thrashed himself into a bad intestinal situation...so the next step should be...

Reece's hands closed around her waist, dragging her attention away from what she should be doing. He lifted her to her feet and secured her left arm with his horse-lifting grip locked around her wrist. Fire and ice, his touch was like peppermint, an utterly inexplicable combination of heat and chill that momentarily cut through the fear of losing Gordy and made her think...so many different things. Primarily it reminded her of one thing: He needed to leave. But Gordy needed to stand up more, and she'd failed at lifting him to his feet twice already.

"My arm can wait," she repeated. And it could wait

outside his grasp. She twisted her wrist free, ignored the deep ache the motion caused, and pointed to Gordy. "He needs to be on his feet."

"He can rest a moment. You're hurt."

He sounded so sincere, genuinely concerned... Which was crap, of course. "He needs to be on his feet," she repeated, "Resting a moment is the last thing he needs." *Don't look him in the eyes. Don't look him in the eyes.*

"Jolie..."

"Reece..." she replied, and looked him in the eyes. Right. No time to waste. She started moving again, toward the stall door so she could get to the supplies and away from him. Something in his touch, in the fact that he had helped them, and the concern in his eyes made her feel weak, muddied her thinking. Roused emotions she couldn't afford right now.

She knew what needed to happen for Gordy, not him. "You can stay here until I get him in a sling. He needs to be in a sling. And don't think you get to tell me what to do just because you went all strongman and carried my horse to the stable. You don't get to dictate anything in here. The circus might be yours to destroy, but Gordy is a Bohannon, so I'll take your help with him, and then you can get the hell out of my stable."

Not calm. Not calm at all. What had happened to her calm? Her arm. Pain and fear did this to her. That and the weirdness of seeing Reece. But it would all go away again soon enough. Losing Gordy on top of everything else would be a pain she couldn't ignore. Sling. She needed one of the horse slings.

Flipping open the lid of the trunk where various first-aid implements were kept, Jolie dug through, using her injured arm even if every second the ache grew worse. The only sling she knew they had was for the big horses...

"Tell me what you're doing." Reece said, apparently deciding it wasn't worth fighting with her.

Good. She didn't have time to fight.

Reece moved to the side of the trunk. "I'll help you if you tell me what you need."

More Good. Be helpful. The sooner Gordy was on his feet, the sooner Reece could go away. "I didn't see him fall," she said. "I don't know how much he could have jarred his insides when he went down, but I saw him thrashing to get up and that could have twisted his bowel. I don't want him fighting colic while his body needs to be focused on healing his leg. We need a sling. And some way to hang it. I'll work on the sling, you see if you can find a couple of pieces of lumber that will stretch across the top of the stall."

He left immediately. Of course he knew the way. The circus might be somewhere new every week, but it was always set up in the same layout. And that layout hadn't changed in the last ten years. She'd changed. He'd changed—God, had he ever—but the circus was the same.

A few minutes later Reece came back with two especially thick posts thrown over one shoulder and found her crouched in Gordy's stall, stringing together belts and harnesses.

"Lay them across the top. This isn't a proper sling, but it should work until the vet gets here." She stretched the leather across Gordy's chest, noting the labored breathing, and fought down another wave of panic. Once she had it in place over the shoulder she could access, she looked at Reece. "Think you can pick him up again? I need to get this around the other side and I need him on his feet, so I need you just supporting that place where his leg is compromised. Then I'll climb the stall and get it all hitched to the lumber."

He scowled at her. What did that mean? A longer look

at her arm told her why he looked so sour, but to his credit he squatted beside Gordy and got him up again, just as she'd asked. Which didn't make up for anything. He would probably pitch some kind of fit when this was over. He was a showman after all. Doctor. Showman. Jerkface.

She'd been upset with him for years, but had thought she'd finally let go of it a few years ago. The strength of her anger at seeing him now surprised her.

Not that she could spare time for reflection. To hell with Reece. She'd help Gordy—they'd help him. He'd survive. Get him up. Get the vet to cast his leg. Take care of him. Not a detailed plan, but it was as good as she had right now. And when Gordy's leg was in a cast, she'd figure out what the next step was. And then the next. She had a job, and right now Gordy was it.

"Hurry…" Reece said through clamped lips, doing his best to keep his head away from Gordy's mouth, should he get bitey again, but he managed to get the little stallion on his hooves and support his chest.

Jolie ducked around the other side and in a few seconds had threaded the makeshift harness through, clipped the ends together and thrown the long tail up and over the wood.

Good thing they were all pretty much acrobats…and that she was good at jumping. Her small stature made her the perfect size for tossing and flying, but made reaching objects in tall cabinets or shelves difficult. Made hauling herself to the stall top require a hop first.

She grabbed the top of the stall with both hands. Pain shot up her left arm and she let go again. It took a few seconds for the buzzing to subside so she could try again.

"Jolie?"

"I'm okay. It's…probably not broken."

He swore under his breath. Like he cared that much. Like someone who'd cut those he'd supposedly loved out of his life for a decade could care at all, let alone enough to swear.

A burst of anger at the bitter memory gave her the strength she needed to pull herself up on the second attempt. She maneuvered herself between the lumber Reece had slatted across the top of the stall, balanced and reached for the leather dangling over the lumber.

As she worked, she looked down and saw Reece scowling up at her again. "What?"

"Hurry," he said.

"You carried him all the way in there, is supporting one end such a chore now?" She looked down, noticed red on Gordy's white fur and howled, "Is he bleeding?"

"Dammit, Jolie, that's *your* blood."

"Oh." She swallowed back down another wave of hysteria and fastened the belts until the little horse was lifted ever so slightly from the floor.

"Too high," he called. "His front hooves aren't on the ground."

"I think the next notch will put too much weight on his leg, though… This is the best we can do. Maybe we can find a tile or bit of wood, something to slide under his good foot so he can stand but keep the weight off the other."

"After we clean your arm."

Back to the arm. "Later. What happened out there? You saw it, right?" Should she give him a sedative? Could she even do the math right now to figure out the right dose, or find a vein to inject it?

"He hurdled a little leap and just landed badly." He let go of Gordy slowly, letting him test the sling, and she waited to climb down until she was certain she wouldn't have to adjust the buckles.

Reece got to that decision before she did then stood and plucked her off the top of the stall. Picking her up again.

She'd forgotten he did that, just picked her up whenever he wanted to. And now that he was twelve gazillion feet tall, he might be even worse about it.

"Good grief, put me down." Being this close to him made her feel more breathless than she wanted to sound. She wanted to sound angry. Angry was better than fragile and girly.

"I'm helping you down."

She couldn't kick him because he might drop her and she already hurt. Though in a way she was grateful for the pain as having something else to focus on had to help keep her from thinking too hard about the past and just what Reece was there to do. "I climbed up on my own, I could've climbed down without your help too."

"You're hurt, and you're too stubborn to let me take care of you...your wound." He set her in the straw, and when Gordy whinnied and tugged at the sling, he lowered his voice. "It needs to be cleaned at the very least. Animal mouths..."

"I know. But it's waited this long. If I'm going to catch some dreaded horse-bite disease, then I'm pretty sure there is no difference in waiting fifteen minutes to clean it or fifty."

Gordy thrashed about, trying to escape the makeshift sling, causing the lumber above to skid on the stall. Jolie watched the wood move enough to be convinced: Gordy definitely needed a tranquilizer. And she needed a shot of something too. Like whiskey.

"Who's going to take care of him if you're sick?"

"I won't get sick. You're the one who's been looking like you were going to throw up."

He ignored her vomit talk. "This is ridiculous. He is in the sling. There is absolutely nothing else you can do for him until the vet arrives. Come with me to Mom's RV and let me treat it."

"No." She redirected his attention. "I have some sedative but I need some help with the math. You do medicine dosage calculations all the time, right?"

"I don't know the dosage for horses," Reece muttered, but reached up to hold the lumber steady.

"I know the dosage for a big horse and the weight differences, so you should be able to figure out what to give Gordy if I tell you that, right?"

"Fine, then we'll deal with your arm." He looked at her, but direct eye contact did something to her insides and she had enough to worry about.

She looked away, told him the dosage for a full-sized horse and the weight differences, and then left him thinking and holding the lumber to run to her trailer where she had the medication in her fridge. When she came back, he stood there still and immediately told her the number.

Flipping the cap back on the needle, she plunged it into the vial and extracted a slightly smaller amount than Reece had told her. Just to be safe. "You can treat my arm when the vet gets here. Gordy needs me. He needs reassurance. The last thing he needs is to be alone and scared."

"Jolivetta Chriselle Ra—"

"You just stop right there, Dr. Reece I'm-Going-To-Act-Like-The-Boss Keightly." She'd poke him in the chest if her arm didn't hurt so much and she didn't have a needle in the other. "I'm not going anywhere. The vet or someone might come in and get the idea of putting him down if I'm not here to stop them. Now, let go of the wood and hold him still. This medicine isn't great in the muscle—it eats it up. Has to go into the vein."

"Do you want me to do it?" Reece asked. Like she hadn't done this a hundred times before.

"No. I want you to hold Gordy." *And stop being bossy. And stop being around. And stop being…everything else.*

Reece let go of the wood, rubbed a hand over his face

like he could wipe off frustration, and slung his arms around Gordy's chest again, his voice gentling a little too. "Why are you so convinced they're going to put him down?"

"He's got leg problems."

"Explain."

"Really bad circulation." Jolie maneuvered to the other side of the horse before adding, "And he's broken that leg before. It was very hard to heal the first time…"

"So it might be kinder if they come to that decision now rather than after—"

"No!" She shouted, causing the horse to flinch. She took a breath and calmed her voice. "It's not going to come to that. Horses can survive broken legs. And the circus is closing anyway! He has time to recuperate."

She went for a vein she had found before, back of the neck, easier to get to and somewhere where she could talk softly and provide comfort. Not that she felt calm and comforting right now. She felt way too much of everything. Worry. Fear. Betrayal. Anger. A disconcerting awareness at Reece's foreign manly scent in the stable… But she channeled worry away for Gordy's benefit and gentled her tone. "We're leaving here and going back to the farm in a few days, and he'll have space to relax and get better. He doesn't need to get better fast so that he can perform."

"It's nothing to do with performing."

"No, it's about taking the easy way out. Gordy's part of the family, and you don't just shoot your family if they get a hangnail." She threaded the needle into the vein, pulled back to make sure blood came into the cartridge, and then injected slowly. "You take care of your family. At least, that's how it's done in my family. You might not be willing to fight for yours, but I am."

The sedation worked almost instantly. She hadn't given Gordy enough to knock him out, but he did stop thrashing and mellowed significantly. With the safety cap back in place, she waved Reece off Gordy's back. "You can go now."

"You know no one is going to put him down if he has a chance to recover." He moved to the door of the stall but didn't leave. "I'm not leaving until you stop acting like a crazy woman and let me get a look at your arm."

If he didn't stop going on about her arm and about Gordy's leg, she might hit him. From the angle she'd have to swing up to hit his chin, and might even be able to knock him out. Providing his jaw was more glass than the granite it looked like. "He has a chance."

"Just wait for the vet." Reece leaned against the jamb.

She slid past him to grab a stool and moved it back into the stall. "I have been taking care of horses forever." Okay, she might be acting crazy—she'd never felt moved to violence before—but Gordy was important. "And I take care of people too. I know what I'm talking about. He can be casted. Sometimes a kind of exoskeleton can be built to support a broken leg. I've read about it, and we have the slings for the big horses. We have one who has a metabolic condition that causes him to get laminitis, and we had to sling him once. This little makeshift sling is taking weight off that leg, and we can get a better one for him set up. It's temporary. So stop preparing me for the worst."

Her throbbing arm needed a break, and so did she. She scooted the stool toward Gordy's head with her feet. He might be sedated but he'd feel her there. She'd comfort him. And maybe she'd absorb a little comfort from keeping near him too. A little comfort would be good right now. "I hope you're not so fast on the plug-pulling for your *people* patients."

....
....

CHAPTER TWO

REECE RUBBED HIS HEAD, a headache starting between his
brows. This was not how he'd pictured their reunion going.
That had gone entirely differently. She'd been wearing
something sparkly for starters.

"Hey…" His brain caught up with the situation now
that the immediate emergency had passed. "You're not
dressed."

"I'm dressed just fine," she bit at him, and then her
voice turned honey-sweet as she began to pet Gordy's
face and talk to him. "It's going to be okay. I won't let
anyone hurt you."

"For the show," he cut in. He'd been waiting at the show
the whole time to see her perform, and only now did it
register with him that she wasn't dressed for the ring at
all. Jeans and a pink T-shirt with a white unicorn and a
rainbow coming from its butt, while funny, wasn't performance attire. "You haven't performed yet. I figured
you'd come at the end, the aerial act maybe, but you're
not dressed."

"I don't perform any more."

"Why not?"

"None of your business." Her words were angry, but
she kept her tone sweet. Not for him, he realized. She
looked back at Gordy and ruffled his ears. The sedative
had taken the fight out of the little horse, but her touch

and proximity soothed him. Despite the drug, he tilted his head against hers and accepted the comfort.

She had the touch. Reece forgot his irritation for a few seconds, remembering the way she'd sat with his head in her lap after the accident, petting his temples in much the same way she that she petted the horse's face now too.

Two people in one body. In the ring she came alive—so full of energy that even when a trick failed she still held the audience in her hands. And the rest of the time she had that gentle touch that soothed any kind of animal. Even teenage boys. She'd been the only one he'd wanted around him after Dad had died.

The pink T-shirt had a growing spot of red on it where she'd clamped her arm to her side, cradling it protectively against her and using her other arm for Gordy.

"Hurts?"

"Adrenalin is wearing off," she murmured, "but I can wait."

"No doubt." He made a note to ask Mom all the things about Jolie that he'd never let her tell him before, when he had been trying so hard to stay in school and keep Jolie off his mind. Something was up with her, and it wasn't just upset about Gordy's accident. It might even be about more than his reason for being there, and the myriad other reasons she had to be angry with him. Not performing any more wasn't something she'd have decided for the last week of the circus. It was older than his decision to close the show down. How much older, he had no idea.

He was saved from thinking further about what kind of knots Jolie might have worked herself into while he'd been away when Mack Bohannon escorted the vet into the stable and ushered Reece and Jolie out—two too many people for the small stall.

"I know that's not a proper sling." Jolie said, gesturing to the small injured horse from the gate, "but I couldn't think of anything else we could do for him that might keep his digestion working properly and keep weight off that leg. We don't have a sling small enough for him."

"I have one." The vet pulled a backpack off his shoulder and handed it to Mack, Jolie's uncle and head of the Bohannon clan. Ultimately, Gordy's future rested with Mack, who dug into the pack and retrieved the sling then proceeded to help the vet swap it with the makeshift one.

"He's going to be okay. He can heal this," Jolie said to Mack, who looked grim. Not the right look. Not one Reece wanted to see any more than Jolie did. Whatever her protestations, she didn't need to watch the play-by-play.

He reached for her shoulder and tried to pivot her toward the door. "Let's get your arm tended to."

"I'm not leaving yet." Mack looked back at her and she shook her head, her chin lifting, "I'm not leaving. You might need me."

As easy as he'd like to be with Jolie of all people, he'd mistakenly thought perhaps time would have made her somewhat less stubborn. She'd always been this way when it came to Gordy, and Reece had started throwing his weight around to get her to mind him all those years ago when her mother had gotten her back when she'd been taken. That had been the first time his father had ever put him in charge of anyone in the company.

She thought him bossy? Well, she made him bossy.

The vet needed room to work and, knowing very well how hard it was to treat a patient when being hovered over, Reece made his decision. He scooped her legs from under her as his other arm caught across her back, and he carried her out of the stable.

Too stunned to say anything for a few seconds, it took them actually leaving the stables for Jolie's indignation and terror to kick back in. "Reece! Reece, put me down. I need to stay with Gordy."

"You need your arm cleaned and inspected." Reece tightened his arms lest she take a mind to thrash free of his grip. "I'm done talking about it. Mom will have first-aid supplies in her RV."

"No. What if they decide to put him down while I'm gone? He needs an advocate. He needs me there to promise to take care of him. See him through this again. I know he can heal." She twisted, testing his hold, and then locked onto him with a baleful glare. "Please." The word didn't go well with the glare or the tone.

"It won't take long."

"It will take five minutes to walk to your mom's RV. If you must have your way, my trailer is closer!" As the words tumbled out, she realized what would convince him. "I have all the medical supplies anyway, I'm the EMT on staff. And I won't fight you if you go there and we do this fast. Or just let me go do it myself and—"

"You're an EMT?" He stopped walking and looked down at her, his eyes going from hers to her mouth long enough to distract her. Kissing…would be bad.

Don't look at his mouth. "Can't you walk and talk at the same time?" Jolie barked at him, startling his gaze back to hers. "I am an EMT, yes." With the stable now officially out of sight, the firm heat of his big body and the prospect of being alone with Reece began to scare her more than Gordy's plight. One crisis at a time, that's all she could deal with. Not knowing what she might say or how she might react when she got her emotions sorted out? Well, that could cause another crisis. "Put me down and let me clean it myself, or start walking. Don't just stand here while they might be making decisions without me!"

"Didn't you have to leave the circus to attend classes

to become and EMT?" What the hell? Why did he care so much about this?

"Do you see my face? This is the face of someone who is freaking out. Put me down or I swear I will belt you with my broken arm...*which isn't broken...*"

Reece scowled, but he started walking again and she almost relaxed. At least she stopped gritting her teeth.

"I took a course over the summer when we were between seasons."

It figured that he'd focus on her dislike of the outside world, like that was important right now. She could do things outside the circus, she just didn't care to. When the circus off-seasoned at Bohannon Farm, as it did every year, it was like living at the circus. The only difference with the summer she'd gone to school had been that she'd had to spend time with a bunch of possibly dangerous weirdos who'd thought mowing the lawn every Saturday, frequenting the mall, and driving an SUV was something to brag about. "My trailer is that way." She pointed with her good arm, and he veered off, following the directions she supplied.

Within two minutes she was inside her cozy little home. "There's supplies in the skinny cabinet above the sink."

Reece put her down in front of the sink and the first thing he did was wash his hands. "Paper towels?"

She gestured to the other side of the counter and then opened the cabinet to start getting out supplies with her good arm, then thought better of it and stuck the bad one under the faucet. It would hurt, but if she was going to have pain she'd either control it or be the one in control of inflicting it.

Number-one rule or dealing with Reece? Don't let him hurt her again. Even if it was that for-her-own-good kind of hurt.

No, especially the for-her-own-good kind of hurt. She'd had enough of that, thank you very much.

"This doesn't look good," he muttered, as he wrapped his hand around her wrist to take control of the flow of water over the wound. In that second she forgot all about her fear for Gordy and about the pain. She even forgot about how angry she was at him for what he was about to do to them all. Skin-to-skin contact was more potent than being carried, especially when it reminded her of how big he'd gotten. Hadn't he supposed to have been full grown when he'd gone off to school? When did men stop getting bigger? Was he still growing? This was ridiculous.

Her chest ached when she looked up at him. "You're too tall. Makes my neck hurt." She pretended that was where the pain was. It was better than give in to the urge to press against him and lean into the strength she'd seen in action. Give in to the urge to keep forgetting the bad things. Soak in the comfort she knew waited in his arms.

Stupid.

That should be rule number two—don't let Reece comfort her ever again.

She pulled her arm from under the water and ripped a fresh paper towel from the roll to blot at it, then applied pressure to staunch the blood that started flowing again. The ache deep in her arm had subsided but it surged back to life when she put pressure on it. If she mentioned that, he'd have her at the emergency room faster than she could say, "Don't put me to sleep, it's just a broken arm." It'd be her front left leg if she were a quadruped, mirroring Gordy's injury. Fate's twisted sense of humor…

He caught her arm again and directed it under the counter light where he could examine the bite. It was well on its way to bruising and there were several ugly punctures and a shallow gash.

"It doesn't need stitches. There are a couple of punctures that I might put a stitch or two into, but if you have butterflies, that can hold for now." He watched her, his voice having lost that edge of irritation as soon as he'd gotten his way. His mouth hadn't got the news that he was less irritated, though. His lips pressed together, hard and cranky. "Probably better anyway, in case an infection does start up—which happens way more often in punctures than cuts, you realize. And the reason we should have gotten this treated faster."

He unfurled his fingers from her arm and her thinking cleared a little. She needed more of that. "You know, I can do the medicine and bandaging. You visit your mom. I need…I need you to go and I can take care of this myself." Him going would help. It had to help.

"I'm almost done." The way he no longer met her eyes said that he felt something at least. It might be a ghost of the connection that they'd once had, but he still felt something.

"I don't care if you're almost done. I want you to be somewhere else. Somewhere I'm not. I will finish up and then go back to the stables. You're messing everything up." Her voice rose as she spoke, reaching to near shrillness at the end. "Because…you're still…"

"You can be calm if you want to be calm." He sure sounded calm. But then she remembered—he didn't really care about them. This was just Doctor Man, who lived to treat patients. Or something.

"I'm trying to be calm. You could hurry up some. You know I need to get back." Gordy needed her. Focus on that. "Except I forgot that you're good at leaving people waiting." *No, don't focus on that. Gordy. Get it together.*

He gave her a look and snagged her wrist again—no doubt to keep her from getting away. She'd have to climb out the window in her bedroom or squeeze through the one over the sink if she wanted to get out. His big body blocked the tiny kitchenette. And he continued to work at his own pace.

She tried deep breaths to calm down. She really was trying, that was the problem. She'd thought she could always be calm, but right now she couldn't. Her heart hammered against her sternum like the beat of so many hooves in the ring. She could hear it, see it pulsing in her vision, and she knew that wasn't good. Her deep breaths got shallow and fast, outside her control.

Everything was out of control.

"They won't euthanize him while I'm gone, right?" she blurted out. "That's the kind of thing that takes time and preparation, right?" More words tumbled from her lips.

Like he knew anything. Or maybe he did. Maybe he was keeping her there forever for a reason. "They'd wait long enough to let people say goodbye if it came to that, right?"

Right? Right? God, she really did sound crazy. And she'd had a plan for speaking to him on the farm, when the dust had settled after they'd all settled in. Later. In the future.

"Take a deep breath. In through your nose," Reece said, his voice firm and demanding. He wanted to control everything. Even how she breathed!

"Jolie," he said her name again. "I think you're having a panic attack. Slow down your breathing."

"I'm not panic attacking." Was that even a term? She'd said it wrong. Everything was wrong. That's exactly the kind of inarticulate nonsense that would make him think twice about even considering her request when she got round to making it. And probably everything she'd said and done since she'd seen him again would add to that thinking twice and thrice, and whatever fourth, fifth and sixth were… Sure, no problem, he'd hand over the reins of his birthright to someone who might be a babbling idiot.

Jolie had no proof she could even lead picnic ants in a straight line to the potato salad. She knew she could do it. Or she thought she could. She'd been so sure before he'd got here. Before she'd fallen headlong into that deep place where she stuffed all the emotions that were too hard to put words to.

It would be better if she knew it in some logical manner that came with charts and graphs. Doctors probably loved charts and graphs!

"I can't breathe." She probably had caught some awful horse-bite disease. Everything was wrong. Everything.

He let go of her wrist suddenly and grabbed her hips. Half an accelerated heartbeat later she was sitting on the counter in front of him, gasping for air and shaking all over, helpless against the onslaught of tears that swamped her vision and poured down her cheeks.

Reece cupped her cheeks, tilting her head until he had her gaze. So blue. So steady.

He said something. His thumbs stroked her cheeks, wiping away the tears as they poured down. She had no idea what he was saying, calming sounds. Comforting sounds. And they reached her. The tears slowed along with her breathing, and behind them she felt a stampede of embarrassment. And confusion. What the heck had just happened…?

"That was a panic attack?" her voice rasped, the raw sound causing a few aftershock hiccups.

He nodded, wrapping his arms around her and pulling her to his chest. Warm. Firm. Right where she'd wanted to be.

"I've had some experience with them."

It was hard to imagine anything rattling Reece like this. "They're awful," she mumbled, drained, ashamed, and wantonly breaking rule number two.

"Yes, they are."

She'd stop breaking rule number two in a second, but right now she needed the hug. And with her face hidden by his chest she didn't have to look him in the eye…

When she didn't say anything else, he added, "They're your family, and they love Gordy too. They're not going to make any decisions while you're getting your injury tended to."

"I know. I'm sorry. I don't know why… I don't know what happened. I don't usually act like a crazy person." She swiped her eyes again and pulled away, before she did something even crazier.

It had just been the shock of seeing him again for the first time. But that shock was gone, it couldn't last forever. So it was done. She willed it to be done and she was the one in control of her emotions…not the other way around. Never again. Focus on one big emotion at a time, that was the key to remaining tethered to her sanity. And right now that one big emotion had to be concern for Gordy. He needed her. She could fall apart later.

Forget that the last time she'd been this scared she'd been sixteen and watching Reece drive away into the world alone, and remember how all the faith she'd put in him—all the worry she'd had for him—had meant nothing. In the end he had been just like her father, who, incidentally, had been good at hugging too.

She should remember all that. If Reece was going to consider her request, it wouldn't be because he cared so much about them. She had to find another angle. "You should finish." Because she'd freaked out before they'd got to bandaging.

He nodded, looked at her longer than she was comfortable with him looking, then resumed treatment—dabbing on ointment, placing a couple of rectangles of gauze onto the wound, which he had her hold in place so he could deal with the tape.

"Don't worry about this. You're just wound tight right now. We all are. I'm worried about him too." A couple of rips of tape later and he replaced her fingers with white cloth tape, guaranteed to hold even if she should bleed again and get the whole mess wet. "If it starts feeling hot or hurting more, tell me."

"I know. Antibiotics." She pretended he hadn't said anything about worrying about Gordy. He could turn his worry on and off like a light switch or he didn't really feel anything. Or Doctor Worry was different from the worry of mortal men who couldn't worry and fret over loved ones while ignoring them utterly.

"If I had my kit, I'd start you on them right now," he muttered, and smoothed down the last strip of tape. "You haven't got any bigger, have you?" He squinted at her in a way she could only deem as judgmental.

"I'm big enough. Not everyone aspires to be a giant's stunt double." Sarcasm: Her Refuge. Her voice-activated ten-foot pole for keeping things away, keeping things from getting to her.

"I'm not judging. I was considering your weight for prescription purposes."

"Oh." Okay, so maybe she wasn't totally done being crazy. But it was easier to jump to a negative conclusion than to think that he cared. He was still here to destroy her *everything*. Time to go. She slid off the counter on the other side of him and hurried to the door. "Lock it when you leave." Not waiting for an answer, she took the stairs at a near run.

"Do you want some pain relievers?" he called from behind her. She heard the question as the door swung shut but didn't go back inside to answer him. Pain relievers? Hell, yes, she'd like some. She'd also like some amnesia pills. And she'd like him to take them too and forget the last ten minutes.

Even if the small part of her mind that was currently sane said that no one would put Gordy down without giving her time to say goodbye, she was still more than half-terrified she'd get back to the stables and find him already gone.

Reece stared at the screen door for several seconds, expecting it to open again and for Jolie to come back for some ibuprofen or something. But she didn't.

He shook a couple of pills out, laid them on yet another paper towel and folded it around the pills so he could stick them in his pocket. Before the night was over, someone would need them. Possibly him. If he didn't know better, he'd say that panic attacks were contagious. That he'd somehow given her the one he'd been fighting all evening.

A mess of paper towels and tape littered the counter, so he spent time tidying it up before he left. That was one thing always ground into the circus kids: keep your living area tidy. When it's small, and on wheels, you had to be as tidy and deferential to everyone else as you could be. And you had to be okay with making things work, even if that meant taking a shower with the garden hose behind the RV because you were on a schedule and all the other showers were occupied. You learned to make the best of things. He could control the physical mess he left behind, and the only speculation he could offer to the emotional devastation he knew he'd leave in his wake? He could only hope that they could make the best of it.

It was their nature. It was *her* nature.

Three years age difference between them, but circus kids grew up fast. Especially Jolie. When they'd gotten her back, she'd never really been a normal little kid. Always looking over her shoulder. Always afraid something would go wrong. Children learned behavior, like worrying, and she'd learned it then and learned it well.

He'd spent the last ten years trying not to think about what she'd learned by him leaving.

He still didn't want to think about that, even with it staring him in the face.

His worry for Jolie could cripple him. It certainly would've had him running back home to her that first week away at school if he'd so much as let his mother mention her name. It had been his only survival tactic. The only way for him to stay in school had been to quit Jolie cold turkey.

She might be the same size, but she'd changed in other discouraging ways. He'd probably played a part in that. Thirty minutes in her presence had dredged up more questions than just how she was going to handle him closing down the circus.

The show music had stopped a while ago, so Mom was either at her RV or the mess tent. She always liked to eat with everyone. Keightly Circus really did band together as a family, which was the hardest part of shutting it down. They ate together. Off-seasoned together. Raised their children together. The elderly performers even tended to retire to the same places…

He flipped the lock on the doorknob and stepped out, giving it a good pull. Locked up. As requested. Now to find Mom and get more information.

An hour later, having received the lecture from his mother that Reece had been dodging for a decade, he walked into the stables with two plates and bottles of water.

He found Jolie alone with Gordy, who was now utterly unconscious. A simple cot had been slid into the remaining space in Gordy's stall and Jolie sat on it, her back to the wall and her legs dangling, eyes fixed on the small white stallion. Though by her glazed look, she wasn't really looking at Gordy.

Reece knew only too well that you could stare right into your past if left to your own thoughts long enough. Usually at the memories you least needed to focus on. The ones you'd probably be better off forgetting entirely.

Since he'd stepped foot onto the lot, when he'd had any time alone with his thoughts, he got images of his father's blood, muddying the sawdust and sand in the ring…

"What are you doing? You look sick. Is the food really that bad?" Jolie's voice cut through his haze. Thinking too hard was contagious too…

"It's fine. I'm fine. Brought dinner. Thought you might be hungry and I'd like to know what the vet said." He nodded toward the cot—it was big enough for both of them to sit on without touching each other, provided it stood the weight. "You mind?"

A suspicious squint answered him, but that was better than the panic earlier. Her green eyes still had that glassy look, like emotion wasn't too far beneath the surface. She was the first to look away, but she held up her good hand for the plate, freeing one of his so he could fish the water bottles from his pockets before he sat. "So?"

"He said front-leg breaks are worse than back, which aside from his circulation issues… I don't really understand." She rested the plate on her thigh, freeing her hands to shuffle the water bottle off to the other side. It must still be hurting. "Not sure if he means that they happen more frequently or if they are harder to splint, harder to heal, harder on the horse, or if it's Gordy-specific…" She gestured to the new harness on Gordy with the toe of her boot. "But that sling is more comfy and it's not bound by notches. They got it perfectly seated. Mack said it's possible he twisted something inside when he fell, so it was good that we got him on his feet so fast. They couldn't feel anything when palpating his belly, but he was out of it by then and couldn't have told them it hurt even if the pain was blistering."

"Prognosis?" He looked at the food, not able to bring himself to take a bite yet. She hadn't either, even if she was using her feet to gesture so her hands could keep hold of her dinner. Well, hand. She wasn't using the injured arm for anything but keeping her water tucked against her thigh.

"Oh…" She breathed the word, her tone confirming the worst, and that she wouldn't agree with it until forced to. "He said it's rough… We would try…"

But.

She didn't actually say it but he still heard it.

He put his bottle down, fished the pills from his pocket and placed them beside her leg. "Anti-inflammatories," he murmured, leaving her to take them or not, and went back to the conversation about Gordy. "So what's the next step?"

"Sit with him. Keep him comfortable. Watch for signs of colic." She took the pills. "And I have both pain medicine and tranquilizers to inject if he gets worse."

"You did really well with the tranquilizer earlier. Hit the vein the first time. Did you take courses on animal care too?"

"No, I learned to care for people, but I've given injections and done blood draws on the horses before. And I read. A lot."

He remembered that. She read anything zoological in nature, didn't matter if it dealt with the horses and dogs that were in the show or wild animals, which had not been in the show since her twice great-grandfather had been mauled by a lion during an act. The circus was always dangerous, but it had got a little less dangerous when they'd got back to their roots and away from the exotic-animal fad popular from the Victorian era.

"Thank you for dinner."

He kept his eyes on the food, but not looking at her didn't keep memories at bay. He made himself eat. It would be a long night, as he had every intention of spending it here at her side. "You're welcome." He looked at her again. Dammit.

The wild auburn curls had been worked into some kind of fancy braid so he could see her clearly even in the dim light of the stable. Still the prettiest girl he'd ever seen in the flesh. Even prettier than when he'd left. She might have cried again since she'd left her trailer—her wide-set green eyes looked bigger, glassy, and heartbroken. There was a little crease between her brows that said she frowned more than she should, and even now, with her expression mostly blank, the shadow of that unhappy crease remained.

"I know it's not the right time for this, but I wanted to apologize," Reece said, feeling his way through the words as he went.

"For leaving us?"

CHAPTER THREE

No. He couldn't apologize for that. "For…" He looked at her again and drew a deep breath. "I mean about the circus. About what I'm here to do. I know it's not what you want, but I want to help you get settled wherever you want to go after Keightly."

"I don't want to go anywhere else," she said.

None of them did. He was the bad guy in this, but for the right reasons. One day she'd see that. "I know you don't."

She put the untouched plate aside and turned on the cot to face him. "Listen. I didn't expect to see you tonight. Actually, I didn't think I'd see you at all until Ginny and Mack's wedding. And what happened to Gordy…I had a plan for how it should go when you came to the farm. What I wanted to say… But it sort of evaporated when I freaked out."

She had a plan? She had pictured him coming back and it didn't involve being a crazy woman? "Don't say you wanted to talk me out of closing."

"I was going to ask you to work with me and change what we do. No more traveling circus, a new future."

That sounded an awful lot like "Please don't close".

"There is no future for Keightly, Jolie. This isn't just about me and what I want to do with my life. It's dangerous. Especially with people getting older, it's getting more dangerous for them. Gordy is an old-timer and—"

"He's not an old-timer," she cut in, the flash of her eyes telling him that the crazy woman might be about to make a reappearance if he didn't watch out. "He's twenty-eight. Miniature horses live much longer than big horses, and we have some big horses on the farm that are over thirty-five. Gordy is firmly middle-aged."

She was still afraid someone was going to announce plans to euthanize the little guy. "Not what I'm getting at."

"Number one, the big-spectacle acts, the ones that are the most dangerous, aren't done by the core troupe any more. We get contracts for the headliners—fliers. We had a Russian bar act a couple years ago. But just because the core group is getting older doesn't mean that they want to give up the life."

"I know they don't want—"

"Number *two*." She held up two fingers, silencing him. "I don't want to keep the circus on the road. I don't even want to keep it a circus."

"Not keep it a circus?" His headache was increasing. "Stop counting lists of supporting…whatever, and tell me what you want to do with Keightly."

"I want to make a circus camp," Jolie said, her voice softening. "At the farm."

"A circus camp."

"The older performers can still teach. I'm proof of that. Just because I don't perform any more doesn't mean I don't know how to do things. I can be the demonstration, they can instruct, and we can make sure to…to…" Her hands flew up, a gesture he knew was meant to summon some word that had temporarily eluded her, and which had always been his cue to finish her thought when her mouth got ahead of her. Not that he could do that any more.

"Circuses are dying." She abandoned that train of

thought and started again. "They're dying out. There were probably thousands in North America, now how many are left? How many close every year? How long before these art forms are no longer even remembered? Sooner, if we don't teach them to children and pass on our knowledge. Plus, we're only half an hour from Atlanta, and people love Keightly in this part of Georgia. They'd love to send their children to circus camp in the summer. Physical activity, fun, a day camp while their parents work. And for the rest of the year we could do the circus-school thing for older kids. Like high school and college age, those who are at their most fit and can best handle the rigors."

"Wait." He lifted a hand to rub his forehead, a headache blazing to life dead center behind his eyes. It wasn't exactly asking him to keep things going as they were, and while he appreciated that… "You make good points. All your points are good, but Mom is done with running things. She's said so over and over again and that's why I'm here. But I don't have time to devote to co-running a circus camp. I have a practice to build and run."

"I'm not asking Ginny or you to run anything. I'm offering. I will run it. I can do it. I'm not a little girl any more." It wasn't that she didn't like being told no, she just wouldn't be told no about *this*. Her fingers twitched then drummed against her legs, trying to calm her indignation. "You do whatever it is you want, focus on your practice. Ginny can retire and participate however much or little she wants to."

"My name is on it, this is my equipment, I'll have to take a hand in it. Plus, there's also no way I want to subject children to that kind of danger."

"I wouldn't just welcome them and throw them on the trapeze without a net," Jolie said, and then winced, realizing how badly chosen her words had been for him. "We'd be safe. Start slow. Probably start with simple tumbling for children without any gymnastic experience. And it's not all acrobatics. You know as well as anyone that there are a blue million different disciplines within the circus that don't even approach performance. Including costume design, set designs, tending animals…"

"People like you who don't perform any more."

"Right." She stopped looking him in the eye, shifting her gaze back to the sleeping Gordy.

Because she'd basically told him to stuff it earlier when he'd asked why she hadn't been dressed to perform. He couldn't tell if she didn't want to talk about that or if she just didn't want to talk about it with him. Screw it, he wanted to know! If it was another of his sins, he had to know so he could fix it. "When did you stop?"

"I stopped when you did."

His stomach lurched. "Why?"

She shrugged. "I just did."

"You had to have had a reason. You loved it…"

She shrugged again. "I didn't want to any more."

"Jolie—"

"I still practice, do different things, it's a good way to keep in shape. I don't do the trick-riding, but I figure the rest of the Bohannons have that market cornered anyway."

She didn't cast blame on him, and that was something he should be thankful for. What could he say if she brought up his past sins? And why was he digging into her history and motivations when he really didn't want her digging into his? Because he was an idiot. Because he couldn't know her without wanting to know every single thing about her.

Because he couldn't say no to her, which was why he had stayed as far away as he'd been able to.

And it was because he couldn't say no to her that he had to get out of there now. Bad plan to stay with her. "Are you going to be all right here on your own tonight?"

"Yes. Someone will come and try to relieve me in a few hours." She looked him fully in the eye again, somehow managing to look even smaller on the cot beside the unconscious horse. "Will you at least think about it?"

He knew what he thought about it. He thought—no, he knew—it was a bad idea. No matter how badly she wanted it.

"Please? Give me some time to show you how it can be. After Gordy is stable enough that he doesn't need me round the clock? After we relocate to the farm?"

After her arm healed? After he told her he had a probable buyer for all the equipment?

He stretched to buy a few seconds in the vain hope the right words would appear, present him some way to let her down easily, but his words were as elusive as hers had been. "Okay. I'll wait until we've settled at the farm, see what everyone else thinks about the idea. Weigh the pros and cons…"

She breathed out slowly, in what he could only term as relief, and leaned back against the wall. "Don't take this the wrong way, but could you also stay away from me for a few days?"

"Why?"

She shrugged. "Because if you're around, I'll just keep wanting to ask you to do it, and then—" She stopped suddenly, her cheeks flaring pink. "Well, not *do it*, obviously, because that would be stupid. Obviously." She was repeating herself so she stopped, shook her head, and then tried again. "I wasn't talking about sex. Obviously."

If she said "obviously' again…

"We don't…not sex. I wasn't talking about doing that. Hah." She shook her head. The more she tap-danced around, trying to clarify, the worse it got. "I meant doing… the camp. I would keep asking you to do the camp…" A great sigh came from her and she stopped talking. Finally. Without more obviouslys.

"Sure," he said, working to keep his voice normal. Unaffected. "I can give you space. You should sleep. Mom's got my number if you think the bite's growing infected. I need to go take care of some things anyway." He walked out.

He had important things to do, like locating his backbone before he just said yes to whatever she wanted to keep from letting her—and everyone else—down.

It was like that. The reason he didn't want them in the circus any more? He didn't want any one hurt. Any kind of hurt. But physical hurt—which could kill—had to trump emotional hurt. The emotional hurt just made you feel like you were dying.

They would acclimate to life off the road and outside the circus, he reminded himself yet again. And if they couldn't, he'd help them find new homes. Somewhere he could stop worrying about them. Somewhere someone else would have to take responsibility when luck turned and those death-defying feats could no longer defy.

Since the second his father had died, that responsibility had passed to him, and even when he hadn't actively been with the circus, he'd felt it. Oh, he'd ignored the hell out of it, but now that he could no longer do that he felt the weight of every life in his hands. And it was about damned time he used those hands to shield them.

He was a man now, not a boy to be shushed and ignored.

And really not a horny teenager who kept replaying Jolie's clumsy words: *I'll just keep asking you to do it.*

There had been moments in Jolie's life when the instant she'd done something, she'd regretted it.

Usually, those moments had involved falling off something. When she'd first started learning the wire, she'd had that feeling a lot. It had always gone away as soon as she'd hit the ground.

Since she'd learned to control her emotions, she'd not experienced this level of regret over anything she'd done.

And that feeling had never lasted for three days before.

She couldn't stop worrying about her sudden anxiety-driven freak-out and the way it painted her. More evidence that she was losing her mind. Her practiced, easy, unflappable calm had abandoned her the second she'd seen him, and even though he'd stayed away, as she'd asked, she couldn't shake it.

The very last show had run last night. Jolie had not attended. The show had ended for her the night Gordy had been hurt.

Today she should be doing what she always did—helping load everything with the others—but Mack had come and told her to stick with her charge. Maybe he heard about the freak-out. Maybe it was in deference to her arm. She had no idea.

So she did what she could in the stables, tried to wipe her mind, and tried to ignore the ache in her arm and the worry over how Gordy would fare during the ride to the farm. There could be no sling in the back of the trailer, not with it bumping down the highway and over potholed country roads. He'd have to lie down.

People came and went, carrying out equipment and moving out the other horses.

Jolie disassembled the cot and set it out, then resumed her vigil from a small stool in the stall. That was something she could do. Now, if only she could stop feeling like she'd just made the biggest misstep in history and at any second she was going to fall. No, actually, it was more like at any second she was going to stop falling. A sudden bone-crunching, sixty-to-zero-in-the-blink-of-an-eye method of stopping.

It might just be a relief when it finally happened. The fall was just killing her more slowly.

If she hadn't turned into a crazy person, Reece could've come today and waved his big stupid arms and impressive shoulders around to move Gordy when he needed it. Or lift him up in the horse trailer if his belly started bothering him when they were on the road. The poor little horse was still under the effect of drugs, and she couldn't tell whether his innards were out of sorts or if he was just too out of it to eat enough for any sort of digestive motility. Any time he flicked his ear, she checked for poo, and celebrated even a little bit of the stuff.

She looked behind Gordy again.

"You need help with him in the trailer?" a deep male voice asked, and this time she recognized it instantly.

Great. He would show up while she had her head right down there by the horse's butt.

"I'm not doing anything!" Jolie blurted out, jerking her head back from Gordy's rear quarters, "Just looking for horse poo." Right, because she wanted to remind him that she was inarticulate. She should've said a clinical word. Who in the world over the age of ten said "poo"?

"I didn't ask what you were doing," Reece said, grinning at her for the first time in over a decade.

"Sorry. I'm really tired." And she'd blame that on her acting like a crazy person this time. "What did you say?"

"I asked if you need help with Gordy."

"I do. Yes. Please." Jolie took a deep breath and peeled herself up off the stool. "I'm stressing about getting him home. And about—"

"Whether he's developing colic," Reece filled in, understanding her fecal fixation, thank God. "Have you changed the bandage?"

"Not since yesterday…I think." Maybe. The past three days were a bit of a blur.

He lifted a leather case and gave it a rattle. "Lucky for you I came prepared this time."

"Lucky for me." She glanced at Gordy again and then stepped toward Reece. "Maybe we could do this outside. I think I need a little air before we get crammed into a horse trailer. Wait, that's what you meant, right? Riding with me and Gordy in the trailer?"

"That is what I meant," he confirmed, stepping to the side to let her pass and then following her out into the sunny spring morning.

They always loaded the animals and outbuildings first, mostly because they were done taking them down first. The Bohannons would likely be on the farm before the workers were even done pulling down and packing up the big top that had put food in their bellies for years.

She tried to put that out of her mind. It wasn't the last time she'd see the tent. It'd go up again for his mother's wedding, whatever Reece decided about the camp. She sat at a picnic table and laid her arm on the sun-warmed wood, then let her eyes wander away from whatever he was going to do.

She added a new rule to her growing list intended to help her learn to traverse this new, overly emotional landscape.

Rule number three—focus on one emotion at a time.

Picking one emotion right now was harder than when her terror for Gordy had had her by the throat. Reece's presence made it hard to think. Not having slept much for the past three days also made it hard to think, and she'd already gone two for two with crazy Jolie appearing whenever Reece did.

Made her not want to ask if he'd come to any decision. To talk about something less like emotional napalm.

"Do you remember when I used to ride Gordy?" She felt him flicking at the tape and within a few seconds the bite was exposed, and the open feel made her look.

"I remember." His voice changed, a softening that gave her some small hope that he had something in his heart for their history, their lineage…other than just the horror and tragedy of his father's death.

"It wasn't long before I was too big for him. For a long time I asked when he'd grow up so I could ride him again. I didn't understand he was different from the other horses," she murmured, feeling the familiar burn return to her eyes. Three days of it springing up. Three days of waiting to fall. Three days of insanity. "He can be such a brat sometimes. He bites the other horses all the time. But this was the first time he ever bit me."

Reece almost reached for her hand but pulled back at the last second in favor of the medical supplies. "He didn't mean to."

Jolie swallowed, shifting her gaze away from him again. It took her a while to work up the will to speak and the ability to trust her voice. "I know."

"It's looking good." He shifted them away from the sad topic and back to something he could control. "The punctures at least. Better than I hoped, but there's more bruising than I like. You should get it X-rayed, just to be on the safe side." Reece uncapped a fresh bottle of water and poured some over gauze pads to clean the wound.

"If it's broken it's just a tiny fracture. That might not show up on the films for a couple of weeks. I'll wait a little bit and see how it goes." She continued shifting the topic. "Have you been staying with your mom?"

"No. I have a short-term apartment leased. I haven't been here at all since that first night, though I meant to come back. One of my professors called to advise me about a doctor in the area who is retiring and wants to transition his practice into the hands of another. He set us up to speak and it's actually pretty close to the farm."

"Who's the doctor?"

"Richards."

"Oh, I know him. He's got great peaches, and planted more at his orchard not long ago. Doing something with apples. I kind of zoned out when he was explaining that part." She shook her head. "Something about apple breeding, which sounded weird and not like something I wanted to know. It might forever ruin me on apples."

Reece applied antibiotic ointment then started tearing strips of tape to get ready for bandaging. But he stopped when she mentioned knowing Dr. Richards. "Have you seen him?"

"Granny Bohannon sees him, and I've taken her to the doctor several times. Practically have to hogtie her to get her there, no matter how bad she's feeling," she answered, and when he didn't immediately respond, she prompted, "I haven't seen him for my own health, if that's somehow weighing in on your decision on whether to get in on his practice or whatever. You wouldn't get me grandfathered in as a patient."

"I'm not worried about that," he said, getting the bandage supplies together and finally moving on to the application stage.

Jolie squinted a little. Lying. He was lying. "You *are* worried about that."

"I'm more worried about other things."

"Are you sick?" Jolie looked him in the eye again. "Or are you worried that I'm going to freak out again?"

"Neither."

"You're lying." She resisted the urge to turn his head so he faced her. "You've looked like you're about to puke at least three times since you came back. So either you're sick or I make you sick."

"You don't…" Reece smoothed the tape down with his fingertips and Jolie finally noticed it wasn't just the hand-pat he aborted to avoid touching her, he was working hard not to touch her even while treating her arm. "It's the sawdust."

Sawdust? "Have you developed an allergy?"

"No. I just don't like the sawdust. Haven't been able to stomach the smell since Dad died." His voice was low and sincere, but gruff like he really didn't like admitting this. "The college I attended? The main old academic building where pretty much all the core classes were was remodeled during my first year. I learned to come in through the back door and take the long way to my classes to avoid it."

Jolie felt her stomach bottom out. All the time she'd spent with him after his father's death and she hadn't picked up on that? He hadn't even looked at her when he'd made this admission, which told her that it was something he felt vulnerable about. Reece still had some of his tells, though she obviously didn't know them as well as she'd always thought she did if this news was such a shock to her.

She'd never met anyone who didn't like the smell of sawdust before. That Keightly Circus used it to the end was a point of pride to them and the deep-rooted circus traditions they'd always tried to preserve while other outfits had grown bigger and more modern.

"So you wouldn't throw up?"

"No. That would have been okay. It was the panic I couldn't handle. Got over the worst of it, no real panic any more. Still makes me queasy, though."

"I'm sorry." She didn't know what else to say, but she did know that he needed some kind of contact—and she just didn't think her over-emotional self could handle him pulling away if she tried to touch him. At least it didn't seem like he was just being difficult any more. "I didn't know."

"I didn't want anyone to know. I still don't," he admitted in a low voice. "Just wanted you to know it wasn't you. But I think you were right about trying to keep some distance right now. It would be easy for things to get confused between us. Taking it slow would be for the best."

"I agree." She pulled her freshly bandaged arm away, stood, and began gathering the refuse. "They've already left with the other horses. We have a trailer to ourselves. We can get him in there and get on the road now if you're ready."

He nodded, gathered his supplies and approached the truck, where he handed his treatment bag to the driver and asked on his way back to her, "Is he tranquilized?"

"I hate that word. Makes it sound like such a peaceful state, and most everyone or everything I've ever seen tranquilized ended up slack-jawed and drooling." Jolie headed into the stables, Reece behind her. "But to answer your question, yes."

She peeked to make sure he was still out of it, that the poo fairy hadn't shown up while she was outside, and then unhooked the sling as Reece worked his magic muscles and lifted the horse to carry him to the trailer.

"You need to prepare yourself. If he's not doing any better after three days…" Reece began, leading where he knew Jolie didn't want to go. They were sitting in the hay in the trailer, Gordy between them, his head in her lap.

"Don't," Jolie whispered, emotion in her voice pulling at his insides.

"I'm not trying to hurt you."

"No, I know you think you're being practical, delivering the hard doctorly advice and whatever, but I'm not giving up on him while there's hope."

Denial. "Is there hope?"

She'd probably held out hope for him for months. He

hoped not, but he didn't know. And he didn't really want to know yet. Her emotional state wasn't the only reason Reece wanted to go slow with her.

"Of course there's hope. He's still alive." She looked at him like he was a monster, but she already had too many weapons to use against him to admit how gutted he would be when Gordy died. Admit how easily she could gut him if she wanted to. She probably didn't know she had any weapons at all, and his only chance was if she continued not to realize it.

"When we get to the farm and we get him situated in his sling, you need to wean him off all the drugs and see how he feels when he's alert."

"He's in pain."

"Yes, he is." Reece gave in to his decision not to touch her and laid his hand over her forearm, where the thin material of her sleeve would keep flesh-to-flesh contact at bay.

It was enough. She looked at him. "He stuck by me when I was in pain." Even with the sleeve barrier, she pulled her arm away. "It was just you, me and Gordy. When I got back. When Mom got me back from that awful group home when Dad left me. Just you and me, and Gordy. And he never left." She looked back at him and resumed petting the sleeping horse. "Dad left. You left. Gordy never left. I won't leave him to the whims of Fate. We're going to fight, and he'll get better."

He didn't know whether she was talking about just Gordy any more, or if she'd included herself in that declaration.

All he knew for sure was that he didn't like being lumped into the same category as her gutless father.

CHAPTER FOUR

REECE DIDN'T LIKE to sort through emotions. He ignored them as best he could until it all became clear without reflection. But nothing regarding Jolie was clear.

Well, nothing except the fact that she could still drive him crazy in every meaning of the word—even when he'd not seen or heard from her for two weeks.

Reece pulled into the long country driveway and reached up to loosen his tie, which seemed to be growing tighter and tighter the closer he got to the farm. The old quote about the road to hell being paved with good intentions rolled around in his head.

The old proverb was embroidered on a pillow in Dr. Richards's office, the practice he'd finalized purchase of in the past two weeks. If Richards didn't take that damned pillow with him when he left, Reece was going to burn it.

The road to hell wasn't paved with anything, let alone intentions. It was a long gravel driveway into the middle of nowhere Georgia.

His mother's wedding would start in about an hour, so here he was, no solution and no idea what he was walking into, or how the temperament of the group would be. All he knew was he'd grown really tired of waiting for a solution to the camp question. Jolie was probably tired of waiting too. If she wanted to open in time for summer, there was definitely a clock on his decision-making process.

The white summer big top had been raised, and Reece pulled up far enough to the side that he wouldn't be disturbing any post-wedding photo ops, and got out. Spring was always a volatile time in the South, and with the weather growing ever hotter, a cold front from the northwest promised something nasty. In the distance he could see black clouds looming, and already the wind had picked up.

He rolled up the windows of his car, grabbed his jacket and wandered into the tent.

No one was inside yet, but flowers and an arch of some sort stood in the ring.

Reece took the opportunity to check for sawdust, and breathed in deeply, braced for the revulsion he expected to follow.

"It's just sand." Jolie's soft voice came from off to the side, refocusing his attention on her.

She sat on the end of the bleacher, her pale auburn curls pinned up on the side by a flower, lots of milky skin on display, a lightly freckled shoulder bared by the filmy pink dress she wore.

No solution there either. The only thing he could think of was: girl next door. "Thank you." It was kind of her to see to that, though she might want to hurt him.

Jolie looked him over, noting the extremely well-cut suit. "You had that tailored? It looks tailored. Your mom will be pleased."

"Does that mean I look good?" Reece wandered over and leaned an elbow on the edge of the bleacher, right by where she sat. His elbow almost touched her thigh, so she slid down the seat a little.

"You look good. If they don't move up the time, though, I imagine no one will look good for it."

"Storm?"

"Storm." She tilted her head toward the entrance he'd come through and added, "I stashed a bucket of gloves, hammers and ropes back there, just in case the wind starts wreaking havoc with the tent." Because even if Reece wasn't going to let her use it, she couldn't just let it fly away in a strong wind.

"Good idea."

"I wasn't sure you'd be here," she murmured, looking back at the ring and decidedly away from him.

"At my mom's wedding?"

"It's been two weeks." She'd made up her mind not to bring up any of the camp business with him today if he came, so she probably shouldn't pick a fight with him because he'd been gone without word again for two weeks. And really it was dumb to be upset about it, and she wouldn't be upset about it if he didn't leave her hanging in limbo again. This time it wasn't about their personal relationship, it was about their possible professional relationship. Which probably meant that it shouldn't actually upset her.

Besides, Reece didn't need her giving him an excuse to abandon everyone again. They were all happy he'd come back, the prodigal son. If she ran him off, they'd forgive her—that's what family did—but it would hurt them and most of Jolie's existence was focused on protecting these people, not unthinkingly hurting them.

So maybe she should take a page out of Reece's book and avoid him.

She stood up, smoothed down the one-shoulder pale pink chiffon dress she'd gotten especially for this wedding, and walked away from him to the stairs so she could walk down. His eyes followed her to the end, and once on the ground she turned in the other direction and walked away from him.

"Do you have something you need to do?" he called

after her, sounding confused. Welcome to her world. He left her in a perpetual state of confusion.

Did she have something she needed to do? Not really.

"Yes," she lied, sort of, not looking back at him. Did it count if that thing she needed to do was find somewhere to continue their decade-long tradition of not talking to one another?

She felt him following and stopped to look back. "What are you doing?"

"Helping?" Reece shrugged, like this was perfectly normal.

"The thing I need to do is be alone. It's your mother's wedding, and having us at each other's throats or acting crazy would be bad."

"So let's not act crazy," Reece said, shrugging again. "Truce for a day?"

"Stop shrugging. It just draws attention to your gigantic shoulders," Jolie grumbled. "Truce? Easier said than done."

He reached up and pushed back a stray lock of sandy brown hair, tucking it behind his ear. The rest of his mane stayed caught in a short ponytail at the base of his skull, but that one lock kept breaking free, making her itch to touch it.

"Do you hate me, Jo?"

What?

Right. He wasn't talking about his hair.

"Sometimes," Jolie murmured, refusing to lie about that, even if it wasn't an admission she wanted to make. "I also don't want to bother you, and I don't want to fight with you…which is kind of a lie because I do want to fight with you. Or actually, I want to yell at you. And maybe kick you in the junk. But that would be bad. Counterproductive. Pathetic. And it's exhausting."

She stopped her random confession because dealing

with any sort of feelings meant she might get uncontrollably teary. Something else she'd discovered in the past two weeks. People weren't supposed to cry *before* the wedding. She should save up her tears for the wake to follow.

He reached up and tugged on his tie, loosening it around his neck.

"You're messing it up."

"You said that before. I'm messing everything up. I know. And I don't care. I can't breathe." Reece worked at his collar until the tie was hanging loose and the top button was unfastened.

Jolie closed her eyes and took a deep breath, seeking strength from somewhere.

He stepped over to her, stopping close enough that even with her eyes closed she knew she'd have to crane her neck to look him in the eye. Nothing touched, but she felt heat radiating off him. "I know you said you want to kick me in the junk, but aside from this unexpected violent streak you've developed you look amazing."

"I don't…it's the dress. It's new." She opened her eyes, forcing herself to meet his eyes.

"I thought it was bad manners for anyone to outshine the bride."

"And you haven't even seen the bride yet."

"I know a tough act to follow when I see one." Reece ran the tip of his finger over the pink orchid pinned in her hair and his voice quieted. "I didn't know I wasn't going to come back when I first left."

Every survival instinct in her roared to life, demanding she step back, put some space between them, not look at him…but closed eyes didn't hold tears well, and the fool seemed bound and determined to make her cry. "Please, don't do this now."

"Can we just pretend for today that I haven't been an ass for the past ten years?" A ghost of a smile danced across his lips. "That I'm just the owner's idiot son? Bossy, opinionated, incapable of keeping his hands out of your hair... And you the big-hearted girl-next-door who puts up with me?"

"I never just put up with you," Jolie whispered, looking down and drawing a deep breath. They were having a moment. That needed to stop. She stepped back and put on her best sarcastic tone. "I suffered you."

"Did you?" Reece grinned despite her sour words.

Jolie mustered a smile and nodded. "Totally. Important distinction." And then she drew a breath. "Okay. I'll sit with you. For a little while."

"Just until you feel moved to violence against Samson again?" He turned, offering her his elbow.

Jolie laughed, unable to help herself. "You've named your manly bits? Good Lord, what an ego." But she slipped her hand through the crook of his arm. "Why would you name him after a mobile phone?"

"Samson is the strong dude from the Bible. Not the people who make electronics."

"Duly noted." Jolie tried to resist the urge to remind him how strong Samson *hadn't* been the only time she'd gotten up close and personal with him. And wait a minute, did that make her Delilah? Okay. Weird.

"Well if I start feeling violent toward him, I'll stay until I've carried out whatever instinct is telling me to do."

The wind picked up, buffeting the tent so hard that the thick vinyl thumped like a drum in the cavernous tent interior and saved her from reflecting too hard on the sudden bizarre ramifications of their genitals.

"If they don't hurry, they might end up getting married in Oz." Her hand tingled where it was wrapped around his arm, and even with the not inconsiderable heels she wore, he still towered over her. A feeling crept in with his presence and proximity that she refused to name. It was a stupid feeling, the kind of feeling that led her to all sorts of bad decisions.

They climbed a few rows up and sat, Jolie making sure she left some space between them, and while they waited for everyone else to get there, he talked. Safe topics.

It began with a story about his first day in residency, and how his size had auto-selected him to wrestle some naked, violent drunk down while others had got restraints on the man, and how he'd never been so happy to see insane amounts of body hair. "It was almost like he had on a fur suit, so that's what I pretended. Actually, I was a little envious at his ability to grow hair."

"You're really stuck on that Samson story, aren't you?" Jolie teased, but by the end of the story he had her laughing and, at least for the moment, distracted from all the crap that had piled up between them.

When the bride and groom entered the big top on foot, Jolie sat up straighter. "I thought they were going to ride in."

"Horseback?"

"That had been the plan." She shrugged. "Maybe they decided—" A crack of thunder stopped her words. Everyone looked up, including Reece.

As if Mother Nature had generously waited for the happy couple to find shelter first, as soon as they made their way to the ring, the sky opened up and rain poured down in such heavy amounts it echoed loudly in the nearly empty tent.

Lightning and thunder arrived, and the winds picked up, rocking the whole thing. Big storms made circus people nervous, but in the spirit of enjoying the wedding, everyone got out of their seats and moved to the outer edge of the ring so they could hear the vows.

Before the pastor had got out the "Dearly Beloved," a

whistle cracked through the air and in that instant forty heads turned in unison toward the direction the storm was rolling in from.

One of the anchor cables had come loose.

"Damn." Jolie took off in the direction where she'd stashed supplies and grabbed gloves, a couple of extra spikes and a hammer. A group ran with her, cousins and circus cousins along with Reece, all dragging on gloves and making ready to do whatever was needed to save the tent.

When another cable snapped free, the rest of the wedding party descended on the northwest side of the tent to hold it down.

Like hang-gliding in a hurricane, they worked between gusts to pound the stakes deeper into the earth. While a group worked on what had come free, others split off with hammers to drive in deeper the spikes that were still set, trying to ensure that they did not come free.

By the time they had the tent secure, every member of the wedding party was drenched and exhausted. All except the bride and groom, who were only severely disheveled, having been kept inside the tent working under threat of death or bodily harm.

Once again everyone gathered around the ring, the windblown bride and groom with the pastor the only three dry people under the big top.

Jolie stepped between Reece and Natalie, another cousin. As it became clear that the meager number of attendees couldn't fill the circumference of the center ring, they stepped inside and the circle of people closed ranks.

There was no bride's side or groom's side, they simply clasped hands and witnessed the joining of two lives.

For the first time in ten years Reece's hand opened beside her and she slipped her hand into his—palms crossed, fingers curling around the edges. Not entwined, not as lovers holding hands. As family. Just as Natalie's hand did on her left, minus that exaggerated tingle Reece always evoked.

But she had to ignore that.

Jolie would never have thought herself one to cry at weddings, and she didn't want to be one of those overly emotional people who did. It was just her stupid inner sixteen-year-old who'd dreamed of a Keightly-Bohannon wedding all those years ago.

That would have been different, of course. She could still remember what her ridiculous sixteen-year-old-self had imagined. Naturally, they would have gotten married on the trapeze, with flowers and vines wound around everything, culminating with her leaping into his arms with some ridiculously intricate trick that no one had ever tried before, spontaneously erupting from her in a flash of romantic inspiration... And then Reece would have caught her and kissed her and tossed her back.

Or the other one, where Gordy was the flower girl.

Every fantasy beyond ridiculous. Not at all romantic. Not like this ceremony, no matter what calamity conspired to interrupt it. In the end it simply stripped away any artifice and left the simple beauty and truth of two people who'd waited for each other...and had finally found their way together.

Her throat thickened. Maybe Reece had been right to leave when he had. Maybe she'd spun some fantasy about their relationship too. Maybe he'd known where she hadn't.

And now they were all so wet that maybe no one would notice a couple of tears on her cheeks...

Reece's hand squeezed, letting her know he'd noticed.

She looked up at him, but he did not look back at her. The way his jaw bunched confirmed for her that he wasn't unaffected now. The strange beast stood there, grinding his teeth. She couldn't even tell if he was reacting to his mother marrying or if she was the only one lost in those old thoughts.

And her doubts grew as the ceremony progressed. At the end hands eventually parted to applaud the new Mr. and Mrs. Mack Bohannon, leaving Reece as the last in the Keightly line. Maybe he was thinking about his dad.

Of course he was thinking about his dad…

"Are you all right?" she asked him as Natalie retrieved her camera and began snapping pictures of the newlyweds.

"They're taking pictures," Reece said, shaking his head.

Jolie nodded slowly. "It's a wedding. I think picture-taking has been the tradition as long as there have been photos."

"Yes, but look at everyone."

She looked at herself, at him, and at everyone else. She saw lots of clothing plastered against bodies, lots of wind-blown hair, and lots of smiles.

But it was definitely out of control.

"You think that the wedding was ruined by the storm." She reached up and turned his head until he was looking at his mom. "Do they look unhappy?"

"No." He wrapped his hand around her wrist and pulled her hand from his cheek. Without warning, he walked to the seats, grabbed his jacket and walked back. A second later he'd wrapped it around her and now busily buttoned it up, like that would keep the exceedingly oversized thing on her. "They look happy," he said when her arms were in the sleeves and he'd gotten her as warm as he could. "But it should have been better."

"It was pretty amazing the way it was."

"The tent almost blew away. We're all soaked. Her flowers are all broken."

"And her heart is full." She shook her head. He couldn't

focus on anything but the parts that were outside his control. "How about me? Do I look happy? Or am I just putting up a good front?" She smiled, though it was a guarded thing. She wasn't going to make this easy on him.

Reece looked at her over the space of several increasing heartbeats. "You were crying earlier."

He caught her arm again and his hands, big and much warmer than hers, closed around hers to warm it.

"I'm okay. A little cold, though, so thank you for the jacket."

"I know you're cold." He chuckled then said, "I'm pretty sure everyone knows that. It was a public service that I put that jacket on you."

"Public service?"

He looked at her now hidden chest, a glimmer of that old flirty light in his eyes.

"I'm sure your cold perkiness was making your male cousins uncomfortable."

Nipples. He was thinking about breasts, even though she didn't have a lot going on in that department. And that wasn't unappreciated. Except for the old rule that predated Reece, and which she should make rule number four, so she didn't forget that it applied to Reece as much as to other men.

She didn't need a man in her life. Better to be alone than with someone who would leave you anyway when he left the circus and the life. A variation on the rule ground into her head by her mother: don't marry a man not part of the circus—he'll only break your heart and abduct your daughter when he leaves.

Only there was no circus now, and she hadn't really revisited that rule.

She glanced over her shoulder to make sure no one was looking at them.

When she looked back, his hand was at the side of her

head, fiddling with the hair clip. He untangled it from the bits the wind had yanked free of the clip before dumping gallons of water on her and unwound the coil of curls. "The mess really is bothering you."

"I like it down."

"Even when it's all wet?"

"Especially when it's all wet…"

Her scalp tingled and the hooded quality of his eyes when he looked at her made everything else tingle too.

Damn rule number four. Their truce was in effect until tomorrow, and why couldn't that truce include all the other bad feelings she wanted a night off from?

Flirting, holding hands, kissing…all good feelings. Feelings she might like to try out again.

Giving in to impulse, Jolie stepped between his legs, where he perched on the side of the ring, and leaned up to press her lips to his stubbled cheek.

"What are you doing?" It didn't come out as a question so much as a gruff and somewhat alarmed statement, but his arms went around her nevertheless.

"Pretending you haven't been an ass for ten years." She slid her arms beneath his and turned her head to rest her cheek in the hollow of his shoulder.

His chin came down to rest atop her head, but his body didn't relax.

"You're warm."

"No, I'm not."

Jolie ran her hands up his spine, over the wet material, which thankfully was thin enough to have started drying. With a slow, drawn-out sigh Reece relaxed against her.

"I think they're doing the cake thing," he murmured into her hair, and Jolie turned her head to look, unwilling to pull back yet.

"I think they're in a hurry to get on to the wake and then on to their honeymoon."

"The wake?"

Jolie leaned back and looked at him, her brows pinched. "Yes…"

"For?"

"Keightly Circus? Did you really think we wouldn't have a wake for it?"

"But this is a wedding."

"And your mom and Mack wanted to celebrate a new beginning while we toasted the past. This is how they met, you know. It's balancing something sad with something good."

"They're moving the flower— What are they doing?" Reece's scowl forced her to pull back so she could see and explain to him properly what was going on.

"They're changing the set for the show."

"Performing…"

"I know you've been gone a while, but think. What do we usually do at a wake?" She wrapped his arms around her middle and stepped back until her back fully pressed into his chest.

What do they do at wakes? "Talk…about people. Drink some toasts…"

"And we give tributes." She shook his arm.

"It's been a long time since you checked on Gordy." He did not want to attend the wake. Not telling him was a dirty trick. Dirty. And if it weren't his mother's wedding day, he'd leave and let her riddle out the enigma of how he felt about this.

"No. Gordy's much better, which you would know if you hadn't stayed away entirely for two weeks." She turned in his arms and laid her hands on his chest. This felt good. Jolie felt right. A wake did not.

"Are you okay? No one's mad at you, if that's what you're worried about."

"I'm fine." The look she gave him said she knew better.

"You're nervous. Your hand is sweaty."

"It's fine. Let's sit." Reece let go and started walking, but Jolie caught his hand before he got too far. Surprise caused him to stop and look at her.

She squeezed his hand. "Don't look so grim."

There had better be actual drinks involved in these toasts. Something to let him turn this off. He let her go ahead of him up the bleachers, and followed.

In the first row someone had set out a line of framed photos. It only took a glance to establish who they were—people Keightly had lost over the years. Some he remembered, some only the older members of the group remembered.

Grandpa. Uncle. Cousin... The wakes he'd attended.

Dad. The wake he'd skipped.

This wake was sounding worse and worse all the time. Mechanically, he sat beside her.

"You'll wish you'd stayed," she whispered, accurately reading his mind. But she still kept her voice low, keeping his discomfort private, like she'd apparently kept the sawdust business private.

"The executioner doesn't usually attend the funeral."

"No one thinks of you that way. They love you, Reece."

She took his hand again, and he ignored the warning in his head that told him he shouldn't be touching her so much. Her hand felt good. Small, but strong. That touch. If this evening was going to go the way he thought it would, he'd need that touch to get him through.

"And as weird as you may feel right now, it's your family too. Everyone wants you here. Well, maybe not everyone—you don't seem to want you here. But everyone else does."

"Even you?"

Jolie nodded, but the sadness never far from her eyes filled in what that nod didn't. She didn't want to want him there. She'd told him to stay away, after all, and he had no doubt that however bothered by everything he was, she was just as affected. He just didn't know whether that was a good thing or a bad thing. All he knew was that it was impossible to ignore.

The lights went down and she scooted a little closer to him. He switched her hand to his other and wrapped the closest around her shoulders. Maybe he could enjoy this part of the wake. Not the performing, because the knot in his gut had already started twisting. But being alone with Jolie in the dark, allowed to smell her hair… That could get him through this.

From somewhere behind the bleachers a spotlight popped on and focused on the ring. A white sheet hung on a frame—makeshift projection screen—and Granny Bohannon strolled up to the still blank screen. He'd always called her Granny, even if she wasn't his grandmother. A heart of gold and a mouth like a sailor in a small, spunky package. The Bohannon women all seemed to be as small as the Keightly men were large. "If Granny's the presenter for the evening, things are already looking up," Reece murmured, wanting her to enjoy things and not worry about his reaction. And it was true. Granny made everything either fun or utterly inappropriate. Usually both.

"She's been organizing the kids for this for weeks," Jolie whispered.

A slide appeared, one he recognized as the oldest in the collection. A very serious-looking performer without a smile. Once they'd gotten a good look at the picture, another spotlight came on, illuminating one of the kids in a replica of the old costume from the photo. The sandy-haired teen tried to juggle and ended up chasing the balls around the ring while Granny narrated…in language that almost made Reece blush.

He couldn't stop the smile that followed. "Start with

the clowns," he murmured to Jolie, who patted his arm again. They all loved to laugh. It was the best way to start off the wake. History, memories, and laughter. People he didn't know, people he did know, and some he wished he knew better.

The first non-clown performer to enter the ring had Reece tensing again. He squeezed her shoulders just a little too tight, not hurting her but making the turmoil he was feeling clear. Luckily, there was no rhyme or reason to the format of the wake. People had been preparing acts, tributes to the old acts from the past, compiling stories to tell and writing toasts. They took pride in every aspect, but there was no schedule or program.

Ten years ago, not equipped to know how to help him, Jolie now realized she'd failed to pick up on all his signals. Failed to help him through his father's death, or even recognize the kind of thoughts he'd been having. She'd thought she'd had him figured out, but if she had then he wouldn't be suffering now.

She'd lost her father too or, well, she'd been lost by her father, but the result had been similar. And she'd gotten over it. That's the only way to make it in life, get through the bad things until stuff got good again.

The sawdust had been a revelation. While she'd seen Reece's personality shift after his dad died, she'd always thought of it as being anger—that was the only emotion he'd ever allowed her to see until he'd made that unexpected sawdust confession.

The bright spotlights reflected off the sand and created a low glow in seats. Enough that she could see the muscle of his jaw bunching and the unnatural rise of his shoulders. But his biggest tell was the look of extreme concentration on his face. He didn't even seem aware that she was scrutinizing him.

Only an idiot wouldn't know he'd been in pain when his dad had died, but she just hadn't picked up on how traumatized he'd been until now.

"If I tell you a secret, do you promise not to tell anyone?" Jolie touched his hand again, trying to draw his attention from the ring.

"No," he replied, keeping tones low. "Maybe later." Because he was concentrating.

"No one is going to be hurt."

"Burns," Reece muttered. "Juggling seven clubs is just as impressive without fire or added danger."

"From a technical aspect, but it's not as exciting."

The look he gave her confirmed what she'd thought: He was escaping back into anger.

Armed with what she'd picked up this evening, Jolie now felt the need to protect Reece. To help him. Her own anger was still there, and still righteous—he had been an idiot to cut them all out of his life as he had done. And since he'd done it once, she had no doubt that he'd do it again, pack them all off at his earliest convenience. But she understood him a little better.

Her father leaving her had driven deep the need to stay within the safety of the circus, and his father dying had driven into Reece the idea that there was no safety at the circus.

Evening turned to night, then to morning. There were toasts, stories, and tributes. And no one got hurt. Reece met a new stepbrother, a fifteen-year-old boy called Anthony who'd come to Bohannon Farm as a ward of the state, part of their program to foster troubled kids. He endeared himself to Reece the instant he introduced himself and asked Reece and Jolie to come with him outside, and immediately bowed out with a slug to Reece's arm and a murmured, "You owe me."

"Did you put him up to that?" Jolie squinted at him, but mostly just looked amused.

Reece shook his head, smiling at Anthony's retreating back. "I did not. But I'm glad he picked up on my desire to escape." He offered a hand to Jolie and when she took it, he started walking toward the trailers.

They walked as close as they could, giving up hand-holding in favor of arms around each other. Before they even made it to the footpath leading to Jolie's trailer, they both knew where they were going. The question in Reece's mind was about whether or not she knew why he wanted to go there.

When she stepped up onto her stairs and turned to face him, the way she looked at his mouth for a few seconds before looking him in the eye was invitation enough.

He slipped his arms around her waist and closed his mouth over hers, kissing her with the longing he'd never lost.

Her soft lips parted in an instant, welcoming his tongue into her mouth.

The hands on his back squeezed, fingers pressing into the flesh in a way that caused a riot of goose-bumps and driving chills under the now dry material. No one else tasted like Jolie. No one else kissed like her either. She'd hold the kiss as long as he did, lack of oxygen be damned. When his heart had sped up to the point that he needed air, he broke the kiss but kept her close enough for them to fight for the same air with big shuddering breaths.

"This is a bad idea," Jolie whispered, swallowing and licking her kiss-swollen lips.

Reece shook his head. "Good idea."

"Bad idea. Bad bad…" She kissed him this time, releasing her hold on him to get at the jacket buttons and shed the bulky material that kept them apart. Freed from it, she pressed tight against him, the gauzy material of her dress leaving very little to his vivid imagination. God, he wanted to feel her. Everywhere.

CHAPTER FIVE

SHE PUSHED HER tongue into his mouth and he barely stifled a groan.

The groan made her pull away, or something did. She felt for the door behind her, flipping the latch and stepping to the side so she could swing the door open. "I don't know whether to invite you in."

"Invite me in. I...am a great guest." He grabbed his jacket and stepped up onto the stairs, which forced her up the remaining couple into the trailer.

"What I mean is I have rules. See, mostly I had one rule, but now I have four. I think. I might have five. Because..." She licked her lips and he closed the door, but couldn't take his eyes off the little pink tongue tracing her lips.

"I like rules." Reece would have said he liked anything at that point. The unfocused look of her eyes as she stared at his mouth made the words mostly meaningless anyway.

He dropped his jacket in the floor, wrapped his arms around her waist and lifted her against him.

No hesitation, she kissed him again, whatever she'd been trying to say. All heat, and deep kisses that made him question whether he'd have another episode like the last time they'd got heated.

The edge of the couch cushions touched the backs of his legs and Reece sat, arranging her legs to straddle his thighs as he leaned back, keeping her close so she could have no doubt how much he wanted her.

"I have rules." She tried again, winding her fingers in his hair and pulling to keep his head tugged back.

He couldn't tell whether the look in her eyes was the heat between them or an impending panic attack. The glazed sexiness was gone. "What rules?"

"Rules about men," she panted, shaking her head.

Freaking out was a sign to stop kissing her.

"I'm not sleeping with you." She blurted the words out before running them through her one-emotion-at-a-time rule. Lust was having a showdown with fear, and she couldn't decide which one to go with. Fear won for control of her mouth at that second.

"Okay." He reached up to pull her hands from his hair then carefully lifted her from his lap and placed her beside him on the couch. "Do you want me to leave?"

"I don't know." She could see both reactions as equally compelling.

Reece shifted, winced, and settled into the cushions again.

"Are you in pain?"

"I'm fine." He took a deep breath and looked at her. "I'd really like to know what you're thinking, though, because a minute ago…we were on the same wavelength. Then you started to panic."

"I'm still soggy."

Reece nodded. "So you want to change before we talk?"

It would give her a chance to think about what she could say to him, what information she was willing to part with… "Yes."

He gestured to the other end of the trailer. "I'll wait."

"Do you want to change too? I don't have much that would fit you, but you could go back to the RV and change."

"I'm not leaving. I want to talk and make sure you're all right. I'm making the most of our truce."

Jolie headed for the other side of the trailer and stripped down to her underwear with her back to him. There wasn't much privacy in the small living space, and she twisted to see if he was looking.

Of course he was looking. "Close your eyes."

"I've seen it all before."

"Do you really want to go there with me? I hear that rodeo riders can last at least eight seconds."

Reece winced.

That zinger had been a decade in the making. He looked away and she went back to changing. With clean underthings and her fluffy pink robe on, she wandered back to the couch, turned on a space heater on the way and sat down, feeling somewhat warmer if not more in control. She may not have changed that much since he'd last seen her, but he'd changed. It really wasn't fair.

"What's with the pink? You seem to wear it a lot now."

"I like pink. It's a myth that redheads can't wear pink." He looked large and out of place on her sofa. And something else, uncomfortable maybe. Angry? No, his jaw wasn't bunching, but he had that look of concentration again.

He looked her over and added, "You turn pink easier than you used to."

"One of the many ways I'm an enigma," she mumbled, and tried to remember why she'd stopped kissing him.

"Tell me your rule about men."

The color in his cheeks rose a little. "So you mean you don't date."

"I don't date," Jolie confirmed.

"How long has that been going on?"

She sighed. "Long enough. I don't need to date. And, honestly, there have been slim pickings with the circus.

We have guest artistes. Mom married one and is now travelling with a new circus family. But I haven't wanted to have to move on with a troupe when they left. So, no, I don't date. Though I am starting to see that I could now. I mean, if there is no need to be on the road any more then there isn't that obstacle when you're getting into a relationship. I don't really need anyone who is in the life any more." She didn't date, but right now she also didn't know how to get control of her mouth. He hadn't asked for all this information. "I'm not signing up for dating sites or whatever. I'm okay with not dating."

"You're not convincing me." He stretched back, keeping those blue eyes fixed on her. "No one who wants to be alone kisses the way you kissed me." He tilted his head in the direction of the big top. "You might be able to sell that line to someone else, but I have a very long memory."

It felt weird to talk about this. She'd gone so long without talking to anyone about these intimate details of her attempted love life, but Dr. Long Memory begged to be reminded. "Then you should remember how the sex went with us."

"I remember. Believe me. It's a dent in my ego that I'm the worst sex you ever had." The way she looked away from him and turned just a little pinker, a little guiltier meant something. "The only sex you ever had?"

She cleared her throat, shifting and straightening her robe so it kept her well covered. "That's not your business."

"The hell it's not if I put you off sex for life," Reece muttered, angrier than he rationally should be to hear those words. He certainly didn't want to hear that she'd been with, well, anyone else. But hearing that she'd been with no one since him...was worse. "You have no appetite for it?"

"I have a fine appetite, I just don't need a man to help me…with that."

"With orgasms, you mean." He tried to keep his mind blank, because this conversation had suddenly taken a new interesting turn and his mind summoned appropriate visuals.

"With orgasms," she confirmed with a grunt, waving a hand. "I don't need help. I can do it myself."

Definitely a mental image he could spend months contemplating…but not if he wanted to get anything else done. "There's m-more to it than that." He stammered, trying to find his cool. He'd had the idea that this conversation would help him understand her, and maybe help her somehow. Not break him.

"I have a toy and I'm not ashamed to say it."

More…fantastic mental images. Images that completely robbed him of words.

"So, however much better orgasms are with a penis, it's covered?"

Stop picturing. Stop, stop, stop.

He leaned forward, turned off the heater, and sat back again. He'd had a point to make… "Okay, but it's still different with someone."

"It's close enough. It can't be all that different." She squirmed around at the other end of the couch, growing pinker by the second, despite her claims. "The mechanics are all covered!"

"Oh, Jolie…you're either fooling yourself or trying to torture me." Maybe both.

The shake of her head that followed was slow, less certain than all this my-orgasms-are-acceptable-as-is talk had been.

"So you're saying that hypothetically, if someone else controlled the vibrator…"

"It doesn't vibrate." She waved a hand.

"So it's…"

"A kind of squishy penis thing."

Reece rubbed his face, trying to relax his brows before she gave him another headache. "So, hypothetically, by your definition if I controlled the…toy, it would be no different for you than doing it yourself." He should be trying to get this out of his mind, not grilling her about it. Only someone stupid would have this fight with her, but he needed her to know he was *right*. What kind of grown woman didn't understand this basic truth? The kind he'd broken.

"Right."

"Fibber. Please, tell me you don't really think that. You're just getting some payback because of how…awful I was the first time we…"

"If I was torturing you, I'd say, 'Here, hold my happy playtime-penis while I have an orgasm.' And afterward push you out the door. But that would be mean to you and meaningless to me."

"Fine."

"What?"

"Get your play…time…penis. Your whatever. Get it."

Jolie laughed, a breathy laugh that said she was picturing things now. "You're joking."

"No, I'm calling your bluff. You're just messing with me."

"Reece…"

"Say it, you're just—"

"I'm not messing with you! But sleeping together is a bad idea."

"You're right, I'm definitely not getting laid tonight. I don't have condoms with me, and unless you are lying about that rule against men in your life, you don't have them either."

"I don't have them."

"Then get your toy."

"Because you've seen it all before?"

"Because I've seen it, and you deserve to see me suffer after you know exactly what it means." A good man, knowing how she responded to dares, wouldn't dare her sexually. But he wasn't feeling like a good man right now. He was feeling like a very frustrated man who had to open her beautiful damned eyes. And maybe vindicate himself a little along the way.

"Is this what they taught you in Playing Doctor School? Because—"

"Hell, no. There will be nothing clinical about this. And I'm still of the mind that it would be insanely hot, but if you want to turn me off the idea fast, keep up the doctor talk. Makes it smarmy and unappea…less appealing."

Jolie watched his face, and then she pointedly looked at his groin. Yeah, he might just suffer from this if she agreed to it. "So you are swearing you won't try to have sex with me."

"I promise you, I will behave myself."

She considered a moment. Pros and cons. Pro: she would get to make him suffer. He'd taken her virginity and then promptly freaked out, had got out of there and run away—like to another freaking state and never came back. Making him suffer and give her an orgasm? That sounded vaguely like justice. Pervy poetic justice…if she didn't have some kind of performance issue. Did women get those? And he would have nothing and suffer and… she wasn't sleeping with him. No matter what he said… and he could be made to want something really bad and not have it. *Like her camp.*

Cons: he might break his promise. He did have a record of broken promises, and he was right about there being no condoms in the house. Which could mean that there might be a little Bohannon in her future. Which actually wouldn't be a con. She loved kids. She just didn't love the idea of being abandoned by a lover or husband or a whatever Reece was.

Too many emotions to think about, especially when the big one that kept distracting her was the idea of more kissing… One emotion at a time.

"Fine. But you should know that I have no good and honorable motives. And no matter how much you want to have sex after, I'm not going to do it. I'm not going to touch your penis. I'm not going to kiss it or anything else. And oral sex seems dangerous. I'm not doing it."

"I wouldn't ask. This is all about me proving I'm right." He stood up, grabbed her off the couch, and marched the short distance toward the bedroom. "But you're going to have to explain the 'dangerous' comment later."

"I know how that thing goes off willy-nilly, like an unstable grenade. And if it's by my face…I would really have to insist on some kind of protective eyewear. Goggles."

"That was one time," Reece muttered, and now had the mental image of her with goggles on, and it was still sexy to him. God, he should put a halt to this nonsense.

"You really have to stop picking me up and carting me around. You're not a caveman. Didn't they teach you any vocabulary at doctor school?"

"Medical school," he corrected again, since he was pretty sure she was calling it doctor school now to annoy him. "I know a lot of big words. You don't want to play Scrabble with me. I dominate."

"I imagine if your opponent gets the letters you want, you just pick them up and move them where you want them to go."

"Don't you?" He put her down at the foot of the bed and began shedding clothes. Probably looked like he wanted to get this over with, and he kind of did…but it was more eagerness. She'd made him stop looking earlier. "Why are you just sitting there? Get the toy. Does it have a name?"

"No. Of course not." She gestured to the bedside table while looking him over. He wouldn't stop her. The point of this completely insane idea was to show her that sex was better with a partner, not a toy.

The way she looked up at him was an encouragement until she said, "Leave the boxers on."

Getting undressed was a little harder for Jolie. Reece stripped without a shred of hesitation, but she couldn't match that. Her boldness almost abandoned her as she reached for her panties and stopped to look at him.

This wasn't the sort of thing she'd ever have pictured herself doing on a dare. But if she was honest, that wasn't all this was. She had his taste still on her lips, and the memory of his warm hand in hers. The idea of being flesh to flesh with him—of feeling the length of his big body melding against hers—awakened a need inside her she'd not felt in a long time.

And she knew he was right there with her. His pupils dilated, his mouth was open, and there was a color on his cheeks she would have called exertion in any other circumstances…they all added up to the same thing. It may have been ten years, his face might have changed, matured, but she could still recognize want in him. He still wanted her. Logically, she knew he'd probably shared that look with a number of other women since he'd left her. And tomorrow she'd no doubt remember that…but right now he wanted her. Not anyone else. She deserved a night of that. Whether or not he deserved to suffer, she couldn't really say.

"Come here." He held out one hand and when she took it and sat on the bed, topless beside him, he guided her mouth back to his.

Something else to think about tomorrow, when she'd probably regret this. Right now she was stuck in some loop of not believing him, wondering if he was right, wanting him to be right, and then wondering if she'd regret finding out.

His breath came fast, and her heart sped up in tandem. Probably some primitive warning system she'd also regret ignoring.

She shut it down. The way his hands gripped and squeezed, greedy for the feel of her, that peculiar trembling low in her belly...all shouted a little louder than that warning system.

They stretched out on the bed, and when the hair on his chest teased her flesh, she was surprised to find her breasts beginning to ache. Kissing had been a great deal calmer when they'd first started doing it. And by the time they'd got around to it affecting her breasts, eager hands had been involved, and sometimes his mouth. But he hadn't even touched them yet, and her body was already responding.

She slid her hands to his head and curled her fingers in his longish sandy locks, pulling his head away. Air, she needed air. Her heart was beating too hard and too fast. As soon as their lips parted she took several great shuddering breaths, all the while staring into eyes as blue as a stormy sea.

He would break his promise. That's what Reece did. The muscles in his arms and back strained and shook with restraint, but it wouldn't last. He'd at least try to break his promise. For the first time she was fairly certain she'd let him.

She closed her eyes, trying to calm down, trying to still her hips and belly, which alternated between writhing into the mattress and quivering. The sensation of his warm hand tracking up the inside her thigh got her eyes open again. "That's not Mr. Happy."

He grinned as she spilled the name of her toy. "I'll get you for the lie later." His smile faded and he just watched her eyes. "Just want to make sure…you're ready."

A tremor of anticipation started deep inside her, and every whiffled breath confirmed for him before his long fingers found her sex and gave a long stroke.

Pleasure lanced through her, and somewhere in the back of her mind Jolie was aware she was supposed to compare this with pleasure she'd had on her own. But thinking was entirely too much effort.

Reece's look of concentration returned, and with it high, tight breaths. If her horses ground their teeth like he was doing, she'd bit them. Okay, yes, he was suffering. She couldn't even take any pleasure in that because the terrible need coiled in her felt like suffering too. It had never been this intense, even compared to how awful it had been that one other time they'd started to make love and he'd…had issues and bailed immediately afterward.

He licked his lips, withdrew his had hand from between her legs, and the fingers that had stroked her went into his mouth, shocking every other thought from her mind. She became aware that he was proceeding with the imitation penis when she felt it gliding, seeking her entry.

His eyes devoured her. She knew before he'd even slid the toy home that it was going to be the best orgasm she'd ever had. No doubt lingered that one waited for her. But she was supposed to do her part too…and slid a hand toward her sex.

Reece let go of the toy, grabbed and pinned her hands above her head.

"What are you—?"

"I'm the one who gets to." He crossed her arms at the wrists and held them with one hand, the other sliding back to the toy and beginning to move it. In and out, slow then fast, twisting and straight, adjusting the angle by the sounds every lick of pleasure ripped from her. But it wasn't enough. Just a pathetic substitute for what she desperately wanted. She wanted to feel the heat of him between her legs, feel the muscles on his back flex as he moved inside her…and she wanted him to feel. Pleasure. And whatever that dark current passing between them even now was…she knew it'd be more.

"Take it away." She panted the words, unable to move her hands and do it herself. The distress in her voice must have reached him. He stopped, breathing as hard as she, and shook his head, confused.

"I want you. I don't want it. I want you." She nodded, backing up her shameless, desperate words.

Reece closed his eyes, shook his head and began slowly working it within her again. "I promised." His hand still held hers, wound together now more than pinned. He opened his eyes and watched her. "I can feel you shaking. Don't fight it. You need it. I need it."

Then he whispered, "I will never break another promise to you, Jolie, no matter what it costs me."

It wasn't true… She'd never be that important to anyone. But the fantasy of it pushed her over the edge. When her climax came, her body bucked, but she kept her head still and her eyes locked to his. He knew she didn't believe him. She could see it in the frown that flashed through his eyes. No barriers existed between them right now.

She'd have expected him to gloat, but there wasn't even a hint of victory in his tortured gaze. He said nothing to taunt her, no *I told you so*.

He simply withdrew the toy, his hand shaking as he laid it behind him on the bed, and dragged her whatever fraction of an inch she was away from him—not satisfied until their flesh melded and his arms held her. Burying his face in her hair and his nose in the nape of her neck, he shuddered and sighed.

Stiff and unyielding, his erection pressed against the cleft of her butt, but he did nothing to relieve himself. Just held her while both their hearts tried to slow back down.

Jolie was the first one to crack. However much she wanted to punish him for the past decade, now she just wanted him to feel what she'd felt. "I could touch you…"

"No. I told you. I'm not going to break any more promises to you. Not now, not ever." He shuddered again, but apparently deciding that he couldn't stay tucked against her warmth he released her and rolled to his back and then to a sitting position at the foot of the bed and reached for his pants.

"You're leaving?"

"I'm removing myself from temptation." He tugged the pants on as he stood, and wrested them over the…impressive tent in his tight boxers.

She hadn't taken the time to admire him before, but he really had stayed in magnificent form in his time away from the circus. "You were right," she whispered, unable to keep from an honorable answer when he was suffering to keep from breaking promises.

"We can talk about that tomorrow." He pulled his shirt on, in a hurry to get out of there, but he did pause to look at her. "Are you okay?" He smiled, a tired, forced grin if she'd ever seen one.

Jolie nodded, pulling the sheet over herself as much for him as for her.

Reece stepped around the bed, bent down and kissed her on the head, then made his way to the door. It closed and she scooted into the warm spot he'd left on her bed and pulled the blankets over her to keep what little of his heat remained.

She should try to figure out what this meant before they

talked about it. But if he remained true to form, he'd beat feet and she'd see him when he came to sell the equipment to some buyer.

Knocking at the door and the sound of his name being called in a frantic manner pulled Reece from fitful sleep. He stumbled out of bed and to the door, then wrenched it open to find Granny Bohannon there, looking wild-eyed.

"Get your doctor things. One of my boys got hurt."

It had been a few months since his last ER rotation, but he shook his sleepiness out and focused. "Hurt how?"

"Fell, got his arm bent around bad somehow. Don't know if it's broke, but we can't hardly get him on his feet. Dammit. I told him to stay the hell off the equipment, but he listens about as good as my fifth husband. And he was the deafest son of a…"

Another bone injury? Reece left Granny cussing at the door, crammed his feet into his shoes, grabbed the bag he'd brought with him for the exams he planned on offering today, and took off out the door behind her. She'd already climbed onto a four-wheeler and gunned the engine, leaving him the seat behind. And she hadn't stopped complaining in a vocabulary blue enough to make high-school boys jealous.

And just what his ego needed: to hold onto a tiny ninety-year-old woman to keep from being dumped off the back of an ATV. He stuck his arm through the handle on his bag and reached behind himself to grab a metal rack in the hope it would save him from an unexpected head injury.

They bounced over the uneven ground, which turned out to be as good as coffee when trying to wake up from staying up all night, staring down the gullet of the beast from your past that kept trying to swallow you whole, and then volunteering for more sexual frustration than he could have imagined before Jolie and her toy…

It didn't take long to reach the barn, it just felt like it. Reece got off when Granny rolled the vehicle to a stop, and followed an especially sober-looking teen into the barn where several people were gathered around boy of about fifteen, leaning against a post, his face ashen from pain.

Jolie knelt beside the boy, helping hold his arm to his chest for stability. So they had gone to her first? Seemed they weren't entirely ready to take what he was offering yet, but at least they had when Jolie presumably hadn't been able to help.

She looked at him long enough to confirm where her thoughts were too. The blush just added to his awareness and difficulty in focusing.

"His shoulder is dislocated," she announced, keeping the arm held in place and shifting her gaze back to the kid. "Anterior dislocation of the humerus."

Reece stooped beside the boy. "How can you tell?" he asked, but a quick examination confirmed Jolie's diagnosis.

"Well, it's in front of where it's supposed to be. Probably hit it on the back as he fell because the ball is in front of the socket." Jolie pointed to a bump that shouldn't have been there. "If it were worse, like a sprain or a break, there'd probably be lots of swelling and bruising by now." She reached up to push her hair back from her face, looking back at Sam and offering the teen a tight smile.

"Good instincts."

"I've had some experience with this type of injury," she murmured, deflecting the praise.

"You've had a dislocated shoulder?"

She nodded but didn't look at him. Because the circus life was dangerous, no matter how much she'd like to pretend otherwise. Right. He could deal with this later.

"Bet that hurts." He shifted his attention to the boy, whose breathing sped up as Reece pulled his arm from the protective fold across his chest and began moving it slightly. Scared, anticipating pain.

Jolie moved around and knelt on the other side of the kid. "Look at me, Sam. Hurts like crazy, I know. And it's about to hurt a lot more for just like…a few seconds. Imagine you're putting all that pain into a ball, and we're going to kick it away. That kick is going to hurt…but then it's going to be gone. Yeah, it's really going to suck, but after it's going to feel so much better. You need to relax and do what Reece says to make that happen. Can you do that?"

So much for his usual plan, which was to say, "You might feel some discomfort…"

"I'll try," the kid said.

"Just keep looking at me," Jolie said, one hand on the boy's cheek to keep him face to face with her.

The muscles liked to spasm when the bones were out of the socket like this, and he'd only ever set an anterior dislocation once, but he remembered how to do it. With the boy sitting there on the dirt floor, his gaze fixed on Jolie's, Reece slowly lifted and rotated the arm, drawing a scream from the kid but causing the head of the humerus to reseat itself.

Jolie winced, but the scream—like the pain—passed fast, as she had promised. Just not before the boy had jerked away from her, leaned to the side and thrown up his breakfast. Or lunch. It was later than Reece had thought when Granny had come banging on his door.

"Breathe, Sam. It's all over." She leaned away from the vomit and stood pretty quickly.

Granny held out a bottle of water to Reece. He smiled at her, uncapped it and handed to the boy. "It's okay, Sam. Natural reaction to extreme pain." He wrapped an arm around the boy's middle and hauled him back from the barf, then pressed the water bottle into his hand. "Drink this. It'll help."

A few seconds later, while they all stared at the kid, the color started coming back to his face.

"Feel better?" Reece asked.

A nod, and he held the water to Jolie so he could use his hands to stand up. Not wanting him to use his newly reduced arm, Reece slung an arm around his waist and helped him stand. "Bet the next time Granny says don't climb on the equipment…"

"I won't," Sam filled in, then muttered, "I'd really like to lay down."

"I'll go fetch the golf cart," Granny announced, and pointed to a chair. "Sit. I'll be right back."

Sam obeyed.

"If you have a sling at the house, or some material we can fake one with, that'd be good too, Granny," Reece called after her.

She waved. He hoped that meant she understood.

Jolie hovered around the kid, and Reece gave them both the necessary aftercare instructions. He couldn't trust the kid to remember, but Jolie really did have a head for this stuff, terminology or no.

"You're good with the kids," he commented, and soon Granny returned with a sling and got them all onto the golf cart for a ride to the big house. Sam sat in the front, and he and Jolie sat in the back with their legs dangling off the vehicle—hers dangled better. He had to work to keep his feet off the ground.

She reached behind him and slid a box from behind him to behind her, allowing him to scoot back enough to keep his feet from banging on the ground.

"I like the kids," Jolie answered finally. "They've been kicked around by the outside world too. It helps them to be here with us."

She really didn't like the outside world.

"But you probably see that kind of thing all the time," Jolie said, hopping off the back of the cart as Granny rolled it to a stop. "You can get callous about that kind of thing. Probably doesn't bother you much any more, right? You see it every day, you get used to it."

She smelled good. His libido, never really normal since the night before, kicked in—memories of her squirming beneath his touch and the disheveled bed steeped in her sweet scent… He couldn't think, and she was probably saying something important to him. Reece stood and turned to grab his bag, and in doing so he saw several of the company members waiting on the big wraparound porch.

"We're here to see the doctor," someone said, taking Reece's attention off Jolie. He counted…eight new patients waiting.

"Got a place set up inside. Used to be a laundry room before we set up the laundry in the pole barn there," Granny announced, but she stuck by the kid, pointed to some building, and gestured for Reece to follow her inside.

When he looked back to tell Jolie he wanted to talk to her later, she was already far enough away that he'd have had to shout for her to hear him.

Later. He'd find her later. Right now he had a family to take care of, and for the first time since he'd come back into their lives, Reece felt like he was doing his job.

A good feeling that would have to hold him through being the village hard-ass again later when he told Jolie no to the camp idea and wrecked the connections they'd reforged yesterday and last night.

But a truce could only last so long.

CHAPTER SIX

AFTER THE LONG task of compiling medical histories for the last generation of performers, and with the extensive list of their profession-related health problems in mind, Reece went in search of Jolie. He still had a couple to see after they got done with the day's chores, but there was a break he could take advantage of now.

If the wake had given him any doubts about his decision, the twisted spines and cartilage-free joints shared by every performer he'd seen so far shored up those doubts.

He found Jolie by following the music to the big top, where she was perched on a wire strung between two portable stands, not exactly a high wire but a good ten feet off the ground.

The leather slippers she wore he recognized from seeing other wire dancers, but the hand guards protecting her palms were new to him.

A slow, sultry guitar solo blared from hidden speakers, but the music paused as she slid her front foot forward on the wire. She looked toward the player, lost her balance and fell.

Reece started forward, and had run several yards down the causeway when he realized she wasn't on the ground—or on the mats below. Thank God she had mats down.

Ever nimble in reflexes, she'd managed to catch the wire on the way and was now pulling herself back up.

Maybe that's what the hand guards were for. The thing bowed and stretched some where her hands put pressure, but she managed to get back on it and onto her feet.

With a few quick, bouncing steps she ran the length of the wire to one of the towers, bent over, grabbed a remote, started the song over again, and approached the wire again.

It was a routine. She was practicing a routine...what other reason would she have for starting the music over? The mats and his curiosity gave him the strength to stand and watch her, when otherwise all he wanted to do was make her get down onto solid ground where she couldn't fall to her death.

Her moves started slow and sinuous, the kind of moves he'd expect in a belly dance or a strip tease. Sexy didn't fly in American circuses, but if she could move like that, she might pull it off. Maybe in Vegas...not that she belonged in Vegas.

Reece stuck to the shadows to keep from interrupting her, but he did stand out enough to look around and see if anyone else was watching.

Just when his thoughts started to scrape bottom, the music picked up and she began a series of heart-stopping leaps, feet high off and back low on the wire. Within the space of a few notes she'd gone from siren on the high wire to something that he'd expect to see in gymnastics. Some combination of beam and bar that at once thrilled and terrified him.

If she fell she'd land on the mats. He repeated the mantra every time his heart stopped.

Now he understood what the hand guards were for—to protect her palms when she swung on that wire. Not just safety gear should she fall.

She let go of the wire three times during different spins and angles. The final one she didn't catch but used it to dismount, and he had never been so thankful for mats in his life.

Another new experience: being both terrified and turned on at the same time. And neither of those reactions did he particularly want to admit to.

The only thing he could admit to right now? She was still a performer—as much as pained him to admit it. She had to want to, no one kept in that kind of conditioning if they didn't want to.

Well, no one but him. He didn't want to perform, but he still wanted to be in the kind of shape he'd have been if he hadn't left. It was part of the life…just how he'd been raised, to value the peak of human performance that highly. If she didn't have an actual routine choreographed with music, he might be able to believe that was her reason too. But it felt more like something else he'd broken when he'd left.

Maybe her wish for the camp was a way to try and satisfy that need. Even believing herself alone in the big top, she smiled. She glowed, though the siren-like quality to her performance was new.

"I thought you'd have interrupted," Jolie said, unwrapping the guards from her wrists and turning to look toward where Reece skulked in the shadows. "Really didn't expect to get to the releases."

"I didn't think you saw me." Reece stepped out of the shadows and immediately took a seat on the raised outside edge of the ring. "The music pause makes you stumble, but you go jumping and leaping and don't get dizzy? Makes no sense."

"I don't know why. I think I have an inner-ear condition."

Reece focused then, brows pinched.

"I'm kidding." Jolie laughed, hanging the guards over

one of the rungs on the tripod ladders up to the wire. "I really don't know the answer. I couldn't at first, but I was convinced it was possible…so I just kept trying. Eventually it got easier."

"I read something about ballet dancers training their brains to ignore the inner-ear signals of dizziness. Maybe it's something like that," Reece said, but he still looked a little freaked out. And tense. "Speaking of conditions, how's your arm?"

"Smooth segue." Jolie stopped beside him and sat. "A little sore but manageable."

"You should get it X-rayed." He reached for her arm and ran the pad of his thumb over the remnants of the bite, a gentle touch that sent a wash of goose-bumps up her arm and down over her chest. Her breasts reacted, small as they were, and she suddenly became hyper-aware of the leotard stretched across the sensitive peaks.

He noticed. And then he made a point of looking at the wire. "The dance…the act? Very sexy. When you weren't flipping around, scaring the hell out of me."

"I had the mats down for safety. And I toned down the sexiness a lot. It's hard to play with those emotions for no one."

"I wouldn't say no one. You knew I was here."

"I also knew you'd freak if I performed for you, and what might that do to my concentration?" She grinned and drew her arm back from his inspecting gaze. "You look like you have something on your mind."

Reece nodded, a smile saved for her. "I do. I'm just blown away a little." He looked at her mouth just long enough to prepare her. "And I decided there was something else I'd rather do than talk."

Jolie swallowed just before his mouth came down on hers and his arms went around her, lifting her from the seat as he stood and covering the short distance to lay her on the oversized mats beneath her wire, pinning her and rousing her recently super-charged passion.

Kissing could happen without promises to stay forever. He wouldn't stay forever, she knew that. He'd leave her again, and them having kissed or having gone to bed together wouldn't matter to him at all when he made the decision to go.

She wouldn't let it go too far. She would stop before her brain entirely turned into hormone pudding.

In a little while…

Nap time. Some people might think the smell of the stables to be the sort of thing you didn't want to sleep with, but Jolie disagreed. None of the horses were allowed to trample in their filth. The stalls were kept clean and as fresh as could be. The strongest scent was the hay, except for right after the horses came in sweaty. There was that odor too. But as hot as it had gotten this week, no one was up to getting themselves or the horses sweaty. Least of all her.

So, naturally, someone would be walking around in the stable, interrupting her nap time. Jolie knew who it was before she opened her eyes. "Reece." She lifted the sleep mask she liked for her stable napping and looked at the massive man looking down at her from the head of her cot. "Seriously, when did you get so big? Big as a horse. I could ride you." She paused, pulled her mask off and sat up, like that would make her not say stupid things. "Okay, that came out wrong."

He smiled. "I could throw you over my shoulder. I know how you like being carried around."

"Oh, yeah, every woman wants her butt in the air for the world to see." She swung her legs off the edge of the cot and reached for her boots. "What can I do for you?"

Reece tilted his head behind him to the many full-sized mounts in their stalls. "Thought we could go for a ride."

"You're here in the middle of the week. That's a new one for you. Sounds like something more than a horseback ride."

He nodded. "We should talk."

It was her turn to nod. "And you think we'll talk better on horseback? Because that seems like a distraction, some kind of sleight of hand to try and distract me from something that you don't want to say."

"Not entirely wrong, but it would also be nice to get out in the fresh air." Reece stepped back from the stall and held the door for her. "I also wanted to check on Gordy." The small horse was sleeping again. "Did you stop his tranquilizers?"

When Jolie stepped out of the stall, he went back in and squatted down to look at the cast holding the horse's leg in place.

This stall was bigger than the ones in the traveling stable, but Reece took up enough room for her to give him the space. She stayed in the doorway watching him. "I stopped his tranquilizers. But he still has some pain medicine and I occasionally give him a mild sedative just to keep him mellow. I don't know if he actually needs them, his mood is pretty good, but I imagine it keeps him from trying to walk around too much. Every now and then he kicks his back legs and tries to buck out of the sling, but the one the vet brought is good. He gives up pretty quick."

"Still on poop vigil?"

"Nope, his belly is doing just fine. The kids are cleaning the stall frequently. Especially since they keep sneaking him apples."

"I was going to ask you about the kids. How many are there?" Reece backed out of the stall and closed the door, taking over in his bossy manner.

Since she had pointed out his reason for asking her to go for a ride, he was now using another method to distract her. "Seven." She cleared her throat and dropped her hands to her hips, planting herself in his path.

"I don't want to go riding. I'm tired. I'm sore. It's hot. I'm borderline cranky. And I'm pretty sure you came here to tell me something I don't want to hear, which I guess I should be grateful for—the fact that you're willing to at least tell me bad news in person."

"Jo…" He stopped her tirade with one syllable, and when she stood staring at him, waiting for him to spit it out, he sighed and gestured her to a bench.

"I don't want to sit. Is that how they taught you to break the bad news to people in doctor school?"

"Medical school," Reece corrected, an edge coming into his voice that said the cool look he wore was more fragile than he'd like it to be. "I want you to sit down so you don't feel like I'm looming over you. I want to talk to you, not intimidate you. That's easier if we're closer to eye level."

"I don't think that's going to help us see eye to eye."

"Stop." He reached for her, like he was going to pick her up and put her on the bench, but then caught himself and drew back again. Old habits did die hard. "Fine. I'll sit. You can stand."

Jolie folded her arms over her chest and looked at him, a little more irritated that his sitting did make him look less intimidating. "I'll stand." And those few inches she had on him in height then would help…

"I am not able to support your camp idea," he said without further preamble. Right to the heart of his decision. "It's not safe. I understand why you want to do it, and I appreciate you wanting to keep Keightly intact, take care of everyone, but it's not the way."

"Because you don't think I can do it."

"I honestly don't know if you could do it, but that isn't why I've come to this conclusion." He frowned, wearing the serious expression she assumed was supposed to show how tortured he was about these hard decisions he had to come to for the greater good…and the idiots who couldn't take care of themselves. "You might manage it just fine, though I have doubts considering how you avoid leaving the safety of the farm. But the real issue is the danger. Someone would get hurt. Add to that what a waste of your talent it would be."

Talent. Right. This was about what was best for her. The man was a walking contradiction. "I'm sorry, is this that thing you do to break bad news to people by saying something good with the something bad so that they don't feel like the bad thing is as bad?"

"No." Reece leaned against the wall behind the bench, watching her in a way that made the height difference no longer matter. "You want to be performing."

"I don't want to be performing," Jolie grunted. "I want to be here, with my family. I want to take care of them. I want to preserve our traditions and our way of life. We can do that here without being on the road." Okay, she did enjoy performing, but that wasn't the biggest part of her life. They were. Even if Reece didn't care about any of that any more.

"You aren't being honest with yourself. You haven't seen yourself perform. You glow. It was always your dream. Didn't change, did it?"

"It changed. I was sixteen. It's not my dream any more. My dream…" What was her dream? The camp. And, well… "My dream is for everything to stay the way it was. But that isn't going to happen. So now my dream is doing the best that I can for everyone. And the camp is a good idea. No, it's a great idea. You think everyone is just going to settle down and retire, but that's not who these people are. They want to do this, but they're going to listen to what you say and not put up a fuss. Because when they look at you they see Henry Keightly, the boss, a man who everyone loved and respected, and who did everything for this family. I look at you and I see…broken promises and control issues."

"Broken promises?" Reece scowled, his own arms crossing now so that they stared over their arms at one another. "You see more than that. What word have I broken lately?"

"Having a good track record for a couple of weeks doesn't wipe out the bad one you've had for a decade. I'm not stupid, I know that you are here now and you'll act fully present and connected to everyone, but as soon as you decide to go somewhere else, you'll go without a backward glance. I remember that part of you very well. Do you want me to tell you what it was like? Because I can tell you—in excruciating detail—just how long it took me to give up on you."

He didn't say anything, but his nostrils flared and his lips compressed. Nothing to say? Well, she had plenty!

"You haven't been willing to have any of us in your life until you thought you could come in here and control us, unless we do what you say we can't be part of your life. That's how it is. That's probably why you became a doctor, so people would pay you to tell them what to do."

"That's not true." Reece spoke quietly, and she remembered that voice. She got louder and louder the angrier she got, but Reece got quieter. "I'm buying a practice fifteen minutes from here and making this place my home."

"And everyone here is going to listen to your orders. Except me. So, what's the solution? Get me to go find some other circus to join, because obviously I should be performing! Should I be offended that you're worried about the safety of everyone but me, who obviously should be performing?"

"Jolie, I'm trying to take care of everyone and do right

by them. And doing right by you doesn't fit into the plan of what's right for everyone else. You're different. And stop saying 'obviously'. I hate it when you say that, like anything about you is obvious. Ever."

"I'm just so darned different…"

"Stop," he ordered again, then changed direction on her. "You know how much all the equipment is worth? I have a buyer. It will endow the farm for a long time, take care of the animals, and the people who take care of the animals will have a wage. It's a lot of money."

"The camp would bring in money too, and allow everyone here to hold onto their pride rather than being put out to pasture."

"You're not thinking clearly. You're just too emotional about this. No one is putting anyone out to pasture." He gritted his teeth—that muscle in the corner of his jaw bunching in time with her rapid heartbeat. "Your dream is for everything to stay like it was? That way you don't have to go out into the world and be part of it. You want this camp so you can still be in the life without actually being in the life. No ties outside the circus. No learning to get along with regular people."

"Are you joking? I'm talking about inviting strangers into my home on a daily basis, forever. I'm talking about pulling back the curtain and showing children that the magic isn't magic. That they can do great things if they work at it, no matter what anyone out there says about them." She knew that world very well, and she knew exactly why she had to stay away from it. "I'm going to do this, no matter what you say."

"Are you?" He stood up again. Sitting no longer worked for him. Or he had decided he needed to be more intimidating to make her agree.

Jolie squinted, not feeling intimidated so much as empowered by finally getting to have the fight with him that she should have had years ago. She stormed up to him, stepped to the side, and then right up onto the bench he'd vacated, forcing him to turn around to keep that intimidating stare. Unfortunately, that also put him in primo chest-poking range, and she was fired up enough that her index finger was already rod-straight and itching to jab him in his impressive torso.

"I know what I'm doing this week. Going to the bank! They give business loans and I'm smart enough to figure out how to get one for this. Though, honestly, with all the supporters we have, if the loan is troublesome I am certain I could finance the camp by contacting a few of Keightly's former supporters. Then I'll buy the equipment from someone lest prone to tyranny than you are. It won't have the Keightly name but the Bohannons are known too. I can keep the Keightly name off everything so your family legacy isn't sullied by my ineptitude. It would have been good for advertising, and to have the iconic tent for the children to perform in, but there are trapeze schools who set up outside, and the free-standing rigging isn't all that expensive."

He didn't flinch from her bench, and to his credit he didn't grab her and put her back on the ground either. He stood his ground, arms still crossed, though his thumbs stuck out in that annoying he-man manner that made her want to bend them backwards.

"So you're just going to stick a sign up by the highway and hope people come? You know if you really want to do this you will have to go to schools to introduce the idea, talk to parents at activities and athletics centers and let people know what's going on. Get insurance for everything—"

"I'm not a shut-in, Reece. I do go out when I need to. I speak the language and everything! I may not like it out there, but I can do it. You act like I'm asking you for charity. I'm offering you the chance to honor two hundred years of history in a venture that *makes money*. Not just uses it up."

"You don't understand how much responsibility this is. And, yes, it might make great wads of money, but this equipment is mine and even if I do nothing for this camp besides supply equipment, at the end of the day it's my responsibility if anyone gets hurt." His voice rose. Finally she'd struck a nerve.

"Fine, then it's settled. I'll get the equipment somewhere else. Go ahead and sell off the big top."

He loosed a loud groan of frustration and turned to walk away from her, enough to presumably give him room to get hold of his hands if they reached out to grab her again. "You remember how it was when Dad died. You remember how awful it was. I know you do. For God's sake, Gordy's hurt because he's a working animal. And we've had a number of really close calls with other performers in the past. Some who were injured badly enough they couldn't perform any more. You don't want to saddle children with that, Jolie. You ignore the danger. Have you seen how many of them have back and bad joint problems?"

"I'm not ignoring the danger, I'm just not going to be crippled by it."

"No, you let yourself be crippled by other things."

She took a breath and forced herself to stop for a few seconds, think about what he was saying. Was that an acknowledgment that he was crippled by the fear of other people dying like his dad had? "You want me to say I have abandonment issues? Fine. I do. I also don't want to go out there and get a job in an office and have a house with a white picket fence, live in a subdivision where it is supposed to look like a community but where everyone's interaction ends at their property line."

"What's so bad about it?"

"Loneliness is a sickness, Reece. People medicate it with materialism and they forget the things that are important."

"There are worse things than being alone."

Her face suddenly felt cold and she knew the angry red face she'd worked up had abandoned her. Jolie could hardly believe he'd just said that to her. "No, there isn't." She'd never say to him that there were worse things than watching your dad die in a horrific accident. Her throat constricted, but it was the burning in her eyes that demanded she summon her anger again. Anger was better than tears. "If you think telling me all the ways that it's too hard for me will do anything but make me more resolved than ever, then you've done a really good job of forgetting everything you ever knew about me. But thank you for reminding me for the thing I forgot about you."

"What's that? That I'm always right?"

"No, that it's stupid to get into bed with Reece Keightly, because the sting lasts longer than he does!"

Done with this conversation, with hoping that he'd do the right thing, Jolie stepped down and stormed toward the door.

"What are you doing?"

"Leaving!" she answered, but didn't turn round. She just raised her voice to make sure he could hear her. Strategic yelling. "I'd think that would be something you'd recognize when you saw it."

Reece watched Jolie leave, the wind knocked out of him as effectively as a punch to the solar plexus. He took a few steps back and sat on the bench again.

Because it turned out that shaming himself for taking her virginity in that way was one thing, and having her say it out loud were wildly different things.

Jolie had more reason than anyone in the world to hold

grudges against him, but she still kept trying to be kind and generous with him. She had taken care of the sawdust for him. Had put down the mats below her wire so he'd be more at ease. Tried to preserve his family history and the Keightly dynasty…but there was still a wound there.

A big one.

She was right to question his staying power.

She was also right that he was a control freak. Letting her buy the equipment and do this without his support—or his input—with his people… At least if he let her use the Keightly equipment and the name, he could keep some constraints on what was taught at the camp. Establish a curriculum that would minimize the possibility that she'd have massive future regrets. Make sure he did the physicals so that the kids were all healthy enough to participate…

He groaned, and then got up and went into Gordy's stall to sit with the little horse, who was actually awake and eating. He did look better. He'd been ready to give up on the little stallion in those first days, but Jolie had stuck it out. She didn't let go of anything she loved without a fight. Which made him wonder: had she ever actually let go of him? He'd denied her the fight. Denied her the closure.

He should go back to his apartment and get ready for work tomorrow. This week and next, Dr. Richards was overseeing him treating his patients. There was no contractual clause demanding that, but Richards wanted that extra bit of reassurance that his people would be in good hands, and Reece could understand that. He felt the same way and wanted Richards to be at ease with the transition and the future care of his people.

Even if the core company no longer bore the Keightly stamp in any form, even if they lived on the Bohannon farm, he'd consider every one of them to be his people until the very end.

* * *

"I'm here to see Reece."

Reece knew that voice. He followed Richards into the exam room, and smiled as soon as he saw the patient. "Anthony, this is Dr Richards, he built this practice."

Anthony introduced himself as Reece's brother, extending his hand. When Richards appeared confused, Reece jumped in and explained about how Anthony had come to be his new stepbrother.

"Could I just see Reece? I have a problem that I would rather…"

"Certainly." Richards nodded and left the room.

When the door closed, Reece rolled a stool over to where Anthony sat and joined him. "Are you worried about Granny? Or are you here for yourself?" Please, don't let the girlfriend be pregnant… Jolie already gave him too much Bohannon drama to deal with.

"I'm here for me." Anthony took a deep breath. "I didn't want to tell Mack and Ginny. Didn't want to tell anyone really. But now I think I have to."

"Well, whatever you say to me as a doctor, I will keep in confidence." Reece maybe shouldn't see his own stepbrother as a patient, but he'd do it this once to find out what was wrong, if nothing else.

"I'm diabetic. Type II. I used to be pretty big, you know, chubby…when I was a kid, before you guys took me in, and then I got diabetes. But as I got older, I lost weight, it got better. I didn't have to take medicine for it any more, so I didn't think I needed to tell anyone about it." His knees bounced in the seat and he looked down a lot.

Reece took the hint to help him out. "But something has changed?"

"I've been using Granny Bohannon's meter to check my blood sugar every day. She knows about my diabetes, but I didn't want to tell anyone else. I didn't think it was important any more."

He could read between the lines: Anthony thought Mack wouldn't adopt him if he knew he had an illness. Reece understood hiding weaknesses. He nudged the kid's foot with his own, making him look at him. "He would have still adopted you. Mack and my mom? They're not like that. You don't need to worry about that."

"Medicine is always expensive. I don't want to be expensive."

Reece would hug him if he knew him better, and if he didn't also know that fifteen was not a hugging age for boys unless it was with someone you had a thing for. Reece resisted the urge. "Anthony? Don't worry about that. It's not always expensive and, besides, you're part of the family. You came here today for a reason, so you tell me what's going on, we'll get it sorted out."

Anthony nodded, still slouching, still looking uncomfortable. "Jolie caught me testing yesterday. And she's in town today, across the street, but she dropped me off here because she said you would help me. I think it's not in control as much again. I have been getting higher blood-sugar numbers when I check it." He sighed, like every word he managed was another nail in his coffin.

"Listen, I don't know what you've gone through in your life before you came to us, but I want to. Like you said, we're brothers now. Brothers look out for one another. So when I tell you not to worry about this, that the only reaction that Mack and Mom are going to have is concern for you, you can believe me. Jolie didn't lie to you about me helping, and I'm not going to lie to you either." Reece wrote some notes on the chart, giving Anthony some space. "We're going to do a little bloodwork and then get a plan formed, figure out how to get this fully under control. Maybe you've just been doing something different, maybe you could do something different, maybe you need some medicine to help you out. There are a bunch of options, and none of them are a good reason to be upset."

Anthony nodded and sat up a little straighter, rolling up his sleeve, ready for the blood draw. "There might be a reason…"

"What sort of reason?"

"My girlfriend likes to bake…"

Reece laughed. "You think that might be the reason?" A shake of his head and he stood up. "It's not easy to find a girl you like who wants to bake for you. She pretty?"

"She's real pretty,," Anthony confirmed, pulling out his phone and turning it on.

Pretty girl picture, front and center. "Oh, yeah, hard to turn down sweets from her. Give me a second." Reece stepped out long enough to request some supplies, and then sat with Anthony again while they waited. "So the bank is across the street. Is that where Jolie is?"

"She's getting a loan to buy the circus stuff from you for the camp. I can't wait. It's going to be awesome. I'm working out upper body now. Jolie said catchers have to be strong in the upper body."

Catchers. Right, Reece's part of the act they'd been working on before he left. He was going to have to pay a visit to the bank… "I hate to make you wait, but the nurse is going to have to come do the blood draw, and then it will take a few minutes to get the preliminary results. I'm going to step over to the bank and check on Jolie."

"You think she's freaking out?" Anthony asked. "She's been running around all morning, but she gets that look when she goes to town."

Funny that he could be so observant about other people but not confident enough to trust those skills when it came to his place in the family. "I'll just be a couple of minutes…"

CHAPTER SEVEN

JOLIE TREATED ERRANDS like a marathon. In order to get all her business in The World done and over with in one day, she'd happily run herself to the point of exhaustion. Today she'd even kept Anthony home from school and managed to get out in the early morning, get meetings done, get back home to pick Anthony up and drop him at Reece's office, and now she'd check "Bank' off her list. As soon as the loan officer got back from wherever he'd gone to.

She wasn't entirely certain what would happen at the meeting, whether or not he would just discuss options with her or whether he'd have her filling out paperwork. Dealing with banks for the circus and the farm had always been the business of Ginny and Mack. No wonder they'd gravitated to each other. They both had to deal with bureaucracy, and while they might not enjoy it, they were at least competent. Another thing she didn't want Reece to be right about.

He'd said she couldn't go out into the world and get students for the camp. It would be the biggest lie of her life if she tried to say that he was wrong about her not wanting to go out into the world at all. But having him say she couldn't was either a dare or forbidding her to, and both possibilities roused in her the wrong reaction. However ridiculous or immature, shining a spotlight on her weakness made her want to prove him wrong.

But it was more than that. She wanted to prove to herself that she could do this. No matter how good her reasons for wanting to stay safely inside the circus life, those reasons were now a road block that kept her from reaching her next destination.

The door opened and Jolie turned in her seat to look at the man walking in.

"Miss Bohannon, I'm Matt Carmichael. There's a man in the lobby asking for you. He didn't give his name but he said that you would know who he is."

"I know who he is," Jolie said. She didn't need to look and see who it was, but stood and offered a hand to the loan officer in his pigeon-grey suit and overly starched white button-down. "He can wait where he is." She shook his hand and then pointedly closed the door and returned to her seat. Let him watch her, the big jerky know-it-all. "I'm not entirely certain what the meeting is for. I've never applied for any sort of loan before, but with the amount of information about loans and the whole process online, I just wanted to talk to someone face to face. Thank you for agreeing to see me on such short notice."

"You're welcome…"

Before he could continue the door swung open and Reece marched in. "I need to speak with Miss Bohannon for a moment."

"Sir, I really must ask that you wait in the lobby."

"It's okay," Jolie said, sighing and standing. "We'll be quick, Mr. Carmichael. Sorry about this."

He was remarkably okay with the situation, and closed the door behind him when he left.

Reece waited until the man was across the lobby, well out of earshot, before he said, "You're going to get in over your head if you get a loan and try to do everything at once. I know you're angry but everything I said yesterday is still valid. You need to figure out if you have a market before—"

"Do you think this is my first stop of the day?" Jolie kept her voice low, not wanting to get into another shouting match with Reece in public, especially at the place where she hoped to get money to finance the operation Reece was trying to shut down. Him rousing her to make an ass of herself in front of everyone would be a great way to set her up to wreck everything herself.

"I've been to the elementary school, the middle school and the high school this morning. I have phone numbers for different athletics teachers and coaches, I have been to the little dance academy and spoken with the owner about putting up advertising on her bulletin board and whether she'd support having me speak to a couple of her classes to get a feel for things."

She looked out the door, caught Carmichael watching her, and the look he gave asked if she wanted to be rescued. Funny that the suit could be her safety net. A quick shake of her head had Reece turning to look at Carmichael too. His look was much less friendly, she expected.

"You did all that today?"

"Not that I have to justify myself to you, because we both know you're not going to support my decision and you're not going to work with me." Jolie tried to affect a cool tone. She was getting a teensy bit better at dealing with the emotional onslaught, but she could really stand to be totally better at it by now. "Your only purpose here is sabotage. So consider me onto you."

Reece shook his head. "Think whatever you like, I'm trying to protect you."

"I haven't had your protection for the past ten years, and I don't need it now," Jolie reminded him, just in case he'd forgotten she was harboring a grudge and had a damned good reason to do so.

"You just don't want to admit it. If you wanted to claim normalcy, you wouldn't be so stressed about being in public. But have you seen yourself? You only uncross your arms when you have to, and then right back they go. You're trying to do too much too fast."

"Only when you're around," Jolie said, but whether it was true or not she really didn't know. She uncrossed her arms. "Just go. I have a meeting to attend. Though if you want me to think you're on my side, you could tell me what the bid you had for the equipment was. You know, since I should know what I'm getting into financially."

He answered without a second's hesitation. "Just over two million for everything. Both of the big tops, the climate control, the seating, all the sleeper cars the crew live in, the trailers the performers don't own, the actual—"

"So much," Jolie muttered, her astonishment wiping out her anger in a flash. She'd thought she'd been thorough in thinking through the details of starting the camp, in considering the money she'd need... And she had for the rigging and the seats, but the climate control hadn't occurred to her. The sleeper rails weren't necessary for them because this year she only wanted a day camp, but if they went to a sleep-away camp later, there would have to be some kind of facilities for sleeping. Her idea of details and the actual details? Not exactly the same.

He looked smug, and considering how clueless she might actually be, Jolie couldn't blame him for looking smug. But was that all she saw on his features? No. No, he looked greedy too. Two million dollars was a lot of money. "That's the real reason, isn't it? You talk a good game about the difficulty of travelling circuses in this day and age, about the danger to the people you supposedly care about, but at the end of the day you're looking for a fat paycheck."

"Stop it." Reece reached over and grabbed her elbow, giving it a shake. "You know me better than that."

When had she crossed her arms again? "No, I don't. I thought I knew you, but I've had ten years to come to grips with the fact that I never really did. And I'm so stupid... I let flirting, old memories, and *hormones* make me forget that basic truth about you. It's all about Reece. Everything is about you."

Such an idiot. Didn't she ever learn? He may have been Reece when he'd left, but he was Dr. Keightly now.

Reece had to work to keep the frustration from his voice. What did he have to do to make her willing to give him the benefit of the doubt? Even as he asked himself the question, he knew the answer: he had to say yes to the damned camp. So he'd just have to keep dealing with her issues until she gave up, because the camp couldn't happen.

"No matter how badly I behaved in the past, I'm here now. I want to absolve myself by doing what is best by everyone. I'm not your enemy." He let go of her elbow and stepped to the door. Making sure his voice was low, he added, "How many people have been injured in training? More than in the performances. Training is the most dangerous time. When did your shoulder get dislocated? Training, right?"

"No, Reece. Not during training. You don't remember, do you?"

He had been around when it had happened? Reece scoured his memory. She'd fallen a few times, but never to any great harm. "When?"

"Never mind," she muttered, nodding toward the door. "Just go back to work or something."

Through the glass, he could see the suit approaching. He'd said what he'd come to say. She'd either listen or she wouldn't. Time to go. "We'll talk more about this later." He stepped out into the lobby.

Jolie called after him in tones anyone who didn't know her would think were sweet, "Thank you for letting me know, Dr. Keightly." Reece knew better. That was the Jolie equivalent of *Screw you, Reece.*

He passed the loan officer, who stepped back into his office, and for a second he considered throwing Jolie over his shoulder again and dragging her out of the bank. But he couldn't do that, not without it affecting his new practice across the street. "Don't sign anything, Jolivetta!" he yelled instead, even if he knew she probably would.

"Are you all right?" the bank official asked Jolie as he stepped inside.

Reece stopped and looked back, half expecting Jolie to say something about how unreasonable he was.

"I'm fine. I'd still like to speak with you about the loan, though the amount has gone down significantly." The door swung shut, keeping him from hearing anything else, so Reece continued out of the bank.

That could have gone much better...

Glad he'd taken a late lunch, Reece came back into Richards's practice, soon to be his practice, and let himself into the administrative area.

All the gray suddenly bothered him. His head hurt. Tension headache, and he didn't need medical school to diagnose that one with how tight his forehead had stayed bunched since the fight with Jolie.

That had been in color. Not like these gray walls. Pale gray floor. Darker gray baseboards and furnishings. He was losing his damned mind—a color bothered him this much?

Finding the door to Richards's office standing open and the room empty, Reece walked in and closed the door.

Thank God. He just needed to sit and close his eyes for a few minutes. Close out the monochrome.

More gray. The same thing happened at his apartment, just with a different color. Beige. Beige, beige, beige.

But the farm had color. Green fields and trees. Red and white barns. Pale yellow farmhouses. Blue Keightly logo everywhere.

Red hair. Pink clothes. Jolie.

He had to find some kind of alternative to her camp idea. With the farm being Bohannon property, he couldn't throw her off and tell her to go and find a job.

He could bring her into the office as some kind of office worker maybe. Somewhere he could monitor her, help her if she started to freak out. A couple of hours a week, just to get her used to it.

Except she would be angry with him for even suggesting it. Probably bring Gordy into the office just to prove a point to him. He rubbed at the tension between his brows.

She'd looked nervous at the bank, but most people who were going to talk loans looked nervous. It was just across the street from the practice, he still had some time. He could go back and see how she was handling it. But dropping in once had been enough, considering how that had gone. She might try and beat him to death with a checkbook if he showed up again.

If she was going to go ahead with the camp without him, God only knew how far in over her head she'd get. Not that she wasn't smart, but she had the kind of creative mind that tilted when presented with math and schedules. He was sure she could handle the simple accounting of taking tuition and setting up paychecks for the performers—all she had to do was get the forms on that from his mother—but the overheads would never occur to her. The light bill, water bill, the cost per day for lunches and snacks. Insurance. Inspectors.

He closed the door and dropped onto the couch. The judgy pillow he hated—the one with the eye-searing embroidered flowers and travel advice about the road to hell—rested at the far end of the couch, setting his teeth on edge. He wouldn't let a piece of gaudy fabric change his plans. Taking care of everyone wasn't about having good intentions. It was his responsibility.

The practice was also his responsibility.

When he'd told her he didn't have time, it hadn't been entirely true. He'd considered the amount of time he would be spending to set up a new practice, but the deal with Richards took away a great deal of that. Sure, he had the patients themselves, but he didn't have to worry about all the other stuff it took to set up a brand-new practice. Or deal with the time and money issues that came while establishing a patient base.

He could help her run a camp if he wanted to.

He just wasn't sure he wanted to.

Teaching would be less dangerous for her on a daily basis for her. And with the amount of safety gear available, it could be reasonably safe for the kids. Some things. Not the trapeze though.

A knock on the door roused him from his chair in the dark.

Richards was back. Patients to see.

Time to stop sitting in the dark and do what *he* had been put on this earth for. He couldn't control her any more than he could control Fate. All he could do was try to steer her in the right direction. That would be easier if she trusted him at least a little.

"Dr. Reece Keightly." Reece introduced himself, extending his hand to the first patient in the office the following Wednesday morning. "Dr. Richards is ill today. Have you been informed about my buying the practice, Mrs. Nolan?"

The woman, who looked every ounce the perky soccer mom, shook his hand and smiled. "I have. Nice to meet you. You're one of the circus people, aren't you?"

That had never happened to Reece before he'd decided to settle here. In Nashville, where he'd gone to school, no one had known he was "one of the circus people." "Yes, ma'am. My family have owned Keightly Circus since the early 1800s."

"So you're the one that closed it?"

He hadn't expected that either. "I am." He hooked the stool from below the counter and sat, facing his new patient. "What am I seeing you for today?"

"I actually came because you're here. My daughter Briona? She's thirteen and such a talented gymnast, but two weeks ago her coach told her our Olympic ambitions were a pipe dream. Said that no matter how hard she practices, she's not capable of that level of performance. And she's just crushed. Doesn't want to train any more, even though she loves it. I've just been beside myself, trying to figure out how to help her get through this, and my sister told me there was going to be a circus camp this year on that horse farm outside town. I know how people will be interested, and that space will be limited...but since you're going to be our doctor now, I thought..."

It took him a minute to recover from his surprise. "Actually, it's not certain that there will be a camp yet, Mrs. Nolan. It's not going to be run by the Keightly family, if it even comes to fruition. Jolie Bohannon, whose family traveled with the Keightly Circus for generations, has been researching whether or not it's viable for the area and it's... she's not certain at all that it's going to happen yet." He looked at the chart, noticed that the nurse had taken vitals and left the reason for the visit blank. "So you don't actually need to be seen for anything related to your health?"

"Well, no. Not today. I'm in good health. We're all in

good health, except for how sad my daughter is about her Olympic dream." The Gymnast Mom, not Soccer Mom, smiled at him. "But could you give me contact information for Miss Bohannon? I'd really like to speak with her. Maybe I can help her arrange the camp, if that's part of what is making her hesitate on the decision. I'm a party planner, but I think those same skills could be useful in… It's not going to be an equestrian camp, right? It's a circus camp. Like with juggling and tumbling and maybe trapeze?"

Everyone loved the trapeze. Except him these past ten years.

"You give me your information and I'll pass it to her," Reece cut in, really not having expected this for his first patient flying solo. "And where did you hear about this again?"

"My sister runs the gymnastics studio. That's where Briona, my daughter, got started in gymnastics. Then she moved on pretty quickly when it became clear she could use a private coach. I just want her to have something else to be excited about, and see other possibilities. The performers for circuses are on those TV talent shows, and in Vegas, and all sorts of places. She'd really like—"

Reece waved his hand, smiling at her to hide his irritation. "I'm sure she would enjoy a circus school, but you should know it is dangerous, especially the trapeze. If I were Jolie, I wouldn't offer trapeze at all the first year. That's the major barrier to the camp now, trying to decide how much could be done safely for all children who might want to come, not just those who could be Olympians."

"Oh, I'm sure that can be worked out. Gymnastics is dangerous too, but you just have to try and do it the safest way possible. And I did some research online. There aren't any in the South, but there are a couple of circus schools in New England and on the west coast. And they all look really wonderful."

Nodding, he stood and held out his hand. "I'll pass on your interest, Mrs. Nolan. Just leave your contact information with the receptionist, and I'll move along to the next patient. Wouldn't want to get behind and have Dr. Richards think the new guy can't cut it."

She laughed and stood, shaking his hand longer than he'd actually have liked.

The ghost of Keightly Circus was haunting his practice. Great. He'd thought it was possible that people in the area would put the name association together, but he hadn't expected them to seek him out when this was Jolie's project. It had also never occurred to him to check out what the other circus schools or camps—if there even were any camps—offered.

On Thursday, he was asked about the camp by three more patients.

Friday, his receptionist fielded calls all damned day. They all wanted to know two things. When did it start? How much did it cost?

Richards officially bowed out on Friday. He made himself available by phone in the case of emergency for the following week, but the practice was now Reece's.

He had to talk to Jolie before the practice became her answering service.

"We're going to have a helluva time keeping the kids off the trapeze at night," Granny said, watching the many cousins working to erect the rigging overhead.

"I thought you had them under lock and key when it got dark," Jolie said, kicking back and propping her feet on the raised edge of the ring. Paperwork surrounded her—loan papers, licensing papers, insurance papers, examples of curricula from the few other schools and camps around the country, and an article she'd printed about the ins and outs of starting a summer camp—all stacked in piles of hand-cramping and head-exploding glory.

Choking up the grip on her ink pen, she bent over the clipboard on her lap, writing yet more letters on blank lines and filling in tiny boxes. The paperwork was going to break her.

"The side of the lock that needs a key is on the outside, not the inside," Granny muttered. "And the biggest rascal is Anthony. He's a Bohannon now, and we love him, but that boy has been a little wild since Mack and Ginny went off on their honeymoon."

A tingle at the back of her head had Jolie first lifting her hand to check that a bug wasn't crawling on her neck. No bug. A ponytail pretending to be a rat's nest, half out of the band and tangled, but no bug.

She looked up.

"Reece," Jolie breathed, surprised to see him there.

"No, Reece didn't do anything." Granny shook her head. "But maybe we should have him talk to Anthony. They're brothers now."

"Afternoon, Granny." Reece stepped around the edge of the aisle and walked up, kissing Granny on the cheek. "I'll talk to Anthony. We're getting to know one another, and I'm happy to lend a hand." He looked at all the paperwork and then back at Jolie. "What's all this?"

"Well, I'm gonna leave you two to your damned fight," Granny announced, just before shuffling off. "Got to get dinner on the table, get all these kids fed." Anyone under fifty was a kid to Granny.

"I'll come and help when I get done with Reece," Jolie called after her, her eyes on Reece, who now had his eyes on the rigging installation currently going on. "They're all using safety gear, and always do. Just in case you're worried."

"I'll count on seeing you when you're done. Knowing you two, that should be some time in October…" Granny shook her head and headed away before she really interrupted.

"I'm not worried," he murmured, and then sat down, eyes fixed on the paperwork again, prompting Jolie to answer.

"Loan papers and license papers and other papers." Spreadsheets. Advice from the principals of each school she'd visited. Lots and lots of papers. "We decided that since no one had come to haul off the equipment yet, and no one had told us to take the big top down, we were going to set it all up for inspectors."

"For the camp?" Reece took a seat on the edge of the ring, his voice too calm to be comforting.

"Yes. Everything needs to be inspected before the insurance people can provide good estimates." Was this the kind of calm that preceded an epic eruption? After their big fight the other night, she'd spent about as much time wanting to see him as not wanting to see him. More proof that Reece made her stupid.

"I see. When are the inspectors coming?"

"Tomorrow."

"On a Sunday? Guess I'll be sticking around, then." He picked up a pile of papers and moved them one row down, where more papers awaited her, and took a seat at Jolie's side when a space was made. "I'd like to be here for it."

Heat. The man radiated heat, which made the way the arm nearest him react so weirdly. Goose-bumps rose. Jolie casually wrapped a hand over her arm and rubbed it. Maybe he wouldn't notice. "Why?"

"I have a compromise to offer." He looked down at her arm, but didn't comment.

"I didn't think your expansive doctor vocabulary included that word."

"There you go, doubting my mastery of the English language again." He smiled and Jolie felt herself laughing a little in return.

"Thrill me. Or prove that you don't actually know what that word means. I'm still open to that being the outcome of this conversation, regardless of what you might dub compromise."

"One year. Trial period." He said the words slowly and then put his arm around her shoulders, sliding her the last remaining inches toward him. "Better?"

Definitely better. And worse. "Better how?"

"You're cold."

"Oh." Jolie nodded, mustering a smile in return to cover the lie. She wasn't exactly cold, but her body would probably just love to react more when pressed against his gloriously muscled torso. "Go on, you sound like you have other qualifications."

He nodded, and with the thoughtful way he looked at her, the way he looked at her mouth, she almost lost the thread of the conversation with the urge that came to kiss him. Memories of his mouth on her flesh, of giving her pleasure over to him and the promise he'd kept and those words that still sent chills through her: *I'll never break another promise to you.* She so wanted to believe him.

She moistened her lips, quite willing to throw the paperwork down and kiss him breathless, right there in front of everyone. Dumb. Dumb, dumb, dumb.

"Qualifications," Reece said, clearing his throat, breaking the connection as he looked back up at the rigging being installed. "You're going to be doing most of the work but I want veto power."

He could switch it off. That must mean that most people could switch this kind of thing off. Probably how he'd kept his cool with her and Mr. Happy. Unfortunately, Jolie's emotions still ran wild in his presence. She dug her fingernails into her thigh, a sharp sensation to override the firm heat and heady male scent wrapping around her. Kind of worked. Sort of. She managed to repeat some words back. "Veto power on what?"

"Curriculum. Number of kids you'll take on the first summer. Length of term. And I want all physicals to go through my practice." He unwrapped his arm and scooted a couple inches away, enough room to put his arm between them and gesture upward. "You're setting up the trapeze rigging and net, so you obviously intend on having an aerial component. I want to be the one who does the physicals to determine fitness level for the more advanced—"

Him breaking contact did wonders to clear her head. Terms. She should think about terms. "Wait. So your idea of the compromise is that with your limitations, I get what? To buy the equipment from you? Use the name? What?"

"You have a knot in your hair."

"I know…" she muttered, frowning at his change of direction. Knowing Reece, if she didn't fix it, he'd start trying to get the band out and that would mean touching again. She needed to be able to think. Jolie reached up to start working on the lopsided curly mass. "Go on."

"You get everything. The big tops. The equipment. The mess tent. The safety gear. The name. Costumes. Lady Calliope. Everything."

Everything? Even the calliope? She managed to drag the band from her hair and dragged the locks over her shoulder to begin combing the tangles out with her fingers, and turned so she could see his face better. "Why?" He was hiding something, Jolie just couldn't figure out what.

"For starters, my practice has turned into an answering service for 'When is the circus camp opening?' calls." Reece watched her working on her hair, pensive frown in place, words slow, the fingers of his right hand unconsciously moving, sliding against one another, and she realized he wasn't lying so much as distracted. By her hair. "Second, if you're going to do it, I want a hand in it."

Jolie got most of the auburn riot under control and stopped touching it, returning him the favor of helping clear his mind…in theory. "You said you didn't. You said you didn't want the responsibility." She tossed the lot back over her shoulder, helping more.

He looked back at the installation, allowing her to study his profile. Still thoughtful. "I'll feel responsible no matter what. Even if you go in entirely the opposite direction. Because it is my decision to close Keightly down that made you make alternative plans. But if you use my equipment, at least you can't have too much of a fit if I make demands and set an uncompromising safety standard."

"I never would have had a fit about that, Reece. I'm not sure when you think I turned into a diva…"

"Divas perform. You don't. So you can't be a diva."

"Why does that bother you so much?" Like a dog with a bone…

CHAPTER EIGHT

"Why don't you perform?"

"I told you. I just don't want to any more."

He shook his head, going silent as he watched the Bohannons zip-lining back down to the ground, the last of the rigging in place.

"I figured I wouldn't see you again until the buyers came to take everything away. That's kind of your thing. Show up after being gone, upset plans…"

"I'm not going anywhere." Reece looked fleetingly frustrated, but turned away from her before she could figure out what had caused it. "I told you. The practice is fully mine now—"

"You say that, but you do disappear after every bump? Though this time it's only been a few days. I suppose that's improvement."

"I've been working. You haven't come to my apartment ever, so don't make it sound like I'm the only one who can make the offer."

Okay, so he had a point there. "I guess I didn't know I could. Or I never considered it because when you go, you're gone in my mind." She frowned, feeling a twinge of guilt. "Do you want me to come visit your apartment?"

"Honestly, Jo, I don't know."

Over the past month she'd done more soul searching than she was comfortable with. But recognizing problems didn't mean she knew how to fix them. She'd just started to embrace the idea that maybe she should tell him the realizations. At least then maybe she wouldn't come off as a crazy person. Not everything. She could seem messed up—there probably wasn't any way to avoid that anyhow, but she would like to draw the line before she got certifiable or psycho.

"The whole thing…after the wedding? That freaked you out, right? That's why you don't know whether you want me around, or is it just not wanting to get too tangled up with me? You don't have to say you'll partner with me over the camp as a way to keep anything relationshippy from happening. I told you before, I can take care of my own—"

"No!" he shouted, cutting her off. "Don't say that again." He stood up, rubbing his upper lip in that way that shouted discomfort louder than his shouty voice did. "That's not the reason."

"Fine!" Okay, so she made him feel uncomfortable. That whole business in her trailer had been his idea, or maybe it had been hers? Whatever—it had made him feel uncomfortable. What was she supposed to do with that? Ignore it? That's how she had worked before she'd become the Most Emo Chick in Circusville. She missed that skill, her calm. Her missing serenity…

As he didn't want to talk about it, she put it aside and asked, "Do you want to put the camp stuff in a contract? I know you like to be official and you're putting off a big sale in order to give us a shot at this."

"Not within the company," Reece said. He exhaled roughly, and held out a hand to her. Handshakes still meant something to him at least. Jolie looked at it and then at his face. Business arrangement. Leave all that bad sex and good sex and all the past and everything else out of it. Just focus on the deal and the future, which would be a business arrangement. Not a sexy business arrangement. She'd file all that under "Weddings Make Her Dumber".

She put her hand into his to shake, but she didn't shake it yet. "Say you promise not to sabotage things." And it wasn't underhanded for her to test how serious he was with the promise.

"I don't sabotage things."

She lifted a brow. "Don't even imply that you're direct all the time."

He caught her meaning because he frowned. "Fine. I promise not to sabotage things."

His promises shouldn't mean so much, not with their history, but if he really meant to never break a promise to her... Her heart squeezed and she gave his hand the fastest shake in the world then pulled away to start gathering up her paperwork. "I'll work on getting you figures and if you want to be here for the inspection tomorrow, you will need to just hang out because I don't know exactly when he's arriving. In the afternoon some time. Also, don't forget about talking to Anthony. I think he's got a girlfriend in town. He's on the phone or the computer all hours of the night. Worrying Granny to death. Generally being fifteen."

"You're not happy that I changed my mind?"

"Of course I am. We can do it the right way now, keep the name, and be everything the community would like us to be. Have the iconic tent."

If she looked at him, she'd say the wrong thing. Like admit that whole week after the wedding she'd been thinking about throwing her rules about men out the window and giving him a chance to redeem himself in a full-contact way that involved no toys... And then he'd gone again and she'd decided that he was a massive jerk and she didn't want to do anything with him. But now he was here, and she wanted to again, but not if he was going to keep looking like he couldn't get away from her fast enough.

"I don't believe you."

"That's okay. We're business associates now. It's not your business to see to my happiness. Just a partnership for the camp."

She felt his hand on her chin before she saw him moving closer.

"I'm not shunning you or anything. I'm just trying to be a good guy. Make the right decisions for the right reasons, which usually comes easier to me."

"I don't know what that means." Jolie sighed, wrapping her hand over his in the hope of steering his grip away from her chin.

"Means I'm avoiding certain subjects because that's not coming easily to me with you."

Right. She pushed his hand away, tired of this suddenly. "I don't know what that means either."

Reece leaned down, not letting her get far. The kiss he claimed was slow, hot and full of want. "Means I want you, and I know it's a bad idea. But I'm having a damned hard time caring about whether it's good or bad." He didn't lean back, staying so close that she could feel his lips brush lightly against hers as he spoke, and the scent of his aftershave enveloped her.

"Why is it a bad idea?" Glad she had not yet picked up her sheaf of papers, she let her fingers find his shirt and curl into the material at the waist. "Because you're thinking of running off and becoming a lawyer or something now that you've got the doctor thing done?"

He kissed her again then straightened back up, but kept his arms around her waist, his voice as gentle as if he were talking to a skittish horse. "I'm not the one who's going to be leaving, honey."

"I'm certainly not going to be leaving." Jolie blurted the

words out and then sorted through his implication. "Are you back on that performing thing again?"

"I found you working on an act, but you don't perform. With this camp? You're going to have to. And when this summer is over, you're going to remember how much you love it, and you're going to want to go back on the road with a new circus."

So rational, like a flowchart. She knew doctors would like charts.

"So your big plan to get rid of me is…say yes to the circus camp, so that at the end of a trial season I'll be bored with it. It doesn't matter whether it's a success or not, you think I'm just going to do all this work to build something and then leave because I want to wear Spandex and walk on a wire."

When she put it like that, it did sound kind of like an ass move. Reece shrugged, unfolding his arms so he could rest his hands on her hips, the better to keep her from getting away from him. "I'm not going to lie and say I like it, but I know how miserable you'd be at a desk job."

Jolie reached up and pushed her hair back from her face. "This is not a desk job." A breeze in the nearly empty tent caught at the curls and ruffled them, so they shined like bright copper where the light reflected. He kept his hands on her hips to keep from putting them in her hair.

"You know, maybe you should give me these little snippets of what's going on inside your head more often." Her angry voice alerted him to the depth of the problem. He looked back at her face. "They make me less inclined to think that I'm the problem, because I tend to do that, you know—blame myself. I always think I'm the problem. But when you think I'm a problem, it just makes me mad."

"I don't think you're a problem." Reece hooked a finger in her a belt loop on her jeans as she twirled out of his grasp and dragged her back to him until her back was to his front and he could get his arms around her waist and hold her still. "I think you have a problem. A problem I contributed to when I left. Maybe a problem I caused. If you're missing out on what you want to do because of me... God, Jolie. You need to move on from that. You need to move on from this. Performing is a young business, but you're still young enough to do it. But time won't stand still forever. In ten years..."

"I don't want to move on from this. I don't think this is something bad that needs moving on from. How else can I possibly get that through to you? And how can you continually degrade me for my fear of the outside world, use it as a reason to say no to the camp, and then encourage me to continue the lifestyle that you believe I've just been trying to use to hide from the rest of the world?" She shoved at his forearms and Reece let go, starting to feel a little of her anger himself.

He sat back down, ready to let her get away if she was so determined to flee. "I don't degrade you. I'm just trying to make you think about your future. And you have this huge stumbling block, blinders that don't let you see there is a whole world of opportunity out there for you."

Grabbing the papers, she began stacking them in crisscross fashion, more orderly than he'd have expected from her.

"You can't have it both ways. Either this camp is in the life, or it's not. If it is, why do I need to go anywhere else? If it isn't, why should you want me to go somewhere else?" She shook her head, straightening and looking him dead in the eye, hurt evident in hers. "Everything I need is here. I don't need to go anywhere else."

He was so tired of hurting her. "Why did you build a routine?"

"I'm just playing when I do that." The way she looked down confirmed that she was holding something back.

"You're not being honest with yourself. I want more for you."

"Still. About. You. You don't even see it. They always say that you fall for a man just like your father. Well, call me a cliché. That's exactly what I did."

He was also damned tired of her holding his going away to college over his head. "You have to forgive me for going to school at some point, Jolie."

Movement in the corner of his eye told him they were no longer alone, though he'd thought that everyone had finished with the rigging and left a while ago. But maybe the shouting had drawn someone back.

"I don't need to forgive you for going to school." She walked to the end of the row and down to the ground and back until she was in front of him, if much smaller now from his higher position. "I was upset when you left for a number of reasons. I was afraid something would happen to you out there. That someone would hurt you. That you'd be alone and no one would be there to help you. The fact that I missed you—that I was afraid you would forget me—was secondary. I was terrified *for you*. But I never begrudged you your education."

More tears in her eyes, and the high color on her cheeks matched the high way she held her head. Reece didn't know what to say. Confessing how much he'd missed her would only make her angrier, so he said nothing.

"For the record, I'm proud of what you've accomplished. Everyone here is proud of you for that. Proud enough that I keep forgetting that despite the fact that you want to be the good guy, as you put it, you still cut us out of your life without any warning. You never looked back, and I definitely feel a grudge about that. That was your choice, and you're back here now, wanting to be the good guy? Well, *you'll* have to forgive *me* if I expect you to be the one who leaves. Again. As soon as you can."

"You're right. I did all that. Nothing I can say will change it."

She reached up and swiped her eyes then started walking again. He watched until she rounded the bleachers and walked out of sight.

A couple of seconds later he saw movement again and looked up.

Anthony.

"So, we're brothers now, right?"

Reece nodded. "We're brothers now."

Anthony took the bleachers at a quick climb and sat at a manly distance from him. "I heard you guys fighting. You okay?"

"Not sure what I am. Aside from an ass." And not sure he should be the one getting comforted by the kid who needed a big brother to lean on, not the other way around.

"She was crying." And Anthony had been torn between which one of them to comfort. Reece would probably have chosen to stay away from the weeping woman too.

"I've probably made her cry more than anyone in the world." He leaned his elbows on his knees. "Even her asshole father."

"I don't know which one her dad is. Hard to keep track of them all, just a sea of red hair."

Reece grinned at the teenager, fleeting though it was. It was hard to hold a grin right now. "Her dad wasn't a Bohannon. Her mom is Mack's sister. Seven brothers, one sister that generation. Jolie's dad wasn't born in the life. He tried it, married into the family, but it didn't go very well. Hard on people to suddenly start living on the road."

"So he left?"

"He…" Reece started to explain and then paused, uncertain how much weight his words carried and whether he should share. But Anthony was family now. Thanks to Mom marrying into the Bohannons, there was now an actual link to the Bohannons that went deeper than simply decades of tradition and traveling together. Besides that, everyone knew the story. Not like it was a secret that could ever be kept…so even though he might not want to be the one telling the story, he did want Anthony to open up to him. He should lead by example. "Her dad left when she was five. But he didn't just leave. He took her with him."

"Like kidnapping?"

"Yeah." Reece tried not to picture the broken little girl who'd been brought back home. "Got all the way from Florida to Chicago before he decided he didn't want her. So he gave her a note with contact information for the farm, dumped her in front of a police station, told her to go inside, and left her there so he wouldn't get arrested."

Anthony looked back in the direction Jolie had left. He'd been with the family a couple of years. Jolie's oddities were probably beginning to make a lot of sense to him.

"What happened to her?"

"I don't know exactly. I know they had to fight to get her back. There's an assumption of something negative about the lives of circus families. If not abuse then at the very least dysfunction. I have never asked but, straddling both worlds now, I can speculate about what happened. Social workers, attorneys, questions about why her father stole his child from her mother only to abandon her far away? Very suspicious." Reece shrugged, dismayed at the lack of details he really had about such a big event in her life.

Anthony looked around the tent, and Reece couldn't read past the scowl the young man wore. Either he was just angry or he was really trying to work through what

Reece had told him. "But wouldn't she have to look abused for them to think that?"

"She was a wild little thing before. Fearless. And clumsy. I've never seen a picture of her where she didn't have some kind of bruises or scrapes. Put it with the other questions...and they put her into a group home for a week or something, until it was sorted out. By the time we got her back...she was different."

Terrified all the time. Wouldn't let go of his hand, even when she'd had to go to the bathroom. Reece could remember standing with one arm in the bathroom stall and the rest of his body outside the door, giving her the most privacy he could because she wouldn't even let go of his hand to go to the bathroom. Just the one good hand, the other had been in that pink sling.

Oh, hell. That had been for her shoulder...not her arm.

"And then you left her too," Anthony filled in, pulling Reece's attention back with a simple statement that ate through his gut.

Reece nodded. And she'd been afraid someone would hurt him. He really was an asshole.

Anthony shook off the scowl on his face, leaned forward to punch Reece in the leg. "Tell her you're sorry, man."

"It's not that simple." Such a good-natured kid. Impossible not to like him. And if Reece ever doubted how much he'd missed his family, being presented with a kid brother intent on taking care of *him*...there was just no way he was leaving again.

"Sure it is. You're sorry." Anthony mustered a smile, shrugging. "Whatever reasons you had for what you did don't matter. You're sorry. Tell her. That's why she talks so much."

"What do you mean?"

"I don't know Jolie real well, but I watch people. She

talks when she's confused, trying to work stuff out." He tapped the side of his head. "And she used to be a lot quieter. Actually, she used to be a lot calmer too. She's been riled up since you got back."

"You watch people, eh?"

"I'm going to be a writer, I pay attention."

"What are you going to write?" Reece asked.

"Deep stuff; it'll blow your mind."

Reece laughed finally and stood up. "I don't doubt it." Presented with a fist, Reece bumped his against it and tilted his head. "Granny won't save dinner if you're not there."

"She'll save food for me. I'm her favorite."

And Reece's favorite too, but he cupped the back of the kid's neck and gave him a light shove toward the exit. "Fine, she won't save me any. And if I'm going to talk to Jolie again, I'd better fortify myself."

And he was supposed to talk to the kid about…something. "Don't stay up so late on the phone with your girlfriend. You might be Granny's favorite, but she'll still chew you up in the foulest language you ever heard if you don't do what she says."

"I mind."

"Two words, man: Manure duty."

A sexy blues instrumental didn't go with the horrific bureaucratic forms in Jolie's lap. But what really could go with this kind of insanity? Funeral-home music maybe.

She switched to a new stack of papers, just for something else to look at. Tuition schedules. She'd based them on the idea of paying back loans. Now she wasn't sure how to do it—just change the destination of the monthly payment to Reece as a wage? It was his equipment, and even if he was going to endow the farm with the money, he should be the one to actually do with it what he would.

Talking to him was unavoidable.

Jolie didn't know what was worse—trying to make it through a single conversation with him without being overwhelmed by some emotion or another, or the hours of introspection afterwards when she relived—

A loud knock on the door rattled her trailer, startling her. She yelped and the very next second Reece had the door open and was standing on her entrance stairs.

"You cried out."

"You almost banged a hole in the door."

He came more fully inside, closed the door and stepped around her piles of paper to sit on the couch.

"Oh, come on in, Reece. Sure. Have a seat. Pay no attention..." Now where was she going to run away to? Maybe she should start talking about all the men she was going to sleep with now that he'd made Mr. Happy seem like Mr. Crappy, Lame and Boring...

"If I'd asked, you might have said no. And I'm here to apologize."

Apologize? She slowly lowered the pages to peer at him over the edge. "For what?"

"Everything."

"Everything?" Well, that cleared it right up.

He nodded, looking her in the eye and then shrugging. "I'm sorry."

Her stomach twisted and she crawled over the papers and onto the couch beside him, turned sideways to face him but stayed far enough away to avoid touching him. "Care to expand on what 'everything' means?"

"For hurting you."

"For not calling? Not writing? For disappearing for ten years?"

He kept eye contact, but the wince told her his apology didn't extend that far. "I had to cut off all contact with you."

Either he just didn't get it or he was trying to get out of actually admitting what had happened…and maybe what had driven him to it. "Why?"

"Because…I just had to." Definitely didn't want to admit anything.

"Were you in the witness protection program?"

He made another face. "No."

"A coma?"

"Jo…"

"Did you get abducted by aliens?"

"Jolie…"

"I know, you were a secret agent and—"

"You've made your point."

She shook her head. "Your turn."

"Nothing I can say will give you any kind of peace. But that doesn't mean I'm not sorry. I want to make things right with you."

"You can't make things right with me without an explanation. If you just want to say you're sorry and have me forgive you…okay. I will stop bringing it up. I won't ask any more. I'll forgive you, and I'll try to forget. Maybe we can even be friends someday… But you can't make it right without telling me the truth. You can't leave this big hole and make it right, even if what you have to say hurts. I deserve an explanation."

"I would have quit school and come back the instant you asked me to," Reece muttered. "I didn't know any other way to stay in school than to just…try to forget you."

The words hurt, but they really shouldn't surprise her. She needed to hear them, she just couldn't look at him while he said them. "Did it work?"

"No."

That was something. Jolie slumped back against the arm of the couch as she listened, her hand going to the fringe of the throw draped across the back, something to play with, something to focus on, something to keep her calm as she listened.

"It wasn't my plan when I left. But before we even got to the campus…I knew I couldn't come back. If I didn't stay away, nothing would ever change. And then someone else would die because that's the nature of the business. And maybe some death would happen that I could have prevented if I'd stuck to my convictions…and I'd have borne more responsibility because I didn't know how to make everyone listen to me. Keightly became my responsibility the instant my father died, and he taught me to protect. But I was nineteen. I couldn't protect anyone."

The truth rang in his voice and reflected in the sadness in his eyes, and she knew how his father's death had hit him. She'd seen him change but hadn't known how to help him. It was the truth to him. He couldn't know she wouldn't have asked him to give up his schooling.

"What are you thinking?"

What was she thinking? "I don't know. Wishing I'd known, I guess. It took me a long time to give up on you." She abandoned the fringe and swiped her cheeks when she realized she'd started crying again. "By the time I accepted that you weren't coming back…I think I was numb. It didn't hurt that much then. I was calm. And I've been having a hard time getting my calm back since you got here. Really would like to get that back. When I'm happy, I'm happier. When I'm sad, I'm sadder. Like…everything is catching up. It's too much. I hate it." Of course her tissues were all the way on the other side of him. She took a wobbly breath and then crawled forward, leaning over him to cram her hand into the tissue box. "And now I'm out of tissues!"

Which just made her want to cry more.

"Stay here." He stopped her before she could lean back,

turned her and when she sat across his thighs he wrapped his arms around her.

"I'm sorry. I keep crying, and I don't mean to. Is this a panic attack too?" She pressed her eyes against the side of his neck, her face hot all over.

"You don't have to be sorry." Reece stretched out as much as he could on the sofa, keeping her on top of him, her face hidden in his neck. His voice was gentle. "I think this is something else."

"I'm crazy."

"You're not crazy. Just let it happen. I'm not going anywhere."

More breaking rule number two. Too overwhelmed to fight it, she relaxed against him and cried long past the point when she even knew what she was crying about, but he never wavered. Never tried to get out from under her.

"Your shirt's all wet." She lifted her head and looked at him. "Do you still want to be in business with a crazy chick?"

"You think this is news? I knew you were nuts the minute I saw your crazy hair. But do you feel better?"

She nodded and he kneaded the back of her head and tugged her forward to press his lips to her forehead.

"I forgive you even if you're an idiot."

He tilted his head until it was his forehead against hers. "Thank you."

"I'm going to get off you before I attack you. I do have one grudge left, but I think we've probably dug deep enough for one night, don't you?"

"What is it?"

She climbed off, fetched a paper towel from the kitchen and blew her nose. "You made Mr. Happy seem very lame."

He laughed as he rolled to his feet. "I'm trying very

hard not to ever say those words, turn them into innuendo, or hit on you…"

"The runny nose is a real turn-off." She blew her nose again. "And the red puffy eyes."

"Not so much." He tilted his head toward the bedroom. "I could sleep, though. If you didn't mind me staying. I'd really like…"

"So you can be here for the inspectors?"

"No. I could stay at the RV and be here for the inspectors." He looked her in the eye and smiled. "You want more confessions? Okay, I just want to stay. You got up before I got done holding onto you."

A nod was all she could pull off. Sometimes words meant too much. A nod didn't amount to promises. When morning came, she reminded herself, everything might look different.

No promises tonight. She didn't want him to fail any tests right now.

CHAPTER NINE

HEAT AT HER back and all around her, Jolie shifted in the bed, aware first of the heat and then the source of it. Reece, at her back, warm breath in her hair.

She grabbed the blanket that was over both of them and tossed it back behind him, as smoothly as she could to avoid waking him, leaving them both covered only in a sheet. She wanted a few minutes to enjoy his presence before things got hard again. They always seemed to get hard again when they each had so many issues bubbling beneath the surface.

The early morning sun hit the windows above their heads, making the pale yellow curtains glow gold. She shifted around in his arms, suddenly struck by an intense need to look at him.

His shoulder-length hair, always tied back from his face, was loose and a sandy lock draped across his forehead. Golden eyelashes fanned his cheeks, hiding those blue eyes she loved.

Carefully, she linked her fingers with his and scooted in until her forehead rested against the two days of beard scruff on his neck. His scent mingled with hers, and her bed became a strange and wonderful place. Full and safe.

She wanted this. She wanted him. For however long it lasted. If she prepared herself for the end before they got started, maybe it wouldn't be so bad when he left. He might stay until the end of the summer, seeing as that's when he was sure she was going to leave. Facing up to the fact that he was wrong might make him leave again.

That wasn't what she needed to think about this morning, it would only lead to dark places, and she had a warm, glowing bedroom and a golden man holding her. Not the time for dark places.

Jolie tilted her head and pressed her lips to his neck—a couple of slow, lingering kisses to encourage him to wake.

He smiled. She didn't see it, but she felt his jaw move against her temple and she leaned up to look at him.

"Morning," he said, stretching until his feet hung over the bottom edge of her bed.

Jolie grinned back and kissed his chin, then his cheek.

When he'd got that pesky stretching out of the way, Reece grabbed her and rolled onto his back so she rested atop him again. Her legs fell to either side of his hips, but that was all the rearranging she had time for. His hands moved to her hair and tugged her head down until their lips met. His tongue stroked hers and his arousal roared to life between her legs, but the cotton pajama shorts she slept in and his boxers kept any accidents at bay. Which meant she could practice moving against him, find out what made him moan.

The last time he'd been in her bed he'd turned her beliefs upside down and had taken no relief for himself. Now she wanted to see that kind of need in his eyes, to make him tremble and shake.

She wanted some kind of reassurance that she could be good enough for him. If he wanted her half as badly as she wanted him, that would be good enough for most people. It was a good starting place…

She knew how to move, the long sinuous rolls of her spine and her hips, until she rode the ridge of his erection through the cloth.

"Jo…" He groaned her name against her lips. "I don't have condoms."

She pulled back, and he relaxed his hold on her hair to let her, but only until she could look him in the eye. She smiled. "I got some the day after we played with Mr. Happy."

"Oh, thank God."

The relief in his voice made her smile. "I would have thought…"

"I've been trying to be the good guy."

"The good guy gets condoms."

"Temptation." He shook his head then rolled them again until she was beneath him. He rose to his knees, suddenly very interested in getting her clothes off.

No slow seduction.

Good. His need gave her confidence.

He dragged her shorts and panties down with one go. Jolie tugged the shirt over her head then reached for his boxers. "I'm tempted to make you stand up so I can properly see wha—"

His boxers were already down and her words died in her throat. "Good God, I'm throwing away Mr. Happy."

This time he laughed, then leaned into her again, pulling her legs around his hips as he claimed her mouth once more.

Reece lifted up enough to give himself a grand view of her beneath him. Her auburn curls spread across the yellow pillowcase, her milky skin and freckles, and the palest, pinkest, most pert…

"I want to be on top," Jolie panted, pulling his gaze back to her rapidly pinkening face.

"You haven't really done this before." No. Don't refer to the other time.

Her brows pinched and she reached up, rubbing her

hands over his chest, making him inclined to do whatever she wanted. Because nothing had ever felt more right and it wasn't rocket science.

His inner caveman screamed that she'd been given to him. His father had given her to him to take care of. She was his. Always had been his. Always would be his. Jolie, his Jolie. He kissed her again.

"I was doing it right when we were clothed...wasn't I?" The question rumbled against his lips between kisses.

She wanted to be in control, which might be another test. And she might need reassurance. "You were perfect."

She'd accused him of being a control freak a couple of times, and then there was the method of their last tryst when he'd controlled the toy... It would be great if he could just act, stop second-guessing, but she was wrong—he wasn't a control freak. Reece grabbed her hips and rolled again. "Okay, if you change your mind..."

"I won't." She sat up and the gloriously slick heat ground against him. Every ounce of him wanted to flip her back over, take her, drive himself into her until she knew she belonged to him. Until he got his reason back. Until that hold she had over him was at least a little weaker...

But he'd always need to protect her. "Where are the condoms?"

She leaned to the side, fished around in the drawer, grabbed her toy and tossed it across the room, then found what she was looking for.

And if she wanted control of the condom, it would have to wait for next time. Reece plucked it from her fingers, tore the foil and slid her down his thighs until he got the thing on.

Sitting up, he grabbed her and dragged her back to him, unable to abide all that air between them. He eased into her. All he had to do was last longer than a few seconds and he'd do better than the other time…but he wanted her shaking and moaning for him, not that damned toy.

After a few tentative, experimental shifts and grinds against him, she found a natural rhythm that made him sweat. Reece grabbed her hips, trying to hold onto some semblance of control. If he didn't…he'd disappoint her again.

"Don't… You liked it," Jolie gasped as he slowed her down. "I want you to like it…a lot."

"I do." He gritted his teeth, tugging her back down with him as he lay back in the bed.

Kissing could always distract her, and he thrust his tongue into her mouth, hands tangling in her hair again. Every rock of her hips got him a little closer to a poor showing. She deserved the best, this was practically her first time as he'd ruined the actual first time.

When he felt his orgasm building at a speed that left him in little doubt that if she kept moving another few seconds he'd be lost, Reece gave in to his need for her orgasm and flipped them again, pulling out before he got there.

The hurt look on her face knocked the wind out of him. "Why? Why did you do that?"

"Jo. I need to… I need… I need to make you come."

Jolie felt him shaking where he knelt between her legs. That and the tortured light in his eyes soothed her. This wasn't because he didn't want her. It was his control issues. Even telling her he needed anything was kind of a milestone.

She nodded, and he crawled back over her, his kiss gentling this time as he began a sensual onslaught that wiped out her ability to worry.

Only golden light today. No dark places.

* * *

Once all the details had been finalized and the night-mare days of form-filling were past, completing the actual physical needs for starting the camp were a breeze. If you counted out the conversation both Jolie and Reece were avoiding. An impending showdown over the trapeze.

First day today, and Reece was going to come for the day, but he hadn't stayed with her last night. The first night in the past couple weeks he hadn't. It had taken a while to get to the bedroom, but once they had, neither had been eager to leave it.

It was better for both of them and their fledgling relationship to try and work together in things.

He'd needed an evening to himself and she'd given it to him.

She needed to be reassured regularly that he wasn't going anywhere, and he gave that to her. Any time she got nervous, so, like…every day.

Reece needed to run the physicals for the kids with exacting demands and limits, and she knew why he needed it…so it was no hardship for her to help. Over two weekends leading up to the opening they'd held an open clinic for the campers and he'd put them through the wringer. Health checks. Endurance trials. Games designed to test speed and reaction times. A little over the top for the kids who were going to be working with choreography, costume and set design…but she hung in there.

Jolie finished getting dressed for opening day in a T-shirt identifying her as an instructor and the equipment she'd need for her tightrope class. Along with a few other miscellaneous bits and pieces she'd need for demonstrations with the older instructors and their classes.

During the past two weeks Reece had also started working with Anthony on the monkey bars, starting slowly with the basics of how to be a catcher—a position they both hoped Reece could eventually hand off to Anthony. He decidedly did not want to get on the trapeze. Jolie didn't think he was afraid so much as he had developed an intense loathing for flying after his father had died. And that was the talk they had been avoiding.

When they'd been working to get her into his family's troupe in their teens, it had taken Reece three months to learn to just catch her with any kind of consistency. Three months of leaping and falling before they'd found the rhythm, learned to time their swings and he could catch her eight times of ten. And when they'd begun throwing tricks, it had taken another several months before each one was better than it was worse.

Anthony would not be ready to catch until maybe the end of the season. Having him in the show planned for the end was a possibility, but the other aerialists needed to practice their tricks with someone who could catch them the rest of the time. She had to have that talk with Reece.

Later.

After no one died on their first day.

With breakfast done, and a full hour before the kids were due to start arriving, Jolie wandered into the big top and found Reece alone on a zip-line, hanging from the canopy as he inspected the rigging. Again. She really shouldn't be surprised by now. This was the third time she'd caught him inspecting the equipment. A socket wrench in hand, he methodically made his way around every part of the connection before him, and then carefully maneuvered himself further down.

Safety Man did not like risks of any kind. And while this was something Jolie could appreciate, she did not want him up there when the parents and kids started arriving. She grabbed one of the megaphones and—once he'd anchored himself again—lifted it to her mouth. "Reece

Keightly, you had an inspector here. And now you're quadruple-checking to make sure it's good?"

He shot a thumbs-up at her.

"Twenty minutes and I'm coming up after you. You promised— no sabotaging the camp! Scaring the parents counts as sabotage."

"Almost done!" he bellowed back down.

Jolie sighed, put the bellowing apparatus down, and headed toward her class area. Most of the seating had been cleared out of the big top to make more room for the different classes to work in the tent at once. Having been a one-ring circus meant that they'd never shared space before.

Kicking off her shoes, she put on the soft-soled leather slippers Angela had made for her ages ago, and which the costuming maven had duplicated for her five students from impressions made during registration.

She limbered up and climbed onto the low wire with the rodless umbrella in hand she preferred for balance. And by the time she'd run the length of the wire a few times, Reece came strolling toward her.

Not knowing any other way to approach the question on her mind, she blurted it out. "Anthony isn't going to be ready to catch when they are ready to start learning to fly."

"I know." He watched her. "Do that little hopping thing. Where you change your feet. What's that called?"

"I don't know terms. It's a ballet thing, but I couldn't keep the language in my head. I tried. Just…didn't work." And it looked more impressive than it actually was, one of the easier things she did. She gave the little hop he'd requested, back and forth a few times, and found him smiling at her when she stopped and took the second needed to restore her balance. "Good to see you smiling. Happens so infrequently in the tent."

He stepped over and took her free hand, and she made the little hop onto the mats. "Are you ready for this?"

"I'm excited. But we still need to talk about the trapeze."

"We don't need to talk about it. I know what I have to do. I promised to be a good…whatever I am, and I will do what is needed. But the sooner I can get Anthony up and running on it…"

She leaned up, wrapping an arm around his neck and urging him down. "Kiss me. Make it count because we can't be kissing when the kids are here." And they still had a few minutes before the Big Excitement began for her, and the Big Scary began for him.

Having made a promise to never break a promise to her gave Jolie a great big stick to hold over Reece's head. Especially as he'd also promised not to sabotage the camp. Had given his stamp of approval on the squad selected for the aerial act. And now he had to do what he absolutely did not want to do. Get on the trapeze.

He looked at a sea of faces, all forty children cleared to attend, that wanted to see the trapeze demonstration. The ones selected for the aerial troupe had been practicing swinging out and letting go of the bar all week, since the opening, safety lines controlling their falls to the net. Reece was supposed to catch Jolie, that's what they hadn't seen. That's what he'd be doing for them until Anthony was ready. Which, naturally, meant he had even more responsibility on his shoulders should one of them get hurt.

While Jolie talked to the kids, explaining what he did to all the non-aerialists who'd just stayed late with their parents to watch, he hooked himself to the safety harness. He hadn't used one to climb the ladder since he'd started flying at eight, but teaching them the safest way possible was important. He hooked into the lines and climbed rapidly to the platform above. Practice swings at ground level had been set up for them to practice hanging, mats beneath and spotters. He'd even used one to make his body remember what the hell it was doing, but he needed a few minutes above ground to get used to everything again.

Just like riding a bike, and possibly just like falling off one.

He unhooked the safety lines and the swing, tuned out whatever was going on with the audience below and stepped off the platform.

Suspended from the bar by his hands, he pulled into the swing. It had been easier to achieve the biggest swing when he'd been fifty pounds lighter.

All he heard was the blood pounding in his ears. Jolie might not get dizzy any more, but he'd been grounded a while. It took effort to remember how to do everything he was supposed to do.

At the height of his swing—as high as he was willing to push it for demonstration—he flipped himself and hooked his legs on the bar. He was the catcher. He wouldn't be doing tricks, he wouldn't be dropping, unless it would hold two hundred but not three when he caught Jolie…and they fell into the net and he crushed her to death. Would blood look the same in sand as it had in the sawdust?

Closing his eyes, he let the swing take him.

It wasn't going to get better. He could do it, but the thrill was well and truly gone.

Reece opened his eyes, pulled up on the swing to a sitting position and gave Jolie the thumbs-up.

She repeated his procedure, wrapping a belt around her middle and hooking safety lines before she climbed to the platform. But she switched things up when she also hooked her megaphone to the belt and carried it aloft.

"So what we're going to do…" She began explaining the mechanics of a simple hand-off. Both hanging by their knees, clasping hands in the middle, and her letting go. The first thing Reece was willing to teach the kids.

He waited on the swing, which now only swung a little. He'd have to work to get it going again when the time came. She talked longer than he'd expected, long enough that the kids were getting antsy before she put the megaphone down and looked at him.

"Scared?" he mouthed at her, standing on the swing but not starting the swing until he was sure she wanted to do this.

She shook her head, unhooked the swing and held it with one hand while holding onto the platform supports with the other. "Ready."

Her pale face said she was lying. Right. Something to make her promise later…to tell him the damned truth even when she didn't want to admit to something. He frowned and looked down at the small audience. If it were anything but a knee hang, he'd call it off. But they were about the safest thing that could be done on the trapeze.

Soon his swing was at height and he lowered himself back to the bar. When he reached the right distance from his platform, he yelled, "Hep!" And she took off. When they met in the middle, she turned over to hook her knees on the bar. When he reached the platform, he did the same.

When they met in the middle again, he caught her wrists, she released the bar, and they swung free. She smiled, but there was no ease in her grin and none of the light that he had always seen when she performed. She really was struggling. "Okay?" he asked, and she nodded. They wouldn't get to talk again until he had caught her.

"Rusty," she assured him and then nodded. "Let go."

Reece hated this part. When they got to the middle, he had to force his hands to unlock and she fell to the net. Normally there would be a partner on the platform to swing out to her again, enabling her return to the platform, but they were a two-person show today. He stayed upside down, watching as she flattened out and bounced a couple of times in the center of the net.

Perfect. Safe. Everything was okay. He rose back up to a sitting position, letting the blood drain back out of his throbbing head.

She exited the net as she'd taught the children, hooked back into the safety and climbed back toward the platform. But by the time she got there she was a little rosier in the cheek. Enough to convince him that she was okay to go again.

As Reece stood and got the swing going again, she explained what they were going to do with the megaphone. And then she explained some more. At least three times she started to put the megaphone down, only to stop and add something unnecessary to her explanation. The third time she put it down she very nearly reached for it again, but changed her mind and reached for the swing hook instead, which she used to retrieve her swing.

They were definitely having a talk when this was over.

By the time she got the swing back, the hook stashed, and had given the lying nod that said she was ready, Reece had his swing high enough. At the height of the swing he slid back to the bar and on his mark called for her to go.

One each, swinging forward and back, and by the time they met in the middle, they were synchronized to catch the trick.

Reece reached, and Jolie let go of the bar, but she didn't reach for him until she'd already fallen out of his reach. His hands closed on air, his stomach lurched, and he watched her flatten and fall onto the net.

He pulled himself back above the bar before he threw up, and watched her exit the net and stop to say something to the kids before she repeated her procedure to get back up to the platform and get ready. She didn't look at him, just announced she was ready and waited.

Reece didn't start swinging until she looked at him.

"What's wrong?" No mouthing anything now, he yelled across to her, regardless of whether or not everyone would hear. This was her camp, she was the one who had insisted on an aerial component, and she had blown that catch.

"Nothing. Just rusty," she yelled back, scowling at him and adding a quick jerk of her head intended to get him moving again.

Reece took a couple of deep breaths, stood, and started the swing going again.

Once more she released the bar and Reece's hands made contact with her arms this time, sliding all the way down to the wrists, where they should lock, but before he could complete the action she jerked her arms free and fell once more to the net.

She'd rather fall than have him catch her?

Reece pulled back up and watched her bounce and then move off the net and march for the other end again. Not again. No.

Before she could get herself secured and climb, Reece swung to the middle of the net and hopped off the bar, letting himself fall into the net below.

He got down and headed for the kids. "Sorry, guys. We're done for the evening. Jolie's getting over a vertigo thing. She thought she was ready, and she wanted to do this for you guys, but her inner ear isn't co-operating." When he got many confused looks in return, he pointed to his ear and explained, "Squiggly bits deep inside your ear that control balance. We'll see you all Monday and the trick will be demonstrated before any of the kids go up on the bar."

Everyone was very understanding of that, except Jolie, who stood out of the way, yanking on the hand guards she wore to try and unbuckle the straps that held them in place. He left the group and walked up to her, his nausea almost a memory now that his feet were on the ground.

"What was that?" He took one of her hands and unfastened the buckles giving her fits.

"I don't know."

"You always say that when you don't want to admit something." He pulled the guard off and held his hand out for her other hand, which she placed in his. "So you can reach your hand into mine. Just maybe not when there's danger involved? Did you think I'd fling you off the net or something?"

CHAPTER TEN

JOLIE SHOOK HER HEAD. "I really don't know what happened."

"All you had to do was close your hands around my wrists." The guard came off in his hands, and she tried to pull her hand back, but his hand clamped down and held her in place.

"I know." Why hadn't she grabbed onto him? They were together now. In a relationship. Having mind-blowing sex, working together…practically living together, and she couldn't make herself reach for him. "I'm sorry."

Reece shook his head, and she noticed that he was pale. "Are you sick?"

"Yes. Yes, Jo. Not catching you? I almost hurled on your head. Twice. You did fine on the knee-hang. I don't get it."

"I don't know. I don't get it either."

"You need to think about it."

"I don't want to."

"Yes, I know, that is how you got through the past ten years, but you have to stop ignoring problems. If we're going to be together, if we're going to try and make this work, as we said we were going to, you have to find some way to trust me."

"I do trust you."

"No, honey, you don't trust me. If you trusted me, you

wouldn't have ripped your arms from my grasp and let yourself fall, instead of relying on me."

Jolie sucked in a breath. She wanted to argue with him, but what good would that do? She'd said she'd forgiven him, and she had…but maybe it would never matter how many promises he kept. Maybe she was too messed up to trust anyone.

"Is it me, or is it everyone?"

She looked up at his quietly spoken question and then stepped in to wrap her arms around his waist. "What do you mean?"

"Do you just not trust me, or do you not trust anyone?"

"I trust you. I do. You've been great. You didn't want to catch but you tried. And I know you've been working with Anthony since he wants to catch for the end of season show. You've been great." She laid her forehead against the center of his chest and mumbled, "I'm reaching now. See?" She shook her arms around his waist. He gave in to the hint and wrapped his arms around her.

"No camp stuff tomorrow. We're going out."

"I have things—"

"Hey…" He waited for her to look up at him and said, "You can do them on Sunday. Tomorrow we're going out."

"Like riding?"

"No. Like out into the world. Date. We're going out, you and me. Not on errands. Not to get groceries or go to the bank. We're going out. Dress casual, wear comfortable walking shoes." He leaned down and kissed her and, as always, she melted into him and her anxiety started to do the same. Before she could get lost in it, he lifted his head and put her back from him. "I'll pick you up at ten. Wear one of your camp shirts."

"You're not staying with me?"

"Not tonight."

He was mad. Which…she couldn't blame him for.

"Ten," he said again, then turned and headed out, leaving her to stare at the trapeze and, eventually, to clean up and shut everything down.

Going out into the world to spend time? Definitely a punishment for not reaching for him.

At least she didn't have to wear heels for it.

"Where are we going?"

Reece looked over at Jolie. That had been the third time she'd asked since he'd wrangled her into his SUV forty minutes ago.

"You say you trust me, but you can't take it that I won't tell you. It's a surprise." Reece shook his head. "If you were paying attention to the highway signs, instead of just sulking and staring at the blur, you'd have figured it out by now." Yesterday had been one of his buttons, but he'd got on the trapeze for her. She could go on a date with him in a public place for him.

"I don't like surprises. And I'm not sulking. I'm listing the reasons that everything is going to be okay." She crossed her arms and frowned but sat up a little straighter and focused immediately on the massive approaching sign. "The zoo?"

"The zoo."

"There will be a lot of people there."

"That's why I wanted you to wear your camp shirt." He looked at the matching Keightly Circus Camp T-shirt he was wearing. "So this is like a business outing too. Good for the camp. Lots of people will be here with their kids, and Keightly has been in the news a lot lately with the circus closing and now with the camp up and running. Have you been here before?"

"No," Jolie admitted, climbing out of the car and pausing to adjust everything, including the hang of her T-shirt so that it looked perfect.

When he offered his hand to her, she had to stop and wipe her hands on her shorts before she took it. Sweaty palms. But no panic attack yet. With the new information she'd given him about her out-of-control emotions since his return, he didn't know whether to expect another panic attack or not. Whether her anxiety at being out in the world would be increased in his presence or decreased, he had no idea.

"It'll be okay." He closed his hand around hers, and then thought better of it and linked their fingers. More secure hold. Maybe the little things would help her. "And you're going to like the zoo. Lots of animals… And we're going to go straight to the kids' area. I don't know what it's called. There's a petting zoo and other things there. So lots of kids. Lots of animals. You can pet a camel or… something else that doesn't bite."

Petting zoos, an idea Reece could get behind. They weeded out the dangerous animals.

She nodded but looked less convinced than he was, and stayed close as he walked them through the ticket booth to the park. Maybe his presence did help her.

It would be great if he could find some simple way to fix his problem with the trapeze.

For the first hour of their visit Jolie stuck to Reece like glue. They wandered through the petting zoo, they ventured out to the see the monkeys, and when she wanted to go back to the child area, he didn't put up a fuss or make her feel bad about it.

Camels, llamas and sheep, and Jolie liked the sheep best. Domesticated animals trumped exotic ones. They could be trained and didn't often eat their owners. But watching the kids with the animals was the best of all. Their glee was an easy emotion for her to identify with and wrap herself in.

And when her eyes skimmed over a little boy of about

five, wandering alone with tears in his eyes, she knew that emotion too. Releasing Reece's hand for the first time since they'd arrived, she walked over to the little boy and touched his shoulder. "Are you looking for your mom?"

As soon as she asked the question he started to cry. Most kids outgrew her by the sixth grade, but she was still taller than a five-year-old, and if she'd learned anything from Reece and their fights it was the importance of minimizing your height when someone was already scared or upset.

She squatted, keeping eye contact, and spoke in her gentlest voice. Soon she had his name, the identity of who he'd been with, and at least a small measure of his confidence. She'd always liked kids. "Don't worry, Drew. We'll find your daddy."

He nodded, swiping his eyes with the back of his hand.

"Do you remember what color shirt your daddy was wearing?"

She felt Reece approaching, and the little boy suddenly taking her hand confirmed it. "It's okay. That's Reece. He's my friend. He'll help us find your dad. What color is his shirt?" she asked again, giving the boy's hand a jiggle until he connected with her gaze again.

"White."

Great. A man in a white shirt. That wouldn't help.

"Don't be scared. Everything is going to be okay." She looked around, but seeing over the crowd was as hopeless for her as it was for the little boy. And Reece didn't know who he was looking for any more than she did.

Surely no one would abandon their kid at a zoo. That wouldn't happen. Who would pay the ticket price and walk through cameras and be on security footage when they abandoned their kid? No one. People who abandoned their children worked to retain anonymity. "He's got to be looking too. Do you see anyone looking?" she asked Reece.

Reece glanced around but shook his head and asked Drew, who still held Jolie's hand, "What's your dad's name?"

"Will you put him on your shoulders?" Jolie redirected.

"My shoulders?"

It took a dose of convincing for both Reece and Drew to agree to the maneuver, but soon Reece had Drew on his shoulders and standing. It took less than a minute before the worried father cut through the crowd and relieved Reece of his tow-headed shoulder-growth. After many thanks, Reece steered her to the cotton-candy stand and got her a fluffy pink treat.

A shaded bench nearby? Even better. She hurried to it and sat, then offered a pinch of the wispy spun sugar to Reece.

"You told me that I have to think about…emotions and things?"

"I asked you to think about them," Reece corrected, but popped the candy into his mouth.

She ignored the semantics and forced herself to look Reece in the eye. "That's what I feel like when I'm…in big public places like this."

"Like Drew?"

"Like I'm lost…or like whoever I'm with will leave me there and I'll be by myself and I won't know what to do. Which sounds really stupid now that I say it out loud."

"Jolie, you had that happen. Well, you had worse. It's not stupid. It's wrong, but it's not stupid." He took another pinch of the cotton candy and held it to her mouth. She took it and while the fruity fuzz dissolved on her tongue he added, "You knew what to do to help Drew. Some outside-the-box thinking but it got the job done. I would probably have just taken him to the office and got the park people involved with finding his father. But, you know, what you did was better. You got Drew involved. He found his own dad. I doubt that he'll even remember this when he grows up. It's not going to leave a scar."

She got the implication. Drew wouldn't have a scar like hers. Referring to it directly felt like one of those things that would rouse emotions. Instead, she returned the favor and held a puff of the candy up to his mouth. He took it and then kissed her fingertips and looped his arm around her shoulders to pull her in close while the sugar dissolved.

"What other situations do you think might scare you? If I left you here and went home, what would you do?"

"Get a taxi, go home and kick you in the—"

He stopped her before she actually said the words by laying a hand over her mouth. "So you could handle that. What other situations do you get worried about in public places?" He slid his hand down to the side of her neck, where he could play with her hair and stroke her skin at the same time.

She lost the small amount of emotion that had come with her realization about her public fear, replaced by the warm, tingly feeling on her skin that came any time he played with her hair. "I…feel like I might not know what I'm supposed to do, and I'll do something wrong. Get into trouble, or make everyone hate me."

"That one I understand. I had it the first couple of years at school. But after I figured out the right comeback for some dude getting in my face and calling me a 'circus freak,' it stopped having any power over me. Different doesn't mean bad. Different is just different." And in a quieter voice he asked, "What did you do that was wrong when you were in the home?"

He would have to put that together. "I…drank out of the garden hose. I didn't know any of the cartoons the other kids knew. I kept asking where their horses were, and where we were going next… Different to kids is bad. Not just to them. It was all different than what I understood, and that confused me and upset me. A lot."

"How did you get your shoulder dislocated?" he asked, his voice so deceptively quiet that she almost missed that he'd linked it with her group home ordeal…

"You remembered…"

"Pink sling," he confirmed with two words.

What could she say about that? She still didn't know why it had happened. "I guess I made Mrs. Barch mad."

"Mrs. Barch?"

"She ran the home. But hated kids, near as I could tell." So naturally she'd made kids her career…

"What did you do to make her mad?" His hand slid into her hair, distracting her a little…probably distracting himself.

"I don't know. I know I say that when I don't want to talk about something, but I honestly don't know. I climbed onto the counter to reach the phone on the wall and the next I knew she jerked me down by the arm. I threw up on her. It really hurt. She sent me to bed for being bad. A couple of days later…Mom and Mack got there. The social worker gave them grief, I guess. Kids whose families aren't in the circus don't get abducted, I guess. But the instant Mom saw my arm, the social worker lady realized she'd put me with someone who'd do that…and then left it dislocated for days without taking me to the emergency room. She'd have gotten into trouble.

"So she sent me with Mom, and they were so glad to have me back they didn't file any complaints." It had taken Jolie most of her life to riddle out exactly what had happened with the social worker, the things you missed when you're little…

Reece scowled so hard Jolie was suddenly more than half-afraid he'd tell her to stop being dramatic or something else that made it her fault. But he let go of her hair, wrapped his arm around her shoulders and pulled her snugly against his side. The kiss he pressed to her temple lasted and lasted, and when he eventually spoke it was against her skin. "I should have asked what happened."

"You were eight." Jolie knew she might never learn to navigate the outside world but maybe she could learn to navigate this man. "You took good care of me. Everyone did. But you and Gordy especially."

He made a sound so contrary that Jolie tugged his head to hers to kiss him and subtly shift the conversation. "Thank you for going along with the shoulder thing. You know I was about a heartbeat away from climbing onto your shoulders."

"You know better than to think I couldn't have picked you up," he joked, but his voice said he was still upset.

"Oh, no I'm sure Strong Man could have, but Safety Man—you remember the other side of your personality? He would not have been very happy if I had. I didn't have any spotters, no safety gear on… What if you dropped me?"

"That's not how it goes and you know it." Reece goosed her ribs, and when she was giggling he stood, picked her up and tossed her over his shoulder.

She laughed and hit him on the butt. "Dirty! My defenses were down!" He didn't put her down, just started walking. "You know when you do these things in public, wearing that T-shirt, you're representing Keightly…" Right across the pavilion…in full view of the adults, who squinted, and the children, who laughed…off they went to the exit.

Jolie braced one arm against his back to hold herself up and waved her cotton candy at the kids they passed with the other so no one would be alarmed, and dropped the sugary stuff into a trashcan as they passed it. "Hey, Hercules, where are we going?"

"Home."

Thank God. And if he knew what was good for him, it had better be for sex.

The trapeze didn't smell like sawdust, but it had the same effect on Reece. He had thought the more he got up on the thing, the better he would do with it, but he still always felt on the edge of panic the whole time. His grim glowers even kind of scared the girls in the troupe. He needed to work on that but taking on one more thing seemed too much right now.

Every evening during the week, before the kids were picked up, Reece came and worked with them on the trapeze. The first two weeks of flying with a catcher, they'd all learned the knee-hang and how to fly back onto the swing when another girl swung out to meet them.

It took another two weeks for Reece's body to re-learn the ins and outs of the whole dangerous business, and for the old muscle memory to adjust to his new, bigger body. Only then did he feel comfortable adding the simple toss to their routine. The extra hour he spent teaching Anthony to catch in the evenings helped. Anthony taking the role was the light at the end of Reece's trapeze tunnel…

Two weeks later Reece added the simple toss to their routine. Things were going well.

With Reece's rigorous physicals and safety standards and Jolie's strict behavior policies it meant that at the rehearsal for the end-of-summer finale show they only had light injuries. The worst had come in the form of a scissor incident in costuming, and it had been when Reece hadn't been around and had only required a couple of stitches.

"How are you doing?" Jolie asked as he stretched his arms and shoulders, preparing to climb the ladder up to the platform.

He turned round so she could push his arm up from the back, stretching his shoulders better. "I'm fine. Have you decided if you're going to do anything during the finale?"

"I don't really want to. I don't want to show up the kids. They've been working hard all summer." She moved to the other arm, repeating the stretch he preferred.

He nodded, looking no less grim as he took to the ladder to get on with today's rehearsal.

Jolie moved off to the stands and took a seat, eyes fixed on the group above. They didn't need her direction today. She simply waited for Reece to climb on the screen and then pressed "Play" on the music that would accompany the aerial act.

The kids had gone for a haunted-circus theme, and every piece of music sounded like a deranged calliope, taking to the minor keys. While she really liked the theme the kids had put together all summer for the show, today, with Reece's mood, it put her on edge.

Anthony was the best at the knee-hang, but he really wanted Reece to be proud of him, Jolie could tell. He also was a little too confident for her liking. Two days ago Jolie had caught Anthony and his girlfriend, Tara, on the trapeze one evening after the camp was closed, practicing together. She'd put a stop to it. But she hadn't told Reece. He was so on edge about the trapeze already.

Reece got his swing where it needed to be, found his mark, and called, "Hep!" which got the first flyer launching on the swing.

He'd started self-medicating with anti-nausea medicine about three weeks ago, and he had been a little late taking them today because of a small emergency at the office. He wasn't sure he'd taken it in time to get the full effect, but the symptoms when he was in the air never started until he'd been at it for a few tricks and had had time to work himself into a mental lather.

It was psychosomatic, and he knew that Jolie would understand—she had waded through a few panic attacks this spring—but he didn't want her to know. It felt like breaking a promise to her if his mind was making him unable to complete the trapeze position he'd agreed to.

The first flier flew from the bar to his hands. Like always, she looked up at him nervously, like he was going to fling her off the swing. The three girls in the troupe always looked at him nervously. The only one who took every flight with extreme glee and confidence was Anthony—the fourth flier, it was a necessary part of learning to catch.

It would let the kids down if Reece couldn't catch. And the camp. Anthony just wasn't ready to do the catching yet but he got his shot earlier with the knee-hangs. He and Tara had worked that trick out very well during classes.

They each got a shot with the same tricks. The girls went, and when it was Anthony's turn Reece marked his swing and yelled, "Hep!" but noticed when he swung back toward his new younger brother that he was standing on the bar.

"Anthony!" he yelled. A combination of his lateness in taking the anti-nausea and vertigo pills and the surprise trick combined to rob him of the ability to say anything else. Anthony launched up at the wrong time, executed a perfect forward somersault, but when the timing was off, it didn't matter how perfect the trick was.

He was close. Reece stretched for Anthony's hands and only got one of them, throwing his swing off balance so that it swung on the diagonal.

Anthony seemed to understand only when their hands were slipping how dangerous what he'd done had been, and let go to let the net catch him.

The wrong point in the swing. The wrong time. Reece could do nothing but watch Anthony fall and pray he hit the net. They learned to fall properly the first day.

Anthony bounced once at the edge and then flew off into the ring.

Jolie had her phone out, dialing 911, before Anthony even let go of Reece's hand. But it all happened so fast. She ran with the phone to her ear, and gave report and instructions as she fell at Anthony's side.

"He's breathing," she called to Reece. And he, ever the protector, unfolded from the swing and fell to the net as soon as it was safe to do so, taking the fastest route down so he could get to them.

Breathing, but unconscious. She dared not move him, but reached to check his pulse, and breathed a tiny bit easier when she found a strong beat with her fingertips.

Reece knelt beside the unconscious teen and began checking for injuries. "More broken legs." His voice rasped. "Looks like the left tibia. Simple."

Jolie didn't even need to look at him to know how he was doing. His skin had turned ashen, but his hands were steady. This had to be like a nightmare for him.

Anthony started to wake up, and Reece found his voice. "*Do not move*, Anthony. You could have a neck or spine injury. I know you're in pain, but be still." And then added to Jolie, "Brace his head with your knees. Don't let him turn it."

He moved on from the obvious bones to Anthony's abdomen, prodding lightly as he watched the kid's face. "You tell me if this hurts, okay?" Jolie watched as well, as Reece's hands moved around Anthony's belly. At the left side, under the ribs, he pressed and Anthony cried out.

Reece stopped pressing, folded one of Anthony's arms up for Jolie to reach and said in tones so level and steady that her hair stood on end, "Keep an eye on his pulse. I need your phone."

"My pocket." She pressed Anthony's wrist, finding the pulse and counting the beats as she alternated between looking at her watch and watching Anthony's face.

Reece walked a short distance away and called, she assumed, 911 again. She heard the "words possible splenic rupture' and noticed that Anthony's pulse rate was increasing.

"Reece? His pulse is speeding up…a little."

He hung up and came back over. "How much?"

"What's happening?" Anthony asked, his voice breathy, scared.

Jolie answered Reece, frowning, "It's gone up from one-eighteen to one-twenty-five." And then said to the youngest Bohannon, "Do you hear the ambulance? Don't worry. Everything is going to be okay. The ambulance is here and we'll get you to the hospital and patched up. But you need to stay calm, okay?"

The paramedics stepped in, and with Reece's help got Anthony loaded onto a backboard and into the ambulance.

"Go with him," Jolie said to Reece, knowing he would be of assistance. "I'll be right behind you."

She should have told Reece that she'd found them practicing. Tara had gotten the message that she could be kicked out of the camp and not allowed back next year for the stunt with the trapeze, but Anthony had had something to prove. And he'd wanted to impress Reece more than anyone. If she'd told Reece, he could have gotten through to Anthony.

This was her fault.

But Reece would blame himself.

Six hours later Reece had yet to speak to Jolie. She moved along beside him through the hospital, everywhere she could go. He was a doctor so they let him into Recovery to see Anthony when he came out of surgery. And he left Jolie in the waiting room with every single person who lived at the farm—even Granny and the brood of young wild things she fostered.

He just couldn't think about her right now or how she'd take it when he told her the camp was done. No more. No show. No next season. Anthony could have died. But, really, any of them could have died. It didn't matter how safe they played it, when it came time for that last show, the safety gear came off. And he'd fallen for it—the idea that these were safe tricks. That this was fine. He should have been listening to his gut when every time he'd got into the swing, he'd almost thrown up.

Reece stayed back with Anthony as they removed the tube in his throat and Reece got to talk to him.

"You know I'm going to kick your ass when you get better," Reece said, taking Anthony's hand and leaning over the bed so he could look him in the eye.

Anthony smiled, and Reece relaxed.

"I thought you'd catch me."

Reece shook his head, but he was so relieved he couldn't do anything but rib him. "I would have if you had told me what you were going to do. But you're lucky. Your spleen ruptured, but they got it out clean. You survived a ruptured spleen, which is fairly badass. You also have a broken leg, and it's a simple fracture. Granny wanted them to put you in a pink cast with flowers, but I intervened. That old lady is so upset she's forgotten how to swear."

"Sign of the apocalypse, isn't it?"

"Sources say." Reece grinned and then did something that probably would have horrified the kid if he wasn't drugged, and especially if chicks were watching. He dropped a kiss on Anthony's head. "We want you around until you're old enough to cuss like Granny Bohannon.

You don't need to impress anyone, you already have. And if you don't believe how many people love you, when they wheel you to your room, I want you to look at the waiting room."

Anthony's eyes squeezed shut and a couple of tears slipped out, but he nodded. "Thanks, Reece."

Reece squeezed his hand.

"If you tell anyone I cried, I'm going to tell them you kissed me."

Reece smirked and let go. "All right, Spleeny." He made his farewells before the recovery nurses kicked him out, and went out to speak with the family.

Later that evening, when the hospital administration made it clear that visiting hours were over, Jolie waited for everyone to exit Anthony's room and then went to speak with him. Luckily, she found him in one of his post-surgery lucid phases and took his hand. "We're going to head home, but Granny is going to be here bright and early in the morning to sit with you. Do you want one of us to stay here with you tonight?"

Anthony smiled a little and shook his head. "I'm okay. Could you call Tara for me?"

"She's been here, honey," Jolie told him, grinning. "And her parents just dragged her home a few minutes ago. But you were sleeping. She knows you're going to be okay. She'll probably bring you something she baked tomorrow…and yell at you."

"Doesn't do any good," he muttered.

Jolie knew precisely what he was talking about: her yelling at him. "Well, it would have been better if you hadn't needed to learn the hard way, but you came through it. Everyone's going to be fine."

"Reece isn't. He's…very upset still."

"Reece learned his lesson the hard way once already."

Again she wished she'd just told him about Anthony and Tara. It was her fault really that Anthony was hurt. She was too lenient…or maybe not intimidating enough. Something. She should have handled something differently.

"His dad," Anthony filled in.

"His dad."

"No one will tell me how it happened."

No one liked to talk about it. Jolie didn't like to talk about it, but maybe if she had used it to scare him the other day this wouldn't have happened. Not talking about things wasn't working out for her on so many levels.

"It was equipment malfunction, a Russian swing. His dad was flying on that one. They take two fliers to get the swing moving fast and high enough, and then the front person lets go and kind of…catapults really fast and far to the catcher. Much further than regular catches." She tried to explain gently and quickly, knowing he needed his rest.

Anthony squeezed her hand. "Something broke?"

"Reece was the additional power on the swing. He wasn't supposed to fly, just be at the back to get it going, and he's really good at that. Has a powerful swing." She had to stop and focus on something to keep the mental images away. "Whoever installed it the last time hadn't done a good job. One of the bolts had stripped and as there were a number of other bolts, he'd just figured he'd change it the next time it was set up."

"Did it break?" Anthony asked, the horror in his voice pulling her attention back to his bruised face.

She nodded. "Before his dad jumped, the swing came loose…at the worst time…and they both pitched off it at a really bad angle, moving fast. It looked like they were both going to miss the net, but somehow only Henry missed it. Reece hit it. I think Henry pushed him or flung him off course somehow. He had the air knocked out of him but his dad hit the rigging and then the ground. He didn't die instantly. There was so much blood…and the EMTs didn't get there in time." Which was why Jolie had studied emergency medicine and was a certified EMT.

It had been so long since she'd even let herself remember it…

"So he checks the rigging every day," Anthony supplied.

"I don't know how to make him stop or even if I should try," Jolie confirmed. "Anyway, he's not mad at you, but he might ride you when you get out of this antiseptic-smelling lock-up, but it's just because he's feeling really protective of you."

Anthony nodded. She squeezed his hand again. "We all are. Now sleep. I'm sure Granny will bring you something in the morning to keep you amused. Or maybe she'll make you write 'I will not pull unexpected tricks on the trapeze' one thousand times. Either way, rest." She leaned up and in to reach his cheek, kissed it, and then went to find Reece.

Jolie walked with Reece to the garage. "We should talk about this…" she said, hurrying to keep up with his longer stride. She wanted to hold his hand, but he had them crammed into his pockets.

"When we get back to the farm."

He knew. He knew and he thought she was an utter failure as a camp director.

The trip home felt like a drive to her execution.

Jolie just wasn't sure whether it was the end of them or the end of the camp.

CHAPTER ELEVEN

JOLIE STOPPED THE car and Reece climbed out and set off for the big top. "Reece, you don't need to go back in there right now."

"I have to," Reece bit out, not looking back at her. "I'm taking down the trapeze."

She ran to cover the distance being eaten up by his long stride and grabbed his hand. "I already locked up the ladders. No one can get up to there without getting the ladders unlocked."

He scowled but stopped and looked back at her. "I'll check. Go to your trailer and wait."

As much as she wanted to make him stop and listen to her, talk to her, just be with him until she knew he was okay, Jolie let go of his hand and did as he requested.

She almost hoped Anthony had told him then at least he'd place the blame on her—where it belonged—not blame himself.

After she reached the trailer and got inside, she stepped back out where she could best see the tent and waited for Reece to arrive.

And when he still hadn't come half an hour later she sat on the stairs and waited.

The good news was that she could now unequivocally say that she had control of her emotions again. Calm. She'd managed to stay calm through the whole thing. Right now she was worried but able to keep the panic at bay.

She folded her arms on her knees and laid her head down, giving him the time he needed despite her natural inclination to run after him.

Reece had to admire Jolie's simple solution to lock up the ladders. She'd climbed them and pulled the tail of the rope ladder up behind her. They draped over the platforms, where no one could get to them without extreme effort and construction ladders locked up in the pole barn.

Checking her solution had taken about a minute, and then he spent the next forty minutes throwing up.

Jolie had gone to her trailer, as he'd asked. He saw she was sitting on the stairs with her head on her knees, waiting for him. Hearing his approach, she lifted her head. "You look like hell."

"Yeah. I need a drink," Reece muttered.

She stood, heading into her home to get him a glass of water. "Or did you mean booze?"

He took the glass and drank it all. When it was empty and his mouth was a little improved, he looked at her. "The camp is over, Jo. No finale show. No camp next year. I'm going to call up the buyer from this spring and see if his offer is still on the table."

The calm with which she took his ruling seemed off. She held out a hand for the glass and took it back to the kitchen. "Are you okay?"

"I'm… No." He may as well tell her. "I've been—"

"It was my fault that he did that," she said quietly, stopping him in his tracks.

Reece turned and sat on the couch, taking up entirely too much room in the small home when he stood around in it. "What do you mean?"

"I caught him and Tara on the trapeze the other evening, and I chewed them both out." Her voice was level, no tears in sight, though she looked haunted by guilt, and there was a small tell about how upset it had made her in the way she kept holding her own hands. "I got through to Tara, but I guess I didn't get through to Anthony. And I didn't tell you because I didn't want you to be upset. I thought I'd handled it…but I hadn't. If it had come from you, he would have listened."

"He might have," Reece said, but shrugged. "Hard to say. It was probably a matter of time. And, really, we're lucky it was family. If it had been one of the kids, they could have sued."

She finally moved to the couch and sat beside him. "Next year—"

"There won't be a next year, Jolie." He needed to stand. She was too close and when she was close he wanted to please and protect her, physically and emotionally. Best she stayed outside arm's reach. "This life is too dangerous. And you're not performing because of it as I thought you would. You teach, and your students are doing great on the wire, but you're not performing except those times you practice your routine, which I thought you were going to perform at the finale, but you said no. So what's the point?"

He turned back to look at her on the couch, silent and frowning. Was it because she worried about him or she was trying to work out how to make him do what she wanted? He didn't know.

"Where does this leave us?"

She probably wouldn't want to wait for a solution to appear, or like the solution he had in mind. "I love you, Jo. But there's no future for us if you're on the road, and there's no happiness for you if you're not in the life. And

I don't even know if I could handle it if you were performing. We tried to preserve the life with the camp, but it can't work. So you tell me, what's the solution? Do you want to come and work at my practice? Make appointments and sit all day at a desk? Good Lord, you're like the ultimate riddle."

"Once again, I am a problem to be solved."

"Stop saying that."

Naturally, he would wait until he could couch it in break-up words before he said "I love you' the first time.

"Sounds like you have made up your mind."

"I have to protect you." He said the words softly, but they may as well have been shouted.

Jolie shook her head. "I'm not your responsibility."

"Yes, you are my responsibility." He laughed, a short, mirthless sound. "And I know how stupid that sounds when I say it out loud, but I'm supposed to protect you. I'm still on that job."

"The job your dad gave you when I was five?" What could she say to that? He'd all but admitted it was insane.

He plowed his hand through his hair. "Yes."

"Is that why you love me? Because I'm your responsibility to take care of?"

"No. That's why I try so hard not to love you. Makes it that much harder to take care of you properly when every time you're sad it's a lance through my chest." He stepped to the door, ready to escape. "I have a list of owners who are looking for a wire act. I'll send it over tomorrow. Email."

"You've been…you've been headhunting a job for me?" She didn't know whether to cry or scream.

"I was just getting a feel for whether there was a market."

"How long? Recently? All summer? When did you take

this little task on your shoulders?" She rubbed between her brows. Some of that old numbness began seeping in and she let it. "You know what? Never mind. I don't want either of us to say anything else. Something we might regret. We'll talk again when we have clear heads."

"My head is clear, honey."

"Are you blaming yourself?"

"I'm blaming everyone. You. Me. Anthony. The people in his past who made that kid feel like even when he was part of a family he had to keep working to make them love him. And I'm blaming the lure of the big top and the thrill of flying." He opened the door and stepped out. "I'll talk to you soon."

At least that would be different this time. He didn't want to hurt her, but he would be man enough to put it to her straight before he left her.

Reece drove his car through the grass to park on the far side of the big top, and he didn't care who didn't like it. There was a trail of dust streaking across the flat Georgia landscape where he'd raced down the long dusty drive. At least driving on the grass wouldn't make life difficult for any asthmatics on the farm.

He wouldn't have had to do this if the whole area hadn't been packed with cars and fans—spectators, he imagined.

Jolie had called that morning and left a message that the season finale recital of Keightly Circus Camp would be going ahead, and had then refused to answer any of his calls when he rang her back.

Inside the tent, all the seating had been installed and it was packed to the gills with people. He saw all manner of dressed performers below the stands, which traditionally served as the backstage area for performers about to come out.

It wasn't a haunted circus. It was a zombie circus.

But no matter how cute it was, it could not go on. "Anyone seen Miss Jolie?" he asked, making the circuit around the tent via that backstage portion. Children pointed in the direction he traveled, and he eventually found her counting heads. Without saying anything to alert the kids, he grabbed her elbow and steered her out of the tent, where he might possibly choke her to death. "Call it off."

"Reece, just listen. There is no trapeze act. These kids have worked too hard to miss their finale. However, all the safety equipment is being used. And you're just going to have to trust me. I know I screwed up with Anthony, but don't take it out on the kids. They need this. They deserve it."

He looked toward the flap and a bizarre little grey-skinned hobo clown smiled at him. And waved. Reece waved back at the little boy then looked at Jolie. "You should have told me."

"Yes. I should have. There's a lot of things I should have told you. And when you said you loved me, even though you said it under duress, I should have believed you."

"You didn't believe me?"

"Not until later." She touched his face and then pressed her thumb between his brows and gave the muscle a little rub. It actually felt good, forcing his brow to relax. "I promise we've taken every precaution that's possible. I know you'll approve of what we've done. It's more camp than circus now. And the only way someone's going to get hurt is if a meteor falls. No trapeze. Please, Reece. Just go and watch the show. I saved you a seat by Granny." She turned to head for the tent again.

"What about the aerialists?"

"They have a new act." She stopped before entering. "And they've worked like crazy the past week to get it ready. It's not on the trapeze. And it doesn't even need a net. Okay?"

He was holding up the show. Reece sighed and walked inside. Once again he'd failed to say no to Jolie. Finding Granny easily enough, he took a seat and tried to relax. Mouth like a sailor and a heart of gold, she laid a weathered hand over his and gave him a comforting pat. "Don't worry, everything's gonna be okay."

"I hope so."

He must have looked sick because she let go of his hand, reached for her purse and put it in his lap. "But if you have to throw up, there's a barf bag in there. I stole it from the hospital." When he didn't say anything, she added, "Them zombies are disgusting."

Over the next two hours he watched the most ridiculously cute zombie-clown parody since the *Thriller* video that he had to laugh. They always started with the clowns.

Then came jugglers with fake bones, balls painted with skulls, sticks modeled like femurs…

Stiff-legged acrobats, who shuffled around before breaking into feats of creepy, contorted tumbling.

And toward the end an oddly placed fashion show where the kid designers talked about the costuming. While the little zombie fashion show was going on, the crew went about in the background, setting something up.

Thick mats went down. Cables suspended from the rigging high above were brought down to dangle and large steel hoops were attached to the ends. Set in the wide shape of a square, so all around the tent everyone would have a good view.

Then he saw his aerialists, minus Anthony, walking out in single file, dressed all in black with gauzy fabric tatters hanging everywhere. While the rest of the show had pre-recorded music with it, he heard the first strains of the calliope as the girls took their positions in the hoops. Mack drove the calliope into the ring with his mother at the keyboard, playing what he could only call music of a haunted carousel.

The stage hands got the hoops spinning. He'd made sure all the trapeze troupe had been gymnasts…except Anthony. Give a gymnast a big spinning hoop to play with? They probably liked it just as well as the trapeze, and at only three feet from thick mats Jolie was right, it would be a miracle if they found a way to hurt themselves badly.

They found artistic ways to arrange themselves within the hoops, each move slowing or increasing the speed of the spin. It was flashy and graceful, and a little bit creepy with the calliope. And as he watched, he forgot the horror that always darkened his circus experience.

Jolie had done it. They'd got off to a rocky start but next year there would be a waiting list a mile long to come to the camp. At the end she made a short speech, giving recognition to all of the former Keightly Circus performers and especially to him, who…

He could fill in that blank. Reece, who had made her beg and plead to be allowed to try it. Reece, who treated her like an incompetent child. Reece, who left for long stretches of time because he couldn't control everyone.

Not that she said any of that. He waved his hand at the applause and circulated through the crowd of parents and performers, giving his congratulations. Then he went to Jolie's trailer to wait for her. She'd left the door unlocked, as usual, so when she finally got back she found him sitting on her stairs with a glass of tea in his hand. The problem was, no matter how long he'd sat there, he didn't know what to say to her. His feelings were all still scrambled in his head.

* * *

"You were right. I didn't see anything there that…wasn't amazing. And the kids deserved their shot to do the show. I hope someone taped the zombie clown *Thriller* dance."

Jolie smiled and came to a stop in front of the stairs, just far away that he couldn't touch her without standing up. "Oh, don't worry, we have the whole thing on tape. It might be one of a kind. Collector's edition."

"About that…" Reece licked his lips. "About next year…"

"Wait. I want to talk about us. Can we talk about us first?" She stepped closer, her courage faltering a little. He'd been smiling at the circus. He'd enjoyed it. She should have stuck with that topic. She could handle that topic…

Reece tilted his head back toward the living room. "Do you want to come inside to do this?"

"No. With you on the stairs, we're closer to the same eye level right now. The height changes inside, nothing that tall for you to sit on," Jolie babbled, then paused, took a breath to find her center again and started over. "I have a speech. And if we go moving around, I might forget it. Or forget how it starts."

"You have a speech?" Reece reached behind him to set the glass of tea inside then focused on her. "I'm ready."

"You said I didn't trust you, and you were right. I didn't. I wanted to, and I tried. I knew you were trying. But it just wasn't coming together for me. When I got on the trapeze with you that day, I couldn't bring myself to reach for you. When we did the knee-hang, it was different. I never had to let go of the bar until you had hold of me securely. But when we did the toss and I had to let go of the bar, I couldn't take your hands, even when they were a sure thing. Not because I thought I would fall, I thought it was possible that you would drop me. And just that possibility seemed so much worse than me deciding to fall on my own. It doesn't make a lot of sense."

Reece waved a hand. "It does. That was about being in control, even if the decision you made was one that could have hurt you. I understand that need for control. Believe me." He was very calm. If that meant he didn't care, he was going to have to reject her twice, because she wasn't going to stop.

"I don't even know when I started to trust you. It wasn't like there was a light-bulb moment when I thought, Everything's okay, I can trust Reece now. He hasn't broken his promises or whatever. The whole summer, and even when we got back from the hospital and…well, we broke up, right? I expected it. I had been waiting for it the whole summer. And then you had that list, and it seemed like you had been expecting it too." She felt tears burning her eyes and had to stop talking for a moment to breathe.

"I could be a total psycho and ask you to get on the trapeze to prove to you that I trust you, but I don't need to do that. I already reached for you…today. I knew you would be mad about the show, but I knew you would come. I know you'll always come, Reece. I know it. Even if you…" Her voice cracked and she squeaked the rest in the most undignified fashion while swiping her cheeks. "Even if you don't want me any more."

He stood, took two steps toward her, reached out, and his hands didn't close. "Are you done with your speech?"

She nodded.

His arms surged around her waist and he picked her up, carried her inside, his mouth on hers before the door closed, and her pants were off before they got to the bed.

Ten minutes later Reece rolled onto his back, dragging her with him. "Sorry. I meant to last and last…"

"It was longer than five seconds," she teased, smiling.

He groaned, "I'm never going to live that one down, am I?"

She scooted up closer so she could tuck her nose beneath his chin. "You do every time. I just like to make sure you don't lose the magic." And then she pulled back to look him in the eye. "And you had it at the show tonight, didn't you? Not the sexy magic, but...you felt it, didn't you?"

"I forgot where I was, who I was...and why I had left. That's the first time that's happened. Yes." He pushed her hair back from her face. "I felt the magic. If you want the camp next year, I'm good with that. I think if you run it like you have done this year—"

"Without the trapeze," Jolie cut in.

He smiled, looking relieved. "Without the trapeze. The hoops were wonderful. I'd rather you stay away from the silk aerialists, though. That's more dangerous than trapeze."

"I agree." She kissed him again and said, "We don't have to make any decisions. I don't want to travel, but I did find out that I can get an agent to arrange corporate gigs and big parties, short-term travel if I do feel like performing. But, honestly, the idea of having a pasture to ride in every day, maybe get a miniature mare and breed them? One day build a house with a foundation? That idea's starting to grow on me. I still don't think I could handle suburbia but...I can handle not traveling. I can make a life, a happy life, outside The Life."

"You work on building a life outside The Life, I'll work on making sure it's happy." Reece didn't propose, but it was as good as she needed.

She sat up, straddling his groin, and gave a slow wiggle. "I owe you an 'I love you.' I'll see if I can find one lying about if you can last longer than ten minutes this time."

"If I can't, I'm sure we can find Mr. Happy around

here somewhere…" he said, rolling her over and kissing her breathless.

Strides may have been made today, but the man still liked to be in charge.

And that was okay. Jolie knew she had all the time in the world to break him of it.

* * * * *

DR PERFECT ON HER DOORSTEP

LUCY CLARK

To our gorgeous Abby. You are such a delight.
Never stop!

—Ps121:7-8

CHAPTER ONE

STACEY WILTON PULLED the car to the side of the road. She looked across at the house, nostalgia rising within her. Turning the key to cut the engine, she unbuckled her seatbelt and opened the door, her gaze never leaving the house. The late-afternoon rays from the sun combined with the blue of the September sky only enhanced the beauty of the place.

It looked so different—smaller, somehow. Which was ridiculous, because houses didn't grow or shrink. And yet it was still the same as her memory recalled. The front garden had been re-landscaped, the large tree she and her sisters had used to climb was gone, and no shade fell over the front windows, but instead the garden was alive with rows of vibrantly coloured flowers, enjoying the spring weather. Stacey smiled. Her father would have loved that.

She leaned against the car and drank her fill of the place she'd called home for the first fourteen years of her life. It was a place she'd never contemplated leaving, but she'd soon learned that life was never smooth. Her mother had walked out, abandoning them all.

Stacey and her sisters had been almost five years old, excited to start school, when their mother had declared that she'd had enough. Their father had been the local GP, working long and erratic hours. He'd employed a young nanny—Letisha—who, many years later, he'd married.

When he'd been head-hunted to run a new palliative care hospice in Perth Arn Wilton had accepted the position without consulting his teenage daughters.

'Why do we need to go?' Stacey had asked him, tears streaming down her face as he'd packed yet another box.

'Because this job is too good to pass up, Stace. I get to be a part of something new and exciting as well as incredibly important. This is the first palliative hospice just for children.'

'But what about all your patients *here*? What about your practice? I was going to become a doctor and then one day work with you here.'

'Stace.' Arn had sighed with resignation and placed a hand on her shoulder. 'It's time to move on.'

'Just because of a job? It doesn't make sense, Dad.'

'Well, then, think of Letisha. You love Letisha, and now that we're newly married it's not really fair to ask her to start her married life in a home where there have been so many unhappy memories. Tish deserves better, don't you think?'

When Stacey had opened her mouth to continue arguing her father had given her a stern look, which had meant the discussion was over.

Stacey and her sisters had packed their lives into boxes, said tearful goodbyes to their school friends, and hugged their neighbours, Edna and Mike, with tear-stained faces.

'I've never lived next door to anyone else,' Stacey had told Edna, who had been like a second mother to her.

'Adventures are good,' Edna had told her. 'And we'll keep in touch. I've given you enough letter paper and stamps to last you for a good two years at least.' Edna had smiled at her. 'We'll see each other again, Stacey.'

'Promise?' Stacey had asked.

'Promise.'

Then the Wilton family had left Newcastle, on Australia's east coast, and headed to Perth on the other side of the country. There they'd settled into their new life, and many years later Letisha had given birth to Stacey's new sister. Indeed, over the years their family had grown from three to six children.

Now, finally, after almost two decades, Stacey was returning to the job she'd always dreamed of: taking over the old family medical practice her father had once run. She hoped it would provide stability for all of them—especially after the events of the past eighteen months. Her father and beloved stepmother had passed away in a terrible car accident, leaving Stacey and her sisters as guardians of their younger siblings. Not only that, but Stacey had been jilted at the altar by the man who'd been supposed to love her for the rest of her life.

No, the past eighteen months had been soul-destroying, and her coming back to a town she'd always regarded as a place of solace was much needed.

'Can I help you?'

Stacey was pulled from her reverie by a man standing just at the edge of the driveway next to the house she was staring at. He was very tall, about six foot four, and wore an old pair of gardening shorts and a light blue T-shirt which he'd clearly used as a painting smock, if the splatters of green, yellow and pink paint were anything to go by. He had flip-flops on his feet, a peaked cap on his head, and a pair of gardening gloves on his hands. A pile of weeds was on the concrete driveway near his feet. How had she not seen him there before?

'Can I help you with something?' he repeated, taking

off his gloves and tossing them carelessly onto the pile of weeds.

Stacey shifted her car keys from one hand to the other. 'No, thanks.'

'Are you sure? You seem to be quite entranced, just looking at my house.' He angled his head to the side, giving her a more concentrated look. 'Are you sure you're feeling all right?'

She waved away his concern and smiled politely. 'I'm fine… It's just that—well I used to live here.' She pointed to the house. 'When I was little.' She called her words across the street, feeling a little self-conscious as one or two cars drove between their impromptu conversation. When the man beckoned her over it seemed like the most logical thing in the world to cross the road and go and chat with a complete stranger.

'You've cut down the tree,' she said, pointing to where the tree used to be.

'Had to. It was diseased.'

'Oh. How sad. I guess it has been a while, but I do have such happy memories of climbing it—and swinging on the tyre swing.' Her sigh was nostalgic as she continued to peruse the garden. 'I really like the flowers. Very pretty.'

'Thank you. I don't mind doing a spot of gardening. I find it relaxing.'

'And painting? The house used to be a cream colour, but I think the mint-green looks much better. Good choice.'

The man nodded. 'I found painting very…therapeutic. I'd never painted a house before, but now I have. Both inside and out. One more thing crossed off my bucket list.'

Stacey gave him a puzzled look. 'Bucket what?'

'Bucket list. You know—a list of things you'd like to do before you pass away.'

She shook her head. 'I've never heard it put like that before. A bit morbid, isn't it?'

The man grinned—a full-on gorgeous smile that highlighted his twinkling blue eyes. Bedroom eyes, her sister Molly would have called them. Eyes that could mesmerise a woman from across the room…or across the road.

'Not morbid,' he continued, shaking his head a little. 'Adventurous. For example, if you had on your bucket list, *Talk to a strange man about bucket lists* then you could go home and cross that right off, feeling like you've actually accomplished something new today.'

Stacey's brow creased further. 'Why would I have that on a list of things I'd like to accomplish before I die?'

The man surprised her further by laughing. Was he laughing *at* her? Or at this bucket list thing he kept gabbing about?

'Never mind.' He held out his hand. 'I'm Pierce.'

She put her hand into his, ignoring the way the heat from this hand seemed to travel up her arm and explode into a thousand stars, setting her body alight.

'Stacey.' If she was the type of person to believe in instant attraction then she might be flattered by his smile. Thankfully she left that sort of emotion and nonsense up to Molly.

'Nice to meet you, Stacey.' Pierce gestured towards the house. 'Would you like to come inside? Take a look at some of the other changes we've made?'

We? He was most likely married, and as this house was perfect for children no doubt he had a couple of those as well. He seemed honest, personable and quite kind, but first impressions could be deceptive. Perhaps she should ask him some more questions, just to be sure.

She knew the Edelsteins still lived next door, as Edna

had called her earlier that morning asking her to make a house call to review Mike.

'He's too stubborn to come to the clinic,' Edna had told her. 'But he'll listen to you, Stace.'

That was how Stacey found herself here, coming to see Mike and Edna. But now she was being invited by a stranger into the house where she'd grown up. Still, she should test the waters before going inside with him. Better to be safe than sorry.

'Do the Edelsteins still live next door?'

He nodded. 'That Edna… She's a talker, isn't she? Yesterday she stood at her fence for a good two hours and chatted to me while I did some gardening. I kept asking if she'd like to come and sit down on the veranda on the swing and have a nice cool drink—but, no, she was quite happy leaning on the fence and telling me all about her gallstone removal.'

Stacey smiled and nodded, pleased with the way Pierce's words held no impatience as he spoke of Edna. 'Same old Edna. And Mike? How's he doing?'

A frown furrowed his brow. 'Not too good, I'm sorry to say. I popped over last night just to check on him after Edna told me he's been getting increasingly dizzy when he stands up. Plus his asthma has flared, due to all the pollen.' Pierce pulled on his gardening gloves as he spoke and started tidying up the mound of weeds, placing them into the gardening recycle bin. 'His asthma meds are only just keeping things at bay.' He shook his head, concern evident in his tone.

Stacey nodded. This information was marrying up with what Edna had told her.

'Of course in typical fashion Mike's refusing to admit there's anything really wrong with him, but if things aren't brought under control soon he runs the risk of contracting pneumonia.'

'You sound very concerned.' Again she watched his expression, and when he met her eyes his gaze was quizzical.

'Of course I'm concerned. That's why I offered to give him a private check-up.'

Stacey's eyebrows hit her perfectly straight fringe. 'You're a doctor?'

Pierce nodded. 'GP. I've been doing locum work at the local hospital in the A & E department—just a few shifts a week while I finish getting things sorted out around here.'

A *doctor*? Her level of trust for Pierce increased. He was a doctor as well as passing her test regarding his neighbours. 'Well, thank you for checking up on Mike. What was your clinical assessment?'

'Clinical assessment, eh?' Pierce pondered her words as he removed his gardening gloves and then snapped his fingers. 'That's *right*. Edna said a doctor used to live in this house and that some of his kids were also doctors.'

'That would have been my dad—Arn Wilton.'

'She said he was the only one who could ever make Mike see sense about health matters.'

Stacey's smile was nostalgic. 'He and Mike were always good friends.'

'Were? Did they have a falling out?'

'No. Not those two. Mates until the last.' Stacey looked down at the ground. 'My father and stepmother passed away eighteen months ago.'

'I'm sorry to hear that, Stacey.'

Pierce's tone was filled with compassion as well as understanding. She met his gaze once more and shrugged, annoyed with the tears that instantly sprang to her eyes. She blinked them away, wondering why she was telling this stranger so much about her life. It had to be this house—the memories it brought back.

'Losing parents is never easy. Mine both passed away almost a decade ago and still there are days when I miss them a lot.' He exhaled slowly, then shrugged one shoulder. 'I have questions. Ones only they would know how to answer.'

'Yes.' The word was heartfelt, as though somehow the loss of parents and the pain it caused had formed a bond between the two of them. 'Instead it leaves us floundering around, trying to figure things out on our own.'

He nodded, but didn't stop looking intently at her, and for some reason Stacey found it nigh impossible to look away. Pierce seemed to be a decent and caring man—a family man content to care for his home as well as his neighbours. She had no idea why he was only working as a locum at the local hospital, but presumably he had his reasons for not wanting to take on a more permanent position. Perhaps he wanted to spend some time working his way through his bucket list.

She paused as a different thought occurred to her. Perhaps he had a terminal illness, or was recovering from one. He didn't look gaunt. In fact he looked positively healthy. Stacey stopped her thoughts. This man was not her patient. He was not a puzzle for her to solve, to figure out what was wrong with him and then try to find a solution. But it was such an integrated part of her personality—especially being the oldest sibling in her family.

'By five minutes.'

She instantly heard her sister Cora's protest, which came every time Stacey stated that fact. Nevertheless, five minutes was five minutes, and Stacey took her responsibilities seriously.

'Anyway...' Pierce was first to break the silence as he

put the lid down on the green recycle bin. 'I didn't mean to take our conversation in such a maudlin direction. You asked about Mike. Chest is extremely tight, asthma meds are providing basic relief, but I think the chest pains might be worse than he's letting on. Edna said he'd been dizzy, but I didn't take my otoscope with me and when I suggested he see someone about it, to make sure it wasn't the start of something a bit more sinister, he growled at me and kicked me out of his house.'

'He always did have a good bark.' Stacey's smile was instant as she followed Pierce towards the house, quietly amazed at how comfortable she was around him. 'Edna asked me to pop over once I'd finished clinic.'

'That's why you're here? To give Mike a check-up?'

'Yes, but I can see Edna's car's not in the driveway, so I'll wait until she gets home.'

'And your question about neighbours was a test, eh?' He grinned, crossing his arms over his broad chest. 'I take it I passed?'

'Yes.'

'Excellent.' He jerked his thumb towards the house. 'Does this mean you feel safe enough to come and take a look around inside?'

Stacey nodded, excitement starting to build. She told herself it was because she was getting the chance to see inside the house, rather than because she was getting to spend a bit more time with the handsome Dr Pierce.

'Where are you working?' Pierce asked conversationally as they crossed the veranda and entered the house.

'I've recently bought my father's old GP practice.'

'The one up the road? Shortfield Family Medical Practice?'

'That's the one. Phillip Morcombe took over the practice from my father sixteen years ago, and when I realised it was up for sale—' Stacey stopped as she stood on the other side of the threshold, her gaze drinking in the living room of the house which held all her earliest memories.

'Oh!' She clutched her hands to her chest. 'That's where my sisters and I used to lie on our stomachs after school and watch half an hour of television.' She pointed to the middle of the room. 'And the bay window. There used to be a curtain that separated it off from the rest of the room and that used to be our secret corner, where we'd spend hours whispering our best secrets to each other. Or we'd curl up with a book and just read.' She smiled. 'Well, Cora and I read books. Molly could never sit still. Still can't.'

'How old are your sisters? You sound so close.'

'You don't know the half of it,' Stacey said with a grin. 'We're triplets. Non-identical,' she added, as a matter of routine. She waited, expecting the usual reaction of, *Wow. Triplets? I've never met triplets before,* or *Can you sense each other's emotions?* or *How far apart are the three of you? Who's the eldest?* but all Pierce did was smile widely.

'What a lot of fun you must have had.' His tone sounded almost wistful. 'So close, so connected.'

Stacey mulled over his words as he headed around to the kitchen and dining room. 'Are you an only child?'

'I was. For quite a while. I was fifteen when my sister was born. She was born very late in my parents' life, but they loved each and every moment they had with Nell.'

He walked into the kitchen and pointed to a framed photograph up on the wall—one of him and a lovely-looking young woman who was staring at him with open delight, as though he'd just handed her the moon.

'That was taken six months ago, at Nell's twenty-first birthday. I'd just given her the keys to this house. Independent living.' There was a thrill of pride in his tone as he looked at the picture of his sister.

Stacey processed his words. 'You've done all this work with the house for your *sister*?'

'It's been Nell's goal. She's been working towards it for so long and we're almost ready…in about another three months' time.'

'You're not married?' Why had that question sounded as though she was fishing for information? 'Er… I… You don't have to answer that. It's really none of my business.'

'Married? Me?' Pierce shook his head emphatically. 'No. *No.* No, no, no, no, no.'

'So that's a no?' she remarked drolly, wondering if his determined answer hinted at matrimonial issues. She tried not to frown, tried not to lump him into the same category as another specific male she knew who had also had deeply rooted issues with marriage and commitment.

'I'd do anything for Nell.' As he said the words he quickly checked his watch, then gasped. 'And that includes going to meet her at the bus stop. Come on, Stacey.' Pierce grabbed her hand and tugged her back through the house, across the veranda and into the garden. 'We're going to be late.'

'We?' She pulled her hand free. 'Er… I'll leave you to it.'

'But you have *got* to meet Nell. She'd love to meet someone who used to live here. She adores this house. She picked it out five years ago and told me that was the house she was going to live in when she was twenty-one. She's very stubborn and adamant, my sister.'

'Well, then, I'll go next door and see if Edna's home yet and——'

'There's no time for discussion now.'

Pierce grabbed her hand again and started tugging her

along with him as he quickened his pace, pointing in the distance to a bus that was drawing closer.

'That's her bus! We've got to make it to the bus stop in time. Usually she can cope if I'm not there to greet her, but her whole routine has been a little out of whack lately—what with her promotion at work and all the new things she's had to learn. Hence me meeting her bus is the one absolute she needs in her life right now.'

Pierce spouted this information quickly as they continued towards the bus stop. When he broke into a jog as the bus drew closer Stacey had no option but to go along with him. As they jogged she had to confess she was rather intrigued at the way Pierce spoke about his sister.

They arrived at the bus stop just as the young woman from the photograph was climbing down the back steps of the bus, stepping onto the pavement. She looked around, anxiety etched on her features, but the instant she saw Pierce running towards her, the anxiety cleared and a wide, beaming smile brightened her face.

'I got scared. I could not see you, Pierce. But now you are here.' Nell, who had shoulder-length blonde hair and blue eyes that matched her brother's, spoke every word perfectly, but with little inflection.

Pierce let go of Stacey's hand before enveloping his sister in a hug. 'Sorry, Nellie. I was gardening and forgot the time.'

He took Nell's bag from her and slipped his arm around her waist as Nell started off down the street, counting her steps. She didn't seem to notice Stacey at all, and as Pierce beckoned for her to follow them, Stacey's sharp medical mind began sifting through the information she knew.

Nell had been born to a more mature mother, and clearly needed a strict routine. She hadn't paid any attention to Stacey, even though Stacey had been holding hands with Pierce. The fact that Pierce hadn't tried to introduce Stacey, instead allowing his sister to continue counting the steps from the bus stop to the house, alerted her to the fact that while Nell might appear to be a beautiful young twenty-one-year-old on the outside, mentally her age was far younger.

It wasn't until they were standing on the front veranda of the house that Nell stopped counting and turned to smile at her brother. 'I got it right. The same number as yesterday.'

'That's great, Nellie.' He removed his arm from his sister's waist and turned to indicate Stacey. 'There's someone I want you to meet.' It was only then that Nell seemed to notice Stacey's presence. 'Nell, this is Stacey.'

Dutifully, Nell held out her hand to Stacey and shook it firmly. 'Hello, Stacey. I am very pleased to meet you.' She nodded and smiled, as though she was secretly proud of herself for getting the greeting correct.

'Good girl,' Pierce said softly. Nell let go of Stacey's hand, her smile increasing at her brother's praise. 'I know this is your house now, Nell, but when Stacey was a little girl she and her sisters used to live here.'

Nell looked from Stacey to Pierce and back again, as though slowly processing the words. 'Really?' Her eyes widened with delight. 'Did you sleep in the same room as me? The pink room?'

Stacey smiled and nodded. 'The room was definitely pink.'

'Why don't you show Stacey your room now?' Pierce encouraged as he opened the door, holding it for the women to precede him.

'Yes!' Nell entered the house and clutched her hands to her chest with the excitement of a child at Christmas.

'I *love* my room. Did you love it, too, when it was your room?'

'Yes. I really did.' Allowing Nell's excitement to affect her, Stacey followed the young woman down the hallway.

Nell was delighted to show Stacey her doll collection, as well as a cupboard full of puzzles. Jigsaw puzzles, wooden puzzles, metal ones too.

'You must be very good at puzzles, Nell.'

'Yes. I am. My brother says that I have an amazing puzzle brain.'

She grinned, and Stacey couldn't help but instantly warm to her.

'He is so funny.'

'Afternoon snacks are ready,' Pierce called, and Nell immediately turned and set off for the kitchen.

'I like afternoon snacks. Do *you* like afternoon snacks, Stacey?'

'I do, Nell.' Stacey smiled as she watched Nell politely thank her brother before sitting down at the kitchen bench to attend to her food. They all ate, Pierce having prepared fruit with cheese and a glass of juice for himself and Stacey as well.

'How was work, Nell?'

'It was good, Pierce.' Nell swallowed her mouthful.

'Nell works as a researcher for a computer company. She solves a lot of their internal programming issues.' Pierce offered the information for Stacey's benefit, but Nell nodded as though to confirm it.

'That sounds impressive,' Stacey added.

'It is.' Nell ate another mouthful.

'Did you do anything exciting today?'

Pierce continued with his questions and Stacey had the feeling it was all part of their routine.

'Yes. I solved the number puzzle Mr Jorgensen could

not do. He said I did it really fast.' Nell preened a little, feeling good about herself. 'I like puzzles.'

Once Nell had finished eating she stacked her plate and glass in the dishwasher before announcing that it was time to watch television. Off she went, leaving Stacey sitting at the table with Pierce. He watched his sister in the other room, a proud smile playing about his lips, and when he looked back at Stacey he saw she was watching him intently.

'Higher functioning autism,' he stated as he drank the last of his drink.

'She's doing very well for herself,' Stacey remarked, finishing her juice.

Pierce nodded as he collected their glasses and stacked them in the dishwasher. 'She is, and I have to say I'm very proud of her.'

'So I can see.' Stacey grinned. 'And thank you for the snack. I can't remember the last time I actually sat and had an after-work snack.'

'It's Nell's routine.'

'What happens if you're at the hospital when she gets home from work?'

'I try to be here most days, but if I'm not at the bus stop to meet her then Edna or Mike usually help out. And if that's not possible, and I know I'm going to be delayed, I'll ring Nell and let her know before she gets off the bus. But thankfully those days are few and far between.'

'If you need further support I'd be happy to add Nell to our practice nurse visitation list.'

He nodded. 'I was going to suggest something like that. I'm so glad you've bought the practice. We all thought it was going to close completely.'

'I know. My father's old partner retired last year, and since then there have been various locums running it.'

'A practice can't survive like that. It definitely needs someone at the helm.'

Stacey spread her arms wide. 'As you see.'

'You're running it by yourself?'

'Uh…with my sisters. Well, sort of. We all own the practice equally and Winifred the practice nurse, who has been there for years, is staying on—thank goodness.'

'Ah, yes. We've met Winifred several times. She's lovely.' Pierce leaned back in his chair and watched her for a moment. 'I take it both your sisters are doctors, too?'

'Yes. We went through medical school together, did all our GP training together.'

'And what do you mean by "sort of"? Your sisters are "sort of" running the practice with you? How does that work?'

Stacey frowned as she thought about Molly's new plans to study surgery. She was proud and delighted with her sister's accomplishments, but it did put her in a bit of a bind.

'Actually, my sister Molly has decided to study surgery.'

He raised his eyebrows at this. 'She's been accepted to a surgical training programme?'

'Yes.'

'Here?'

'Yes, at Newcastle General. A place came up at the last minute so she took it. Effective immediately.'

He nodded. 'Good for her.'

Pierce leaned one elbow on the table and rested his head on his hand, giving her his undivided attention. She shifted in the seat but forced herself to remain calm and collected as she placed her hands in her lap.

He continued just to sit there, watching her as though she were a complete mystery to him. When he raised a questioning eyebrow she spread her hands wide. 'What? Is there something on my nose? Do I have milk on my lip?'

Pierce smiled and shook his head. Good heavens! Did the man have *any* idea just how lethal that small, gorgeous smile of his could be? The way it caused the corners of his eyes to crinkle with delight? The way it made her feel as though he wasn't trying to judge her, just trying to understand her? For all intents and purposes this man was a stranger to her, and yet for some reason she felt so comfortable around him. It was an odd sensation, but with both Cora and Molly telling her to loosen up, to step outside her comfort zone, start living her life for *her* instead of everyone else, and with Pierce smiling at her so acceptingly, Stacey found herself telling him things she usually wouldn't tell anyone.

'Yes—yes, it *is* good for Molly. She's always wanted to do it. But it does leave me somewhat in the lurch. Cora, my other sister, is over in Tarparnii at the moment, working with Pacific Medical Aid.'

'An excellent organisation. I have…friends who do a lot of work with them.'

Stacey wondered at his hesitation. Were they his friends or weren't they? 'Are you interested in going to work there, too?'

He shrugged. 'Maybe. One day.'

'It's not on your bucket list?'

Pierce grinned. 'There are a lot of other things on my bucket list so I'll attend to them first.' He gestured to the house. 'And first on the list is to get this place completely shipshape for Nell and her soon-to-be housemates.'

'She has friends who are moving in, too?'

'Two other fine young ladies who she works with. Loris is in a wheelchair, which is why I need to finish getting all the ramps made, and Samantha has high-functioning Asperger's.'

'Sounds like it's important for me to get to know all of them.'

'Yes. Your medical practice will be the closest one for all of them. But where Nell is concerned, if she knows you on a more personal level then she's more likely to come to you when she needs help.'

'And we'll help in any way we can.' She smiled politely.

Pierce nodded with thanks, then looked at her thoughtfully. 'Hang on a minute. If Molly's studying surgery at the hospital, and Cora is overseas, then who *is* running the clinic with you?'

'Molly does a day here and there, and she's promised to find me a locum to cover for her.'

There was silence between them for a minute, with the clock on the mantel ticking loudly. Pierce continued to watch her intently, leaning his head on his hand. Stacey started to feel highly self-conscious as he just looked at her…stopped everything and *really* looked. What did he see?

'All right.' Pierce straightened up and slapped his hand onto the table, making her jump. 'I'll do it!'

'What? What will you do?' Stacey asked, startled by his abrupt behaviour.

'Call your sister. Tell her the search is over.'

'What search?' Stacey stared at him as though he'd grown an extra head.

'The locum search.' He stood and held out his hand to her. 'Dr Pierce Brolin, at your service.'

Stacey shook his hand, still a little dazed. 'I'm not sure I underst—'

'I'm coming to work for you. I'm your new locum.'

CHAPTER TWO

STACEY UNLOCKED THE front door of the family medical practice and headed to the light switch, illuminating the reception area and waiting room. It was early. Just after seven-thirty on a Monday morning. And although her first patient wasn't due to walk through the doors for another hour she'd been too nervous to sleep.

She sniffed. The air still smelled faintly of paint, and she quickly located the air filters she'd purchased last week and switched them on. If it wasn't for the rain outside she'd open the windows, but the September weather was giving them the runaround—one day sunny, the next pouring with rain.

Stacey walked through the practice, opening blinds and switching on the equipment that needed to be on. She refused to dwell on the second consulting room—the one which would be assigned to Pierce Brolin, whose first official day in the clinic would be starting in about an hour's time.

Had she done the right thing? It was true she needed a locum. It was true that Pierce was not only available but also extremely willing. His credentials were certainly impressive—especially his extensive experience in autism spectrum disorders—so she couldn't understand why he wasn't working in his chosen specialty.

'I'm more than happy to fill the gap while you wait for your sister Cora to return to Newcastle,' he'd told her when they'd met last week to sign the legal contracts.

It had been on the tip of her tongue to ask him *why* he was happy to help out here and there, but it really was none of her business. Perhaps he was content to get things settled for Nell without having the stress of a full-time workload hanging over his head. All that mattered was that Pierce was a qualified doctor who was willing to help her out.

She had to leave it at that, had to keep her emotional distance from him, because he was definitely an enigmatic man who was able to make her feel as though she were the most important person in the world. The way he smiled at her, the way he shook her hand, the way he gave her his undivided attention when he talked… All of those little things were things that Robert had never done.

She closed her eyes as an image of Robert's stern face came to mind. Her ex-fiancé, although professing to love and care about her, had never really shown it. She'd always rationalised it—Robert wasn't the demonstrative type—but now that she'd had quite a bit of time to reflect on her failed relationship she'd come to realise that he simply hadn't loved her as much as he'd said.

He'd never held her hand in public, never leaned over and whispered something intimate in her ear, never looked at her across a crowded room as though he wanted everyone to instantly disappear just so he could be alone with her.

When she'd been sitting at her consulting room desk, with Pierce on the other side, carefully reading the locum contract, Molly and Winifred both hovering around and chatting, Stacey had been far too aware of him. His broad shoulders, his thoughtful brow, his twinkling blue eyes when he'd lifted his head and looked at her, somehow making her feel as though he could see right into her soul…

And that had been the moment. That one true moment in time when nothing else seemed to matter. Her mouth had instantly gone dry, the other people in the room had disappeared from her view and it had been just the two of them, Pierce had stared into her eyes and she'd stared back into his. Neither of them had moved, and she could have sworn that the spinning of the earth had actually slowed down, capturing them both in a bubble of time. It had been an odd sensation, but for that one split second Stacey had felt…*accepted*. Without reservation, without condition.

She shook her head, clearing it of the image. 'And he'll be working here,' she murmured as she made herself walk into the consulting room he'd been assigned.

Even now she could picture him sitting behind the desk, looking up at her as she came in to speak to him about something, their eyes meeting and holding once more. Did she yearn for that sensation again because he'd made her feel accepted? Or did she fear the sensation because he'd so easily been able to penetrate the fortress she'd worked hard to put in place after Robert had broken her heart?

She glanced around the room, opening one or two of the cupboards to ensure they were properly stocked with everything he might need. She wanted today to go well, for Pierce to be happy working here.

After she'd left his home over two weeks ago Stacey hadn't been sure which way to turn. She'd known basically nothing about the man, and yet there he'd been, offering his services to help her out. Was he just being kind or was he a bit loopy?

All she could remember doing at the time was murmuring a polite reply to his declaration that he was going to work with her and then excusing herself. Her thoughts had been in such a jumble that she'd almost forgotten to check on Mike Edelstein—which had been the main reason for her being in that part of town. She'd walked out to her car to retrieve her medical bag, and been surprised to find Pierce waiting by the Edelsteins' front door by the time she reached it.

'We may as well review him together,' he'd stated, before knocking on the door.

Stacey had barely had time to collect her thoughts before Edna had opened the door and welcomed them both inside.

The other woman had hugged Stacey close. 'It's good to see you again, love,' Edna had said as she'd embraced Stacey. 'Although I wish it was in better circumstances. But at least now that you're here we might finally get Mike to see some sense, eh? He always had time for you, Stace.'

Mike had indeed been happy to see her, but when Stacey had insisted upon giving him a check-up he'd fussed about, telling her she was blowing the entire thing out of proportion.

He stabbed a finger at Pierce. 'If this young whippersnapper hadn't been hanging around the side fence the other day he never would have heard me coughing.' Mike glared at Edna. 'At least that's what he *said*. But chances are Edna dragged him inside because she was stressing over nothing.'

'Mike—' Stacey began, but Mike was in full swing, his words peppered by coughs.

'Came right over, he did. Sticking his nose in where it doesn't belong, telling me I had problems with my lungs.

Well, of course I do. I've had asthma for most of me life, and I know when it's bad and when it's good and right now it's fine. Just fine, I tell you.'

But the instant Mike finished protesting his body was racked with a coughing spasm.

Stacey instantly rubbed Mike's back, encouraging him quietly to relax and breathe slowly. Her soothing tone must have done something, because Mike's bluster seemed to disappear.

'There's one thing I want to remind you of,' she said as she placed her medical bag beside his comfortable lounge chair.

'Yeah? What's that?' he asked, lifting his chin and meeting her gaze, pure stubbornness reflected in his eyes.

'You may be stubborn, but I'm my father's daughter—which therefore means that my stubbornness trumps yours every time.'

Edna laughed. 'She's got you there, Mikey.' And then, as though everything was now right with her world, Edna declared that she'd go and put the kettle on.

With resigned reluctance, Mike agreed to the check-up.

'Pierce was right,' Stacey said as she packed away her stethoscope and closed her medical bag once her review was complete. 'Your asthma is very bad and your ears are red. Your throat's not the best, either. You'll need some antibiotics, and I want you up at the hospital first thing tomorrow for a chest X-ray to check you're not on the way to contracting pneumonia. Spring is notorious for ailments such as chest infections, and right now it's the last thing you need—what with the rabbit jumping season quickly approaching.'

'Oh, we don't compete any more,' Edna said in a loud whisper as she carried in a tray of tea and biscuits. 'Our ol' Vashta passed away a few years ago. What a champion that rabbit was.' Edna sighed and looked wistful for a moment, before shaking her head once more.

'But you still go to watch, don't you?' Stacey asked, 'I was telling the children about it just last night and all of them were eager to go. Lydia was even asking if we could get a rabbit ourselves. She adores them.'

'Really?' Light shone in Edna's eyes as she'd placed the tray on the table and stood next to Stacey.

'I was also hoping that if I was stuck at the clinic, or if Molly was in surgery, you two might be able to take the children to the rabbit jumping show for me?' Stacey's tone held a hint of pleading, and as she watched them closely, knowing Mike had always loved to help others, especially when it concerned his favourite animals, she saw a flicker of light come back into his old eyes.

'Lydia's interested, eh? How old is she now?'

'She's seven—and just as stubborn as me.'

'Hmm…' Mike stroked his chin with thumb and forefinger. 'Seven, you say? Seven's just about the right age to start.'

Edna reached out and held Stacey's hand as they both watched Mike closely. He contemplated this information seriously for a moment or two before nodding.

'OK, then. I'll go to the hospital and take the antibiotics and do whatever else it is you want me to do—but only because it's important that I'm there to instruct little Lydia right from the beginning. There are many responsibilities that go hand in hand with wanting to raise a champion jumper. This isn't a normal pet we're talking about. She has to be one hundred per cent committed to the entire process.'

'Excellent. I'll inform Lydia when I get home tonight. She'll be ecstatic. But…' Stacey levelled Mike with her best no-nonsense look '…you must do everything I, or

Pierce, or any other doctor who treats you prescribes. Deal?' She held out her hand, never once breaking eye contact with Mike.

Mike sat up a little straighter in his chair and held her gaze before he reached out and shook hands with Stacey. 'Deal.'

Edna squealed with delight and clapped her hands. 'Mike agreeing to treatment *and* the chance to pass on our love of rabbit jumping to the next generation!' She kissed Mike's cheek and then gave Stacey a big hug.

Stacey smiled before packing up her equipment into the medical bag and handing the prescription for antibiotics to Edna.

'Well played,' Pierce whispered close by.

Stacey hadn't realised he was standing so close. She looked at him over her shoulder.

'Gotta have a few tricks up your sleeve when it comes to persuading Mike to do something.'

'So I see.'

He accepted the cup of tea Edna offered him, as did Stacey. Mike started to breathe more easily, thanks to the medication Stacey had given him. He relaxed back in his chair, a smile on his face, as he regaled them with anecdotes about his beloved sport of rabbit jumping and exactly what he'd need to teach Lydia.

By the time they left Mike was settled and Edna was happy.

'It's good to see that you have an excellent bedside manner,' Pierce said as he walked her across the road to her car.

Stacey unlocked it and stowed her medical bag in the back seat. 'Thank you.'

'I'm going to enjoy working alongside you, Dr Stacey.' And then he'd taken her hand in his, gently shaking it, and the action had been more slow and intentional than in a normal brisk business handshake.

'*Very* much.'

Stacey closed her eyes and rubbed her hands together, the memory of that hand-shake, the memory of his deep, sensual tone, still managing to make her tremble. What was it about him that seemed to tilt her world off its axis? When she thought about Pierce she had the oddest sensation of excitement, of anticipatory delight. But she'd had those sensations once before, with Robert, and look how *that* had turned out.

Opening her eyes, she turned away from Pierce's consulting room, forcing herself to stop thinking about the way it had felt to have her hand wrapped securely in his, or the way his eyes had seemed to be able see right into the depths of her soul. He was just another doctor who was helping her out. Nothing more. The slight buzz of awareness she felt whenever she was around him was simply because she was grateful.

There was no need for her to try and figure him out, to understand why he was content to work in part-time jobs, helping out here and there in a medical capacity. The fact of the matter was that his help was needed and she'd accepted it for the next three months until Cora's return. Where or what Pierce Brolin did after that was nothing to do with her.

She headed to the kitchen and turned on the coffee machine, checking there was sufficient milk in the fridge to get them through the rest of the day. 'Business,' she told herself sternly. 'It's all just business.'

'Knock, knock.'

Stacey gasped at the sound of the deep male voice, spinning around so fast she bumped her hip against the fridge door.

'Pierce!' She rubbed at her hip.

'Are you OK? Sorry. Didn't mean to startle you. I thought you would have heard the bell as I opened the front door.' He twirled a small key chain around his finger before putting the keys into his trouser pocket.

'I was…thinking.' *About you*, she added silently, and quickly turned away, busying herself with making coffee.

'So I heard. It's all just business, right?'

Stacey closed her eyes for a second, unable to believe he'd heard her talking to herself but glad that at this moment he couldn't see her face. 'Something like that.' She needed to change the subject. 'Can I get you a drink?' She turned to face him. 'Tea? Coffee?'

'No, I'm fine.' He pulled out a chair and sat down at the small kitchen table. 'Thought I'd get in early and go over my patient notes for the day.'

'Fair enough.'

'How about you? Couldn't sleep?'

She frowned for a moment, knowing she could never tell him that she'd awoken around five-thirty that morning from a dream in which he'd been caressing her cheek, his gaze intent on hers, seeing into her soul once more and making her feel more alive than she'd ever felt before.

'Er…busy thoughts.' Well, that was sort of true.

'Aha. Anything to do with rabbit jumping?'

When she angled her head to the side in slight confusion, he elaborated.

'I was talking to Mike last night—who, I must say, is doing much better. Anyway, he mentioned that you've recently bought two potential champion rabbits.'

Stacey forced herself to relax and nodded. The rabbits. A very safe topic. 'Yes. Lydia and George insisted on having one rabbit each.'

'How old is George?'

'Nine. He said if Lydia was old enough to get a rabbit then he was doubly old enough because he was two years older.'

Pierce watched as she moved around the kitchen, making herself a cup of coffee. How was it she could perform the simplest of tasks with such grace? All her movements were fluid and seamless, and he was entranced. In fact ever since he'd met Stacey Wilton he'd been intrigued. Bit by bit he was discovering more about her, and each new piece of the puzzle was unique as well as confusing.

George? Who was George? He'd presumed that the seven-year-old Lydia she'd mentioned was her daughter. Did Stacey also have a nine-year-old son? If so, where was the father of these children? She didn't wear a wedding ring, and there had been no mention of a husband. He tried to remember whether Mike or Edna had said anything, but Mike had been far more interested in discussing the rabbits rather than the children.

'Sounds fair.' He kept his tone at a neutral level whilst his mind tried to compute any new information he might uncover. 'I know Nell's very interested, but I don't think we'll be buying a rabbit any time soon.'

'She's more than welcome to help Lydia and George if she likes. We only live two blocks away from you, so our houses are within easy walking distance.'

'Thank you, Stacey.' He seemed genuinely surprised by the offer. 'That's nice of you.'

She pulled out a chair and sat at the opposite end of the table to him. 'Having Nell come round might actually prove a worthwhile diversion for Jasmine.'

'Jasmine?'

'She's just turned fourteen, so at the moment she's nothing but hormones.' Stacey slumped forward a little and sighed.

A fourteen-year-old as well! Stacey must have been a young mother. Either that or she was older than he'd initially thought. He managed to hide his surprise. 'Ah. I remember that phase with Nell—which, believe me, wasn't easy. Trying to explain hormones and why she would feel such extremes in her emotions was difficult, especially as our parents had passed away only a few years before. But we figured it all out in the end.'

Stacey sipped her drink. 'That helps put things with Jasmine into perspective. The teenage years are the worst, in my opinion. But of course Jasmine doesn't think I understand. She's still mad at me for dragging her away from all her friends in Perth, three-quarters of the way through the school year, to the other side of the country.'

'I guess it's not easy for you—especially without your parents around.'

'No.' She sat up a little straighter and stared down into her coffee cup. 'Cora keeps telling me that Jasmine will settle down, and Molly's really good with her, but she blames me for everything at the moment, whether it's my fault or not.'

'It's just a phase, Stacey. She'll grow out of it.'

'Let's hope she does that before I lose complete and utter patience with her.'

Pierce chuckled. 'Where are the kids now?'

Stacey checked the clock on the wall. 'Probably finishing off their breakfast and getting ready for school.'

'How do they get to school?' Did she have a nanny?

'Molly's on a late shift. She and I usually co-ordinate if we can, but now that Jasmine's a little older she's responsible for getting George and Lydia to school each morning.'

'Jasmine won't be tempted to cut class if there's no one to check up on her?'

'Oh, gosh. I hadn't even thought of that.' She stared at him for a moment, holding his gaze, the despair slowly disappearing from her face.

Did the woman have any idea just how beautiful she was? Especially when she looked at him like that, all vulnerable and soft. Right at this moment in time he didn't really care how many children she had, or what sort of shenanigans she might be facing at home. All he was aware of was how lovely Stacey Wilton was. She was the reason why he'd been unable to sleep that morning, with his thoughts turning to what it might be like to work alongside her, to see her on a regular basis, and whether or not something else might be brewing between them.

Then she blinked, and with an abruptness that startled him she stood and finished her coffee before taking the cup to the sink and washing it.

'At any rate, I'd best go and review my own set of patients before the busy day begins,' she mumbled.

And within another moment, Pierce found himself alone in the small kitchen.

'Uh…' She poked her head around the door. 'Just let me know if you need help with anything. And er…welcome to Shortfield Family Medical Practice.' She didn't quite meet his gaze as she spoke, and as soon as she'd finished her little spiel she headed off once more.

Pierce exhaled slowly and pushed both hands through his hair. Stacey Wilton was a whirlwind of a woman— buying her own medical practice, moving her family across country, juggling a full-time job and three children. She was dynamic, thoughtful…and incredibly sexy.

He hadn't wanted to think of her in such a way, especially as they would be working together for the next few months, but he'd come to accept it as fact. The way she held herself, the way she walked with a slight swish of her hips, the way she occasionally tucked her shoulder-length brown hair behind her ear… Her eyes were the blue of the sky on a cloudless day, and her lips were… Well, whenever he thought about the shape of her mouth his gut would tighten, because the urge to actually see what those lips tasted like was a thought he hadn't been able to dismiss at all.

It wasn't as if he lusted after every new woman he met—in fact quite the opposite. After Catherine had ended their engagement six years ago he'd tried to date, but as soon as they discovered he was his autistic sister's sole guardian most women would usually choose not to see him again. Catherine, of course, had been different. She'd been instantly loving and accepting of Nell. But even that had had its flaws.

He stood up quickly, almost knocking over his chair, determined to control his thoughts. There was no point in reflecting on the past—not now, when he was at the beginning of the next junction of his life. Just three more months. By then Nell would be completely settled at the house, along with her two housemates, and he could finally accept his dream job—the job he'd been offered several times already but had been forced to decline. Until Nell was ready there was no chance he'd ever be able to leave.

As things stood, he'd been putting his plans into place for a long time, ensuring Nell understood as much as possible about what would be happening, teaching her how to talk on the internet chat channel he'd set up and other things like that. He wasn't going to leave his sister in the lurch—she was as much a part of him as his arm or his leg—but the chance to finally complete his research, to work with other staff who shared his passion for understanding as much as possible about autism spectrum disorders, would be brilliant.

He'd already completed a lot of research, written and published several scientific papers on the positive and negative effects of independent living in the autistic adult, and he knew he'd figured out how to provide the right amount of independence and support for Nell—support which could be given via computer or phone. He was so close to achieving his goal, to finally being able to accept the position he'd been coveting for years. The last thing he needed was to form some sort of romantic attachment to a woman who was clearly devoted to her own family.

Stacey was lovely. There was no denying that. But he still had no idea whether or not she was married. And so Stacey Wilton, for several reasons, was off-limits—even to his thoughts.

CHAPTER THREE

OVER THE NEXT week Stacey couldn't believe how easy she found life working alongside Pierce Brolin. It really was as though he'd been sent from heaven just when she needed him most. He was even still working two shifts per week at the hospital, determined to honour his commitments.

'Nell was asking to see you again,' Pierce mentioned on Thursday afternoon, after they'd finished a hectic clinic.

Stacey had ventured into his consulting room to see how he'd fared during the busy day, and when he offered her a chair she gratefully accepted.

'Oh, that's nice. How is she?' Stacey sat down, sighing with relief at finally being off her feet.

'More interested in meeting your rabbits than in seeing you, if I own the truth.' He grinned as he spoke and Stacey laughed, the lilting sound washing over him. He swallowed and ignored the effect. They were colleagues and friends. Nothing more. 'How about dinner this Saturday night?' Friends could have dinner.

Stacey thought for a moment. 'Are you sure you're prepared for all of us to come?'

'The whole gaggle,' he confirmed. 'I'd like to meet the

children and the rabbits, and if your sister's free ask her to come along, too. The more the merrier.'

Stacey frowned for a moment. The children *and* her sister? Didn't he realise that they were one and the same? Well, apart from poor George, who was clearly not a sister.

'Nell won't be upset with having too many people in the house? We're a pretty rowdy bunch.'

'She's usually pretty good with people if she's been properly prepared. Plus it's good for her to stretch her boundaries. It's one of the reasons why she's desperate to live independently, and the more people she knows and can rely on the better it's going to be for her.'

'True. I've read your papers on the subject. Very interesting.' She tried not to colour as she spoke, not wanting to confess that she'd actually looked him up on the internet and discovered a link to his scientific papers. In fact he appeared quite the expert on the subject of adults with autism and their integration into society.

'Thanks.' He nodded once, acknowledging her praise, but quickly continued. 'So you'll all come?'

Stacey thought over his invitation. 'Well, I'll tentatively accept on behalf of us all, but if I can let you know definite numbers tomorrow that would be great.'

'Glad to see you don't rule the roost with an iron will.'

'No. We're very much a democracy—except when it comes to bedtime.' She shook her head and chuckled. 'George always has to push the limits.'

'That's what nine-year-old boys do, I'm afraid.' Pierce joined in with her laughter, his curiosity about Stacey and these children still highly piqued.

During the week he'd discovered that Stacey wasn't married, or involved with anyone, because he'd overheard one of their more senior patients asking her when she was going to settle down and get married.

Stacey's answer had been polite. 'Not just yet, Mrs Donahue.'

Even though he'd tried to ignore his naturally inquisitive nature, he hadn't been able to stop himself from trying to figure her out. While he respected her privacy, there was something about Stacey—something about the way she seemed to be so tightly wound, taking life very seriously. He knew from talking to Mike and Edna that Stacey and her two sisters had recently turned thirty-one. That was hardly old, and yet she seemed so much older in her mannerisms and in the way her life seemed to be so closely structured.

Perhaps that was the reason he was interested in getting to know her a bit more. Perhaps he'd unconsciously decided to help her to find life a bit more vibrant, a bit more happy during his time here. For the moment, though, he realised the conversation they'd been having had come to an end, and it would look silly if he just continued to sit in the chair opposite her and stare, as he was doing right now.

'OK, then. Saturday night around six o'clock—family approval and patients willing?'

He stood from the chair and came around the desk, aware that Stacey was watching his every move. He leaned on the desk and crossed his legs at the ankle, trying to ignore the way her light visual caress made him want to preen.

'Uh…sure.' She looked down at her hands for a moment, clearing her throat. 'What would you like me to bring? Drinks? Dessert?'

'Don't bring a thing.'

'But I have to.'

Her words were serious, absolute, and it took a moment for realisation to dawn on him. She needed to bring something, to feel as though she was contributing. Those were the rules of polite society and Stacey Wilton adhered to them. Pierce was probably more slap-dash, more than willing to take care of all the preparations and give Stacey the night off, as it were, but he could see that being told to do nothing was stressing her more than being asked to contribute. It reminded him of his mother—always busy, always willing to help, always putting others before herself—and for a moment a wave of nostalgia swept over him.

'In that case, how about dessert?'

She visibly relaxed, and Pierce was pleased to see the smile return to her face.

'Excellent. Dessert it is.'

'I'm looking forward to it.'

'You may regret saying that,' she said, chuckling and held up her hands. 'George likes making desserts, and his favourite colour is blue. Needless to say we've been having a lot of blue-coloured desserts of late, so don't say I didn't warn you.'

Pierce laughed at her words and nodded. He was about to reply when the bell which was over the front door to the clinic tinkled, alerting them to the fact that someone had just walked into the waiting room.

She checked her watch. 'A bit late.'

When Stacey started to rise from her chair he immediately held up a hand to stop her. 'Don't stress. I'll deal with it. You rest.'

As he headed off before she could protest Stacey watched his purposeful, long stride. So bold, as though he knew exactly where he was going in life and how he was going to get there. If that really was the case, she envied him.

Although as far as she was concerned she *did* know exactly where her life was headed—especially as Lydia was only seven years old. Stacey's life wasn't her own, and there was nothing she could do about it. Cora had her research into island diseases and her work in the Pacific island nation of Tarparnii to contend with, Molly was following her dream of becoming a general surgeon, and Stacey—dependable, sensible Stacey—was stuck at home raising her half-siblings.

She knew she shouldn't complain, and most days she was able to handle these negative emotions, but today, being asked out to dinner by a handsome man, and for one moment pretending that he was asking her and only her, had reminded her of what life had been like before her parents' death. That was the way things had been a few years ago when she'd met Robert, when he'd taken her to the most lavish restaurant in Perth, gone down on bended knee and proposed to her in front of an entire restaurant full of guests.

'I love you', he'd professed. 'Be my wife?'

Of course she'd said yes. She'd loved him. But the instant her father and stepmother had been so cruelly taken from them Stacey's life had all but disappeared, with everyone simply expecting her to take over. Unfortunately Robert hadn't anticipated Stacey and her sisters becoming the children's legal guardians. He hadn't been able to understand why the younger children hadn't gone to live with Cora or Molly, and when Stacey had informed him that they would all be staying together—that the younger children needed all of their older sisters, that they all wanted to grieve together—he'd been unable to comprehend it.

Robert had therefore made his own decision and decided to call off their wedding. Unfortunately, he'd forgotten to tell her he'd changed his mind until she'd turned up at the church, dressed in white, sad because her father wasn't there to give her away. The groomsman had briskly apologised to her and then handed her an envelope which Robert had given him only twenty minutes earlier. In the envelope had been a short and concise note in Robert's bold handwriting, informing her that he'd changed his mind. There had been no apology, no other explanation.

Stacey shook her head, clearing her thoughts and swallowing over the lump in her throat. She blinked back the few tears that were starting to sting her eyes and forced herself to take five soothing breaths. Of course, as she'd belatedly realised, there'd been far too many things wrong with their relationship—such as the way Robert had always made her second-guess herself, or made her feel guilty for ruining their scheduled dates because her clinic had run late.

During this last year and a half she'd scooped up what had been left of her dignity, finished off her contract with Perth General Hospital as an A & E consultant and decided that a more sedate pace of life was in order. Seeing her father's old Newcastle GP practice up for sale had been the godsend she'd been waiting for. It had been her dream job when she'd been an innocent fourteen-year-old, wanting to follow in her father's footsteps. With so many things going wrong she'd been determined to make *this* dream become a reality.

It was only because Cora and Molly had supported her, as they'd always done, that the dream had even been realised. It hadn't been easy, uprooting the children and moving so late in the year, but everyone had coped well except for Jasmine. She frowned as she imagined what

Jasmine's retort might be when Stacey told them all that they'd been invited over to Pierce's house for dinner. But it was their first official invitation since moving here, and it would be good for all of them.

Stacey had a hunch that Jasmine would be delighted to meet Nell—especially as the school Jaz had attended in Perth supported integration of children with disabilities. But when she finally arrived home that night, and sat down at the dinner table to enjoy the delicious meal of spaghetti bolognaise and salad which Molly had prepared, Jasmine's reaction was exactly as predicted the instant Stacey told them all about the invitation.

'I don't want to go!' Jasmine shouted.

'Well, *I* want to go,' Molly countered, giving Stacey a wide, beaming smile and waggling her eyebrows up and down as a means of indicating that she thought Pierce was cute.

Stacey ignored her antics.

'How sweet of Pierce to invite us all. Sorry, Jaz.' Molly put her arm around her half-sister's shoulders and pressed a quick kiss to her cheek—a move Jaz wouldn't tolerate from Stacey. 'Looks as though you'll just have to stick it out and come too.'

'I'm old enough to stay home by myself,' she retorted hotly, slamming her knife and fork onto her plate. 'I'm not a baby any more.' As she said the words she glared at Lydia, who was innocently enjoying her dinner and not paying one bit of attention to her sister's tantrum.

'No one's saying you are,' Stacey returned, but no sooner were the words out of her mouth than Jasmine pushed her chair back from the table and ran off to her room. Stacey closed her eyes and sighed. 'If Jasmine really wants to be treated in a more adult fashion then she's going to have to accept the responsibilities of being a part of this family—and that means attending events and accepting dinner invitations rather than having tantrums.'

Molly nodded. 'I'll speak to her when I'm finished eating.'

'Thanks, Mol.'

They both knew Molly would get much further than Stacey. It was basic psychology. Jasmine needed someone to blame for all the pain she was feeling and Stacey had been chosen as the winner. Most of the time she was fine with that. She understood Jasmine far more than the young girl realised, and knew that time really would heal the wound of losing her parents. But sometimes being on the end of her sister's cutting words was difficult to cope with.

'So we're all going, then?' It was George who asked the question, looking expectantly at his big sister.

'We are, George,' she confirmed, and the little boy grinned. 'We also need to make a dessert, so would you be able to hel—?'

'I'll help. I'll help,' he volunteered quickly, and Stacey blew him a kiss of thanks.

'What about Flopsy and Andrew?' Lydia asked.

'Yes, the rabbits can come, too.' Both Lydia and George cheered at this news, the two of them having taken to their new pets with the utmost joy. 'And, speaking of which, don't forget to feed them before you head off to brush your teeth.'

'Yes Stacey,' George and Lydia said in unison.

'Will we meet his sister?' George continued.

'Pierce's sister? Yes. Her name is Nell.'

'Nell.' George tried the name out. 'I like meeting new people.'

'Me, too,' Lydia agreed, slurping spaghetti into her mouth.

'Me three,' said Molly, following suit and slurping her own spaghetti—but not before giving Stacey a little wink. It was code for *Everything will work out fine. Stop stressing, sis.*

Stacey relaxed a bit and was pleased when, the following day, she was able to formally accept Pierce's invitation.

'Excellent,' he said. 'Nell's super-excited. She wanted to know why you all weren't coming over tonight, as she doesn't want to wait until tomorrow.'

Stacey chuckled as she made them both a cup of coffee. 'She wants to see the rabbits, doesn't she?' she stated. 'Flopsy and Andrew will be coming, too, so please reassure Nell.'

'Andrew?' Pierce raised an eyebrow.

Stacey shrugged. 'Lydia named him. She said he looked like an Andrew.' She chuckled and finished stirring their coffees.

'Lydia sounds like quite a character.'

'Oh, she is. Determined to be an actress or an astronaut. At the moment she can't decide, but her determined spirit never wavers.'

Pierce laughed as he gratefully accepted the coffee. 'I can't wait to meet her and the rest of your posse.' It was true. He had a sense that meeting the rest of the people who mattered most to Stacey would help him piece together more of the puzzle surrounding her.

'Posse?' She joined in his laughter, amazed at how light and free she felt, even though they had another hectic clinic scheduled. To have these few moments with Pierce was like a recharge for her internal battery. 'I just hope the noise we naturally generate doesn't scare Nell.'

'Thank you for being concerned about my sister's well-being,' he remarked after taking a sip of his coffee. 'I do appreciate it.'

This thoughtfulness of hers was yet another facet of Stacey's personality, and one he'd been aware of from their first meeting. She gave and she gave and she kept on giving to others, and it made him wonder just who in her life gave back to her. No doubt she was close to her sisters, but it sounded as though Molly was now super-busy and Cora was still overseas, so who did Stacey rely on for support? His natural protective instincts were increasing where Stacey was concerned and he was finding it difficult to stop thinking up ways he could help her.

They both stood at the kitchen bench, sipping their coffees, the silence quite companionable, so when the bell over the front reception door tinkled Stacey jumped, startled out of her reverie.

'Let's get Friday underway,' she remarked, quickly drinking the rest of her coffee and trying not to burn her tongue in the process.

'I'm really excited about tomorrow night,' Pierce said as they headed towards their consulting rooms. 'In fact, why don't you come over around four o'clock and Nell can show the children her puzzles. She's become quite good at sharing.' He straightened his shoulders, brotherly pride evident in his stature.

'That's great. Has it been difficult to get her to the point where she is happy to share her things?'

He shrugged one shoulder. 'It's been more of an on-going thing all her life. Our mother was determined that Nell's autism would never be used as an excuse for bad manners, so Nell was taught from a young age the importance of being polite—and that included sharing. Like anyone, she has good days and bad days. But for the most part she no longer has a tantrum if people put a puzzle piece back in the wrong spot.'

'What does she do now if they do?'

'She waits until the person has finished playing with the puzzle and then she fixes it up before packing it away.'

'Good strategy.'

'It works. So—four o'clock sound good?'

She nodded. 'That gives us plenty of time to get crazy Saturday morning done and dusted and to organise the rabbits.'

'Crazy Saturday morning?'

'George goes to soccer, Lydia has ballet at eight o'clock and then gymnastics at ten, and Jasmine has a guitar lesson.'

'Guitar?'

'Electric guitar.'

'Oh, that sounds…fun—and noisy.'

Stacey grinned. 'Actually, she's pretty good.'

'She can bring her guitar if she likes. Give us an after-dinner concert, perhaps?' At Stacey's grimace he chuckled. 'Or not.' He stopped outside his consulting room door and placed a hand on her shoulder. 'Listen, if I don't get a chance to speak to you for the rest of the day, given just how hectic our clinics are, I'll see you tomorrow at four.'

Stacey was having a difficult time focusing on his words as the simple touch of his hand on her shoulder was enough not only to cause a deep warmth to flood throughout her entire body but for her mind to comprehend little of what he was actually saying. It had been so long since a man had been nice and kind and supportive, and it was…exciting.

Usually she just battled on with her day, her week, her life, sorting things out to the best of her ability, trying to make everyone around her happy. But at the moment it felt good to actually have Pierce standing by her side, offering his support. She had the sense that he was someone she could talk to and confide in. He also had an understanding of what it was like to raise a sibling— in her case more than one. Pierce had had to raise Nell after their parents had passed away, which couldn't have been at all easy.

Long after Pierce had dropped his hand from her shoulder the memory of his warm touch and the way his blue eyes had twinkled with calm reassurance were enough to get her through the rest of the day. However, by four o'clock the following afternoon Stacey's nerves were taut with stress once more.

Thankfully Molly had driven the short distance from their house to Nell's house, with the two rabbits safe in the cage on the back seat of the mini-van, placed between George and Lydia. Jasmine sat in the far corner, listening to her music on headphones and generally sulking.

'Is this where you used to live when you were little girls?' George asked as they climbed from the car.

'Yes,' Molly answered, handing Stacey the car keys as Stacey waited politely for Jasmine to precede her. The surly girl was clearly resenting being forced to come.

'You never know what's going to happen, Jaz,' Stacey said softly as Molly and the two children made their way up the path towards the front door, carefully carrying the rabbit cage. 'You might actually enjoy yourself. They really are very nice people. Especially Nell.'

As she spoke the words she sincerely hoped that Jasmine wouldn't kick up a fuss, because despite Pierce's reassurances she didn't want to test Nell's ability to cope with chaos.

With sullen steps and her arms crossed over her chest, Jasmine walked ahead of Stacey towards the front door.

Stacey only remembered to lock the car at the last minute. She was a little disconcerted about their descending *en masse*, about her family creating too much noise, about seeing Pierce in a more social capacity. *No.* She wouldn't dwell on the latter. They lived and worked in a fairly close-knit community, and as doctors at the family medical practice it was only right that they become friends.

Nell stood at the front door with Pierce, formally welcoming everyone, even though Stacey could see that she was more interested in the rabbits.

'Please, come in to my home,' Nell invited warmly.

'Wow!' George and Lydia remarked as they stared at the ornate ceiling before doing a slow perusal of the room.

When Lydia spied the puzzles she relinquished her hold on the rabbit cage and raced over to where Nell had set them up on the floor. 'I love puzzles,' she declared, before tipping one over and starting to figure out how all the little wooden pieces went back in.

George continued his visual observation while Stacey introduced Jasmine to Pierce and Nell. The teenager managed the smallest glimpse of a smile when she shook hands with Nell.

'Right on time,' Pierce stated, grinning widely at Stacey.

She smiled back, feeling highly self-conscious and trying desperately to ignore the butterflies that had just been let loose in her stomach simply because she was in close proximity to him.

'Are you going to marry Stacey?' George asked, breaking the silence.

'What?' Stacey and Pierce said in unison.

CHAPTER FOUR

'GEORGE!' STACEY WAS gobsmacked. She looked at Pierce in shock, then back to her brother. 'What on earth made you say that?'

George stared at her with his big eyes—eyes that were so like their father's. 'Well...the last time we went to have dinner at a man's house was when you told us you was going to marry him.'

George's tone was a little indignant, and the puzzled frown on his face indicated that he wasn't sure what he'd done wrong.

'But then,' Lydia chimed in from the lounge room, where she was busy finishing off the puzzle, 'he decided *not* to marry you and you had to tell everyone in the church that he wasn't coming.'

'He didn't *want* you,' Jasmine added, and her words were spoken in a tone which was designed to hurt.

'Jasmine! That's cruel.' Molly's chastisement of the girl was instant. 'Apologise to Stacey.'

'What?' Jasmine spread both her hands wide. 'Why do *I* have to apologise and Lydia and George don't?'

'Because you know better,' Molly interjected.

Stacey watched the conversation going on around her—her siblings arguing, the rabbits getting agitated in their cage, Pierce looking back and forth between them all as if he was at a tennis match—and all she could focus on was her increased heart-rate hammering wildly against her ribs. She saw Jasmine's mouth move, the framing of an apology on her lips, but the sound of the words didn't register, only the thrumming of the blood reverberating in her ears.

What must Pierce think of them all! No sooner had they stepped over the threshold than a family squabble had erupted. If this was Jasmine's way of making them all wish they'd left her behind at home, then it was starting to work. Emotional punishment, especially from her siblings, was the one thing Stacey wasn't good at dealing with.

'Stacey? Stace?'

She was vaguely aware of Molly calling her name, but mortification at the situation was getting the better of her and before she knew what was happening Stacey had whirled around on her heel and exited the house. She walked quickly down the street, moving as though on automatic. For a moment she thought no one was following her, and was extremely grateful, but a second or two later she heard a deep male voice calling her name.

Stacey didn't stop, didn't look back, and even when Pierce fell into step beside her she didn't speak a word. Thankfully he didn't try and stop her, didn't ask her to slow down, didn't offer placating words. Instead he seemed content just to walk beside her, matching her fast pace with ease. When she turned down a small lane which led to the park, he simply continued on alongside her.

She made a beeline for the swings—her favourite. The equipment at the park had been upgraded since she'd been here last, but apart from that everything was exactly the same. The familiar childhood setting calmed her somewhat, and when she finally sat down on the swing, instantly pushing herself up, she started to feel the consuming tension abate.

Pierce sat beside her on the other swing, and after watching her for a moment he followed suit and started swinging back and forth, not bothering to speak or initiate conversation. After about five minutes of swinging to and fro in silence Stacey started to slow down, her breathing more natural, her head cleared of its fog. Pierce slowed down as well and soon both of them were just sitting on the swings, rocking slowly back and forth.

'Sorry,' she ventured.

'No apology necessary.'

'I hope Nell's all right and that our silly sibling squabbling didn't upset her.'

Pierce nodded. 'Nell will be fine. She was absorbed with the rabbits, eager to get them out of their cage.'

'Good.'

'Wait a second.' Pierce held up one finger. 'Did you say *siblings*? Squabbling *siblings*? George and Lydia and Jasmine are your *siblings*?'

'Yes.' She looked at him with slight confusion, then her eyes widened slightly. 'I thought you knew that.'

'Nope. I thought they were your children—or at least that some of them were.'

She shook her head. 'Nope. We were seventeen when Jasmine was born, so I *could* have been old enough to be her mother. But my father married our nanny, Letisha, when Cora, Molly and I were thirteen.' Stacey looked down at the ground. 'My mother walked out, abandoned us, when we were almost five.'

'How terrible for all of you.'

Stacey shrugged. 'Letisha's the only real mother we can remember. She looked after us for so long, and then when Dad was finally divorced he could admit he had feelings for Tish.' Stacey smiled sadly. 'They died together in a car crash. I don't think my father could have survived being left alone again.' She kicked the ground with her foot and dragged in a breath. 'Anyway, by the time the three of us had finished medical school we had three new siblings: Jasmine, George and Lydia.'

'And now, with your father and your stepmother gone, you're raising your siblings.'

'Yes. Although the three of us share legal guardianship of the younger three on paper, I seem to have become the designated parent in practice. Though in fairness Molly and Cora are very helpful.'

'But you're the disciplinarian?' He nodded, understanding what she was saying. 'It's not easy to discipline a sibling.'

'No. It's not.' She sighed and shook her head. 'I know psychologically that Jasmine is just going through a phase, that she needs to take her grief out on someone and that someone is me—especially as I've just uprooted her from her school friends and brought her to the other side of the country. I know how she feels because that's exactly what my father did to me when I was fourteen. He took us from Newcastle to Perth.'

'But coming back home was the right decision?'

'I know it is. And I know Jasmine will forgive me one day, just as I forgave my dad. But I wish—' She stopped and gritted her teeth, trying to control the tears she could feel pricking behind her eyes.

'You wish what?' His words were soft and encouraging.

'I wish she *liked* me.' She spoke softly. 'Just a little bit. Just every now and then.' Stacey sniffed, still working hard to gain some sort of control over her emotions.

'At least she gets along with Molly, and Cora is splendid with her.'

'Except Cora's not here and Molly's embarking on a new career path, leaving *you* to carry the burden of a grieving, angry young girl.' Pierce nodded, completely understanding the situation. 'It's not easy when you're thrust into the parental role when all you'd rather do is be their sibling, comfort them and cry with them and not be expected to have all the answers.'

'Exactly.' She dragged in another calming breath. 'I just hope Lydia and George don't develop over-active hormones when *they* enter their teenage years. It's not an easy time for Jasmine. I understand that.'

'But she has to realise that this isn't an easy time for you either. How long is it since your parents passed away?'

'Eighteen months.'

'Well, that's not going to be easy for any of you—regardless of how old you are. Plus, it sounds as though you've had more going on than just the loss of your parents…at least from what George said.'

'Being jilted at the altar, you mean?' There was no point in beating about the bush, especially now, thanks to her siblings and the way they'd blurted out her past hurts.

He stared at her for a second. 'Oh, Stacey. What an idiot.'

'You weren't to know.'

Pierce reached over and took her hand in his. It seemed like the most natural thing in the world so she let him. Warmth spread up her arm and somehow filled her entire being, right down to the tips of her toes, and she just let it. Right at this moment she was tired of always being in control, of bottling up her own emotions and private thoughts.

'No, not me. *Him*. What an idiot he was to let you go.'

Stacey looked at her small hand sitting inside his big one. 'How could you possibly know that?' Her tone was soft, her words tinged with confusion. 'You barely know me.'

'I met you three weeks ago, Stacey, and although I don't profess to know *everything* about you the essentials of your personality are quite clear.'

'They are?'

He gave her a lopsided smile and she had to work hard to calm the butterflies in her stomach. It was bad enough that the touch of his skin against hers was causing her heart-rate to increase. Did she have no control over her senses where Pierce was concerned?

'Stacey, from the way you stood on the opposite side of the road, gazing with fond nostalgia at the house, I knew you were someone who had a big heart. The memories the place clearly holds for you are important, and you didn't shy away from that.'

She stared at him for a moment, then glanced down at their hands, at his thumb gently rubbing over the backs of her knuckles. She wished he'd stop, but at the same time she wished he'd never stop. Was he feeding her a line? Was he being nice to her because he wanted something from her? If so…what?

It had taken her quite a while to figure out that Robert had had his own agenda when it came to their…union. He'd wanted a smart, pretty wife—someone who understood his work and who was dedicated to helping him climb the career ladder. What he *hadn't* wanted was an instant family.

'And if you want more examples of how I know your character,' Pierce continued, his tone as intent as his words, 'let's start with your concern for Edna and Mike, or of the way you talked about sitting in the bay window sharing your secrets with your sisters. But most importantly for me it was the way you interacted with Nell. As far as I'm concerned that's always the biggest indicator of a woman's true nature, because the instant a woman discovers I'm guardian to my little sister, and not only that but she has a learning difficulty, it's usually enough to make them head for the hills.'

'A *woman's* true nature?' she couldn't help quizzing.

It wasn't until Pierce looked into her blue eyes that he realised she was turning the tables, lightening the atmosphere, wanting to remove the spotlight from herself.

'There's a story there,' she said.

Pierce nodded and slowly let go of her petite hand. 'Of course there is, and it's one which has been repeated time and time again.'

'Which begs the question have *you* ever come close to matrimony?'

He nodded. 'I was engaged. Catherine was her name.'

'Was?'

'Still is, actually. She's alive and well, but—'

'But she couldn't take the responsibility of being guardian to Nell?'

Pierce shook his head. 'No. No, quite the opposite, actually.'

'Really?'

He exhaled slowly and looked down at the ground for a moment. 'Catherine was…*is*—' he glanced at her as he corrected himself '—the type of woman who loves to be of use. She loves helping others, being there for them. She's a brilliant doctor, ended up becoming an eye surgeon, but I guess the best way to describe her is that she needs to be needed.'

'So when she found out you had a sister with a disability she was happy about that?'

'Yes, and I thought, *Wow, here's a woman who likes me, who likes Nell, who loves being with both of us, who understands what we're about.*'

'What went wrong?'

Pierce paused. 'She accepted a job overseas, working with Pacific Medical Aid like your sister Cora.'

'Was this before or after your engagement?'

'It was two weeks before our wedding?'

'She just went overseas?'

'She said that we didn't need her as much as other people needed her. That being married would tie her down, would stop her from reaching her true potential which was to help as many people as she could.' Pierce met Stacey's gaze. 'Hard to argue with someone who only wants to do good in this world.'

'And is she doing good?'

'I believe she's presently in Iran, giving the gift of sight by performing cataract operations on those who otherwise could never afford it.'

'She sounds like quite a woman.'

He nodded. 'She sends me a Christmas card every year.'

'It's good that you keep in touch.'

'It is.' He nodded.

Stacey watched him for a moment, wondering if he still had feelings for Catherine. It was clear from the way he spoke of her that he admired her. Could she ask? They were being quite open with each other so why not?

'Do you...?' She hesitated for a moment, then took a breath and plunged right in. 'Do you still have feelings for Catherine?'

'Friendship feelings? Yes. Romantic feelings? No. But I wish her every success and happiness.'

'And yet you sound so forlorn.'

'I do?' He sat up straighter and chuckled. 'Sorry. I'm supposed to be the one cheering you up.'

'Then consider me cheered. You have performed your friendship duties well.'

'Friendship?' he queried.

'Isn't that why we're having dinner tonight? To build friendships not only for Nell but for each other?'

Pierce angled his head to the side. 'I guess I hadn't thought of it like that.'

'Perhaps because you're always so busy considering Nell's needs first and your own second.'

'I'm sure you know all about that, what with having so many siblings. But I think we could definitely be friends.' He spread his arms wide. 'We're off to a good start. We're swinging together.' He winked, implying a cheeky *double entendre*.

She laughed. 'Literally.'

'Yes. So, *friend*, tell me something about you that a lot of people—*sans* siblings—wouldn't know.'

Stacey sighed thoughtfully for a moment, then nodded. 'I love cheesy music videos.'

'Huh? That *is* surprising.'

'They're just so funny. The over-acting, the bad colour saturation, the strange vision of the film-maker. Sometimes the videos have absolutely nothing to do with the lyrics, and that just makes it even more ridiculous and funny. Some of the ones from the eighties are classics—especially with special effects which were considered so cutting edge at the time but nowadays are completely woeful.'

Pierce nodded, as though seriously considering her

words. 'Cheesy music videos? I'm beginning to understand the appeal.'

'OK. Now it's your turn. Tell me something not many people know about *you*.'

Pierce opened his mouth, hesitated, then closed it again.

'Come on,' Stacey urged. 'Friends share.'

He nodded, but exhaled and closed his eyes before confessing, 'I like...to sew.'

'Sew?'

'If I hadn't had a passion for medicine and helping people I would have been a fashion designer.'

'Really?' Stacey couldn't help but chuckle at this news. 'Are you being serious or are you pulling my leg?'

He kept a straight face for a whole five seconds before grinning. 'Pulling your leg. I like to garden.'

'Well, that's hardly a secret. Your whole neighbourhood can tell you like to garden simply by the way you attend to those flowerbeds.' She swung back and forth a little. 'I liked the sewing story better, but if you ever feel like bringing your gardening skills over to my house then please feel free. I do not have a green thumb whatsoever.'

'Perhaps I can give you some pointers. We could do some potting and planting and then head inside and watch cheesy music videos.'

Stacey laughed, unable to believe just how light and happy she felt. How was it that Pierce had not only been able to shift her bad mood but make her feel optimistic?

'Gardening lessons?' She nodded. 'I might actually look forward to them.'

He stood from the swing and held out his hand to her. 'I hope you do.'

Stacey accepted his hand, but as she stood from the swing she over-balanced slightly and fell towards him.

Pierce moved quickly and caught her, with one strong arm about her waist.

'Uh…sorry.' Stacey placed her other hand on his arm to steady herself, trying to ignore the instant warmth which flooded her body, her senses shifting into overdrive as she breathed in his spicy scent.

'You all right?'

His words were soft, his breath fanning her cheek, and when she lifted her head and looked at him she realised just how close her face was to his. Her gaze dipped to look at his mouth, lingering for a second before returning to meet his eyes.

'Uh…' She sent commands to her limbs, telling them to move, her legs to support her, but the sluggish signals took a few seconds to be received. 'Yeah. Yeah, I should be fine.'

As she shifted her weight, Pierce continued to hold her hand. 'Did you twist your ankle? Hurt yourself?'

'No. I just stepped wrong. The ground's a little uneven.'

He smiled at her. 'OK.'

They took a few steps away from the swings before he released her, shoving his hands into the pockets of his jeans as they headed back down the path. Stacey racked her mind for something to say, trying to get her brain back into gear rather than fixating on the way being so close to Pierce had made her feel.

They'd been doing so well, chatting and sharing as friends. She didn't want to be aware of him. She wanted their relationship to be one of easygoing colleagues and friends. She didn't want to dream of him, to wonder what it might be like to have his arms holding her securely, to have him gazing down into her eyes, to have his lips pressed against hers.

'Uh…' She stopped and quickly cleared her throat, astonished that her voice had broken with that one brief sound. 'Um…will Nell be all right with you leaving her like this? I mean, she doesn't know any of my family and—'

'Nell will be fine. Part of her preparation for living independently has involved developing a sort of *script*, I guess you'd call it, for when a visitor comes round. But with two rabbits there for her to play with I doubt she's given anyone else a second thought.'

'Well, that's good.'

'Plus, I'm sure your sister Molly will have everything under control.'

'Probably better than I ever could.' She sighed, thinking of the way Jasmine responded so positively to Molly.

'I doubt that's true. One day soon Jasmine will realise everything you've done for her, she'll see you in a different light, and she'll appreciate you much more.'

They were almost back at the house by now and Pierce started to slow his pace. He wasn't sure he was ready to go inside to the noise and bustle just yet. Chatting quietly, intimately with Stacey had been relaxing, and he couldn't remember the last time he'd allowed himself to relax.

'Oh, I hope so.'

Stacey, too, didn't seem in any great hurry to re-enter the house, and they stopped just outside Edna and Mike's place.

Stacey looked up at the fading light of the balmy September day. 'Hopefully Jasmine's been able to engage Nell in conversation.' Stacey looked across at the house. 'I hate to see her hurting.'

'Of course you do. She's your little sister and she's been through some fairly intense life changes.'

'But George and Lydia seemed to have coped.'

'Because they're younger. Child-like comprehension is sometimes a godsend, and at other times, it's an enviable reality.' He leaned up against the fence between the two properties.

Stacey watched him in the late-afternoon light. 'Did Nell understand about your parents' death?'

'It took her a while, and sometimes she was quite confused when she couldn't find them, or when she'd find me quietly crying because I missed them so much.'

Stacey pulled her lightweight cardigan around her and crossed her arms in front in an effort to stop herself from touching him. She wanted nothing more than to reach out and place a reassuring hand on his arm or, worse, to throw her arms around his waist and hug him close, desperate to let him know that she really did understand exactly where he was coming from and what he felt. Just because they were adults, it didn't stop them from wanting to see their parents again.

'It can get rather wretched sometimes,' she agreed, surprised to find her voice catching on the words. 'I often wonder where I'd be now if my parents hadn't died...if I didn't have the children to constantly consider. No doubt I'd be stuck in a loveless marriage with Robert who, as it turned out, only wanted to marry me because I fitted all his criteria. He might have professed undying love for me, but it was only another lie to secure what he wanted.'

Pierce looked at her for a moment, then shook his head. 'Yep. He was an idiot. What I mean is—and if I may be so bold, given I don't know the circumstances—your ex-fiancé sounds quite thick.'

Stacey's smile was instant. 'Thank you.'

Pierce held out an open hand towards her. 'I mean you're intelligent, caring, thoughtful and incredibly beautiful. What sane man *wouldn't* want you?'

Stacey wasn't sure what to say. His warm, sweet words washed over her, making her feel cherished…and she couldn't remember the last time she'd felt cherished—if ever. They stood there, simply looking at each other, drinking their fill. Butterflies started to churn again in her stomach as the atmosphere between them began to intensify. The need to draw closer to him, to touch him, was starting to become overwhelming, and when she edged a little closer to where he stood she found that he was doing the same.

His gaze flicked down to encompass her mouth before returning to her eyes. He opened his mouth to speak, but before he could say another word Edna's front door opened and she came running out, all in a frantic tizzy.

'Edna?' Stacey called, and the other woman yelped with fright, clearly not expecting to find two people chatting near the bottom of her driveway. 'Is something wrong?'

'It's Mike. He's got pains. I was just coming to get Pierce and call the ambulance,' she said, indicating the cell phone in her hand.

'I've got my big emergency bag in my car,' Stacey remarked, fishing her car keys from her pocket.

'Thanks,' Pierce called over his shoulder as he headed inside with Edna.

By the time Stacey joined him he'd placed Mike in the recovery position. He accepted a stethoscope from Stacey and listened to Mike's heart.

'Ambulance is on it's way,' he informed her as she wound the blood pressure cuff from the portable sphygmomanometer around Mike's arm.

'BP is elevated,' she responded a moment later. 'How do his lungs sound? Asthma?'

'Not asthma. Probably an angina attack.' Pierce met

and held her gaze for a moment, his eyes clearly saying, *Let's hope that's all it is.*

'I'm not…an…idiot,' Mike puffed, his eyes shut. 'Silence…speaks…volumes.'

'Shush, Mike,' Edna said, bossing him around. 'Let the doctors do their work.'

'You've always been very astute, Mike.' Stacey gently rubbed his arm, wanting to reassure him in any way she could. 'Try and focus on your breathing for me. Slow, calm breaths. We're going to set up an IV, just to get some fluids into you, so that by the time the ambulance arrives you'll be in a better state to receive further treatment.'

'What's…wrong?' he panted, reaching out for his wife's hand. Edna dutifully held it, but when she looked up at Stacey, there was fear in her eyes.

'We're not sure at this stage, Mike,' Pierce added as he reached into Stacey's well-stocked emergency bag, which was more like a huge backpack, pulling out the equipment they'd need for inserting an in vitro line into Mike's left arm. 'But rest assured Stacey and I will do everything we can to help.'

'Where is it painful?' Stacey asked Mike, and he told her the pain was down his right arm and across his chest. 'You're doing a good job of controlling your breathing. Well done. Is the pain constricting when you breathe in or out or both?'

'Both.'

'Is the pain stabbing or constant?' Stacey opened the tubing packet while Pierce inserted a cannula into Mike's arm.

'Constant.' He paused. 'Sometimes stabbing.'

'Any other pain? Headache? Tingling in your legs?'

'No.'

'Good.'

By the time they'd finished inserting the drip, Edna still sitting by her husband's side, holding his hand as though she was never letting go ever again, they could hear ambulance sirens in the distance.

Pierce looked across at Stacey. 'Are you OK to hold the fort for a moment? I just want to check on Nell. No doubt the sirens are going to bring the others out to see what's going on.'

'Good point.' Stacey nodded, and wasn't surprised to find Molly walking into Edna and Mike's house less than three minutes later.

'Mike? Mike?' Molly knelt down by his side. 'Ah… look at this. Stacey's got you all ready for the ambulance. Isn't she great?'

'She really is,' Pierce remarked as he re-entered the house. 'Ambulance is just pulling into the driveway. Time to get you mobile.' Pierce ran through what would happen, so Mike and Edna were completely aware of the procedure.

'I can go with him, can't I?' Edna asked as Stacey performed Mike's observations once more, pleased to announce that his BP was starting to level out, thanks to the IV drip.

'That's good news,' Pierce told him as the paramedics came into the house.

Stacey spoke with Molly, making sure her sister was all right to stay with Nell and the children.

'They've spent a lot of time playing with the rabbits and they're just sitting down to do some puzzles. Jasmine's been really good with Nell.'

Stacey sighed with relief. 'I was hoping she would be.'

'George and Lydia are having a turn with the rabbits in the back yard,' Molly continued, talking as though she was giving a patient debrief. 'And I've checked the kitchen—Pierce has pre-cooked an amazing meal, so I'll save you both some and we'll just get on with our night of getting to know Nell.'

'Sounds like a good plan,' Pierce remarked. 'Once Mike's all settled we'll head back.'

'Agreed.' With a brisk, formal nod that would serve her well in the surgical world, Molly kissed both Edna and Mike on the cheek before heading next door.

After they'd assisted the paramedics in settling Mike in the ambulance, Edna rode along with him and Stacey and Pierce followed in Stacey's car. Stacey couldn't help but be impressed with Pierce's cool, calm and collected bedside manner. Mike hated fuss at the best of times, and to work alongside a doctor who could communicate with her via looks, nods or a brief well-chosen word was excellent.

It made her think about her long-term plans for Short-field Family Medical Practice. At the moment there was enough work for one full-time doctor and one part-time doctor, but patients who had been fed up with seeing locums were now returning to the family-oriented practice, and that meant longer waiting lists. That wasn't what Stacey wanted. Even though Cora was due to return at the end of the year, chances were they would soon be requiring more than two doctors to work at the clinic—especially as she already had plans for Winifred, their nurse-receptionist, to start conducting immunisation clinics.

Pierce seemed the obvious choice to approach with regard to a partnership. He would be close to Nell and could keep an eye on her, he was amazing with the patients and he worked exceptionally well with her. Good doctors were hard to find, so she accepted the silent challenge to persuade Pierce to stay permanently at Shortfield Family Medical Practice.

Of course there was the added advantage that he was dreamy to look at, that he made her laugh and that he could ignite an instant fire deep within her. But that was completely beside the point...wasn't it?

CHAPTER FIVE

THANKFULLY, DUE TO their prompt action, Mike was only in hospital for six days, admitted for a mild myocardial infarction.

'You were lucky this time,' stated Brian, the cardiac specialist at Newcastle General. 'But it means big changes, Mike.'

Mike groaned. 'I don't have to eat those fat-free bran muffins Edna keeps wanting to force down my throat, do I?'

Stacey chuckled at her friend's resigned tone. Pierce joined in and she looked across at him. They'd both known Mike was going to be discharged that morning, so had come to listen to what the specialist had to say and also to offer moral support to both Edna and Mike. Going to hospital could be scary enough, but sometimes being discharged could be equally unsettling.

'See? Even Brian's telling you to listen to me and to stop sneaking foods which are bad for you,' Edna chastised, before staring at Mike. 'I love you, Mikey. I need you.' She took his hand in hers. 'And if eating fat-free bran whatever means that I get to be with you longer, then that's what we'll eat. *Both* of us.'

Mike raised his wife's hand to his lips and kissed it,

glistening tears in his eyes. 'That's what we'll do, love,' he finished.

Stacey couldn't believe how blessed she was to be witnessing such an intimate connection between her two friends. After over forty years together they were still deeply in love, and she immediately missed her own parents. When she glanced across at Pierce, who was on the opposite side of Mike's bed, she could almost sense that he felt the same as her, except about his own parents.

'Good to hear,' Brian continued. 'Besides, the only reason you're going home now is because Pierce lives next door to you and Stacey's going to check on you every day.'

'What about district nurses?' Edna queried. The consultant stared at Edna, then shook his head.

'Mike? Listen to a district nurse? I'd feel sorry for the nurse.' Brian chuckled. 'From all those years of playing hockey and football with Mike, I know, Edna, that it's best if someone he loves comes and bosses him around—especially with regard to anything medical.' Brian placed a hand on Mike's shoulder. 'You're a cantankerous old man now, Mike. We both are. And it's best we take steps to protect others from ourselves.'

Mike grinned at his old friend. 'Too true.'

Stacey laughed and walked across to Mike's bedside and kissed his cheek. 'I love you, Mike,' she said. Then she whispered in his ear, 'And you're the closest thing I have to a father. *Please* take care of yourself. I need you.'

When she straightened her eyes were glistening with tears. She'd only meant to encourage him, and yet here she was, standing before the head of cardiology, blubbering.

Mike looked at her firmly, then took her hand in his and gave it a squeeze. 'I'll not let you down, girl,' he promised, his voice choking with a mixture of determination, sincerity and love.

Edna hugged Stacey. 'It's perfect timing that you're back. We need you and you need us. It's right that you're back where you belong.'

And that was exactly how Stacey felt as she walked into her clinic on Friday morning, four weeks after taking it over. Coming home to Newcastle *had* been the right decision, although Jasmine would probably disagree.

As she walked through the clinic, switching on various machines to warm them up, Stacey was surprised to find Pierce in his consulting room, given it had only just gone seven o'clock. She stopped by his open door. 'Good morning. You look as though you've been here half the night.'

He looked up from his computer screen and smiled at her as she walked in, coming to stand near his desk. 'No. Just half an hour or so. I was just finishing up an article I promised I'd write for the team at Yale.'

'Yale? Yale as in the prestigious American university?'

'Yes. Presently the team there are leading the world when it comes to understanding autism and autism spectrum disorders, but there's still so much we don't know about adult autism.'

'Which is where you come in?'

'Sort of.'

'As I've mentioned, I've read your articles. They're good.'

'Thank you.' He used the computer mouse and clicked a few times before switching off his monitor. 'At any rate, the article is now done and on its way to Professor Smith for his approval.'

'I'm sure he'll do more than approve. Have you worked with the Yale team for long?'

Pierce nodded as he stood from his chair, linking his hands behind his back and pulling downwards. Stacey tried not to stare.

'For quite a while.'

'I'm surprised they haven't offered you a job.'

'Well...' He shrugged, then lifted his hands over his head.

Stacey had been about to ask him some more questions, but the words didn't make it as far as her lips as all she was conscious of was the way his trousers dipped and his white and blue striped shirt rose up. He hadn't bothered to tuck it in and she was treated to a glimpse of his firm, smooth abdominals. Good heavens! Did the man work out every day?

She curled her fingers into her palms in an attempt to stop her itching need to walk over to him and feel just how firm those abs really were. Stacey swallowed, her lips parting to allow the pent-up air to escape, only then realising that her heart-rate had increased, and her breathing was more shallow than normal.

It wasn't until he lowered his hands, the shirt sliding back into place, that she realised she hadn't heard a word he'd said—if he'd said anything at all. Quickly she raised her gaze to meet his, hoping he hadn't noticed she'd been openly ogling him. He raised an eyebrow and she noticed a soft, slow smile tugging at the corners of his mouth. It wasn't a teasing smile but one of interest.

Interest? He was *interested* that she'd been ogling him? Mortification ripped through her and she quickly looked away.

'Stacey?'

She headed towards the door, unable to look at him. 'Yeah?'

'Stacey...'

His tone was a little more urgent and she stopped in her tracks before glancing at him over her shoulder. She swallowed.

'Er...' She cleared her throat, unable to control her rapid breathing.

He walked over to her and stood quite near. She wished he hadn't, because as soon as she breathed in, hoping to gain some sort of control over her wayward senses, all she was aware of was the fresh spicy scent which surrounded him. That and the warmth emanating from him made for a heady combination. The breath she exhaled was jittery and, knowing it probably gave him every indication that she was highly aware of him, Stacey sighed with veiled embarrassment and closed her eyes.

What must he think of her? First she'd ogled him and now she was behaving like a complete ninny, all flustered by his nearness. Her mind had gone completely blank—except for the image of him standing there, stretching his arms above his head.

'Stacey?'

'Hmm?' Her eyes snapped open and she realised with a start that he'd actually moved closer than before. When he reached out a hand and tucked a lock of hair behind her ear she gasped, her body starting to tremble not only at his nearness but at the way he'd touched her with such tenderness.

His fingers trailed slowly down her cheek. His gaze firmly locked with hers. It was as though they were in their own private world, just the two of them, time standing still. With her heartbeat thrumming wildly within her ears, she idly wondered if he could hear it.

'Your hair is so soft.'

His words were barely a whisper, but they made her tremble with the realisation that perhaps she wasn't the only one experiencing emotions of awareness. Then again, maybe Pierce gave out random compliments to women as part and parcel of his personality.

'Erm…thank you.' Her words were a little stilted, due to the lack of oxygen reaching her brain simply because of his touch. She needed to move, needed to put some distance between them, and when Pierce dropped his hand back to his side, still staring at her as though he wanted nothing more than to stand there and look into her blue eyes for the rest of the day, she forced herself to edge back.

Unfortunately she hadn't realised how close she was to the door frame and bumped into it.

'Oops.'

'Are you OK?' He put out a hand to steady her.

Stacey cleared her throat and nodded, not trusting her voice not to betray the way he made her feel. She jerked her thumb over her shoulder, indicating the hallway leading to the kitchen. Pierce smiled, as though he knew exactly what was going on, as though he understood exactly why she was unable to speak, and by the delight which was still in his eyes it appeared he really didn't mind at all.

Stacey turned, sighing harshly—more at her own foolishness than anything else—and made her way to the kitchen. Coffee. If she had a coffee perhaps she'd be able to think more clearly.

She sensed rather than felt him following her, so abruptly changed her mind and took a detour into her consulting room. Now that she didn't have his hypnotic scent winding its way around her, or the warmth of his body so near to her own, or the touch of his fingers sliding through her shoulder-length brown hair, Stacey rebooted her brain and forced herself to speak as though nothing out of the ordinary had just happened.

'I'll just put my bag down,' she called.

'Right. I'll switch the coffeemaker on so it can warm up,' he returned.

She almost laughed at the absurdity of their conversation. Polite, professional, impersonal. They were colleagues and new friends, and none of that meant they should be staring deeply into each other's eyes like lovestruck teenagers!

After taking a few calming breaths, Stacey squared her shoulders and walked into the kitchen, determined to focus on one thing—coffee.

'Is the machine ready yet?' She barely spared him a passing glance as she went to the fridge for the milk, noticing he'd already placed two cups on the bench.

'Stacey—what just happened?'

She turned and glared at him, almost dropping the milk. 'What do you mean?'

Pierce waved one hand in the air. 'You ogled me. I caressed your hair. Surely you haven't forgotten already?'

She closed her eyes for one long moment, trying to suppress the tingles and nerves and flutterings of desire she could feel returning. The coffee machine dinged, signifying that it was ready to use. Glad of something to do, Stacey worked on automatic pilot to produce two coffees, adding milk to her own and letting him sugar his coffee himself.

'Like any normal person, when they experience a situation which makes them feel mildly uncomfortable and self-conscious, I *had* planned to forget it, actually.' She forced herself to meet his gaze, even though it was incredibly difficult, and was proud of herself for accomplishing the task. 'Clearly you feel otherwise. So—all right—let's discuss it.'

'Are you always so amenable to doing what everyone else wants?' Pierce stirred sugar into his drink, watching her closely.

'What do you mean?'

'Well, you don't want to talk about those amazing few moments when I invaded your personal space and lost all self-control by touching your hair, and I do.'

As he spoke Stacey felt the fire she'd only just managed to get under control ignite again. They'd known each other for almost a month now, had been working side by side. They'd cared for their patients, met each other's families, shared meals together and she'd learned a lot about him in such a short space of time—especially about the way he treated others. She had to admit that Pierce was quite a man when it came to conversing easily…just as he was doing with her now. The way he could so openly admit that he wanted to touch her hair, be so self-assured, was an admirable quality.

'What I want,' Stacey finally replied as she picked up her coffee cup and held it in front of her, as though she could hide behind it, 'is to take the shortest possible route back to rational thought, which will undoubtedly promote a comfortable working atmosphere. Hence why I was going to push the…you…invading…personal space thing…to the back of my mind and pretend it never happened.'

Pierce leaned a little closer, invading that barrier again. 'But it did.'

His rich, deep baritone caused vibrating tingles to flood through her.

'What if I want to touch your hair again? What if I want to caress your beautiful smooth skin?'

He breathed out slowly, his words unhurried, and she found it difficult to look away from his hypnotic gaze. Was that what he wanted to do? Really?

'What if I want to run my thumb over your lips…?' He stared at her mouth for a good few intoxicating seconds as he continued to speak. 'What if I want to watch them part with the anticipation of feeling my lips pressed against them?'

Her eyes widened at his words and she couldn't help flicking her gaze between his mouth and his eyes, wondering if he was being serious, wondering if he was just teasing, wondering if he actually meant every word he was saying and was about to follow through with a demonstration. The nervous knots caused by his close proximity and her secret need to have him do exactly as he said tightened in her belly.

It *was* there. The attraction she'd been trying to fight could no longer be denied—not now that he'd spoken so openly about it.

Her tongue slipped out to wet her pink lips and she watched as Pierce's gaze took in the process. A slow, deep sigh was drawn from him. He stood there for another half a minute, his jaw clenching a few times, as though he was trying desperately to control some inner urge— even though he was still invading her personal space, still holding his coffee cup in front of him as though in need of protection from his own emotions, just as she was.

'But you're probably right,' he remarked in his normal tone, before swallowing a few times, his Adam's apple working its way up and down his throat above his open-necked shirt. He took two steps back, determined and sure-footed. 'Perhaps it *is* best if we ignore this attraction…'

He gave her a lopsided grin which did absolutely nothing to settle her nerves.

'At least for now. Winifred will be in soon, as will our plethora of patients, and we both have work to accomplish before that happens.'

Then, with a nod, he turned and walked from the kitchen, whistling as though nothing untoward or life-changing had just happened. Stacey watched him go with a mixture of confusion, uncertainty and heightened sensuality.

She shook her head. 'What on earth just happened?'

As though by some unspoken mutual agreement, Stacey and Pierce kept their distance from each other for the rest of the day. Friday clinic sessions were usually hectic, and that evening when she finally arrived home after finishing off the paperwork, long after everyone else had left, Stacey collapsed onto the sofa.

'Whatcha doin', Stace?' Lydia asked as she came over and sat on her sister.

'*Ugh.* What have you been eating?' Stacey asked as she pulled the girl into her arms. 'You're so heavy.'

'Jaz bought us chicken schn—'

'Schnitzel,' Stacey supplied.

'With vegetables from the chicken shop. It was superyum. There's a plate of food for you and Molly. George and I put it together and put some plastic wrap on it.'

'Thank you, Lyds.' Stacey hugged her sister. 'How grown-up of you.'

'George and I ate at the table, but Jaz got angry at *nothing* and took her dinner to her room.'

Stacey frowned at this news, making a mental note to check Jasmine's room later on, hoping to find an empty plate. This wasn't the first time Jasmine had taken her food to her room to eat. It had started a month or two after their parents' death. Molly had wondered whether their sister was in danger of anorexia or bulimia, but Cora had assured them both that Jasmine was eating. However, since Cora had left for Tarparnii Jasmine had become even more withdrawn. Stacey guessed that *any* change—

and Jasmine had certainly had a few—was difficult for her to cope with.

'Why is she like that? Angry at nothing?' Lydia asked, her words filled with innocent confusion. 'Am I gonna be like that when I become a teenager?'

Stacey smiled and kissed Lydia's cheek. 'No. You might get a little moody every now and then, but Jaz is… confused. She can't understand why Mum and Dad died.'

'I can. It's because the angels needed help in heaven and they chose the two best people for the job.'

Stacey's eyes filled with tears at Lydia's words. She hugged her sister close again, wanting to absorb that innocence and hold onto it for as long as possible.

'That's beautiful, Lyddie,' Molly said from the doorway, instantly coming over to kneel on the floor beside the sofa.

'It is,' Stacey replied.

Lydia scrambled out of Stacey's arms and flung herself at Molly. 'There's chicken schnotzel in the kitchen. George and I made a plate of food for you and Stacey.'

Molly hooted with laughter and stood, whizzing Lydia around in her arms. 'Schnotzel, eh? Thank goodness you kept it safe. Come on, Stace. We'd best go eat our schnotzel.'

Stacey giggled as she hefted herself from the sofa, feeling less exhausted than when she'd walked through the door. Glad it was Friday night and she could stay up a bit later, Lydia went off to play with George while the two women sat eating in peace.

Molly looked closely at her sister. 'So… Interesting day?'

'Full day. Lots of patients. Lots of hay fever and sinus problems. Plus there seems to be a gastro bug making the rounds.'

'Yeah. A few bad cases came in to the hospital when

I was in the emergency department just before I left—although it could have been food poisoning. I'll check later on, when I head back.'

'You're on call tonight?'

Molly shook her head. 'Just early tomorrow morning. Split shift. The work of a surgical registrar is never done—which is why, when we get the time, we high-tail it back home to enjoy some chicken schnotzel for dinner and to catch up on sleep. And we don't feel at all sorry for the poor doctors we leave behind to cope—like Pierce.'

'Pierce?' Stacey sat up a little straighter in her chair. 'He's doing a shift in the ED tonight?'

'Yeah. He said someone wanted to switch with him and he was fine with that.'

'He's doing a night shift?'

'Yes. What's the problem with that?'

'Oh. Nothing. He was just in very early this morning at the clinic.'

Molly raised an inquisitive eyebrow. 'Worried about the man's sleeping habits?'

Stacey looked down at her meal, knowing if she kept looking at Molly she'd soon be spilling the beans about what had occurred between them that morning. 'He's an employee…sort of. So of course I'd be concerned about his lack of sleep. I mean, I wouldn't want him doing house calls or treating patients when he's half asleep, now, would I?'

'No. No. Of course not.'

Molly stared at her sister and Stacey looked back across at her.

'What?'

'Is that the *only* reason why you're so concerned about him?'

'Yes.' The word was high-pitched, and sounded false even to her own ears.

'Or is it because the two of you...shared a moment?'

Stacey's eyes widened. 'How could you *possibly* know that?' she squeaked, her knife and fork clattering to her plate. She leaned forward and said in a softer tone, 'What did he tell you? What did he say?'

Molly grinned wildly at her sister and slowly forked another mouthful of chicken into her mouth. She chewed with equal slowness and swallowed before shaking her head from side to side. 'Pierce didn't say anything. You just confirmed a hunch I had—especially after watching the two of you together last weekend at dinner. You were both so cute, so friendly, but with...something more buzzing between you which neither of you wanted to acknowledge.'

'Molly!'

'And then tonight,' Molly continued, as though Stacey hadn't protested, 'he told me three times what a great doctor he thinks you are. He's too much of a gentleman to kiss and tell.'

'There was *no* kissing,' Stacey pointed out.

'But you wanted there to be, didn't you?'

It wasn't a question, it was a statement, and Stacey realised there was no way in the world she could pull the wool over her sister's eyes. Molly knew her as well as she knew herself.

She felt all the fight seep out of her. There seemed no point in denying there was an attraction existing between Pierce and herself. She sat back in her chair and momentarily covered her face with her hands, nodding in affirmation. 'I *did* want him to kiss me. Oh, Molly.' She stared at her sister. 'What am I going to do?'

CHAPTER SIX

As Pierce sat at the nurses' station in the Emergency Department, glad of a quiet night so far, he couldn't help but think of the way he'd actually touched Stacey's hair that morning. What he'd told her had been the truth—he'd thought about touching her hair from the first time he'd seen her. It had looked so soft and glossy in the sunshine that day, as it had bounced around her shoulders, her fringe framing her face perfectly.

He'd been determined to keep his distance, to ensure that his relationship with Stacey remained one of a working friendship. But the night her family had come for dinner, the way he'd felt the need to follow her to the park to ensure she was safe, then having her open up to him about her life, had only intrigued him even more.

Who *was* Stacey Wilton? The *real* Stacey Wilton? What were her dreams and hopes for *her* future? He, of all people, knew what it was like to live for others, always putting your own life on hold for everyone else—and he only had one sibling to consider. Stacey had five.

After Mike's admission to hospital last week he and Stacey had returned to his house, where Molly had been in full organisational mode. It hadn't felt awkward, walking into Nell's house and seeing it full of other people. It had felt right, somehow. It hadn't felt awkward eating the dinner he'd prepared and which Molly had reheated, sitting alongside the sisters, all of them chatting quietly but happily. It hadn't felt awkward when he and Stacey had rinsed the plates and stacked the dishwasher, tidying the kitchen together. Everything had felt...*right*.

Along with that, Nell had loved spending time with the rabbits, and she had definitely formed a bond with George, Lydia and especially Jasmine. Pierce had discovered that out of the Wilton triplets Stacey was indeed the oldest—'By five minutes,' Molly had told him. 'And she never lets us forget it.'

He'd liked watching the easy interaction between the sisters. The tight bond they shared was quite evident. Still, all he could see was Stacey, giving her time to everyone else. Accommodating Cora's desire to head off to work as a doctor in Tarparnii. Encouraging Molly's desire to study surgery. Assisting George and Lydia as they entered the world of raising a championship rabbit jumper.

'She's quite a woman, our Stace,' Mike had said one evening, when Pierce had dropped by to check on him, and had been pleased with the other man's progress. 'She's always putting others ahead of herself. For as long as I can remember—even when she was little.' Mike had thrown some poker chips onto the table. 'I call.'

'We often worry—especially after what that terrible Robert did to her.' Edna's indignation was fierce. 'She stood at the front of that church, wearing her wedding dress, calmly told everyone there wouldn't be a wedding and apologised for any inconvenience. Molly or Cora would've been happy to make the announcement, but Stacey insisted on doing it, on making sure they didn't have to bear her burden.' Edna shook her head. 'Goodness knows whether she'll ever get married now.' She looked at her cards. 'I fold.'

'It'll be tough for her,' Mike added. 'Those kids need a stable environment, and she's doing her best to provide it for them.' Then he pointed to Pierce's cards. 'You gonna call or fold, boy?'

Pierce looked absent-mindedly at his cards, more focused on the way Stacey was constantly infiltrating his thoughts rather than on playing the game. He'd already realised she was the type of woman to put others before herself, and it made him want to do something nice for her—something unexpected, something *just for her*. But what? 'Uh…fold.'

Mike shook his head. 'Easy victory. Your mind's not on the game tonight, boy.'

'I'll go put the kettle on,' Edna said as she stood from the table and headed into the kitchen. 'You go sit in your comfy chair, Mike. Time to put your feet up!' she called.

'Yes, dear,' Mike replied, and rolled his eyes. 'Help an old man up, Pierce.'

'You're not that old,' Pierce protested, but still did as he was bid.

'She's tying you in knots, isn't she?'

The question was rhetorical and Pierce looked at Mike with a frown.

'Oh, don't give me that. I've seen the two of you in the same room together—those sneaky little looks you both have. You like her. She likes you. I get it. I've been there, too, you know. Might have been a long time ago, but my Edna had me in a right tailspin and I had no idea how to pull out of it.'

'How *do* you pull out of it?' Pierce asked as he tucked a blanket around Mike's legs and made sure the television remote controls were within easy reaching distance.

Mike laughed, then coughed. 'Sometimes, boy, you've

gotta fly right through it. No pulling up, no manoeuvring around it. Gotta go through it.'

Pierce shook his head. 'I've been down that road, though. It didn't end well.'

'Your fiancée left you and broke your heart—but that was a while ago and you're over it now. Edna told me.'

'Edna has a way of getting information out of people.'

Mike grinned. 'That's my girl.' He rested his head back and closed his eyes. 'So you're not gonna do anything about the way Stacey makes you feel?'

'I don't know.' Pierce paused, then looked at his friend. 'I've been head-hunted by a hospital in America.'

Mike opened his eyes. 'Really?'

Pierce smiled. 'Edna didn't manage to wheedle *that* titbit out of me.'

'What about Nell?'

'That's why I've spent so long setting up her independent living situation. Her new housemates will move in soon, and Nell's ready for that. She wants to do it. She knows I'll be overseas. We'll talk over the internet, and she'll have a network of people around her who are available whenever she needs them.'

Mike thought this over. 'How long are you going for?'

Pierce shrugged. 'At least six months—*if* I take the position.'

'When did they offer it to you?'

'Four years ago.'

'*What?*'

'I keep turning them down. They keep offering.'

'They must want you to work with them badly?'

Pierce nodded. 'They do.'

'Do you want to go?'

'Yeah, but—' He spread his arms wide. 'And that's always been the problem. There's always been a "but".'

'So for years you've not been able to go because of Nell?'

'Correct.'

'And now that Nell is finally settled and all ready for you to leave you're not sure because…?'

'Because what if this attraction between Stacey and myself is more than just an attraction? What if this is it? The one! What if she's the woman I'm meant to spend the rest of my life with?' Pierce began pacing up and down in front of Mike, then stopped and spread his arms wide again. 'Do you see my dilemma?'

Mike shrugged. 'You've put those Americans off for four years, laddie. What's a few more months? You've promised Stacey you'll stay until Cora gets back and you're not going to leave her in the lurch. It's not your way. So why don't you see whether this thing between you and Stacey *is* real? Give it a chance.'

'And what if it is? Does that mean I *never* get to go to the States?' Pierce raked both hands through his hair. 'Everything was going along just fine. I should have known that that would be when I finally met the woman of my dreams.'

'Your dreams, eh?' Mike chuckled. 'Then you've got nothing to worry about.' His grin widened as Edna came back into the room, carrying a tea tray. 'Dreams always come true.'

'Pierce…? Hello…?'

Sister was snapping her fingers near his face and Pierce instantly looked at her. 'Sorry. I was miles away.'

'Daydreamer!' She chuckled. 'Can you review these notes, please? Plus we've just had another drunk brought in by the police. Non-abusive, passed out in the middle of the road. I've put him in Cubicle Twelve.'

'Thanks.'

Pierce took the first set of case notes from the pile Sister had handed him and tried desperately not to think about the way he'd felt when he'd caught Stacey ogling him. Her visual caress, the way she'd responded when he'd touched her hair, when he'd later leaned towards her, looking deep into her eyes and realising he'd never felt that alive for years… Just that one moment…it had been intoxicating. It was also why he'd forced himself to walk away. Too much of a good thing could cause an addiction. But perhaps Mike was right. Perhaps he *should* give this attraction with Stacey a chance, see exactly it might lead.

The thought excited him and he smiled, thinking of what he might say to her the next time they met. If they had another tension-filled moment like the one they'd shared that morning he was determined that he wouldn't be the one to walk away. He wanted to know what it was like to kiss Stacey—well, perhaps it was about time he found out.

The insistent ringing of Stacey's cell phone woke her with a start. She sat bolt upright in bed and, having had years of practice at being instantly awake, quickly connected the call, her voice sure and firm—as though it *wasn't* half past two in the morning and she *hadn't* been sound asleep.

'Dr Wilton.'

'Stacey? It's my Gary. There's something wrong. I think he's eaten something, but he has a temperature and he's vomited, and I wasn't sure whether I should ring the ambulance because he's refusing to see a doctor, saying it's just food poisoning, but this is really bad and I didn't know what to do, and—'

'It's fine. Give me your address. I'll come over now and assess him,' Stacey interrupted, and quickly wrote down the details with the pen and paper she always kept on the bedside table. Initially she'd had no idea who Gary was, because her mind had still been coming out of the fog from her dream…a dream in which a tall, dark and handsome Pierce had brushed her hair from her face, leaned forward, pressed his lips to hers, kissing her with such tender passion…

Even now, as she did her best to reassure Gary's wife Nanette—who, it turned out, had been at school with her—Stacey could feel her cheeks still flushed with heat from the memories floating around in the back of her mind. As she ended the call and dressed she tried desperately to focus her thoughts on Gary's symptoms, planning several strategies in order to cope with a variety of possible scenarios. If Gary hadn't been able to keep any fluids down then his electrolyte levels might be low and he might require hospitalisation.

Out in the family room, Stacey collected her fully stocked emergency medical backpack from the locked cupboard and left a message for Molly on the whiteboard to let her sister know she'd been called out. Then she collected her handbag and car keys before heading out, thankful that Nanette and Gary didn't live too far away.

'Sorry for calling in the middle of the night.'

Nanette rushed out to meet Stacey, her words tumbling from her mouth as Stacey collected her backpack from the car and both women headed inside the house, which was lit up like a Christmas tree. Nanette had her two-year-old daughter in her arms, the child clearly having been woken from her sleep with all the ruckus and was not happy about it.

'That's what family practices are for, Nanette. To form bonds with the community. Which way?' Stacey's tone was firm and direct, yet she was also trying to reassure Nanette. She needed her to be calm, but given what she could remember of her old school friend that might be impossible.

'I didn't know what to do,' Nanette dithered. 'And I couldn't remember the name of your partner at the GP practice, who I saw the other day when one of my kids was sick, so I called your practice number and the answering machine gave me a cell phone number, and it turned out to be yours, but then I wasn't sure whether to call the ambulance or just take Gary to hospital myself, but when I tried to move him, to get him closer to the front door, he groaned so badly that I started trembling, and—oh, Stacey, I'm so glad you're back in Newcastle. Help my Gary. *Please?*'

Stacey continued to follow Nanette through the house, heading to the bedroom at the back where she could hear Gary groaning.

'What's *wrong* with him?' Nanette kept asking, and Stacey had to use all her mental control to block the other woman out and remain calm as she introduced herself to Gary.

The man was lying quite still, sweating and clammy to the touch. Stacey pulled out her stethoscope and lifted Gary's shirt, talking him through what she was doing. She listened to the sounds of his stomach, not wanting to palpate the abdomen, given he was already in so much pain.

She asked him about the times he'd been ill, about the type of pain he was experiencing, and after she'd taken his blood pressure and temperature she pulled her cell phone from her pocket and called for an ambulance, letting them know her suspected diagnosis.

'Appendicitis!' Nanette's high-pitched shriek made their daughter start to cry and Nanette quickly jiggled the toddler up and down, whispering soothing words.

'Is there someone who can look after your children for you, Nanette?'

'Oh. Oh. Uh… Yes. OK. This *is* happening?'

'Yes, it is.' Stacey took Gary's temperature again. 'We'll have you sorted out in next to no time,' she told him, giving him something to help with the pain.

Within another twenty minutes Gary was being wheeled on an ambulance gurney towards Trauma Room One.

'What have we got?' a deep male voice asked as Stacey quickly washed her hands before pulling on a disposable gown and a pair of gloves.

She let the paramedics give the debrief as she tried desperately to ignore the way her entire body seem to fill with trembles at the sound of Pierce's tone, but it was impossible. She was so incredibly aware of him, of memories of the way he'd tenderly touched her hair, of the way he'd stared into her eyes, of the dreams she'd had of the two of them together, and as she turned to look at him a fresh round of excitement burst forth when he smiled brightly.

'Hello, Stace.' He seemed a little surprised to see her but his smile was wide and genuine. 'No sleep for you tonight, eh?' he said as he walked over to where Gary was being transferred from the paramedic's gurney to the hospital barouche.

'No. I'm Gary's GP, and his wife called me because she was concerned. I'll just see him through to diagnosis. It'll help his wife to feel more relaxed if she knows I'm helping to look after her husband.'

He nodded. 'Fine by me if it's fine by the hospital,' he stated.

'I'm registered here.'

'Excellent.' Pierce hooked his stethoscope into his ears, ready to listen to the sounds of Gary's abdomen.

Stacey looked at her patient, pleased she'd been able to convince Nanette to go and wait in the patients' lounge as Gary had turned exceedingly pale.

'I think he's going to be sick again,' Stacey warned, and the nurses were on the ball with their assistance, attending to Gary as Pierce finished his consult.

'Right. Let's get some fluids into him, boost electrolytes, and an injection of Maxalon to help stop the vomiting. Cross, type and match. We also need to lower that temperature. Get the on-call surgical registrar down here.'

Stacey and the rest of the Emergency Department staff started carrying out Pierce's orders.

'Molly said there have been quite a few cases of food poisoning presenting at the Emergency Department?'

'That's correct. But in Gary's case I think it's something a little more sinister.' Pierce had come around the barouche and was once more listening to the sounds of Gary's abdomen.

'Definitely appendix?'

'Definitely,' he confirmed as the surgical on-call registrar walked into the room.

'What do we have?' he asked.

'Forty-five-year-old male,' Pierce began, giving the registrar a breakdown of Gary's vitals. 'Initial suspected food poisoning, but all symptoms indicative of appendicitis with possible signs of peritonitis. Bloods have been ordered, but I don't think we can wait too much longer for the results.'

'Right.' The registrar performed his own set of examinations, listening to the sounds of Gary's abdomen before nodding and hooking his stethoscope about his shoulders. 'OK, Gary. We're going to get you to Theatre as soon as possible.' He turned to Pierce and Stacey. 'I'll go see if I can find a theatre that's free and get the paperwork started. Next of kin?'

'Gary's wife is in the patients' waiting room. She's quite distraught,' Stacey supplied.

'And who are you?'

'I'm their GP.'

'Excellent. Fetch the wife from the waiting room so I can explain the operation to her and her husband and get the consent forms signed.'

Stacey nodded as the registrar left the room.

'Brisk and to the point,' Pierce murmured. 'Your sister has a much better bedside manner.'

'I'm sure he's a good registrar,' she offered as they watched the nurses perform Gary's observations once more.

'Oh, he is. There's no doubting that.' Pierce stood beside her, speaking softly so only she could hear. 'I'm just saying that you Wilton women have a certain way about you that makes everyone feel more…calm, more relaxed. It's nice.'

He smiled at her—that cute, sexy little smile that she was coming to adore. Then he winked.

The intimate action, as though linking them in their own private bubble, caused Stacey's heart-rate to instantly increase. How was it possible that with such a small gesture he was able to tie her insides into knots and make her tremble all over?

Stacey licked her lips and gave him a little smile in return, before lifting the curtain which afforded Gary and the team the privacy they needed and slipping through before Pierce turned the rest of her body to jelly with another of his full-watt smiles.

When she'd licked her lips his gaze had dropped, taking in the action, before he'd looked into her eyes for a brief second longer. It was why she'd forced herself to move, to step away from his presence—because that one look had said so much. It had said that he wanted to hold her close, that he wanted to feel her touch, that he wanted to press his mouth to hers and take them both on a ride that would send them soaring to the stars.

Stacey took some deep breaths and gave her hands a little shake as she headed to the patients' waiting room. She needed to get her mind off the way Pierce made her feel and on to the job she needed to do—which was to care for her patients. Ever since yesterday morning…when he'd caressed her hair, when he'd gazed into her eyes, when he'd stared longingly at her lips…Stacey had been hard-pressed to think of anything but that.

Before entering the waiting room she mentally picked up her thoughts of Pierce and shoved them into a box, promising herself she'd take them out later and pore over every nuance and action. For now, though, Nanette and Gary needed her at her best, supporting them and helping them. She entered the waiting room and was surprised when Nanette grabbed her and hugged her close. Stacey gave her old school friend a brief rundown on what was happening to Gary and told her that he'd need surgery.

'So I was right to call you?' Nanette blubbered as Stacey offered her yet another tissue.

'You were absolutely right. Now Gary can get the treatment he needs.'

'Can I see him?' Nanette asked.

'Of course. The surgical registrar needs to talk to both of you and Gary needs to sign the consent forms.'

Nanette grasped Stacey's hands firmly in her own. 'You'll stay with me, won't you?'

'Of course.'

At this news Nanette nodded and reached for another

tissue, wiping her eyes and blowing her nose. She pasted on a bright smile. 'How do I look?'

'Like a woman who loves her husband,' Stacey returned, momentarily envious of the connection Nanette and her husband had.

Why hadn't she realised sooner that Robert's words, his professions of love and his actions, hadn't exactly matched up? Perhaps it had been because she'd been desperate to make a connection, to try and find the sort of love that her father had found with Letisha. She'd believed in things that hadn't been there, she'd made excuses for Robert's behaviour, telling herself that he was stressed from working so hard in his pursuit of becoming the hospital's next CEO. One thing Nanette and Gary's easygoing love was showing her was that she was too good to settle for second best. Didn't she deserve to be with a man who loved her so wholly and completely? With a man who would cherish her for who she was?

Nanette's smile brightened naturally at Stacey's words and she nodded with eagerness. 'OK. Let me see my gorgeous husband.'

Stacey stayed with Nanette and Gary while the surgical registrar explained the operation, and after Gary had signed the consent form he was wheeled off to Theatres. Stacey took Nanette to the theatre patients' waiting room, where there was a tea and coffee machine, comfortable chairs and some up-to-date magazines to read.

She'd just settled Nanette with a cup of coffee when Pierce walked in.

'OK. Gary is heading into Theatre now. They'll perform a scan of his abdomen in there and then start the operation. They're just waiting on the report on the bloods, but for the moment everything is under control.'

Nanette sighed at this information and visibly relaxed.

'How much longer will things take? I mean, will he be able to come home later today?'

'No,' Stacey and Pierce answered in unison.

'He'll be in hospital for at least a few days,' Pierce added.

'Are you sure you want to stay and wait?' Stacey asked, putting a hand on Nanette's arm, concern in her tone. 'You could go home, get some rest, and we can call you when—'

'No.' Nanette cut off her words. 'I appreciate what you're saying but I'm staying right here. The kids are all sorted out with my neighbour, and I'm not going home to an empty house only to sit there and wait for my phone to ring.' She put her hand on Stacey's and gave it a little squeeze. 'You don't have to sit with me, Stacey. I know you need to get back to bed or see other patients or whatever else it is you doctors do during these crazy hours of the morning.'

'She *does* need to get home and get some more sleep. *I* may have the morning off, but poor Stacey here will have a plethora of housecalls to make once the sun comes up—and all without her trusty and faithful sidekick.'

Stacey's lips twitched at Pierce's words and she raised one eyebrow. 'Sidekick, eh?'

Nanette giggled, and it was good to see the other woman finding a small bit of lightness in her otherwise dark emotions.

'Absolutely. You're the superhero. I'm just your companion.'

'Companion?' Both eyebrows shot up this time and the smile increased.

'How about…assistant? Better word?'

Stacey shook her head slowly from side to side. 'How

about none of the above? I don't want to be labelled a superhero. Too much pressure.'

Pierce spread his arms wide, as though she really were passing up a once-in-a-lifetime offer. 'Suit yourself.'

Nanette giggled again, then sighed—a long, relaxing type of sigh, indicating that a small part of her tension had been eased. 'Both of you go. I'll be more than fine here. I've got magazines to read—' She pointed to the small table. 'And free tea and coffee and these chairs,' She patted the armrest of the one she was seated in. 'Not too bad for a quick kip, and I have no children to bother me, so all in all a few pluses.'

'Now, *there's* a real superhero.' Pierce held out his hand to indicate Nanette.

The woman smiled and blushed a little beneath his gaze before literally shooing them both from the room.

'She's a nice lady,' Pierce commented as they headed back to the Emergency Department. 'How do you know her?'

'School. She was the year ahead of us.'

'And yet she knows you? I didn't think teenagers stepped outside their bonds of social hierarchy all that much.'

At the nurses' station Pierce sat down and picked up a pen, knowing he should probably stop chatting to Stacey and get back to the mound of case notes Sister had asked him to review. However, if it was a choice between paperwork and chatting with Stacey the decision was a no-brainer. Getting to know Stacey a lot better was presently top of his list of things to do.

'There wasn't too much hierarchy at our school. And besides, *everyone* knows us.' Stacey sat on the edge of the chair next to him and spread her hands wide. 'We're the Wilton triplets. Twins often get remarked upon, especially if they're identical, but triplets—let's just say we're used to being something of a novelty.'

'And do you have some psychic connection that lets you read each other's thoughts? I've heard that twins can have a bond like that. Surely it's greater in triplets?'

'I wouldn't call it a psychic connection, per se.' She thought for a moment, then shrugged. 'It's difficult to explain. I guess it's more like sharing an…emotion. I think it would be the same for any people who spend a lot of time together. The three of us have been together since birth, and I guess we…*feel* that essence of the emotion in each other.' She shook her head. 'It's so difficult to describe.'

'Like intuition?'

'Sort of but…*more* so.'

Pierce scratched his head, the corners of his mouth pulling upwards. 'You're right. You're not explaining it well.'

He tried not to chuckle when she snatched the pen from his hand and shook it at him.

'Listen, buddy. I've had very little sleep, so don't pick on me.'

Pierce couldn't stifle his laughter any longer, and the sound of his mirth warmed her through and through. What was it about him that constantly knocked her off balance, regardless of the time of day?

He held up his hands in surrender. 'Sorry. You're right, of course. Time you were off back home so you can get some rest.' He stood and told the duty sister that he'd be back soon. 'I'll walk you out to your car.'

'That's not necessary. You're needed here.'

'Not at the moment.' He indicated the eerily quiet Emergency Department. 'We're past the "danger hour", and apart from Gary the night hasn't been too bad. So…' Pierce crooked his elbow in her direction. 'If you will allow me, Dr Wilton, I would be most pleased to escort you safely back to your car.'

Stacey looked around at the staff, wondering if they were all watching Pierce being a little bit silly but also incredibly charming, but most of them were too busy to notice. So as not to hurt his feelings, and feeling quite silly herself, whether due to lack of sleep, the release of tension from the past hour or so, or simply the fact that being around Pierce often made her feel delightfully free of restraint, Stacey curled her fingers around his elbow, resting her hand on his arm.

'Why, thank you, kind sir.'

He nodded politely in her direction before they headed off towards the doctors' car park, which was situated right next to the emergency parking bays where the ambulances arrived.

Neither of them spoke for a few minutes but Stacey didn't feel uncomfortable. The sky was cloudless, the stars were shining bright in the moonlight, but the breeze was quite chilly and she actually found herself snuggling a little closer to Pierce, drawn towards his natural body warmth.

'Cold?' he asked, and before she knew what was happening he'd manoeuvred their positions so that instead of offering her his arm in a gentlemanly manner he'd placed his firm, muscled arm about her, his hand resting at her waist, drawing her to him as they walked slowly along the path. 'Better,' he stated as he snuggled a little closer.

Stacey felt highly self-conscious at being embraced by him.

He breathed in and slowly exhaled. 'How can you smell so utterly delicious at such a time of the morning? Or perhaps,' he continued, 'you always smell this good.' He breathed in deeply again. 'Beautiful Stacey,' he whispered, and his sweet words caused goosebumps to flood her entire body.

When they reached her car Pierce gently turned to face her, leaning against the driver's door and bringing his other arm around her. She was now standing firmly in his embrace. Pierce was embracing her openly…here…in the doctors' car park. Granted it was almost four o'clock in the morning, and there was no one else around, but they were on display for all to see.

Stacey couldn't help glancing over her shoulder. She wasn't used to being demonstrative in public, especially because it had been one of the main things in her relationship with Robert that he'd been adamant would never happen. No public displays of emotion or affection. Pierce was so incredibly different…and she liked it a lot.

Pierce adjusted his legs, drawing her body closer to his. 'You *are* beautiful, Stacey. Do you know that?'

She lifted her hands to his chest, unsure whether she was trying to draw him close or keep him at bay. 'I… I'm…I don't know,' she replied, shaking her head as though she didn't believe a word he said.

'Well, *I* do.' Pierce looked down at her. 'Do you have any idea what you've done to me?'

'I'm sure I haven't *done* anything.'

He smiled. 'That's not what I meant, but when you say things like that, with your tone becoming all hesitant and awkward—well, it just makes it even more difficult for me to resist you.'

Stacey shook her head and closed her eyes, wanting him to stop saying things like that. Couldn't he see that they made her feel uncomfortable, that she wasn't used to receiving compliments?

'Why not?' he asked, gently brushing his fingers across her cheek, and it was only when he asked the question that she realised she'd spoken her thoughts out loud. 'What did that jerk of an ex-fiancé do to your self-esteem?' He cupped her cheek. 'Open your eyes, Stacey,' he commanded softly, and to her surprise, she found herself obeying. 'I don't care what any man may or may not have told you in the past, please believe me when *I* say that you are a beautiful, strong, intelligent woman and I would really like to get to know you better.' He raised his eyebrows.

She shook her head again. 'Pierce. Don't say things like—'

'I'm being honest here, Stacey,' he interrupted softly. 'I'm attracted to you and I want to spend some time with you, getting to know you.'

'We spend a lot of time together already.'

'Apart from at work,' he clarified. 'I'm happy to have your siblings around, if you feel as though you need a buffer, but I would also like to take you out on a date— just the two of us.' He was silent for about fifteen seconds, and the atmosphere between them became a little strained when Stacey didn't immediately respond. 'What do you think?' he prompted.

'Um…' She swallowed, her heart beating wildly against her chest. 'You're really serious about this? About this thing—?'

'Can't you feel it?' Pierce pressed her hand to his chest. 'My heart is pounding, Stace. It always does when you're nearby. I catch a glimpse of your smile as you talk to a patient and I'm swarmed with jealousy because I want you to smile at *me*. I hear you laugh on the phone when you're chatting with your sister and the sound relaxes me.'

'Really?'

'Yes, Stacey. Really.' There was intent in his words, as though he was desperate to make her believe he wasn't just feeding her a line. 'Other men may have put you down, may not have wanted to be seen in public with you—and, yes,' he continued before she could say a word, 'I'm aware of how you're self-conscious about showing even the slightest bit of affection in public. I want you to know that I'm not embarrassed or ashamed to be seen holding your hand, or putting my arms around you or… kissing you in public.'

As he spoke his gaze dropped to encompass her mouth. Her lips parted at his words, her heart-rate now completely out of control, every fibre in her being trembling with anticipatory delight. He sounded sincere. In fact he almost sounded slightly offended that she didn't believe him. But somehow he seemed to understand that things had been very different in her past relationships—especially with Robert.

It was nice to have him say these words to her, to reassure her. And yet she still felt as though something was holding her back…but what? Everything she'd seen of Pierce—his interaction with her family, his concern for Mike and Edna, his devotion to his sister—indicated that he was a good man and, as the old adage went, a good man was hard to find. Perhaps she should stop trying to fight him and instead accept that he was really interested in *her*. That he honestly did want to spend time with her simply because he liked her.

The realisation, the sensation of believing Pierce was telling her the truth, made her heart fill with gladness.

'Do you want me to kiss you, Stacey?'

His words were barely a whisper, but they seemed so loud, echoing around her body in sync with the pounding of her heart.

'Yes.'

The single word escaped her lips before she could stop

it. For a split second she thought Pierce hadn't heard her at all, but within the next moment his lips curved upwards with delight and his head began its slow descent.

'That, my gorgeous Stacey, is excellent news.'

And without further ado he captured her willing mouth with his own.

CHAPTER SEVEN

THE FEEL OF his lips on hers made her knees go weak and she slid her arms up and around his neck, clinging to him as he continued to bring her dormant senses to life. Robert had always maintained that kissing wasn't all that important in a relationship, that intellectual compatibility was far more necessary for a functioning and enduring life together. At the time Stacey had believed him, but now, with the way Pierce was filling her with light from the soft, sweet pressure of his touch, she knew she'd been oh-so wrong.

There was warmth in his touch, tenderness in the way he held her close. He'd called her beautiful and at the time she hadn't really believed him. But now, with the way he was pressing his lips to hers, taking his time, not wanting to rush a second of this unique and powerful experience, Stacey was starting to believe he might have actually meant it.

Pierce thought she was beautiful! Accepting this filled her with a sense of wonder and confidence and she opened her mouth a little more, deepening the kiss, wanting to create some of the sensations she'd only dreamed about. He was here. This was real. And she was going to enjoy it.

Pierce's reaction was a deep, warm groan which signified his approval of the manoeuvre. She was delightful, delectable and utterly delicious. How was it possible he hadn't experienced such wonderment combined with innocence before? There was a freshness to her reaction, unstudied and raw, and with the way she was exerting control over the situation, showing him exactly what was contained beneath that quiet, calm exterior, he couldn't help but become even more enamoured with her.

The way her mouth opened to him, the way she responded to him—it was…*giving.* It was then that he truly accepted the fact that she'd always been a giver, always putting others before herself, offering to them the things they desired. As he continued to savour the sweetness of her mouth he couldn't help the thread of confusion which passed through him. Stacey was giving him what he wanted, a heartfelt response, because giving to others was what she knew how to do.

Well, this time, he wanted her to *take,* to allow him to make her feel unique and special and cherished. Naturally, as they were standing in a car park, there was no way that things could progress now, but he had the sensation that where Stacey was concerned taking things nice and slow was definitely the way to go.

He eased back slightly, breaking his lips from hers, not surprised to find both of them breathing heavily from the sensations coursing through them. Good heavens, she was precious. Her eyelids were still closed, her face still angled towards his, her perfectly pink lips parted to allow pent-up air to escape.

Pierce marvelled in her beauty, and the need to explore her smooth, sweet skin was too much for him to resist. He brushed small butterfly kisses on her eyelids, delighted when she gasped in wonderment. Then he slowly made his way down her cheeks, tasting the freshness of her skin. The subtle scent of her perfume combined with the release of endorphins to provide a heady combination, and it was one he knew he could easily become addicted to.

With an all-encompassing tenderness she'd never felt before Pierce pressed kisses from her cheek around to her ear, where he lingered for a moment, causing her body to flood with a new mass of tingles. Then he worked his way down her neck and she found herself tipping her head to the side, granting him as much access as he wanted. He brushed her hair from her neck with the backs of his fingers, not wanting anything to hinder his exploration, his fingers trailing in the silky strands as though he couldn't get enough of the feel of her hair. How was it possible that such a simple action could fill her so completely with needs she'd never even known she had?

It wasn't until he kissed lower, brushing aside the top of her shirt collar, clearly intent on exploring further, that Stacey started to feel a sense of propriety return. She opened her eyes and tried to shift in his embrace, but Pierce spoke against her skin.

'It's all right, Stace.' he breathed. 'I'm not going to ravish you right here. I just want you to *feel*.'

'I do,' she whispered back. 'But…we're…out…in the open and…oh—' Her words were broken off as Pierce pressed kisses along her collarbone, clearly thrilled with her response to his touch as he made his way around to the other side.

'You are exquisite,' he murmured, taking his time, not wanting to rush the exploration.

Stacey tipped her head further back. Her eyes were open as she stared up at the stars, but the sensations he was evoking made it impossible for her to see clearly. It was evident that the attraction between them was incredibly powerful.

When he finally brought his mouth back to hers Stacey's hunger had intensified, and she opened her mouth wider than before, plunging her tongue into his mouth, wanting him to see exactly how he'd affected her senses, heightening them beyond belief. With a passion and urgency she'd never felt before she surrendered herself to him and to the emotions he evoked.

She threaded her fingers through his hair, making sure he didn't break away from her just yet, loving the feel of his arms firmly around her, encompassing her, making her feel secure as well as utterly sexy.

Was this how other people felt when they were kissed by someone who really desired them? Was this what she'd been missing out on? How was it possible she hadn't known that *this* was the way to kiss an attractive man? Or that this was the way a man kissed a woman he found attractive?

Feeling as though her lungs might completely burst if she didn't drag some oxygen into them, Stacey jerked her head back, needing to make a sharp clean break in order to breathe.

'Stacey…'

Her name was a caress upon his lips and she liked the way it sounded. She also liked that he was as breathless as her, as invested as her in all these new and crazy emotions.

'You really *do* like me.' Her words were an astonished whisper, filled with awe and happiness.

'Yes. Yes, I do,' he stated with a slight chuckle, and she immediately closed her eyes and buried her face in his chest.

'Sorry. Clearly I'm a little…knocked off balance by all of this. I keep blurting my thoughts out loud.'

'Is this a common occurrence?' he queried, dropping

a kiss to her head, his fingers sifting through the silkiness of her hair.

'No. That's what's so confusing. Usually I'm quite in control of my faculties.' She eased back and looked up at him. 'But you…' She swallowed and smiled up at him. 'You make me feel alive.'

'That's a good thing, Stacey.'

'I know, but I'm clearly not used to it. Hence the unusual behaviour.'

'I'll let you in on a little secret,' he said, dipping his head closer to her ear. 'I like that you're a little unusual because that means you're unique.' He kissed her cheek.

She sighed and snuggled closer to him, wrapping her arms around him and resting her head against his chest, loving the words he was saying. Having been one of three all her life, it was refreshing to hear that he thought her unique.

The cool breeze, which he'd been oblivious to while he'd been memorising each and every contour of her face, whipped up around them, with a hint of saltiness from the sea not so far away.

'It's late…or rather early,' he murmured. 'And you need to get home.'

Stacey gasped. 'You're still on shift. How could we have forgotten?'

'If there'd been a problem they would have called.' He patted the cell phone in his trouser pocket. 'Besides, I haven't heard any sirens…except for you.' He chuckled and waggled his eyebrows at her.

'That's a very cheesy line,' she stated, smiling up at him and sighing once more.

'I thought you liked cheesy?'

'I do. I really do. But you're right. I'd best get home.

House calls start in exactly...' She paused and squinted at her watch, unable to see the time. 'Some time soon.'

Pierce's warm laughter washed over her.

'Where are your keys?' he asked, releasing her from his embrace with obvious reluctance.

Stacey picked up her handbag, which had at some point slipped from her shoulder unnoticed to land at their feet. She dug around in the bag and eventually pulled them out.

'Amazing what you can find in a black hole,' he commented as she pressed the button to unlock her car. 'All women's handbags are black holes. I'm convinced of it. Even Nell's—although someone at work bought her an inner purse organiser which she absolutely loves. Still, it only means she can carry even *more* things around with her.'

Stacey chuckled as he opened the car door for her. He leaned forward and pressed another kiss to her lips. 'Drive safe.'

'OK. I hope the rest of your shift is uneventful.'

'You and me both. I'll give you a call when there's news of Gary.'

'Thanks. I'd appreciate that.' She smiled at him.

'And once we've discussed our mutual patient we can discuss exactly how we're going to spend the rest of our weekend—after you've finished the housecalls, of course.'

'We're going to spend our weekend together?'

'Why, yes, Stacey. That's what people do when they date. They spend time together.'

'Date?' The word squeaked from her lips and she stared at him with surprise.

Pierce chuckled once more, and was about to say something when his cell phone rang.

'Go. You're needed,' she told him.

He leaned forward and pressed a firm and secure kiss

to her lips before extracting the phone from his pocket, then he winked at her and started jogging back towards the emergency department as he answered his call.

Stacey sat in the car and started the engine. 'We're *dating*?' She stated the words out loud as she buckled her seatbelt. '*I'm* dating?' She switched on the car's lights. 'Pierce and I are dating.' She tried to state the words with absolute firmness, as though it was the most natural thing in the world. 'This is good,' she remarked as she headed out of the car park and onto the road. 'Moving forward is good.'

Stacey seemed to float through the next week with a large smile plastered to her face. Her sister Molly was delighted at this turn of events.

'You're dating Pierce? *Really* dating? Really putting yourself out there and doing something just for you?' Molly was gobsmacked.

'Yes.'

'And you're not overthinking things?'

'Nope. Just going with the flow.'

'Uh-huh.' Molly didn't sound as though she fully believed her, but she grinned wildly just the same.

When Stacey spoke to Cora over the internet chat line Cora knew something was different even before Molly blurted it out.

'You look really…happy, Stace,' she said, her tone laced with curiosity. 'What's going on over th—?'

'She's dating Pierce!' Molly squealed, jumping up and down and clapping her hands with utter delight.

From there, Stacey was plied with a barrage of questions from Cora—so much so that Cora demanded that the next time they were scheduled to talk Pierce should be there so she could 'meet' him.

'So I'm being served up for Cora's approval, eh?' Pierce said at the end of the week.

They'd just finished a hectic clinic day and were relaxing in the kitchen with a soothing cup of herbal tea. Winifred had just left and the front door to the surgery was locked. It was just the two of them, and although she still felt highly self conscious about being alone with Pierce, Stacey was more than happy to have a bit of time with him.

They'd shared several meals together over the past week, with all of Stacey's siblings and Nell, too. George and Lydia had been demanding, craving adult male attention—especially when he spun them around in the back garden or gave them shoulder rides so they could pretend to be giraffes. And he was incredibly patient with them as they showed him the progress they'd made in training their rabbits in the art of professional rabbit jumping.

Nell enjoyed playing with the rabbits, and was getting good at making Andrew jump over obstacles. She still loved playing games, now openly including the other children, and liked to help in the kitchen when it was time for dinner. As setting the table was one of the things she did every night, she continued to do that job whenever she came to Stacey's house, and George and Lydia were more than happy to hand over the task.

Jasmine was perhaps the one who had surprised them all the most, by insisting on taking over Nell's afternoon routine. 'You and Pierce work late. Nell needs someone right there for her when she gets off the bus. George is nine, so he can stay at home with Lydia—or they can come with me, too.'

'But she has an afternoon snack. You'd have to prepare that too,' Stacey had cautioned.

'Hello?' Jasmine had waved her two hands in front

of Stacey's face. 'What are these? They're hands. I can prepare food with them. I'm not a little kid, you know.'

Stacey had talked this over with Pierce, who'd admitted that it *would* be good for someone to take over meeting Nell from the bus as sometimes he just wasn't able to get away from the clinic on time. And so Jasmine had taken over this responsibility and so far was doing exceptionally well.

Stacey had hoped that helping out Nell would stop Jasmine from being so surly with others, but it hadn't. And she'd stopped acknowledging Pierce's presence altogether.

'She's probably jealous,' Molly had said to her one night as they'd tried to figure out how they could handle the matter. Stacey had disciplined Jasmine, and given her consequences, but Jasmine simply didn't seem to care.

'Jealous? Of what?'

'Of Pierce. She probably thinks you've got less time for her now.'

'Has she said something?'

Molly had shaken her head. 'Not to me. I'm just spitballing ideas here.'

Stacey had closed her eyes and shaken her own head. 'How do we reach her, Molly? What do we need to do to let her know we're on her side?'

Molly's phone had rung and she'd quickly pulled it from her pocket. 'Sorry, Stace. I'm second on call.'

'Sure.'

Stacey had waved Molly's words away and within another ten minutes her sister had gone, heading towards the hospital to assist with the patients involved in multiple car crash on the M1. As this was the main road from Sydney to Newcastle, Stacey had had no idea when Molly might return to finish their conversation. Once again she'd been left holding the ball, needing to make most of the decisions and carry out the majority of discipline.

Stacey wanted to talk to Pierce about it—see if he had any ideas—but it wasn't his problem. Besides, if she did speak to Pierce about her younger sister and Jasmine found out she might stop going to see Nell, not wanting anything to do with Pierce or his sister. That risk was too great, so Stacey was left to try and figure it out on her own.

'Do you think Cora will like me?' Pierce asked, bringing her thoughts back to the present.

Stacey smiled as she placed her arms around his shoulders, delighted that she was allowed to touch him in such a familiar way. 'I have no doubt about it.'

'Excellent. Then that leaves only Jasmine.'

'Jasmine doesn't like *anyone*, Pierce, so don't take it personally. I'm trying not to.'

'She's nice to Nell, for which I am very grateful,' he remarked. He thought for a moment, then said, 'How about a picnic next weekend?'

Stacey considered it. 'The weather's supposed to be nice. King Edward Park?'

'Perfect.' He kissed her a few more times. 'Just like your mouth. Perfect for mine.'

She smiled and sighed into his embrace, more than happy for him to take his time exploring the contours of her 'perfect' mouth. Pierce was always saying such lovely things to her—telling her she had luscious hair and that he loved running his fingers through it, or that she was beautiful, precious and deserved to be loved not only for the pureness of her heart but also because of the sadness in her eyes.

'I'm not sad,' she'd replied after Pierce had whispered

the compliment near her ear the other evening when he'd been kissing her goodnight.

Pierce had brushed her loose hair behind her ears and kissed both of her cheeks. 'I'm getting to know you better, Stacey and I can't believe the weight you have to carry on those slim shoulders of yours.'

He'd placed his large warm hands onto her shoulders as he'd spoken, massaging gently, releasing endorphins that had made her want to melt into his arms for ever and never leave.

'I care about you, Stacey. More and more every day. But the sadness which you've buried deep down inside is dangerous.'

'Dangerous?' She'd tried to laugh off his words, but the sound had been hollow even to her own ears.

'If we're not careful sadness can consume us.'

'You sound as though you know what you're talking about.' She'd eased back from his massaging hands and he'd instantly stopped the motion.

'I do.'

'Grief over your parents' loss?'

'Yes. The death of a loved one can leave such a wide and gaping chasm, and if we're not careful—if we don't take the time to heal the wound from the inside out but just keep changing the dressing and applying a new bandage to the wound—then infection can set in.'

He'd brushed the back of his fingers across her cheek before pulling her closer into his arms. They'd stood there for a while, with Stacey revelling in the feel of his arms wound tightly around her, before he'd finally spoken again.

'I understand the brokenness, the pain, the desolation that grief can bring, whatever the circumstances which have caused it. Along with all of these comes loneliness, and whilst I know you have a very supportive family, and you seem more than willing and able to shoulder the lion's share of that responsibility, at times you seem so lonely.'

'Lonely?' She'd eased back slightly and looked up at him. 'I've never been alone in my life. I'm one of three. I wasn't even alone in the womb! And let's not forget I have five siblings.'

'And yet sometimes…' He'd exhaled slowly, his words filled with understanding. 'You're so lonely. I just wanted you to know that I've been there, too.' He'd bent his head and brushed his lips across hers. 'The weight of your world is not yours alone to carry. Please let me help you in any way I can.'

His words had held promise, his touch had held promise, even the taste of his lips on hers had held promise…so why was she having such a difficult time letting go of the chains that bound her? Had she been carrying the responsibility for her family for far longer than she'd realised?

When her father had married Letisha, when they'd had Jasmine, hadn't it been Stacey who had helped the most, wanting to do everything she could to make things easier for her stepmother? Cora and Molly had been delighted with their new sibling, and indeed, when George and Lydia had rounded out their family, the triplets had loved having younger sisters and a brother to entertain. But whenever they'd been asked to babysit it had been Stacey who had taken charge.

Have I always done this? she asked herself later that night. Now that he'd pointed out the wound Stacey had thought already healed, especially since returning to Newcastle to connect to her roots, she was more than aware of the way both Molly and Cora really did leave it up to her to call the shots.

She wanted to talk to Molly about it, but her poor sister

had been rostered on with such long shifts that as soon as she arrived home she'd quickly eat something before collapsing into such a deep sleep Stacey hadn't the heart to wake her.

She loved her siblings—all of them—and would do anything for any of them. They'd do the same for her... wouldn't they?

She tried not to fixate on the question as she went about her daily life, happy that George and Lydia were settling into school but with increasing concern for Jasmine's declining behaviour.

Indeed, when she informed everyone they would be having a picnic in the park the following weekend they'd all been excited except for Jasmine. Even the information that Nell was looking forward to seeing her there hadn't changed Jasmine's attitude.

'I have no idea what to do,' Stacey confessed to Cora during one of their internet chats. 'She really seems to hate me.'

'That's because you're the disciplinarian.'

'How did I get *that* job?'

Cora laughed. 'I don't know. I guess as you're the oldest triplet we've always just naturally looked up to you. At school whenever there was a problem you always came up with a solution. Some people are born leaders, Stace, and you're one of them. Just look at how you've held us all together over the past eighteen months. And when you decided to buy Dad's old practice Molly and I gave our blessing because we trust your judgement. We knew you would have figured all the angles, weighed up the pros and cons.'

'And yet I've hurt Jasmine the most by uprooting her from her friends.'

'The practice would have closed down if you hadn't

bought it when you did. It's necessary for that community to have a functioning, working medical practice and you've put the needs of the many ahead of the needs of a fourteen-year-old girl who will one day forgive you.'

'Will she?'

'Did you forgive Dad when he followed his dreams and took us all to Perth?'

'Yes, but—'

'You followed your dreams, Stacey. You did what you knew was right deep down in your heart. Jasmine isn't collateral damage. Far from it. Just look at how she's helping more with George and Lydia, how she's helping Pierce's sister. Those are *good* things.'

Stacey sighed. 'I guess.'

'You've held us all together for so long—plus you've had your own personal emotional dramas to contend with. And although Molly and I are always there for you—and we know you know this—you still need those moments of solitude.'

'But I don't *want* solitude.'

'Don't you?' Cora was surprised. 'I always thought that sometimes, with the three of us living in each other's pockets all our lives, you just needed some space to breathe.'

'Do you?'

Cora thought on this for a moment. 'I think I find my solitude in adventure.' She spread her arms wide, indicating the military-style truck behind her. 'Just to speak to you like this I have to borrow a truck, drive an hour through rough, dirty tracks that any ordinary four-wheel drive would get stuck in, and then head to the top of a mountain where the satellite transmission is strongest.'

'And I appreciate every time you've done this. I know it must cut into your valuable work there in Tarparnii.'

'But you see, Stace, that's my point. I *like* going four-wheel driving—just like Molly loves dancing and going on clown patrol and joining in with every social activity any hospital runs. That's *her* solitude. Yours is to contemplate the meaning of life.' Cora smiled at her sister. 'And I know Jazzy's causing you concern, but perhaps she's just trying to find her own place—her thing she likes the most.'

'Her solitude?'

'Her happy place,' Cora offered.

Stacey sighed. 'I hope she finds it soon.'

'What about you?'

'What *about* me?'

'Have you found *your* happy place?'

'What do you mean?'

'You're different, Stace.'

'I am?'

'Yes.' Cora threw her arms in the air. 'Can't you see it? Feel it?'

'Feel…what?'

'Pierce! Stacey, I'm talking about *Pierce*. Even over the internet chat I could see he was dreamy. You've picked a winner there.'

Stacey's smile widened as she tucked her hair behind her ear. 'Oh, Cora. He makes me feel so…tingly and shiny and…and…'

'Happy?'

'Yes. That's why I guess I've been feeling guilty about Jasmine—because for the first time in a long time I'm… happy.'

'Don't feel guilty, Stace. Accept it. Draw strength from the way Pierce makes you feel. You deserve a world of happiness—especially after you-know-who.'

'It's OK,' Stacey replied. 'You can say his name now,

because with the way Pierce makes me feel I've realised that whatever it was I had with Robert it certainly wasn't love.'

'Wait. wait, wait!' Cora clasped her hands together and stared at her sister. 'What are you saying? Are you saying that you're *in love* with Pierce?'

Stacey's smile was bright and wide and filled with delight. 'I...I...think so.'

Cora squealed with excitement. 'Oh, Stace, really? This is wonderful, great—and a whole heap of other awesome adjectives.'

Stacey laughed, loving her sister and wishing she was there in person so they could hug.

'Say it again,' Cora demanded, clapping her hands.

'I think I might be in love with Pierce Brolin,' Stacey stated, and even as she said the words out loud she knew that it was far more absolute than she was willing to admit even to her sister.

She didn't just *think* she was in love with Pierce. She *knew* it with all her heart... But for now, although she adored her sisters and the close bond they shared, she needed to keep that intimate piece of information to herself.

CHAPTER EIGHT

'I SEE YOU and Stacey are spending a bit more time together,' Mike said as he tossed some poker chips into the middle of the table. Edna had already lost all her chips and gone off to make them a cup of tea.

'Yes.' Pierce had been wondering when Mike might bring up the topic of Stacey. 'I see your chips and I raise you.'

Their friendly poker games had been going on throughout Mike's recovery which, Pierce had to admit, was good. Mike was adhering to the diet his cardiologist had recommended and was also looking forward to the rabbit jumping competition George and Lydia were planning to attend.

Mike considered his cards, then tossed the same amount of chips into the centre of the table. 'Call. What have you got?'

For a moment Pierce wasn't sure whether Mike was talking about the cards or about the fact that he'd been spending more time with Stacey. Mike was very protective of all the Wilton children, taking on the role of family patriarch with pride.

'I have got a full house,' Pierce remarked, placing his cards on the table.

Mike chuckled and didn't cough once, which Pierce was pleased to note.

'That you do, boy. If you're serious about Stacey there'll definitely be a full house. Are you up to taking on that level of responsibility again? Raising siblings?' Mike placed one hand over the pile of chips in the centre of the table.

Pierce had thought about it—especially as he was spending more and more time not only with Stacey but with the rest of her siblings. She was a package deal. He couldn't have one without the other. He was the same. He would always have Nell in his life. But she was now at the stage where one of her housemates, Samantha, had moved in, and the event they'd meticulously planned and structured for many years could now finally take place: Nell living independently.

But Stacey…beautiful, wonderful Stacey. She responded to his kisses as though she'd never been kissed before, as though she'd never felt this way before, and, he'd had to admit he felt a connection with Stacey that he hadn't felt with any other woman before.

'Well?' Mike brought Pierce's thoughts back to the present.

Pierce looked down at the cards neatly laid in a row. Full house. Was he ready?

'I wanted to find out whether this thing between Stacey and myself was something special—whether it was worth pursing.'

'And is it?'

Pierce reached out, lifted Mike's hand from the pile and pulled all the chips towards him. 'Yes.'

Mike gaped. 'But what about the job? The one they're constantly bugging you to come over for?'

Pierce shrugged. 'Some dreams aren't meant to come true. I learned that lesson a long time ago.'

'Hmm…' Mike looked at his friend. 'I hope you're right.'

Pierce nodded. 'Stacey's worth it.'

'Your feelings are that strong?'

He thought about Mike's question for a moment. *Were* they that strong? *Was* Stacey worth sacrificing his main chance to head over to Yale and lead a team of researchers? He'd been wanting to do that for so long now, but Nell had always come first and there had been no way he was going to choose a job over his most beloved sister. Now Nell was settled and he was free to go, to follow his dream—the one he'd been aiming towards for such a very long time.

And yet there was the way Stacey was able to see into his heart, to understand everything he'd already sacrificed for the love of a sibling, and the way she felt in his arms—as though he'd finally found *his* home, the place where *he* belonged… Were his feelings strong enough that he would never have regrets at turning down the only job he'd ever really wanted?

Pierce's answer was a firm nod in the affirmative, yet for some reason he couldn't bring himself to speak the word *yes* out loud once more. But he was certain he was falling in love with Stacey, and he was prepared to love and accept not only her but the rest of her family, just as she loved and accepted Nell.

'I hope you're right, boy,' Mike remarked as he shuffled the deck of cards. 'Ready for another hand?'

Pierce eyed his huge pile of chips, then looked at Mike and smiled. 'Sure. What have I got to lose?'

Mike's answer was a wise old chuckle. 'If you're not careful? Everything.'

* * *

The following Saturday the sun was shining brightly, making the early October day perfect for a picnic in the park. Unfortunately, by the time they all arrived at King Edward Park, it had become clear that several other people had had the same idea, and all the council-provided barbecues were already in use.

'We'll have to queue for the barbecue,' joked Samantha, Nell's new housemate, as they spread picnic blankets beneath a large shady gum tree. Nell was already getting excited and pulling a Frisbee out of the bag she'd brought with her.

'Come on, Jasmine,' she ordered, reaching for Jasmine's hand and tugging the surly teenager along. 'Come and play Frisbee with me.'

Jasmine did as she was bid, not looking at anyone but not grumbling about it either.

'Jasmine's still not happy?' Pierce asked, placing a supportive arm around Stacey's shoulders.

'Cora says she's searching for her happy place.'

'Perhaps Cora's right. I think everyone searches for their happy place.'

They stood there for a moment, watching Jasmine let Nell boss her around. Stacey wondered whether there was something more to Pierce's words. Had he found *his* happy place? Was he happy? With her?

'She's incredibly good with Nell,' he continued, and Stacey detected no unhappiness in his voice so allowed herself to relax into his embrace.

He put his other arm around her, enfolding her against him. She closed her eyes, allowing herself to breathe in his strength, to breathe in the feel of his supporting arms around her. She'd never understood before how others could draw strength just from receiving a hug from someone else—not until she'd met Pierce. But when he hugged her like this she *did* draw strength from him, and for the first time since they'd moved to Newcastle she saw a glimmer of hope that everything would turn out all right.

'Are you two going to cuddle and kiss *all* day long?' Lydia demanded, wrapping her arms around Stacey's waist.

Pierce instantly broke the contact and bent to scoop Lydia up, then placed his free arm over Stacey's shoulder, bringing Lydia into their hug.

'What's wrong with that?' Pierce asked as he kissed Lydia's cheek. The little girl wrapped her arms about his neck and snuggled into him.

'You smell nice,' she told him.

Pierce sniffed her hair. 'So do you.'

Lydia giggled. 'That's 'cause I've got Stacey's perfume on.'

'Ah…is that what it is?' Pierce sniffed Stacey, then Lydia, and nodded his head. 'Yep. Two gorgeous girls… perfectly ripe for…*tickling*!'

And with that he tickled Stacey's neck before doing the same to Lydia. The little girl let forth a peal of laughter and Stacey chuckled, her heart delighting at the way Pierce seemed to fit so perfectly with her family.

Although Molly had been called to an emergency a few hours ago she had hopes of joining them later. But with almost all of the people she loved the most nearby Stacey really did feel as though *this* was her happy place. *Her* family—complete with Nell and Pierce.

It was as though she hadn't realised there were pieces of her life missing—not until she'd met this man and his sweet sister. She was still constantly delighting in the sensations and emotions spending time with Pierce evoked, but in the back of her mind there were questions. Questions about what the future might hold and where this relationship was going. About what Pierce really wanted from his life. Was he willing to take on her ready-made family? Or did the thought put him off, as it had Robert?

Pierce had told her about the research team—the ones he wrote his articles for. And he'd told her they'd offered him a job—the same job—several times over. Now that Nell was settled and beginning to live her life of independence was Pierce going to head overseas? To lead the team of researchers? Or did he plan to stay here?

The turmoil of her thoughts kept her awake at night. Her life had been affected by indecision, questions and trauma, and it had made her the sort of person who needed to know where she was going, to map out a path of what the future might hold. If she could deal in absolutes then so much the better, but she had also had to learn how to adapt when life threw her curve balls.

'I *said*…' George remarked, tapping her on the arm. 'When are we going to cook? I'm hungry.'

Stacey snapped out of her reverie and looked at her brother. 'Your default setting is "I'm hungry".' She ruffled his hair and smiled. 'There are bananas and apples in the picnic basket. Have one of those to tide you over.'

She glanced at the rectangular brick barbecues provided by the council for everyone to use. All of them were still being used. She glanced over to where a new family was arriving at the park, looking around to stake out their piece of shady grass. The dad carried a portable barbecue and a gas bottle.

'We should have brought our own barbecue, too,' George grumbled, pointing to the family who'd thought ahead.

'Possibly,' Pierce agreed, 'but the point of coming to the park isn't just to eat a barbecued sausage, George.'

'It isn't?'

Pierce laughed. 'Come on. I think there's a football in the bag. Let's go kick it around.'

'Can I come, too?' Lydia asked.

'Yeah, Lydia's really good at football,' George agreed, his grumbling stomach momentarily forgotten as he raced over to the bag Pierce had pointed to. Pierce released a squirming Lydia from his arms and she ran off after her brother.

'They really don't stand still at that age, do they?' Pierce commented as he leaned over and pressed a contented kiss to Stacey's waiting lips.

'You're thirty-six and *you* don't stand still,' she pointed out with a chuckle.

'You're probably right,' he agreed, kissing her again before winking and jogging off to join George and Lydia on a free patch of grass.

Stacey sat down on the blanket next to Samantha, who was more than happy to sit quietly and absorb the atmosphere. Stacey watched as the family who'd brought their own barbecue hooked up the gas cylinder and began to cook their food. A few of the other barbecues were now being vacated, but at the moment she was in no hurry to rush over there and claim one. Pierce was right. Today wasn't just about barbecuing food but about spending time together, in the sunshine, enjoying each other's company.

She slipped on her sunglasses, watching as Jasmine threw the Frisbee at Nell, who didn't manage to catch it and had to run after it. Jasmine laughed and the sound washed over Stacey like manna from heaven. For this moment in time her little sister was happy. Perhaps that was enough for now.

Stacey closed her eyes, filled with a quiet contentment.

A loud scream jolted her eyes open and she pulled off her sunglasses, her heart pounding wildly.

'What?' She blinked a few times and in the next instant a loud whooshing noise seemed to surround the area, shaking every fibre of her being.

'Stacey!' She heard her name being called and scrambled to her feet. Samantha, too, was on her feet, staring, aghast, at what was happening. Panic seemed to engulf the entire park, with some people screaming, others running, and some, like her, standing and staring, trying to take everything in at a glance.

'What do I do? What do I do?' Samantha's high-functioning Asperger's was starting to show itself.

Stacey's mind clicked into doctor mode and she handed Samantha a set of car keys. 'Go to my car and get the big emergency bag from the boot. It's a big red backpack with a white cross on it.'

'OK. OK.' Glad of something to do, Samantha started to focus, and she quickly took the keys from Stacey and did as she was asked.

Stacey stood on the picnic rug and gazed out at the scene. The world seemed to pause as she took in her surroundings, her quick mind piecing together exactly what had happened.

Pierce, Lydia and George were all standing together. Pierce had grabbed their hands, ready to lead them from any danger. Jasmine was standing further away, her hands covering her open mouth, her eyes staring off into the distance in complete shock.

Stacey followed the line of Jasmine's gaze, her own eyes opening wide as she realised why her sister looked so distraught. Nell lay sprawled on the ground, the Frisbee nearby. Nell wasn't moving.

All of this registered in Stacey's mind within one glance.

The next thing to register was the cloud of black smoke filling the air, caused by a flaming ball of gas. The man and woman who had been cooking on the portable barbecue had been thrown to the ground as well, the man writhing and yelling in pain.

'Gas fire!'

Pierce's words broke through Stacey's haze, speeding her thoughts back to normal. He was walking quickly towards her, dodging people as they ran past him. Panic was beginning to grip the entire park. He was still holding onto George and Lydia's hands.

'There must have been a damaged regulator or hose and a fat fire has ignited it,' he called to her.

When they reached the rug George wrapped his arms around Stacey's waist and Lydia just stood and stared. Stacey pointed to where Nell lay on the ground.

'Pierce! Look!'

She watched as he turned, his expression changing from one of controlled concern to one of complete despair as he took in the vision of his beloved little sister lying still on the grass.

'Go!' she urged when he stood still for a split second, his world clearly falling apart. 'Check her. I'll bring the medical kit over.'

'Uh…' Pierce nodded as though his mind was unable to compute which action he should take next. 'Yeah…yeah.' With that he all but sprinted over to where his sister lay.

Stacey turned her attention to her siblings. 'George, Lydia.' She bent down to hug them both, her words fast and stern. 'I need you to stay right here. *Right here.*' She pointed to their rug, which was on the opposite side of the park from where the explosion had occurred.

People were beginning to gather their belongings and leave, others were on their cellphones, hopefully calling the emergency services, others were taking photographs. There was a hive of activity, but the first thing Stacey had to do was to make sure her brother and sister were out of harm's way. Their safety was paramount.

'Wait for Samantha to get back from the car and then do exactly as she says.'

'Yes, Stacey,' they both answered, their little eyes wide with fear.

People were everywhere, and when Samantha came rushing back with the large emergency kit, Stacey nodded her thanks.

'Can you stay with the kids, please?'

Before Samantha could answer, Stacey took the backpack and raced over towards the man who was still screaming, writhing around on the grass. She could smell burning clothes and flesh. Whilst only seconds had passed since the explosion it felt a lot longer, with her mind trying to process too many things at once. For now, though, Pierce was attending to Nell, and although Stacey wanted nothing more than to check Nell herself, she had to prioritise.

The initial fireball which had scared them all was still burning, but thankfully the man hadn't put the portable barbecue beneath any trees, so although it was extremely hot the flames were now shooting upwards rather than billowing outwards. The man had stopped rolling and she realised he was no longer on fire, but his body might be going into shock or worse.

She knelt down beside him, placing the emergency kit nearby. She called to her patient but received no response. She pressed two fingers to his radial pulse, relieved when she felt it—faint, but there. She was fairly sure he hadn't sustained any spinal damage, especially with the way he'd been rolling on the grass before losing consciousness. She opened her kit and quickly pulled on some gloves before finding a soft neck brace to help secure the man's spine, knowing that paramedics would replace it with a more rigid one. She called to the man again, telling him what she was doing, but he remained unconscious.

'Are you a medic?' she heard a woman ask.

'Yes.' Stacey glanced up for a moment.

'Good. I'm a volunteer firefighter.'

'Excellent.' Stacey inclined her head towards the blaze. 'You OK to deal with that?'

'My friends and I are. All the emergency services have been called. My friend's just getting an extinguisher from my car.'

'Great. Thanks.'

True to her word, the firefighter and her friends concentrated on dealing with the blaze, keeping it contained. Less than five minutes had passed since the initial eruption, and even as she concentrated on her patient Stacey could also hear several other people taking charge, marshalling families together and generally controlling the situation. It was good, because it made it far easier for her to concentrate.

Nell wasn't lying too far away and she could hear Pierce speaking to her and Nell talking back. Stacey breathed an inward sigh of relief to know that Nell was OK.

'You're all right,' she heard Pierce say. 'You've just hurt your ankle, so I want you to stay as still as possible. I'm going to get some bandages from Stacey's medical kit and take care of it.'

Stacey glanced over and saw Pierce kiss his sister's forehead before looking over his shoulder at her. Their gazes held for a brief second and she could see the relief in his eyes. His sister was going to be all right.

Stacey was also aware of Jasmine in the background behind Pierce. She was still standing in the same spot, hands still across her mouth, as though she were unable to move or think, horror reflected in her eyes. Stacey wanted nothing more than to put her arms around her, to tell her that everything would be OK, to comfort her when she needed it most, but instead Stacey called again to her patient, still receiving no response.

'Trev? Trev?' A woman crawled along the grass, coming towards Stacey. 'Trev! Get away from him!' she demanded, her words slurred, her eyes narrowed and filled with all the protectiveness of a possessive lioness.

'I'm a doctor,' Stacey told her. 'His name is Trev?'

'Yes.' The woman's attitude changed to one of hope as she came closer, reaching out to touch his head. 'What's wrong with him? Why isn't he moving?'

'I want to find out, but I need you to stay back. Give him some room.' Stacey kept her tone firm and direct. She mentally ran through what needed to happen next: do Trev's obs and assess the severity of his burns.

Thankfully, due to the volunteer firefighters, the blaze was now almost under control.

As she looked down at Trev, Stacey knew she was going to need further assistance. 'Pierce. I need you,' she called, glancing over at him before checking Trev's airway was clear.

'Acknowledged. I've just finished Nell's bandage.' Pierce wrapped Nell in a big hug and whispered something in her ear before he looked over and called to Jasmine, who was still rooted to the spot, unable to move. 'Jasmine? Can you come and help Nell, please?'

Jasmine shook her head from side to side before turning and running away.

'Jasmine! *Jasmine!*' he called, but the teenager wasn't listening. Pierce looked across at Stacey, unsure what to do.

Stacey stared wide-eyed at her sister's retreating back. There was nothing she could do. She couldn't go after Jasmine, which was her initial instinct. She needed to stay with her patient. She just had to trust that Jasmine's common sense would kick in at some point and she wouldn't stray too far from where they all were.

'I'll have to deal with her later.' The words were like dust in her mouth and her heart broke that she couldn't be there for Jasmine when she needed her most. 'Get Nell over to the rug with the others. Samantha, George and Lydia can look after her,' Stacey called, knowing she needed to focus completely on Trev rather than having her attention diverted by other personal matters.

'Right.' Pierce stood and scooped Nell up into his arms, carrying her over to the rug, where George and Lydia instantly rallied around her. Poor Samantha was doing her best to try and marshal some of the other children together—especially the two boys who had been kicking the football around with Pierce and were now quite distraught about their father—the man called Trev.

'I want to see my mum!' one of them yelled.

'What's wrong with my dad?' the other one questioned.

Stacey closed her eyes for a split second, focusing her thoughts on Trev and Trev alone. When she opened her eyes Pierce was coming round to Trev's other side.

'Status?' He pulled on a pair of gloves and reached for the stethoscope.

'Airway clear. Burns to hands, arms, both legs, and minor damage to the face. No response to calls. Trev?'

she called again as she reached into the emergency medical kit to find a bag of saline and a package of IV tubing. 'We'll replenish fluids to avoid the possible complication of shock.'

'I love that you have such a well-stocked emergency kit,' Pierce commented as he unhooked the stethoscope. 'Heart-rate is mildly tachy. Pain meds?'

'Suggest ten milligrams of IV morphine followed by methoxyflurane.' Stacey's hands were busy, opening the packets of tubing and then looking for the best place to insert the line.

'Agreed. Allergies?'

Stacey looked over to where Trev's wife was sitting, rocking back and forth. Someone had had the presence of mind to wrap a blanket around her. 'Is Trev allergic to anything?' Stacey asked.

'Left arm isn't as badly damaged as the right arm,' Pierce commented as he assisted Stacey with setting up the drip.

She looked over to where the volunteer firefighter was standing back. The fire situation was now under control, the gas in the bottle having almost expired.

'Can you help?' Stacey called the woman over, indicating the saline bag, which would need to be held.

The woman nodded and made her way to Stacey, pleased to be of further assistance.

'Is Trev allergic to anything?' Pierce asked Trev's wife the question again, sharing a brief concerned look with Stacey.

The woman was clearly shocked at what had happened but hopefully wouldn't go into shock completely. The right side of her face was starting to droop, which might indicate nerve damage. First, though, they needed to stabilise Trev as best they could.

'Uh… Um…allergies? Um…I don't know. Is he going to be all right?'

'Does he take any regular medication? Has he had any alcohol today?'

'He's had two light beers and…uh…he takes…um… fish oil tablets. The doctor said his cholesterol is high.'

'Has he had any operations? Been hospitalised?' Pierce asked.

'No. No. He…uh…no.'

Stacey nodded and pulled out a pre-drawn syringe labelled 'morphine'. 'Check ten milligrams,' she stated.

'Check,' Pierce replied, and as soon as the saline drip was working Stacey administered the medication while Pierce told the still unconscious Trev what they were doing.

'Is that going to help him?' his wife wanted to know, watching everything they did with eyes as wide as saucers.

'It's going to relieve his pain,' Stacey offered, before they set to work on carefully bandaging the worst of Trev's leg wounds. She was ecstatic when the faint sounds of sirens could be heard in the distance. Whether police, fire brigade or ambulance, she didn't care—at least help was on the way.

Pierce took Trev's pulse again. 'A definite improvement.'

'And just in time to be transferred to an ambulance. Trev, help is here,' she told him as Pierce continued to perform neurological observations.

Stacey had just finished applying the last bandage when the paramedics came racing over. Pierce gave them a debrief while Stacey pulled off one set of gloves and pulled on another, moving quickly over to where Trev's wife sat, still staring at her husband.

'What's your name?' Stacey asked as she checked the side of the woman's face.

'Rowena.'

The word was barely a whisper, and the side of her mouth was drooping down. Stacey reached for a penlight torch and checked the woman's pupils, relieved when both responded to light.

'What are they doing to Trev?' Rowena asked, trying to look around Stacey, who was blocking her view.

'They're transferring him to a stretcher so they can get him into the ambulance. Just sit still for me a moment, Rowena.' Stacey spoke calmly but with a firmness that made Rowena look at her. Stacey pressed gloved fingers gently to Rowena's face, looking carefully.

'What is it? What's wrong?' she asked.

Stacey lifted the blanket off Rowena's shoulders and checked her right arm and side, realising there were several cuts and abrasions down the left side of Rowena's body. 'Rowena? What happened when the fire started? Do you remember?'

'Uh…' She looked at Stacey with scared eyes. 'What is it? Just tell me.'

'The left side of your face is drooping. That's why you're slurring your words.'

'I'm slurring?'

Rowena immediately went to lift a hand to touch her face, but Stacey stilled her arm and Rowena winced. Stacey immediately felt her ribs, gently checking to see if any of them were broken.

'Does it hurt when you breathe in?'

Rowena tried for a deep breath and immediately winced in pain. 'What *is* it? What's *wrong* with me?' The paramedics were securing Trev to the stretcher and

Rowena's gaze followed her husband's supine form. 'Oh, why did this happen? *Why?*'

'Can you remember what did happen?' Stacey prompted again.

'I heard Trev yelling and I looked over and it was as though he was on fire—but only for a moment, and then he just dropped and…and…started rolling and yelling and…and…he was moving at an odd angle and it was all blurry and then I crawled over and you told me to get back.'

'Do you remember falling down?'

Stacey also thought back to that moment when the world around her had seemed to slow down. Where had Rowena been? Stacey looked over to where two folding chairs were still on the ground, unpacked. They were the new kind of folding chair, with firm metal rods for stabilisation. Had Rowena landed on the folded-up chairs? Had she stumbled or been thrown backwards slightly, and ended up breaking a rib and possibly damaging a nerve in her face? Stacey could definitely remember seeing her lying down, so the scenario wasn't completely absurd.

Trev was now securely strapped to the stretcher, his neck in a firm neck brace, an IV pole holding the saline drip up high, releasing life-giving fluid to a patient who still hadn't regained consciousness.

'Where are they taking him? I want to go with him,' Rowena stated.

'I need to finish checking you over,' Stacey told her as she took Rowena's pulse, knowing the woman's elevated reading might well be due to the fact that she was highly concerned about her husband.

'But I can walk. I can move. I can stand.' As though to prove it, Rowena tried to get to her feet but instantly wobbled.

Stacey put out a hand to steady her. 'Perhaps just stay still for a moment and let us get organised.' Stacey beckoned to one of the paramedics, who instantly came over, his own emergency medical kit on his back. 'This is Rowena,' she told the paramedic, whose green jumpsuit declared his surname was Wantanebe. 'Suspected L3 L4 fracture, possible damaged facial nerve. Neck brace, Penthrane green whistle, then stabilise and stretcher.'

'Yes, Doctor.'

'Pass me a stethoscope, please?' She held out her hand and had the instrument immediately provided for her.

She was listening to Rowena's breathing when Pierce came over, Trev now being secure in the ambulance.

'How are things going?' he asked as he knelt down beside Stacey, the stethoscope from her own kit still slung around his neck.

'Breathing is a little raspy on the left due to possible rib fracture.'

'How's my Trev?' Rowena asked anxiously.

Pierce smiled warmly at her. 'I'm pleased to announce he regained consciousness a moment after we'd secured him in the ambulance.'

This news definitely seemed to calm Rowena down. 'That's good, right? That's good, yeah?'

'It *is* good news,' Pierce confirmed as he pulled on a fresh pair of gloves and reached for a bandage. 'Let's get you stabilised and into the other ambulance. Is there someone who can come and be with your boys?' he asked.

It was only then that Rowena even seemed to remember her children, and Stacey was thankful the paramedic had already secured a neck brace in place, otherwise Rowena might have done some damage with the way she tried to whip her head around.

'Jeremiah and Lucas? Where are they? Oh, how could I have forgotten them?'

'They're fine.' Stacey needed to calm Rowena immediately. 'Our friend Samantha is looking after them. Just over there. On the rug under the big eucalyptus.'

She pointed to where Samantha seemed to be surrounded by several children, including Rowena's boys, George and Lydia, Nell, and thankfully Jasmine, too. Stacey wasn't sure when her sister had returned to the rug but she was relieved to see her there.

'They're all right? They didn't get hurt?'

'They're both fine. Do you want them to come in the ambulance with you?'

'Yes, and I'll…I'll call my neighbour to come and get them from the hospital.'

'That sounds like a wonderful plan,' Pierce told her, his deep voice sounding like a comfortable blanket.

Rowena seemed more capable of relaxing now, and even managed a small lopsided smile in his direction. What was it about this man that seemed to cause women to relax and melt? Was it the sound of his rich baritone? Was it the comfort in his gaze? Was it the tug of his lips into a reassuring smile?

As they managed to settle Rowena onto a stretcher and get her and her boys installed in the ambulance Stacey felt the beginnings of fatigue starting to set in.

'You're not coming with us?' Rowena asked, looking at Stacey from the stretcher.

'We'll meet you at the hospital,' Stacey consoled her. 'You're in good hands.' With a warm smile, she waited while Pierce closed the rear doors of the ambulance, then stepped away from the road, able finally to turn her attention to her own situation.

Why had Jasmine been so scared? Was Nell really

OK? Were George and Lydia traumatised? Had Samantha coped all right?

She turned around, expecting to find Pierce next to her, but instead he was already heading over to where Nell was sitting on the picnic rug, still looking completely dazed. He carried her emergency kit on his back and the instant he reached Nell's side he knelt down and opened the bag.

'Let's take a closer look at your ankle,' he told her, brushing some hair from his sister's eyes.

'What happened? Why was there a fire?'

'She's been asking the same questions over and over,' Samantha volunteered as Stacey knelt down next to Pierce.

'She does that when she's upset. Even if you give her the answer it's too much for her to process.' Pierce gave his sister a hug. 'It's OK, Nell. Pierce is here. Pierce will look after you.'

'Always?' Nell's voice was soft, small and very little. It was as though the child within her was all that was available, and it showed just how vulnerable Nell really was when her world was unbalanced from its axis.

Stacey watched as Pierce smiled brightly at his sister. 'Always.'

She understood the bond between brother and sister and she was incredibly proud to see it. He was an honourable man who understood the importance of family. As she watched him tenderly review Nell's ankle, re-bandaging it and then scooping her up and carrying her to his car, Stacey felt her heart fill with a quiet, unassuming love. She wanted this man in her life. No. She *needed* Pierce in her life. She loved him with all her heart and she never wanted him to leave her.

CHAPTER NINE

AT THE HOSPITAL they met up with the burns registrar, who was able to give them an update on Trev.

'They're taking him to Theatre now, to debride and clean his wounds as best as possible, but the full extent of his injuries won't really be known for a few more days.'

Pierce nodded. 'Thanks for the information. We'll let his wife know.'

'Is Nell back from Radiology?' Stacey asked as they walked out of the Emergency Surgical Suite back towards the Emergency Department.

'No. The orthopaedic registrar told me they'd page me when she was done.'

His walk was brisk, but his shoulders seemed to be drawn further back than before and there was a constant furrow to his brow. They headed to the cranio-facial unit, where Rowena had been taken after admission. Thankfully her neighbour had come and collected her boys, so at least she didn't have to worry too much about them and could concentrate on what was happening to her.

'What about *your* children?' Rowena asked Stacey and Pierce after they'd passed on the news about Trev's condition.

'Sorry?' Stacey frowned, looking at the other woman blankly.

'Well, it must be difficult for the two of you to look after your own children when both of you end up here at the hospital all the time.'

'Oh. Those children.' Stacey nodded, belatedly realising what Rowena was talking about.

Before she could say another word, Pierce indicated the physical space existing between himself and Stacey.

'We're not married and those aren't our children,' he stated matter-of-factly.

Stacey's brow was once more creased in a frown, but this time it was because she didn't understand his tone. Yes, what he'd said was accurate and true—but it had been the *way* he'd said it…as though there was no possibility of the two of them ever being anything more than they were right now… Which was what? Boyfriend and girlfriend? Forever dating but never moving forward?

She remembered the first day she'd met Pierce. When she'd asked him if he was married, his answer had been an emphatic no. Was that how he felt? Did he still think like that? That matrimony wasn't for him?

She pushed the thoughts aside, knowing she was probably overthinking things again. And besides, Pierce was no doubt still very worried about Nell. She quickly informed Rowena that the children they'd been with at the park were her siblings, and that their friend Samantha had taken them home. There was no need to add that Molly had been at home and had called Stacey to say that both George and Lydia were safe with her. Jasmine, however, had refused to leave Nell's side.

'Oh.' Rowena settled back onto the pillows and closed her eyes. 'That makes sense, I guess. Still, you two make a good couple.' And then she closed her eyes, the medication she'd been given causing her to doze off.

Pierce's pager sounded, and when he'd checked the number he stated, 'It's Radiology. Nell's X-rays are ready.'

Stacey nodded and together they spoke with the craniofacial registrar before heading back to Radiology. As they headed down one of the hospital's long corridors she looked at him with concern.

'Pierce?'

'Hmm?'

He didn't slow his pace, and when Stacey put her hand on his arm, indicating he should slow down for a moment, he glanced over at her with a hint of impatience.

'Pierce, what's wrong?' When he simply stared at her, looking at her as though she'd just grown an extra head, she tried again. 'Are you worried about Nell?'

'When am I *not* worried about Nell?' The words were wrenched from him, and he turned and started walking again. 'Even when Mum and Dad were alive I was always there for Nell. *Always*.'

'And that's what makes you such a good brother,' she added as she caught up with him.

Pierce exhaled slowly, adjusting his pace a little so he wasn't hurtling along the corridor like an out-of-control freight train. 'At the end of the day it's all about family.'

'And Nell's OK. Yes, she's hurt her ankle, and that's going to upset her routine, but she'll adjust. You'll help her. We all will.'

'I know.' Pierce raked a hand through his hair, then stopped, looking down at Stacey. 'You're right, of course. The main point is that she's fine. No point in thinking what might have been, or how much worse the situation could have—' He stopped and shook his head. 'If a broken or—fingers crossed—badly sprained ankle is the worst thing that happens to her today, I'll take that.'

Stacey put her hands on his shoulders, wanting to reassure him, to help him. 'And you're not alone. You have me and Molly, and Jasmine and George and Lydia to help, and no doubt Samantha's going to be there to support Nell, too.'

Pierce nodded and drew her into his arms, but before he did Stacey looked into his eyes and saw such doubt as she'd never seen in him before. Doubt? Was he still doubting that Nell's ankle was only sprained? Did he think it was indeed broken? Or was there something else going on in his head that she simply wasn't privy to?

His arms around her, however, felt as warm and as strong and as comforting as always, and she quickly dismissed her thoughts. He was her strong, dependable Pierce once more. But he was also a man who was very concerned for his sister, and that made her love him all the more.

'Thank you, Stace.'

He pulled back and brushed a kiss across her lips, right there in the middle of the hospital corridor. She still wasn't used to such public displays of affection, but she was learning not to care what everyone else might think. She knew in her heart that the way she felt about Pierce was like nothing she'd ever felt before. And if she wanted to experience the full scope of what those emotions might be she couldn't be concerned with what other people might think of her relationship with him. It was no one else's business but their own.

'That's what friends are for,' she murmured as he kissed her again. When he smiled at her, the doubt she thought she'd seen had vanished and he was back to being his usual jovial and optimistic self.

'You,' he murmured, kissing her mouth once more before pulling back and taking her hand in his, 'are a very good friend, Dr Wilton.'

'I try my best, Dr Brolin,' she returned, and they headed to Radiology for the verdict on Nell's ankle.

When they arrived it was to find Jasmine sitting on Nell's hospital bed, teaching Nell a hand-clap game.

Nell seemed enthralled, determined to figure out the movements and then laughing along with Jasmine when she made a mistake.

'It's so good to see her laughing again,' Pierce murmured as he let go of Stacey's hand.

'I made a mistake.' Nell grinned widely when she saw Pierce and Stacey walking towards her.

Stacey smiled back at Nell, her heart warming to see Jasmine interacting with others again, but as soon as Jasmine realised Stacey was in the room she clammed up tight, the laughter disappearing, the smile slipping from her face.

Stacey frowned, completely perplexed by her sister's behaviour. Thankfully Pierce didn't seem to notice as he walked over and kissed the top of Nell's head.

'How are things going here?' he asked.

'I made a mistake,' Nell said again, laughing a little, before encouraging Jasmine to do the hand-clap routine again. Jasmine acquiesced and Stacey and Pierce watched as the two girls did the routine. When Nell managed it faultlessly, she cheered and wriggled in bed with delight. 'I solved the puzzle!' It was only after she moved that she winced in pain, having temporarily forgotten that she'd hurt her ankle.

'Steady, Nellie.' Pierce put a hand on her shoulders. 'Nice and still, remember?'

'Oh. Yes.' She nodded earnestly, but still wanted to do the hand-clap routine again and again.

'Let's see how *slowly* we can do it, Nell,' Jasmine suggested, and Stacey could have kissed her sister.

She had no idea what was really going on inside Jasmine's head, but she was a good girl at heart. Of that there was no doubt.

'Pierce. There you are,' said the radiographer as she came back into the room. 'Did you want to have a look at the X-rays? I've got them up on the screen.'

'Thanks.' Pierce and Stacey headed over to the computer monitor and stared at the X-rays. 'She *has* broken it.' His tone was a little despondent.

'But it's a clean break,' Stacey pointed out.

'Six weeks in a plaster cast. Crutches. Protective medical boot after that.' Pierce raked a hand through his hair again and that look of doubt returned to his eyes. What could it mean?

'Her recovery should be uneventful, and at your house ramps have been installed for Loris's wheelchair, so that will make it easier for her to manoeuvre about with her crutches.'

'I'll have to call her work and let them know what's happened. Once she's OK to go back I'll organise taxis to take her to and from the office. Then—'

'Pierce.' Stacey interrupted, taking his hand in hers and giving it a gentle squeeze. 'Breathe. It's OK. You don't have to figure out all the logistics right this second. Just be with Nell, reassure her. She'll be fine because she has you.'

He looked down at her as though he'd completely forgotten she was there. 'She doesn't take to change easily,' he said softly, so Nell couldn't hear him. 'The slightest thing, if it isn't handled correctly, can set her off. And once she's unsettled it can take days, weeks, even months to bring her back around.'

'I understand.' She gave his hand what she hoped was another reassuring squeeze. 'But you're not alone any more. I'm here—along with my plethora of siblings.' Stacey pointed to Jasmine. 'Just look at the two of them connecting. Jasmine talks more to Nell than she does to *anyone* else at the moment. This is a good thing—for both of them. Jasmine will be able to help Nell adjust.'

'Yeah. Yeah, you're right.'

He returned the squeeze on her fingers before releasing her, but Stacey could tell he was still very upset. He thanked the radiologist and asked if he could take Nell round to the plaster room to get the cast sorted out.

'The sooner I can take her home, the better,' he rationalised.

'Absolutely.' The radiographer was fine with that, but as Stacey had been the one to admit Nell officially, given that Pierce was her brother, it was up to her to sign the necessary forms.

'Can I stay with her?' Jasmine's sullen tones were directed at Stacey.

'Sure. You'll need to get off her bed when we wheel it, but that would be great, Jazzy. Thanks.'

'Yes. Thanks for keeping Nell company,' Pierce added, placing one hand on Stacey's shoulder and smiling gratefully at Jasmine.

As they watched, Jasmine's gaze seemed to hone in on Pierce's hand before she glared at them both and carefully slid from Nell's bed. She glanced towards the door, then back to Nell, as though she really wanted to bolt, to leave, to be anywhere except where she was right now. But she also knew that wasn't at all fair to Nell. Instead, she gave Stacey one more glare before pointedly refusing to look at her any more.

'I am completely perplexed by her behaviour,' Stacey told Pierce quietly as they stood off to one side in the plaster room, watching as Nell had her ankle plastered into position. The young woman was delighted to have chosen a pink cast, but the decision had only come after a lot of debate and discussion with Jasmine.

'I think I know what might be causing it,' he remarked.

'Really?' Stacey turned to look at him.

'It's me.' Pierce took his time, turning his head from what was happening to his sister to look at Stacey. 'She resents my presence.'

'No. She was like this before you and I…you know…'

That small, sexy smile twitched at the corner of his mouth and she was instantly swamped with a flood of tingles, which then set off a chain reaction of sparks igniting in every part of her being.

'Before you and I…what?' he asked, his tone deep and intimate.

'Pierce.' She playfully hit his arm, feeling highly self-conscious and trying to stop her cheeks from blushing.

His warm chuckle surrounded her and she couldn't help but sigh at the sound. How was it he could make her feel so completely feminine with just one look, one sound, one touch? 'It's nice to see your smile,' she whispered.

'You didn't answer my question,' he continued, his deep drawl thrilling her so much that another wave of tingles surrounded her.

Stacey met and held his gaze, wanting to capture moments like this when he seemed less burdened, more playful, less troubled, more sexy.

'Before you and I…?' he proffered as a lead-in.

'Became…*involved*,' she finished, and smiled at him.

'Involved, eh?'

Stacey giggled, but Pierce nodded towards Jasmine.

'See? As soon as you laughed she glared across at us. She doesn't like me.'

'She doesn't *know* you,' Stacey remarked.

Still, it probably wouldn't be a bad idea if she tried once more to talk to Jasmine, to try and get her to open up. Perhaps with everything that had happened today the pressure might have built up enough for the teenager to explode.

'Jazzy's a lot like me. Cora says that's why we clash. We both store our stress in a bottle—shoving everything down, adding pressure to stop things from affecting us. But in the end those bottles become too full and the pressure gets too great, so that one tiny little innocuous event ends up having an over-dramatic and out-of-proportion response.'

'So in order to deal with this it's best to let her "explode"?'

'It's best to let her proverbial *bottle* explode, to release the pressure—because once the pressure's released only then is there any room for the clean-out to begin.'

'Your psychology professors would have been thrilled with such an explanation.'

'Shh,' she chided. 'This is how I've explained it to Jasmine over the years, so she can hopefully begin to understand what's happening to her and start to deal with the small things by herself.'

'Will she see a psychologist?'

Stacey shook her head. 'I've tried.'

'Would you mind if I had a go?' he asked as the plaster technician began tidying up, now Nell's ankle was firmly secured in the pink plaster cast. 'Why don't I take Jasmine to the pharmacy to pick up a pair of crutches? You can organise the paperwork for Nell's discharge. We'll meet you back in the ED.'

'OK. It's just as well you're here, because otherwise Nell would have needed to stay in overnight for observation.'

The words were nothing more than a throwaway comment as Stacey reluctantly left his side and headed towards Nell and Jasmine. As he'd presumed, Jasmine was a little reluctant to spend any time alone with him, but when Nell seemed eager to have her collect her crutches Jasmine agreed.

'Thanks again for staying with Nell,' Pierce started as they walked along the hospital corridor.

'Yeah.'

'She doesn't have many close friends.'

'But she goes to work. She has a job.'

'A job that has been carefully structured in order to keep Nell's world as smooth as possible. A lot of the people who work with her are nice and polite, but they're not really her friends—or not what you and I might call friends.'

'I don't have *any*.'

Instead of contradicting her, telling her she had a lot of people who cared about her, who loved her, he didn't say anything. Jasmine looked at him expectantly, a little puzzled as to why he hadn't stated the obvious.

They walked on in silence until they reached the pharmacy. Pierce handed over the request for the crutches and when they had them they set off back the way they'd come.

'Ever been on crutches?' Pierce asked, a slight lift to his eyebrow.

'No.'

He smiled. 'Want to have a turn?'

Jasmine looked at him with stunned amazement. 'But I can't. They're Nell's.'

'Not yet.'

'Stacey will get mad.'

'I don't think so.' Pierce shook his head. 'Don't be too hard on your sister. Her life isn't all that easy.'

'But she's got everything she wants. She wanted to move back to Newcastle, so we did. She wanted to open up our dad's old surgery, so she did. She wanted to find a husband, so she did.' Jasmine gestured angrily to him.

Pierce's eyes widened a bit at the last statement but he didn't say anything. Instead he stopped walking and Jasmine followed suit, crossing her arms in front of her and adopting a stance that indicated she just didn't care.

He adjusted the height of the crutches so they were right for Jasmine and held them out to her. 'Here you go. They don't sit directly under your armpits, just a little lower. There. That's it.' He gave her some basic instructions to follow and waited for her to accept the crutches.

Her wide eyes conveyed her scepticism but she did as he'd suggested, fitting the crutches into place and then starting off carefully, keeping both feet on the ground while she adjusted to the feel of these foreign objects.

'Sometimes,' he said as they started slowly along the corridor, 'we all need a little help. Even Stacey.'

'Stacey's perfect. Always has been.'

'Stacey's heart is breaking.'

'Why? What did you do?' Jasmine's snarl was instant and she nearly overbalanced on the crutches. She concentrated and righted herself.

'*I* didn't hurt her.'

'Not yet.' The angry words were out of Jasmine's mouth before she could stop them. 'You'll hurt her. Robert hurt her.' Jasmine swallowed, starting to choke up a little. 'I heard her crying once. She thought everyone was asleep but I wasn't. She was in pain.' Jasmine angrily brushed a tear from her eyes. 'I don't want to be in pain like that. *Ever.* I'm going to be stronger than Stacey.

I'm going to make sure that no one can make me cry. I'm going to make sure that I can stand on my own two feet and not need anyone else to prop me up. Like Nell, I'll be independent.'

'That sounds very lonely.'

'Nell's not lonely.'

'Because she allows other people to help her.' He indicated the crutches. 'It's all about balance.'

As he said the words to Jasmine he wondered if his own life was out of balance. Certainly today's events had jolted things a little.

Pierce waited for a moment, then started walking slowly again. Jasmine followed, still using the crutches. 'Have you ever asked Stacey why she was crying?'

'No.'

'Why not?'

'Because…because…' Jasmine started to pick up her pace on the crutches, hopping along quite confidently now. 'She wouldn't tell me anyway. I'm just a *kid*. They all stop talking when I come into the room. They hate me.'

'Maybe they're protecting you. Show them you're ready to listen.'

'How do I do that?'

Pierce grinned widely. 'You're a smart girl, Jasmine. You'll figure it out.' Then he looked up and down the corridor. 'Hey,' he said conspiratorially. 'There aren't many people in the corridor. Want to see how fast you can go on those crutches?'

Jasmine stared at him with shocked delight. 'Can I do that?'

Pierce waved her words away. 'Why not? Look around you. Assess the risks.' He ticked the points off on his fingers. 'And stop before you fall over.'

Jasmine smiled brightly, reminding him a lot of her gorgeous big sister. 'Isn't it silly?'

'Sometimes a bit of silly is good for the soul. Ready?'

The teenager nodded and checked the long corridor to make sure she wouldn't be getting in anyone's way.

'OK. Go!'

Pierce walked beside Jasmine, keeping well clear of the crutches. By the time they neared the ED Jasmine was laughing. He looked up and saw Stacey standing in the corridor, watching her sister use the crutches, watching her sister laughing. Stacey grasped her hands to her chest in delight. However, the instant Jasmine saw her sister she lost her rhythm and would have come a cropper if Pierce hadn't been there to steady her.

'Well done!' He picked up the crutch she'd dropped and accepted the other one from her as Jasmine quickly tried to school herself back into sullen teenager pose number one.

Stacey came over and placed her hands on Jasmine's shoulders. 'Are you OK?'

'Fine.'

Jasmine tried to shrug Stacey's hands away, but this time Stacey wasn't letting her. Instead she pulled Jasmine close, wrapping her arms around her sister.

'It's so good to see you laughing again. I've missed that sound so much.'

'You're not mad?'

'Mad?' Stacey pulled back. 'Why would I be mad?'

'Because I was being silly with the crutches.'

Stacey looked at Pierce and then back to her sister. 'Well, sometimes a little bit of silliness is good for the soul.'

'Here.' Pierce held the crutches out to Jasmine. 'Why

don't you take these to Nell? You can demonstrate how to use them, but don't let her have a go on them just yet.'

'OK.' Jasmine accepted the crutches, a little perplexed as to why she was being given such responsibility, but doing it nevertheless.

'The nurse is with Nell,' Stacey remarked, jerking her thumb over her shoulder. 'I've signed the papers, so as soon as Nell is ready she can go home.'

'Thank you.'

'No.' Stacey slid her arms around his waist and hugged him close, not caring who saw them or what anyone said. Pierce had helped Jasmine to laugh again, and that not only filled Stacey with hope for her sister but also filled her heart with love for this wonderful, caring and clever man. 'Thank *you*.'

Pierce wrapped his arms around her, delighted she didn't seem to care who saw them. Given the eventful day they'd had thus far, everyone he cared about was safe. Yet there was one niggling thought that continued to churn around in his mind.

I didn't hurt her.

Not yet.

Jasmine fully expected him to hurt Stacey, to break Stacey's heart…and he had the sinking feeling she might be right.

CHAPTER TEN

THANKFULLY NELL RESPONDED well to the analgesics Stacey had prescribed, so now she was asleep, her plastered leg propped up on a few pillows, Pierce was able to relax a little. Jasmine was insisting on sleeping over in the spare bed in Nell's room.

'I'm not leaving her,' Jasmine said in a stage whisper when Stacey tried to beckon her from the room. 'I want to make sure she's OK through the night.'

Jasmine raised her chin defiantly and crossed her arms over her chest, almost daring Stacey to forcibly remove her. Instead Stacey's eyes filled with tears of pride, and for the second time in as many hours she hauled her sister close in an embracing hug.

'You're such a little warrior. I love that about you.' Stacey sniffed and then released Jasmine. 'Of course you must stay. I'm so proud that you want to—so proud of the way you protect Nell. Thank you, Jaz.' Stacey cleared her throat before making sure the spare bed in Nell's room was made up. 'Just sleep in your clothes and I'll bring you over some clean ones in the morning. Call me if you need anything.' She waited while Jasmine climbed into the bed. 'Is your phone charged?'

'Yeah.' Jasmine's puzzled eyes continued to stare at Stacey. 'Why are you being so nice to me?'

Stacey laughed a little at that and bent to kiss Jasmine's forehead. 'Because I love you, silly.'

With that, Stacey left the two girls to sleep, having already said goodnight to Samantha, who'd been very eager to get to her own bed after such a hectic day.

'Cup of tea?' Pierce asked as she walked into the kitchen.

'Yes, please.'

In silence he made the tea, both of them lost in their thoughts. 'Shall we sit on the veranda?' he asked, and when she nodded he carried their cups outside. Stacey sat down on the porch swing before accepting the cup from him.

They sat there for a while, with the clear night sky spread before them. When she'd finished her tea Pierce took her cup from her and slipped his arm around her shoulders. Stacey leaned closer, more than content to snuggle close to the man who had stolen her heart. Closing her eyes, she breathed him in, wanting to memorise every detail, every sensation he evoked within her. How was it possible she'd ever thought herself in love before?

With Pierce, she felt…*complete*. And because of that she felt confident. She didn't care who saw them together, who commented on their relationship or where things might end up. Pierce had helped her to realise she was a good person, and that at times she was too hard on herself, mentally berating herself when things didn't work out the way she'd envisioned. He made her feel like a person of worth, someone *he* wanted to spend his time with, to share his life with.

As she sat there, relaxing in his arms, allowing herself to dream of a perfect future side by side with Pierce, she felt him tense. 'What is it?' she murmured softly.

'Huh?'

'You just tensed.'

'Oh. Did I?' He shifted on the porch swing, almost overbalancing them. Forcing a laugh, he stood up and walked out to the garden. The grass was soft beneath his feet. Soon summer would come, the grass would dry and turn brown, but for now, thanks to the lovely spring weather they'd enjoyed, everything was good. 'I was just thinking about Nell…about how things could have been worse.'

'But they weren't.'

'I know, I know. But worrying about her is a hard habit to break.' He exhaled harshly. 'There are just so many things that will need to change now, and any change can trigger a decline into tantrums. She becomes so single-minded, she can't understand why I can't change things back.'

He spread his arms wide.

'When our parents died she kept demanding I go and pick them up. For months, Stacey. *Months.* Every single day. And every single day when I had to tell her that I couldn't do it, that I couldn't just get in my car and go and pick them up like she wanted me to, my heart would break. Months this went on.'

'Oh, Pierce.' Stacey stood and walked over to him, wrapping her arms about his waist and hugging him close. 'What you must have gone through—and here I am complaining about Jasmine's attitude when really I have nothing to complain about at all.'

'Your challenges are different, but you still have every right to complain, Stace.' His tone was gentle as he dropped a kiss to her head, but then he unhooked her arms from about his waist and walked further into the shadows of the night. 'My mind is trying to process everything, trying to consider every angle, every contingency that needs to be put in place in order to make Nell's recovery as smooth as possible.'

'I know everything's a bit of a jumble now, but it'll work itself out.'

'What if she endures a setback? What if this event means she's unable to live independently?'

'Well, Samantha's here now, and Loris is due to move in within the next few weeks, isn't she?'

'Yes, but that is also change. And too much change…' He stopped and sighed again.

Stacey watched him for a moment, her mind trying to process what he was saying. She understood that too much variety wasn't good for Nell, but things wouldn't always go to plan in the future—wasn't it best simply to deal with things as and when they arose? In fact, now that she thought about it, with Nell's second housemate due to move in soon it would mean that the three-bedroom home was quite full.

'Where are you planning to live?' The question left her lips before she could stop it and she quickly tried to explain. 'Sorry. I'm blurting things out again. But it just occurred to me that once Nell's other housemate moves in there'll be no room for you.'

'Correct. Initially I planned to rent somewhere nearby—just a one-bedroom flat—until after Christmas, and then I was due to head overseas.'

'But you're not going now?' Even as she said the words the thought of Pierce living on the other side of the world choked at her heart.

'I haven't planned on it. And I'm glad I *did* turn down the job when they re-offered it to me.'

'When, exactly, did they approach you?'

'They emailed me a few weeks ago and asked me to start next month.'

'What did you say?'

'I said no, of course.'

She frowned as she thought things through. 'How long have they been offering you this position?'

Pierce shook his head and walked towards the flowerbeds. 'Does it matter?' He bent down and breathed in the scent of the flowers.

'Yes, it does.'

At the insistence in her voice, he turned to face her. 'Why?'

'Because it's clear to see that you leaving and working alongside such an accomplished research team, working through a lot of the questions still surrounding adult autism, is something close to your heart. If they've been holding this job for you, offering it to you on a regular basis for years, then it's important that you go.'

As she spoke the words out loud Stacey felt as though she'd just plunged a knife through her own heart.

When Pierce didn't say anything, she swallowed and forced herself to continue. 'You write articles for them. You research on your own with limited resources. Just think of all the good you could do working alongside those other brilliant minds, utilising their funding, pooling your knowledge, making a real difference in the way society at large treats adults who are trying to integrate permanently into a normal functioning world.'

Pierce's answer was simply to shake his head.

'Hang on. You said you turned the job down a few weeks ago?'

'That's right and after tonight's events, I'm glad I did.'

'Why did you turn it down? Isn't this your dream job?' Pierce looked up at the star-lit sky for a moment, but before he could speak Stacey continued. 'Did you turn it down because of my medical practice?'

'I promised to help you until the end of the year, when Cora returns.'

'And I thank you for that. But it sounds to me as though the university wants you desperately, Pierce. And if that's the case, then go.' She tried to stop her voice from breaking on the last word and quickly cleared her throat in case he'd heard. 'I can get a locum in.'

'I *am* your locum, and I take my responsibilities seriously.'

'So do I—and I will not be the one to stand in the way of you accepting your dream job.'

Pierce stared at her as though she'd grown another head. 'Are you trying to get rid of me?'

Stacey closed her eyes, glad that it was dark and he couldn't see the tears she was desperately trying to hold back. 'If I have to.' She breathed in slowly, then let it out, unable to believe what she was about to say. 'If I have to fire you in order to get you to take that job then I will.' There was determination in her tone.

'But what about Nell?'

Stacey clenched her jaw, knowing that what she was about to do was for his own good. 'You've put everything in place as far as Nell is concerned, and while her fractured ankle might be a bit of a setback, and bring its own new level of logistics, you've still taught her how to cope with big changes. Plus it's not as though you'd be leaving tomorrow. I'll help you organise things, and we will be there for Nell, helping her every step of the way. Shortfield Family Medical Practice isn't only her closest GP surgery but my family and I are also her friends. We love Nell.'

'I know.' Pierce walked towards her and placed his hands on her shoulders. 'And I thank you, Stacey. I thank you from the bottom of my heart for the way you genuinely love my little sister.' He looked down into her face, half in shadow, half lit by the glow of the moon. 'You look so beautiful. You *are* so beautiful—not only physically but also within your heart.' He shook his head. 'You've changed my life and…and…it would be wrong of me to leave.'

'You have to.' She bit her lip to stop herself from crying. It was breaking her heart to say these words to him, especially when the last thing she really wanted was for him to leave her.

'No. Catherine left me to further her career, and I thought it was incredibly selfish of her. It's just a job, Stacey. I'm not going to sacrifice what's important to me simply because of a job.'

'You couldn't be selfish if you tried, Pierce. And where Catherine's concerned you've told me yourself she's done amazing work, helped so many people. But when you think back to your relationship, perhaps she simply used her career as an excuse because she knew deep down inside that things weren't right.' She swallowed. 'I lied to myself where Robert was concerned, telling myself he'd change after we were married, that I could live with my career always playing second fiddle to his, that I could be restrained as far as being demonstrative in my love for him went. I was willing to settle and it was wrong of me. Robert hurt me when he left me at the altar, and I wish he'd been more upfront with me, telling me his decision *before* I left for the church, but in hindsight his selfish actions saved us both from a lifetime of misery.'

She closed her eyes again, a single tear falling from her lashes to roll down her cheek.

'I couldn't bear it if you always regretted putting me before this job.'

She trembled when Pierce brushed the tear from her cheek.

'I won't.'

'You can't say that. It's been your dream, and you've already devoted so much of your time to it. I've read the articles you've written and you can do so much more with the research team behind you.' She looked up at him, not caring that a few more tears slid down her cheeks. 'Go. Do the work you're meant to do.'

'But, Stacey—'

'No. You're fired, Pierce.'

'You're not serious.' He laughed without humour as she stepped away from his touch.

'I am.'

'No. You're just doing this because you think it's the right thing to do. Well, you can't push me into this decision, Stacey. I'll be turning up to work next week, same as always.'

'No, you won't.'

'But you won't be able to cope.'

'Of course I'll cope. I'm the queen of coping.' She sniffed and brushed away a few of the tears from her cheeks. 'I know what it's like to work in your dream job. I'm doing it right now. Running my dad's old medical practice has been my dream since I was fourteen years old, and although my selfishness might have caused some of my family members—namely Jasmine—a lot of pain, the thrill of finally being where I'm meant to be, of achieving those life-long goals—'

She broke off and smiled.

'It's…amazing. For the first time in my life I know I'm exactly where I need to be and it feels great.' She shook her head. 'I won't be the one to deny *you* experiencing that same sensation, and I'm sure if Nell had a full grasp of the situation then she wouldn't want that either. Both of you have worked so hard to get her to this stage of independent living. Years and years of work, and Nell is ready for you to go. It's what she's expecting and you risk confusing her further if you *don't* go.'

Before he could say another word she turned and headed into the house, wiping at her eyes in order to clear her vision. She located her bag and car keys before turning and heading back out again.

'You're leaving?' Pierce was half on the veranda, half on the threshold as she walked past him.

'I need to.' Before she made a complete fool of herself and begged him not to listen to a word she was saying.

'Stacey—wait.'

She unlocked her car and put her bag inside before turning to face him, the driver's door between them.

'What about us? Isn't what we feel for each other worth pursuing?'

She reached out and placed a hand to his cheek, determined she wouldn't cry. 'If you love someone, set them free.' She smiled lovingly at the man who had stolen her heart, now and for ever more. 'You are going to be amazing. You are going to achieve such great things—and those great things are going to help so many people. I could never stand in the way of that.'

Her voice broke, and before she completely lost her resolve to set him free she turned from him, climbed into the car, shut the door and started the engine.

'Stacey!'

She tried not to hear the pleading in his tone as she carefully reversed out of the driveway, only belatedly remembering to switch on her headlights. Even though they lived only a few blocks from each other she still had to pull over to wipe her tear-filled eyes because she couldn't see properly.

When she reached her house she headed quietly for her bedroom and, uncaring that she hadn't changed or brushed her teeth, she lay down on her bed and allowed the tears to fall. She loved him. She loved Pierce with all her heart. But she could never live with herself if he sacrificed his own dreams for her. His dreams were his, and he deserved the chance to achieve them.

'If you love someone, set them free. If they come back to you, they're yours. If they don't, they never were.' She recited the quote into her pillow, hoping amongst hope that one day Pierce would return to her—because she would always be waiting for him.

'Good morning, sleepy-head,' Molly remarked as she came into Stacey's bedroom. 'Or should I say good afternoon?' Molly put a cup of tea on the bedside table, then walked to the window, where she opened the blind to let a bit of midday light flood into the room.

'What?' A groggy Stacey lifted her head from the pillow, trying to open her bleary eyes. 'What time is it?' She put out a hand to search for her bedside clock, but nearly upset the cup of tea in the process.

'Steady on. It's half-past twelve.'

'Oh, my goodness—Jasmine!' Stacey sat bolt upright in bed. 'I was supposed to take her clean clothes and pick her up hours ago.'

'Chillax, sis. It's fine. Jaz called and asked if she could stay until later this afternoon. She said she was having fun helping Nell adjust and teaching her, with Samantha's help, how to use the crutches properly. Still, I thought you were probably going to go and check on Nell anyway, and besides, it gives you more time to play cutesey kisseyface with Pierce.' Molly grasped her hands theatrically to her chest and then sighed dramatically. 'Oh, most beloved, take me in your arms and kiss me until I see stars.'

'Knock it off, Molly.' Stacey slumped back down onto the pillows.

'Wait. I know *that* tone. What's wrong?' Molly came over and sat on Stacey's bed. 'What's happened?'

'It's over.'

'Between you and Pierce? But how? But why? But yesterday everything was peachy.'

'I'm not sure I want to talk about it right now, Molly.' Stacey rested her hand across her eyes. 'Would you mind doing Nell's check-up when you pick up Jasmine?'

'Isn't that the coward's way out? Besides, Nell will be expecting you.'

'Ugh!' Stacey picked up a spare pillow and put it over her face, yelling her frustration into it.

She knew Molly had a point—that Nell would be confused if Stacey didn't turn up to do the check-up and right now the last thing Nell needed was to have even more instability—but the thought that Stacey would probably bump into Pierce when she went was something she simply didn't want to face right now.

Molly lifted the pillow off her. 'I *hate* always doing what's right. I hate it, Molly.'

'Are you afraid you'll see Pierce when you go?'

'Of course I am.' Stacey flicked back the bedcovers and stepped out of bed, heading to the bathroom. When she came back it was to find Molly sipping at the teacup. 'I thought that was for me.'

'You're clearly in no mood to drink a relaxing cup of peppermint tea. You need coffee, my soul sister, so why don't you have a shower and I'll make you one? Then George, Lydia and I, along with the rabbits as a diversion for Nell, will come with you to the Brolins' house and run interference for you so that you don't have to speak to Pierce.'

Stacey relaxed a little and rushed over to hug her sister, almost making Molly spill the tea. 'Thank you. I knew I could count on you.'

'Always.'

Stacey got dressed and had something to eat, while Molly organised the children and the animals, then drove them all round to Nell's house.

'I just love walking up this path,' Molly said. 'It really does bring back so many wonderful memories. I'm glad someone we love is living in this house and making it her home. It's like the house is ready to make the next generation of memories.'

Stacey didn't reply. She was too focused on looking around the garden, half expecting Pierce to pop out from behind a bush, wearing the same gardening clothes he'd been wearing that first day she'd met him. It seemed so long ago, yet in reality she'd known Pierce for less than two months. Still, in her heart it felt as though she'd known him for a lot longer.

When she entered the house she looked around quickly, but still there was no sign of him. Jasmine and Nell were seated at the table, doing some puzzles. Samantha was in the kitchen baking.

'I like baking when I'm feeling stressed or a little out of sorts,' the woman told them as she checked the cupcakes she had in the oven. 'Besides, I know these ones are Nell's favourite, because when I bring them to work she tells me they're her favourite, so I thought, why not make some to help cheer her up?'

'Good idea,' Stacey remarked, smiling as Nell's eyes lit up upon seeing the rabbits, as well as George and Lydia but more so the rabbits. Stacey wasn't going to ask where Pierce was, or even if he was there. She was just going to do her job and then, if Molly wanted to chat, Stacey would head next door to check on Mike and Edna. But thankfully it was Jasmine who gave her the information she sought.

'Pierce isn't home at the moment. He got called into the hospital this morning and that's why I said I'd stay with Nell.'

'Oh.' Stacey was both relieved and disappointed at the same time. She didn't want to see Pierce and yet she yearned to see him. She loved him so much. 'Right, well…Nell, let's get your check-up over and done with. When you've finished that puzzle I need to check your blood pressure and your foot—'

'And listen to my heart?' Nell asked. 'Can I listen to my heart? Pierce sometimes lets me listen to my heart. It goes ba-dum, ba-dum.'

Stacey smiled. 'Of course you can listen to your heart.'

The check-up didn't take too long, and when Samantha asked if they'd like to stay for Sunday afternoon snack-time Molly raised a questioning eyebrow in Stacey's direction.

'Sure. Why not?' she remarked, hoping against hope that Pierce didn't return from the hospital while they were still there.

Thankfully she managed to enjoy a leisurely afternoon tea and say her goodbyes to Nell and Samantha.

Jasmine was quiet on the drive home, and it wasn't until they walked in the door and waited while George and Lydia took the rabbits back to their hutch, that she turned to Stacey and demanded, 'What's going on with you and Pierce?'

Stacey blinked, a little taken aback. 'Pardon?'

'Pierce looked half sick this morning, all pale and grey, as though he'd eaten something terrible. I asked him if he was OK and he just said, "Yeah." But I could tell there was more wrong than he was saying. And then when you came you were like a mouse being chased by a cat, and *you* looked all pale and grey, too.'

Molly placed her hands on Jasmine's shoulders, then kissed her sister's cheek. 'She's not just a pretty face.'

Jasmine merely stared at Stacey, as if to say she wasn't moving until she got an explanation.

'Well...uh...Pierce and I are...well, we're going to stop seeing each other for a while.'

'You're not going to stop me from seeing Nell?' Again there was that defiant, adamant tone.

'No. Of course not. Nell needs you—well, needs all of us—now more than ever.'

'What? What do you mean?'

Stacey took a deep breath, then looked at Molly, and then back to Jasmine. 'Pierce is heading overseas.'

'What?' Molly and Jasmine spoke in unison.

'Nell will soon be living independently, just as she's always wanted.'

'And Pierce will be free to do whatever he wants?'

There was disgust in Jasmine's tone, and Stacey held up her finger in reprimand.

'Pierce is an amazing man who has done a lot of research and written many scientific papers on the subject of adult autism—especially with regard to integration.'

'I know what integration is,' Jasmine said, before either of her sisters could explain. 'Remember the school I went to in Perth? The school I loved? My friends I loved, whether they had a disability or not?'

'Yes. Of course. Well, Pierce has been offered a job in America and...he's going to take it. When he's there,' she went on before Jasmine could say another word, 'he'll continue his work with regard to integration with an experienced team of researchers. The work he can do there will help thousands and thousands of adults with autism to be better accepted by society.'

Jasmine pondered Stacey's words for a moment, then crossed her arms over her chest and glared at them both. 'I don't see why he has to go to America to do that,' she said, then turned and stomped off to her bedroom.

'I get the feeling Jasmine really does like him,' Molly remarked as they both braced themselves for the ritual slamming of their sister's bedroom door.

Stacey slumped down into a chair and rested her head in her hands.

'Does he have to go?' Molly's question was quiet.

'Yes.'

'Do you want him to go?'

'Yes.'

'What? Why? I thought you were in love with the man.'

Stacey lifted her head and looked at her sister. 'It's *because* I'm in love with him that I'm making him go. He deserves the chance to fulfil his own dreams just like me moving here, or you doing surgery, or Cora going to Tarparnii, or Nell living independently. Pierce has dedicated all his time and effort to Nell. He's a good man, with a big heart.'

'Will the two of you still stay together? I mean nowadays long-distance relationships aren't that difficult to maintain thanks to internet chats and emails and stuff.'

'I don't know.'

With that, Stacey stood and headed towards her own bedroom, to lie on her bed and cry some more.

CHAPTER ELEVEN

By the end of November Stacey was worn out. She went to work early in the morning and returned late most nights. She'd started a night clinic in an effort to catch up on the overflow of patients but also to give her time to ferry her siblings around to their various after-school activities. Most nights she collapsed into bed with exhaustion.

Molly helped at the clinic as much as she was able, but after an hour or two was often called in to the hospital, leaving Stacey and Winifred to cope with whatever patients were left.

'You can't go on like this,' Winifred said late one evening, giving Stacey a big hug. 'You'll work yourself into an early grave.'

'I know. But the new locum will start soon and then, come Christmas-time, Cora will be home.'

'It's a shame Pierce took that job in America before his contract here was up.'

'I fired him,' Stacey told her.

'What? Why would you do that?'

'Because he never would have left to follow his dreams otherwise.'

Winifred sighed and patted Stacey's arm. 'You really love him, don't you?' she stated.

'Yes.'

It was as simple and as complex as that. Yes, she loved him. Yes, she missed him. Yes, she wanted him back, to have her arms around him, to have his mouth pressed to hers.

'He'll be back before you know it,' Winifred promised. 'Go on home, love. I'll lock up.'

Stacey hoped Winifred was right—that Pierce would be back sooner rather than later. Before he'd left for the States he'd tried to contact her, but she hadn't wanted to take his calls. He'd emailed her but she hadn't wanted to read them. Cutting herself off from him was the only way she knew how to make the pain in her heart decrease.

Two weeks after Nell had broken her ankle, two weeks after Stacey had fired him and told him to head overseas, Pierce had been due to leave. The night before his flight she'd gone to bed early, not wanting to dwell on the way her heart ached for him. She'd awoken to the soft sound of someone knocking on her bedroom window and cautiously she'd peeked through the curtains, her heart swelling with love when she'd seen Pierce standing there.

Pulling on a dressing gown and slippers, she'd headed outside to see what he wanted, instantly concerned that something had happened to Nell.

'Is Nell all right?'

'Nell's fine. I'm not.' He'd hauled her into his arms and pressed his lips to hers in one swift movement that robbed her of breath. 'I've missed you these past weeks, Stacey. Why didn't you return my calls? My emails?'

'Pierce.' She tried to pull away from his arms but her efforts were half-hearted at best, because with all honesty that was the place she wanted to be the most. 'I can't do this.'

'What? Let me hold you? Let me kiss you? Stacey, I'm

not going to see you for…I don't even want to think about it. I need this—these memories—to get me through.'

'I know, but I—'

He silenced her with another heart-melting kiss, and this time Stacey couldn't help but cling to him. 'Oh, Pierce.'

'I don't know how to do this,' he told her.

'Do what?'

'Be selfish.'

'I know. You're the most giving man I've ever met.'

'And yet here I am, doing what *I* want to do.'

'For a change,' she finished. 'And, for the record, you're not being selfish. You're following your dreams and you deserve the chance to do it.'

'But what if this *isn't* my real dream? What if my dream has…changed?'

'You won't know for sure until you get to America.' She shook her head and kissed his lips. 'You'll have a great time,' she encouraged him, trying desperately to instil enthusiasm into her voice.

'It would be far greater if you were to come with me,' he said, but Stacey shook her head.

'It's not my dream, but I believe in you.'

He kissed her again. 'And that, my beautiful, wonderful, most beloved Stacey, is worth everything.'

'What time does your flight leave?' she asked.

'I need to leave for the airport in an hour.'

'Come and sit with me.' And so the two of them sat on the chairs on her small veranda, content to hold each other and look at the stars, thankful the October night was not too warm for cuddling.

When finally it came time for him to leave, Pierce kissed her with such passion that she swooned.

'Please take my calls while I'm overseas.'

'No.'

'What? Why not?'

'I can't bear to hear your voice or to see you over the internet because it'll just make me miss you more.' And she wasn't sure whether she'd be able to cope with that.

'OK, then. What about emails and text messages?'

Stacey thought about this for a moment, then nodded. 'Yes.'

'Good.' He exhaled happily before kissing her once more, then walking over to the hire car parked in her driveway.

She was glad he hadn't asked her to take him to the airport, because there was no way she'd ever be able to say goodbye to him and then watch him get onto a plane and leave her. Even this, standing in her own driveway and crying as he drove away, was bad enough.

Now, six weeks since he'd left, Stacey still found it difficult to get out of bed every morning, knowing she wouldn't be seeing him at the clinic. Her dreams were always of him, and she lived for his emails, loving the excitement she read in his words about the research he was doing and the staff he was working with.

Nell's ankle had healed nicely, and all in all she'd coped with the disruption to her usual routine quite well—so much so that she'd refused to go back to catching the bus to and from work and now had a standing arrangement with the taxi company to pick her up every morning and drop her home every afternoon.

Jasmine still went round every afternoon after school, sometimes with George and Lydia and sometimes just by herself. Then, on Friday afternoons, Nell would join the rest of the Wilton family as they all headed over to Mike and Edna's for dinner, bringing the rabbits with them.

Mike would offer instruction and coaching in the art of encouraging rabbits to jump higher over an obstacle.

All in all, Stacey's days were jam-packed with family and patients and longing for Pierce, but when December arrived the days seemed even longer. More patients. More ferrying her siblings to and from their various after-school events. More stress, and most of all more missing Pierce.

'Cup of tea?'

Stacey opened her eyes where she sat, slumped on the sofa after another hard day at the clinic. She was surprised to see Jasmine standing before her, holding a piping hot cup of tea out to her.

'Oh, Jazzy.' Stacey was overwhelmed at the thoughtful gesture, but sat up straight and sighed with relief as she accepted the cup. 'You are a life-saver, my gorgeous sister. Thank you.'

Jasmine looked as though she, too, was about to burst into tears, and after Stacey had taken the cup the teenager hesitated for a moment, before sitting down next to Stacey.

'Mmm. That is a perfect cuppa.'

Jasmine grinned with happiness at the praise.

'It's good to see you smiling. That also helps in so many ways.' Stacey brushed her sister's hair back from her face. 'I've been so worried about you.'

'I was…' Jasmine bit her lip, hesitating.

Stacey waited intently.

'That day in the park, when Nell got hurt…'

'Yes?' It was a day Stacey could never forget. So much had transpired that day. So many emotions. 'What about it?'

'I thought I'd caused Nell to get hurt.'

'What?'

'I threw the Frisbee too far and she tried to get it, and it landed near that barbecue where the man was cooking, and if I hadn't thrown it there Nell wouldn't have been near it, and Nell getting hurt is all my fault.' Jasmine broke down into tears, covering her face with her hands.

Stacey instantly put her cup on the table and gathered her sister close. 'No. No, sweetie. It wasn't your fault. Not at all. There was absolutely no way you could have known what was going to happen. It was an accident. Not your fault at all. Oh, poor Jaz. Have you been carrying this burden with you all this time? Oh, honey.' Stacey started crying as well, feeling her sister's pain keenly.

'I was so angry at you for taking me away from my friends, for bringing us here. I wanted to punish you, and then when I saw Nell lying there…I…I…all I wanted was you. I wanted you to pick me up like you used to and cuddle me close and tell me everything would be all right.' Jasmine spoke through her tears, hiccuping now and then. 'I know Nell's OK now, but…but…'

Stacey fished around in her pockets for some tissues and managed to find two clean ones. 'I'm always here for you, Jaz. No matter what the circumstances. You're allowed to be angry with me, or Cora or Molly or any of us. You're entitled to your own emotions and to be able to show them. That's OK. We're sisters. We'll always work it out in the end because we love each other.'

'Pierce said you love me. He said that things are really difficult for you. And until he said that I hadn't really thought about it like that, you know? And now he's gone, and you're working lots, and you're really tired and you're unhappy, and I don't like seeing you like that. So I couldn't talk to you about Nell, but it was getting too much. That bottle you talk about—it was building up too much. And then…I just couldn't hold it in any more.'

A fresh bout of tears accompanied her words and Stacey held her sister, dabbing at her eyes.

'It's OK. I've got you. Everything's going to be all right,' she crooned, and after a while Jasmine stopped crying and blew her nose. Stacey followed suit and they both smiled. 'I do love you, Jaz. You're my sister. We're family. We're all we've got.'

'We've got Nell and Pierce now, too.' She covered her mouth with her hand. 'Oh, I forgot. Molly told me not to say his name around you in case it upset you too much, but—'

'It's fine. Molly's just being protective.'

'Do you need protecting?' Jasmine sat up straighter. 'Because I'll protect you, too.'

Stacey felt another wave of tears coming on—tears of happiness at seeing that fierce and determined spirit of her sister's shining forth yet again. 'Thank you. But I'm doing all right at the moment.'

'Do you miss him?'

'Of course. But it's important for people to follow their dreams.' She'd tried to keep her words strong but even she had heard the wobble in her voice. This time it was Jasmine who offered the hug, holding her big sister close, and Stacey loved every moment of it.

Jasmine sniffed. 'I love you, Stacey.'

'I love you, too. Always.' They both blew their noses again and then laughed. 'Look at us. Red eyes and red noses. We must look a sight.' Stacey stood and pulled Jasmine to her feet. 'How about some ice cream?'

'But…you haven't even had dinner.' Jasmine pointed to the kitchen. 'I've made a plate of food for you.'

'Thank you. You've been such a wonderful help. But at the moment I need ice cream. Comfort food.' Stacey headed to the kitchen. 'Want some?'

'Yeah.' Jasmine watched as her sister pulled out an ice

cream tub and scooped some into bowls. 'I've never seen you like this before. All "break the rules", like.'

'Then it's about time you did.'

And that was how Molly found them an hour later, when she arrived home from the hospital, exhausted. Stacey had finished her ice cream, then eaten her dinner, and Jasmine had kept her company.

'Kids asleep?' Molly asked as she kissed her sisters on the cheek.

'Yes,' Jasmine replied. 'George put himself to bed tonight—he was so tired after his karate lesson—and Lydia fell asleep with a book still in her hands.'

They all chuckled.

'Typical Lydia,' Molly remarked as she reheated her dinner. 'Oh, I had a thought earlier today. How about next weekend we all do something together? A family activity. I'm not on call, and the kids will all be finished school for the year, so we should celebrate by doing something super-fun.'

'How about ice-skating?' Jasmine suggested.

'I'm not sure Nell knows how to ice-skate, and although her ankle has now healed I wouldn't want to risk her falling over and injuring it again.'

'Good point.' Jasmine nodded, pleased that Nell was automatically included in their family plans.

'How about bowling?' Molly suggested a moment later.

'Bowling?' Jasmine's eyes lit up. 'I used to love it when Mum took us bowling. Yeah. Let's go bowling—Nell will love it.'

'Plus,' Molly added, hugging Stacey close, 'the local bowling alley has cheesy music videos.'

Stacey grinned and hugged her sister back. 'Sounds like the perfect tonic for me. The cheesier the better.'

The following weekend, with the children excited

about being on school holidays for six weeks, Stacey completed her house calls in record time—especially as Jasmine had volunteered to come along and help out. They picked Nell up from her house—Samantha and Loris declined the invitation to join them—and then went home, where they met an excited George and Lydia bouncing around in the corridor.

'Where's Molly?' Stacey asked.

'She's in the bedroom on the telephone. She said she had some loose ends to tie up.'

'Oh?' Stacey hoped her sister hadn't been called in to the hospital, but thankfully when Molly appeared a moment later she assured her sister that everything was fine and that they should head off before they missed their booking.

At the bowling alley they all enjoyed the game—Nell perhaps most of all. And seeing the delight on the young woman's face Stacey wished Pierce was there to see it. She took a photo on her phone of Nell's smiling face after she'd knocked all the pins down, then sent the picture to Pierce's phone.

'You all right?' Molly asked as she came and sat down next to Stacey while Lydia had a turn at bowling.

'Sure!' Stacey offered the word with fake brightness, pointing to the cheesy music video on the television monitors scattered around the bowling alley and the black lighting which made the fluorescent bowling balls stand out like neon. 'Glad I didn't wear white or I'd be glowing brightly under these lights, but the music videos are definitely worth it. Oh, the eighties! Those fashions! That hair!'

'It's fun.'

'It is. It was a good idea, Molly. Thank you.' Stacey hugged her sister.

'Uh…well, you may not want to thank me too much.'

Molly whispered the words in Stacey's ear and she felt a prickle of apprehension work its way down her spine. Stacey eased back and looked at her sister.

'Why?' she asked cautiously.

'Um…well…' The music video changed on the screen and Molly pointed to it. 'Look. Let's watch this one. Hey, kids. Let's watch this music video.'

'What's going on? Why are you acting so stran—?' Stacey wasn't able to finish her sentence as her eyes widened at what she was seeing on the television monitors.

It was Pierce. Larger than life. On every single television monitor in the bowling alley.

'What? But…how?'

Then she stared in utter shock as he started lip-syncing to one of her favourite songs—a song about love, trust and dedication to each other.

'Pierce made you a cheesy video,' Molly remarked quietly.

'He…*what*?'

'Just watch.'

And she did as Pierce, dressed in an all-white suit, holding a large bunch of red roses, was seen to be looking high and low for his one true love, searching for her everywhere, singing to the camera, his handsome face radiating an earnest and honest desire to find her. Stacey's jaw dropped open in stunned disbelief as she watched him knocking on the door to her house, but receiving no reply.

'When was this filmed? And…*how*?'

'We live in an age of digital technology, Stace,' Jasmine offered.

'Yeah. It's not hard,' George added, like the wise old man he was.

Nell was clapping along in time to the music, thoroughly delighted at seeing her big brother on the television. At the end of the video Pierce was still searching, and there was a shot of him walking to the front of the bowling alley. Stacey sat up straighter in her chair—then the television monitors went blank. But the music continued playing over the loudspeakers.

Now everyone in the bowling alley had stopped bowling and they were all pointing and gasping in delight as the man from the video walked into the bowling alley, dressed in the pure white suit which became bright white beneath the black lights. He still carried the enormous bunch of red roses—Stacey's favourite—and headed slowly in her direction.

She stood, belatedly realising she was trembling. When he reached her side he smiled at her and held out the roses. A few people around them started clapping, but Stacey didn't hear them. All she was aware of was Pierce, standing before her, smiling brightly and placing the roses into her arms. What did it all mean?

She didn't have to wait long to find out.

When the music ended Pierce held out his hand for hers. Stacey shifted the roses onto one arm and gave him her hand, loving the feel of her hand securely in his. She bit her lip, her heart pounding with love for the man before her.

'Stacey. I've missed you so very much. Too much to be apart from you any longer. You encouraged me to follow my dreams and you were right when you said I'd feel a strong sense of accomplishment when I was finally in the right job in the right place at the right time…and that dream job is working alongside you in a small family-run GP clinic in Shortfield.'

'What?' She gaped at him. 'But what about Yale and your research and—?'

'All still good. All still happening. But happening on both sides of the world. I'm setting up a sister study at Newcastle General Hospital. I'll work part-time there and part-time with you at the clinic…but I'll be working *full time* in the best relationship, the happiest relationship I've ever had the pleasure to be in.' He shook his head slowly from side to side and gazed down into her eyes. 'I've missed you, Stacey. So much it started to physically hurt to be so far away from you.'

'Oh!' Stacey tried to blink back tears of happiness, not wanting to miss a second of seeing his handsome face, of hearing his perfect words.

Then, to her further astonishment, he released her hand for a moment to unbutton his white suit jacket, revealing a white T-shirt beneath. On the T-shirt was painted, in fluorescent pink writing, the words *Will you marry me?*

He went down on bended knee and took her hand in his again. 'I love you, Stacey, and I intend to spend the rest of my life showing you that. I adore you. Please, will you do me the honour of becoming my wife?'

Stacey opened her mouth to speak but found her words choked with pure emotion, so she quickly nodded and tugged him to his feet, desperate to have his lips pressed against hers. 'Yes,' she finally whispered, just before he kissed her.

'I've missed you,' he returned. 'I love you. So very much.'

'You are my everything,' she told him, smiling with happiness when he tenderly brushed away a few escaped tears with his thumb.

Then somehow the flowers were removed from her arms and Pierce was hugging her close, kissing her passionately in front of anyone and everyone who happened to be in the bowling alley. The round of applause and whoops of joy from their siblings went unnoticed as both Stacey and Pierce only had eyes for each other.

'How did you like the music video?' he eventually asked when Nell had insisted on finishing her bowling game.

Stacey sat on her fiancé's lap, her arms around his neck as though never letting him go again.

'Cheesy enough for you?' He chuckled.

'It was the perfect blend of tacky and ridiculousness. I can't believe you went to so much trouble just for me.'

'You're worth it.' He shook his head again.

'I still can't believe you're here. You're actually *here*. When did you fly in?'

Pierce checked his watch. 'About three hours ago. I had the idea for the video and Molly helped make it happen. We knew you'd be out on house calls this morning, so it seemed the perfect opportunity to do all the photography then.'

'But I still don't know how it was edited together so fast and—' She held up her hand. 'You know what? I don't want to know.' She pressed a kiss to Pierce's lips. 'I just want to enjoy.'

It was a lot of kisses later when Stacey looked deeply into his eyes and said softly, 'You once told me you could see loneliness in my eyes, my sad eyes, and it was true. It was there because something was missing from my life— something just for me, something precious and rare. And that's you. You were what was missing from my life.'

'Marry me soon, Stacey,' he remarked as he kissed her yet again, unable to get enough of her delectable mouth.

'Of course. And that, my love, will be a definite dream come true.'

EPILOGUE

THE WEDDING WAS held outside in Nell's backyard a few weeks after New Year. Pierce had waited only the least amount of time it took to have their banns read before he married the woman of his dreams.

'Do you remember how we used to pretend that we'd get married in this very back garden?' Cora asked as she made the final touches to Stacey's hairstyle before putting a garland of flowers carefully in place. 'Oh!' She gasped. 'You look just like we always imagined. Like a princess at a small backyard wedding with our closest family and friends and we have Mike ready to walk you down the garden aisle, giving you away.'

Molly clutched her hands to her chest before tying Lydia's sash, which had come undone again. All of Stacey's sisters, including Nell, were with her, getting ready. George was with Pierce in the room down the hall. The wedding celebrant was an old family friend of her parents and the garden was filled with their closest friends.

'Nervous?' Jasmine asked, and Stacey wrinkled her nose.

'No. Not even worried. I get to marry Pierce today. My handsome prince. This time it's the real deal.'

Molly took one of her hands and Cora took the other,

all the triplets standing together, grinning at each other, sharing incredible emotions.

'This is right, Stace. He's so perfect for you.'

'And you're so perfect for him.'

'Thank you.' Stacey looked to the two women who had been with her for ever. They were sisters, and sisters were never wrong.

Jasmine rallied Lydia and Nell into position as Edna came in to check everyone was ready.

'Pierce is impatiently awaiting your arrival,' Edna told them as Mike came to offer Stacey his arm.

Both Edna and Mike looked at her.

'Oh, your father would have been right proud to see this day,' Mike told her.

'So proud,' Edna agreed, and kissed Stacey on the cheek. '*We're* so proud—aren't we, Mike?'

'Yes. We're proud of all of you.' Mike's gaze encompassed them all. 'And of little George, of course,' he added, which made Lydia giggle, and the sound of Lydia's giggle made the rest of them giggle too.

It was just the tension release they all needed, so that when the music started Stacey proudly took her place at the bottom of the garden.

Her smile only increased when she saw Pierce standing there, waiting expectantly for her. She floated towards him, not caring whether she walked in time to the music, not caring if anything went wrong. Pierce was looking at her as though she were the most stunning woman in the world, and she knew in her heart that was exactly what he thought because he'd told her so—quite often.

'You look…*wow*!' They were the first words out of his mouth as she came to stand beside him, her simple white sundress and flat white shoes enhanced by the wild flowers in her hair and bouquet. *Au naturel*. No fuss. No big puffy dress. Not this time. *This* was her dream wedding. Simple. Casual. Family.

'You look pretty wow yourself,' she told him as she took in his light grey suit.

'Ready to get married?'

'To you? Absolutely.'

She reached for his hand, linking her fingers with his, unable to believe such a pure, perfect happiness as this existed, and that it was a happiness that, for them, would last for ever.

* * * * *

FLIRTING WITH THE SOCIALITE DOC

MELANIE MILBURNE

To Alan and Sue Beswick for their continued support
of the Heart Foundation in Tasmania.

This one is for you. At last! XX

CHAPTER ONE

EVEN THE DISTANCE of more than seventeen thousand kilometres that Izzy had put between herself and her best friend was not going to stop another Embarrassing Birthday Episode from occurring.

Oh, joy.

'I've got the perfect present winging its way to you,' Hannah crowed over the phone from London. 'You're going to get the biggest surprise. Be prepared. Be very prepared.'

Izzy gave a mental groan. Her closest friend from medical school had a rather annoying habit of choosing the most inappropriate and, on occasion, excruciatingly embarrassing birthday gifts. 'I know you think I'm an uptight prude but do you have to rub my nose in it every year? I'm still blushing from that grotesque sex toy you gave me last year.'

Hannah laughed. 'This is so much better. And it will make you feel a little less lonely. So how are you settling in? What's it like out there?'

'Out there' was Jerringa Ridge and about as far away from Izzy's life back in England as it could be, hot and dry with sunlight that wasn't just bright but violent. Unlike other parts of New South Wales, which had suffered unusually high levels of flooding, it hadn't rained, or at least with any significance, in this district for months.

And it looked like it.

A rust-red dust cloud had followed her into town like a dervish and left a fine layer over her car, her clothes, and had somehow even got into the small cottage she'd been assigned for her four-week locum.

'It's hot. I swear I got sunburnt walking from the car to the front door.' Izzy glanced down at the tiny white circle on her finger where her engagement ring had been for the last four years. *Not sunburnt enough.*

'Have you met any of the locals yet?'

'Just a couple of people so far,' Izzy said. 'The clinic receptionist, Margie Green, seems very nice, very motherly. She made sure the cottage was all set up for me with the basics. There's a general store run by a husband and wife team—Jim and Meg Collis—who are very friendly too. And the guy who owns and operates the local pub—I think his name is Mike something or other—has organised a welcome-drink-cum-party for me for tomorrow night. Apparently the locals grab at any excuse to party so I didn't like to say I'd prefer to lie low and find my feet first.'

'Perfect timing,' Hannah said. 'At least you won't be on your own on your birthday.'

On your own...

Izzy was still getting used to being single. She'd become so used to fitting in with Richard Remington's life—*his meticulously planned life*—that it was taking her a little while to adjust. The irony was she had been the one to end things. Not that he'd been completely devastated or anything. He'd moved on astonishingly quickly and was now living with a girl ten years younger than he was who had been casually employed to hand around drinks at one of his parents' soirees—another irony, as he had been so adamant about not moving in with Izzy while they'd been together.

This four weeks out at Jerringa Ridge—the first of six one-month locums she had organised in Australia—would give her the space to stretch her cramped wings, to finally fly free from the trappings and expectations of her aristocratic background.

Out here she wasn't Lady Isabella Courtney with a pedigree that went back hundreds of years.

She was just another GP, doing her bit for the Outback.

'Have you met the new doctor yet?' Jim Collis asked, as Zach Fletcher came into the general store to pick up some supplies the following day.

'Not yet.' Zach picked up a carton of milk and checked the use-by date. 'What's he like?'

'She.'

He turned from the refrigerated compartment with raised brows. 'No kidding?'

'You got something against women doctors?' Jim asked.

'Of course not. I just thought a guy had taken the post. I'm sure that's what William Sawyer said before he went on leave.'

'Yeah, well, it seems that one fell through,' Jim said. 'Dr Courtney stepped into the breach at the last minute. She's from England. Got an accent like cut glass.'

Zach grunted as he reached for his wallet. 'Hope she knows what she's in for.'

Jim took the money and put it in the till. 'Mike's putting on a welcome do for her tonight at the pub. You coming?'

'I'm on duty.'

'Doesn't mean you can't pop in and say g'day.'

'I'd hate to spoil the party by showing up in uniform,' Zach said.

'I don't know…' Jim gave him a crooked grin. 'Some women really get off on a guy in uniform. You could get lucky, Fletch. Be about time. How long's it been?'

Zach gave him a look as he stuffed his wallet in his back pocket. 'Not interested.'

'You're starting to sound like your old man,' Jim said. 'How is he? You haven't brought him into town for a while.'

'He's doing OK.'

Jim gave him a searching look. 'Sure?'

Zach steeled his gaze. 'Sure.'

'Tell him we're thinking of him.'

'Will do.' Zach turned to leave.

'Her name is Isabella Courtney,' Jim said. 'Got a nice figure on her and pretty too, in a girl-next-door sort of way.'

'Give it a break, Jim.'

'I'm just saying…'

'The tyres on your ute are bald.' Zach gave him another hardened look as he shouldered open the door. 'Change them or I'll book you.'

Zach's father Doug was sitting out on the veranda of Fletcher Downs homestead; the walking frame that had been his constant companion for the last eighteen months by his side. A quad-bike accident had left Doug Fletcher with limited use of his legs. It would have been a disaster for any person, but for a man who only knew how to work and live on the land it was devastating.

Seeing his strong and extremely physically active father struck down in such a way had been bad enough, but the last couple of months his dad had slipped into a funk of depression that made every day a nightmare of anguish for Zach. Every time he drove up the long drive to the homestead his heart rate would escalate in panic in case his dad had done something drastic in his absence, and it wouldn't slow down again until he knew his father had managed to drag himself through another day.

Popeye, the toy poodle, left his father's side to greet Zach with a volley of excited yapping. In spite of everything, he couldn't help smiling at the little mutt. 'Hey, little buddy.' He crouched down and tickled the little dog's soot-black fleecy ears. He'd chosen the dog at a rescue shelter in Sydney when he'd gone to bring his dad home from the rehabilitation centre. Well, really, it had been the other way around. Popeye had chosen him. Zach had intended to get a man's dog, a kelpie or a collie, maybe even a German shepherd like the one he'd worked with in the drug squad, but somehow the little black button eyes had looked at him unblinkingly as if to say, *Pick me!*

'Jim says hello,' Zach said to his father as he stepped into the shade of the veranda.

His father acknowledged the comment with a grunt as he continued to stare out at the parched paddocks, which instead of being lime green with fresh growth were the depressing colour of overripe pears.

'There's a new doctor in town—a woman.' Zach idly kicked a stray pebble off the floorboards of the veranda

into the makeshift garden below. It had been a long time
since flowers had grown there. Twenty-three years, to
be exact. His English born and bred mother had attempted to grow a cottage garden similar to the one
she had left behind on her family's country estate in
Surrey, but, like her, none of the plants had flourished
in the harsh conditions of the Outback.

'You met her?' His father's tone was flat, as if he
didn't care one way or the other, but at least he had responded. That meant it was a good day. A better day.

'Not yet,' Zach said. 'I'm on duty this evening. I'm
covering for Rob. I thought I'd ask Margie to come over
and sit with—'

Doug's mouth flattened. 'How many times do I have
to tell you I don't need a bloody babysitter?'

'You hardly see any of your old mates these days.
Surely a quiet drink with—'

'I don't want people crying and wringing their hands
and feeling sorry for me.' Doug pulled himself to his
feet and reached for his walker. 'I'll see people when I
can drive into town and walk into the pub on my own.'

Zach watched as his father shuffled back down the
other end of the veranda to the French doors that led
to his bedroom. The lace curtains billowed out like
a ghostly wraith as the hot, dry northerly wind came
through, before the doors closed with a rattling snap
that made every weatherboard on the old house creak
in protest.

These days it seemed every conversation he had with
his dad ended in an argument. Moving back home after
five years of living in the city had seemed the right idea
at the time, but now he wondered if it had made things
worse. It had changed their relationship too much. He'd

always planned to come back to the country and run Fletcher Downs once his father was ready to retire, but the accident had thrown everything out of order. This far out in the bush it was hard to get carers to visit, let alone move in, and without daily support his father would have no choice but to move off the property that had been in the family for seven generations.

The day Zach's mother had left had broken his father's heart; leaving Fletcher Downs before his time would rip it right out of his chest.

Popeye gave a little whine at Zach's feet. He bent back down and the dog leapt up into his arms and proceeded to anoint his face with a frenzy of enthusiastic licks. He hugged the dog against his chest as he looked at the sunburnt paddocks. 'We'll get him through this, Popeye. I swear to God we will.'

The Drover's Rest was nothing like the pubs at home but the warm welcome Izzy received more than made up for it. Mike Grantham, the proprietor, made sure she had a drink in her hand and then introduced her to everyone who came in the door. She had trouble remembering all of their names, but she was sure it wouldn't be too long before she got to know them, as she was the only doctor serving the area, which encompassed over two hundred and fifty square kilometres.

Once everyone was inside the main room of the pub Mike tapped on a glass to get everyone's attention. 'A little bird told me it's Dr Courtney's birthday today, so let's give her a big Jerringa Ridge welcome.'

The room erupted into applause and a loud and slightly off-key singing of 'Happy Birthday' as two of the local ladies came out with a cake they had made, complete with candles and Izzy's name piped in icing over the top.

'How did you know it was my birthday?' Izzy asked Mike, once she'd blown out the candles.

'I got a call yesterday,' he said. 'A friend of yours from the old country. She gave me the heads up. Said she had a surprise lined up. It should be here any minute now. Why don't you go and wait by the door? Hey, clear a pathway! Let the doc get through.'

Izzy felt her face grow warm as she made her way through the smiling crowd of locals to the front door of the pub. *Why couldn't Hannah send her flowers or chocolate or champagne, like normal people did?*

And then she saw it.

Not it—*him*.

Tall. Muscled. Toned. Buffed. Clean-shaven. A jaw strong and square and determined enough to land a fighter jet on. A don't-mess-with-me air that was like an invisible wall of glass around him. Piercing eyes that dared you to outstare him.

A male stripper.

Dressed as a cop.

I'm going to kill you, Hannah.

Izzy went into damage control. The last thing she wanted was her reputation ruined before she saw her first patient. She could fix this. It would be simple. Just because Hannah had paid the guy—the rather gorgeous hot guy—to come out all this way and strip for her, it didn't mean she had to let him go through with it.

As long as he got his money, right?

'I'm afraid there's been a change of plan,' she said, before the man could put a foot inside the pub. 'I won't be needing your…er…services after all.'

The man—who had rather unusual grey-blue eyes—looked down at her from his far superior height. 'Excuse me?'

Izzy had to speak in a hushed tone as she could feel the crowd starting to gather behind her. 'Please, will you just leave? I don't want you here. It will spoil everything for me.'

One of the man's eyebrows lifted quizzically. 'Let me get this straight...you don't want me to step inside the pub?'

'No. Absolutely not.' Izzy adopted an adamant stance by planting her hands on her hips. 'And I strictly forbid you to remove any of your clothes in my presence. Do you understand?'

Something in those eyes glinted but the rest of his expression was still deadpan. 'How about if I take off my hat?'

She let out a breath and dropped her arms back by her sides, clenching her hands to keep some semblance of control. She *had* to get rid of him. *Now.* 'Are you *listening* to me? I don't want you here.'

'Last time I looked it was a free country.'

Izzy glowered at him. 'Look, I know you get paid to do this sort of stuff, but surely you can do much better? Don't you find this horribly demeaning, strutting around at parties, titillating tipsy women in a leather thong or whatever it is you get down to? Why don't you go out and get a real job?'

'I love my job.' The glint in his eyes made its brief appearance again. 'I've wanted to do it since I was four years old.'

'Then go and do your job someplace else,' she said

from behind gritted teeth. 'If you don't leave right now, I'm going to call the police.'

'He *is* the police,' Mike called out from behind the bar.

CHAPTER TWO

ZACH LOOKED DOWN at the pretty heart-shaped face that was now blushing a fire-engine-red. Her rosebud mouth was hanging open and her toffee-brown eyes were as wide as the satellite dish on the roof of the pub outside. He put out a hand, keeping his cop face on. 'Sergeant Zach Fletcher.'

Her slim hand quivered slightly as it slid into the cage of his. 'H-how do you do? I'm Isabella Court-ney…the new locum doctor…in case you haven't al-ready guessed.'

He kept hold of her hand a little longer than he needed to. He couldn't seem to get the message through to his brain to release her. The feel of her satin-soft skin against the roughness of his made something in his groin tighten like an over-tuned guitar string. 'Wel-come to Jerringa Ridge.'

'Thank you.' She slipped her hand away and used it to tuck an imaginary strand of hair behind her ear. 'I'm sorry. I expect you think I'm a complete fool but my friend told me she'd organised a surprise and I thought—well, I thought you were the surprise.'

'Sorry to disappoint you.'

'I'm relieved, not disappointed.' She blushed again.

'Quite frankly, I hate surprises. Hannah—that's my friend—thinks it's funny to shock me. Every year she comes up with something outrageous to make my birthday memorable.'

'I guess this will be one you won't forget in a hurry.'

'Yes…' She bit her lip with her small but perfectly aligned white teeth.

'Is there a Dr Courtney around here?' A young man dressed in a courier delivery uniform came towards them from the car park, his work boots crunching on the dusty gravel.

'Um, I'm Dr Courtney.' Isabella's blush had spread down to her décolletage by now, taking Zach's eyes with it. She was of slim build but she had all the right girly bits, a fact his hormones acknowledged with what felt like a stampede racing through his blood.

Cool it, mate.

Not your type.

'I have a package for you,' the delivery guy said. 'I need a signature.'

Zach watched as Isabella signed her name on the electronic pad. She gave the delivery guy a tentative smile as she took the package from him. It was about the size of a shoebox and she held it against her chest like a shield.

'Aren't you going to open it?' Zach asked.

Her cheeks bloomed an even deeper shade of pink. 'I think I'll wait until I'm…until later.'

There was a small silence…apart from the sound of forty or so bodies shuffling and jostling behind them to get a better view.

Zach had lived long enough in Jerringa Ridge to know it wouldn't take much to get the local tongues wagging. Ever since his fiancée Naomi had called off their relationship when he'd moved back home to take care of his father, everyone in town had taken it upon themselves to find him a replacement. He only had to look at a woman once and the gossip would run like a scrub fire. But whether he was in the city or the country, he liked to keep his private life off the grapevine. It meant for a pretty dry social life but he had other concerns right now.

'I'd better head back to the station. I hope you enjoy the rest of your birthday.' He gave Isabella Courtney a brisk impersonal nod while his body thrummed with the memory of her touch. 'Goodnight.'

Izzy watched Zach stride out of the reach of the lights of the pub to where his police vehicle was parked beneath a pendulous willow tree. *Argh!* If only she'd checked the car park before she'd launched into her I-don't-want-you-here speech. How embarrassing! She had just made an utter fool of herself, bad enough in front of *him* but practically the whole town had been watching. Would she ever live it down? Would everyone snigger at her now whenever they saw her?

And how would she face him again?

Oh, he might have kept his face as blank as a mask but she knew he was probably laughing his head off at her behind that stony cop face of his. Would he snigger as well with his mates at how she had mistaken him for a— Oh, it was too *awful* to even think about.

Of course he didn't look anything like a stripper, not that she had seen one in person or anything, only pictures of some well-built guys who worked the show circuit in Vegas. One of the girls she'd shared a flat with

in London had hung their risqué calendar on the back
of the bathroom door.

Idiot.

Fool.

Imbecile.

How could you possibly think he was—?

'So you've met our gorgeous Zach,' Peggy McLeod,
one of the older cattleman's wives, said at Izzy's shoulder, with obvious amusement in her voice.

Izzy turned around and pasted a smile on her face.
'Um, yes… He seems very…um…nice.'

'He's single,' Peggy said. 'His ex-fiancée changed her
mind about moving to the bush with him. He and his
dad run a big property out of town—Fletcher Downs.
Good with his hands, that boy. Knows how to do just
about anything. Make someone a fine husband one day.'

'That's…um, nice.'

'His mum was English too, did you know?' Peggy
went on, clearly not expecting an answer for she continued without pause. 'Olivia married Doug after a whirlwind courtship but she never could settle to life on the
land. She left when Zach was about eight or nine…or
was it ten? Yes, it was ten, I remember now. He was in
the same class as one of my sister's boys.'

Izzy frowned. 'Left?'

Peggy nodded grimly. 'Yep. Never came back, not
even to visit. Zach used to fly over to England for holidays occasionally. Took him ages to settle in, though.
Eventually he stopped going. I don't think he's seen his
mother in years. Mind you, he's kind of stuck here now
since the accident.'

'The accident?'

'Doug Fletcher rolled his quad bike about eighteen

months back. Crushed his spinal cord.' Peggy shook her head sadly. 'A strong, fit man like that not able to walk without a frame. It makes you want to cry, doesn't it?'

'That's very sad.'

'Zach looks after him all by himself,' Peggy said. 'How he does it is anyone's guess. Doug won't hear of having help in. Too proud and stubborn for his own good. Mind you, Zach can be a bit that way too.'

'But surely he can't look after his father indefinitely?' Izzy said. 'What about his own life?'

Peggy's shoulders went up and down. 'Doesn't have one, far as I can see.'

Izzy walked back to her cottage a short time later. The party was continuing without her, which suited her just fine. Everyone was having a field day over her mistaking Zach Fletcher for a stripper. There was only so much ribbing she could take in one sitting. Just as well she was only here for a month. It would be a long time before she would be able to think about the events of tonight without blushing to the roots of her hair.

The police station was a few doors up from the clinic at the south end of the main street. She hadn't noticed it earlier but, then, during the day it looked like any other nondescript cottage. Now that it was fully dark the police sign was illuminated and the four-wheel-drive police vehicle Zach had driven earlier was parked in the driveway beside a spindly peppercorn tree.

As she was about to go past, Zach came out of the building. He had a preoccupied look on his face and almost didn't see her until he got to the car. He blinked and pulled up short, as if she had appeared from nowhere. He tipped his hat, his voice a low, deep burr in the silence of the still night air. 'Dr Courtney.'

'Sergeant Fletcher.' If he was going to be so formal then so was she. Weren't country people supposed to be friendly? If so, he was certainly showing no signs of it.

His tight frown put his features into shadow. 'It's late to be out walking.'

'I like walking.'

'It's not safe to do it on your own.'

'But it's so quiet out here.'

'Doesn't make it safe.' His expression was grimly set. 'You'd be wise to take appropriate measures in future.'

Izzy put her chin up pertly. 'I didn't happen to see a taxi rank anywhere.'

'Do you have a car?'

'Of course.'

'Next time use it or get a lift with one of the locals.' He opened the passenger door of the police vehicle. 'Hop in. I'll run you home.'

Izzy bristled at his brusque manner. 'I would prefer to walk, if you don't mind. It's only a block and I—'

His grey-blue eyes hardened. 'I do mind. Get in. That's an order.'

The air seemed to pulse with invisible energy as those strong eyes held hers. She held his gaze for as long as she dared, but in the end she was the first to back down. Her eyes went to his mouth instead and a frisson of awareness scooted up her spine to tingle each strand of her hair on her scalp. Something shifted in her belly…a turning, a rolling-over sensation, like something stirring after a long hibernation.

His mouth was set tightly, as tight and determined as his jaw, which was in need of a fresh shave. His eyes were fringed with dark lashes, his eyebrows the same rich dark brown as his hair. His skin was deeply tanned and it was that stark contrast with his eyes that was so heart-stopping. Smoky grey one minute, ice-blue the next, the outer rims of his irises outlined in dark blue, as if someone had traced their circumference with a fine felt-tip marker.

Eyes that had seen too much and stored the memories away somewhere deep inside for private reflection…or haunting.

'Fine, I'll get in,' Izzy said with bad grace. 'But you really need to work on your kerb-side manner.'

He gave her an unreadable look as he closed the door with a snap. She watched him stride around to the driver's side, his long legs covering the distance in no time at all. He was two or three inches over six feet and broad shouldered and lean hipped. When he joined her in the car she felt the space shrink alarmingly. She drew herself in tightly, crossing her arms and legs to keep any of her limbs from coming into contact with his powerfully muscled ones.

The silence prickled like static electricity.

'Peggy McLeod told me about your father's accident,' Izzy said as he pulled to the kerb outside her cottage half a minute later. She turned in her seat to look at him. 'I'm sorry. That must be tough on both of you.'

Zach's marble-like expression gave nothing away but she noticed his hands had tightened on the steering-wheel. 'Do you make house calls?'

'I…I guess so. Is that what Dr Sawyer did?'

'Once a week.'

'Then I'll do it too. When would you like me to come?'

Some of the tension seemed to leave his shoulders

but he didn't turn to look at her. 'I'll ring Margie and make an appointment.'

'Fine.'

Another silence.

'Look, about that little mix-up back at the pub—' she began.

'Forget it,' he cut her off. 'I'll wait until you get inside. Lock the door, won't you?'

Izzy frowned. 'You know you're really spooking me with this over-vigilance. Don't you know everyone in a town this size by name?'

'We have drive-throughs who cause trouble from time to time. It's best not to take unnecessary risks.'

'Not everyone is a big bad criminal, Sergeant Fletcher.'

He reached past her to open her door. Izzy sucked in a sharp breath as the iron bar of his arm brushed against her breasts, setting every nerve off like a string of fireworks beneath her skin.

For an infinitesimal moment her gaze meshed with his.

He had tiny blue flecks in that unreadable sea of grey and his pupils were inky-black. He smelt of lemons with a hint of lime and lemongrass and something else... something distinctly, arrantly, unapologetically male.

A sensation like the unfurling petals of a flower brushed lightly over the floor of her belly.

Time froze.

The air tightened. Pulsed. Vibrated.

'Sorry.' He pulled back and fixed his stare forward again, his hands gripping the steering-wheel so tightly his tanned knuckles were bone white.

'No problem.' Izzy's voice came out a little rusty. 'Thanks for the lift.'

He didn't drive off until she had closed the door of the cottage. She leant back against the door and let out a breath she hadn't realised she'd been holding, listening as his car growled away into the night.

'So what did your friend actually send you for your birthday?' Margie Green asked as soon as Izzy arrived at the clinic the next morning.

'I haven't opened it yet.' *Because I stupidly left it in Sergeant Fletcher's car last night.*

Margie's eyes were twinkling. 'What on earth made you think our Zach was a male stripper?'

Izzy cringed all over again. Was every person in town going to do this to her? Remind her of what a silly little idiot she had been? If so, four weeks couldn't go fast enough. 'Because it's exactly the sort of thing my friend Hannah would do. As soon as I saw him standing there I went into panic mode. I didn't stop to think that he could be a real cop. I didn't even know if Jerringa Ridge *had* a cop. I didn't have time to do much research on the post because the agency asked me to step in for someone at the last minute.'

'We have two cops…or one and a half really,' Margie said. 'We used to have four but with all the government cutbacks that's no longer the case. Rob Heywood is close to retirement so Zach does the bulk of the work. He's a hard worker is our Zach. You won't find a nicer man out in these parts.'

'I'm not here to find a man.' Why did every woman over fifty—including her own mother—seem to think younger women had no other goal than to get married? 'I'm here to work.'

Margie cocked her head at a thoughtful angle. 'You're here for four weeks. These days that's a long time for a young healthy woman like you to be without a bit of male company.'

Izzy's left thumb automatically went to her empty ring finger. It was a habit she was finding hard to break. It wasn't that she regretted her decision to end things with Richard. It was just strange to feel so…so unattached. She hadn't looked at another man in years. But now she couldn't get Zach Fletcher's eyes or his inadvertent touch out of her head…*or her body*. Even now she could remember the feel of that slight brush of his arm across her breasts—the electric, tingly feel of hard male against soft female…

She gave herself a mental shake as she picked up a patient's file and leafed through it. 'I'm not interested in a relationship. There'd be no point. I'm on a working holiday. I won't be in one place longer than a month.'

'Zach hasn't dated anyone since he broke up with his ex,' Margie said, as if Izzy hadn't just described her plans for the next six months. 'It'd be good for him to move on. He was pretty cut up about Naomi not wanting to come with him to the bush. Not that he's said anything, of course. He's not one for having his heart flapping about on his sleeve. He comes across as a bit arrogant at times but underneath all that he's a big softie. Mind you, you might have your work cut out for you, being an English girl and all.'

Izzy lowered the notes and frowned. 'Because his mother was English?'

'Not only English but an aristocrat.' Margie gave

a little sniff that spoke volumes. 'One of them blue-blooded types. Her father was a baron or a lord of the realm or some such thing. Olivia Hardwick was as posh as anything. Used to having servants dancing around her all her life. No wonder she had so much trouble adjusting to life out here. Love wasn't enough in the end.'

Izzy thought of the veritable army of servants back at Courtney Manor. They were almost part of the furniture, although she tried never to take any of them for granted. But now was probably not a good time to mention her background with its centuries-old pedigree.

Margie sighed as sat back in her chair. 'It broke Doug's heart when she left. He hasn't looked at another woman since…more's the pity. He and I used to hang out a bit in the old days. Just as friends.'

'But you would have liked something more?' Izzy asked.

Margie gave her a wistful smile. 'We can't always have what we want, can we?'

Izzy glanced at the receptionist's left hand. 'You never married?'

'Divorced. A long time ago. Thirty years this May. I shouldn't have married Jeff but I was lonely at the time.'

'I'm sorry.'

Margie shrugged.

'Did you have children?'

'A boy and a girl. They both live in Sydney. And I have three grandchildren who are the joy of my life. I'm hoping to get down to see them at Easter.'

Izzy wondered if Margie's marriage had come about because of Doug Fletcher's involvement with Olivia. How heartbreaking it must have been for her to watch him fall madly in love with someone else, and how sad for Doug to have the love of his life walk out on him and their young son.

Relationships were tricky. She knew that from her own parents, who had a functional marriage but not a particularly happy or fulfilling one. That was one of the reasons she had decided to end things with Richard. She hadn't wanted to end up trapped in an empty marriage that grumbled on just for the sake of appearances.

'Sergeant Fletcher asked me to make a house call on his father,' Izzy said. 'Has he rung to make an appointment yet?'

'Not yet,' Margie said. 'He might drop in on his way to the station. Ah, here he is now. Morning, Zach. We were just talking about you.'

Izzy turned to see Zach Fletcher duck his head slightly to come through the door. Her stomach did a little freefall as his eyes met hers. He looked incredibly commanding in his uniform; tall and composed with an air of untouchable reserve. How on earth she had mistaken him for anything other than a cop made her cheeks fire up all over again. She ran her tongue over her lips before she gave him a polite but distant smile. 'Good morning, Sergeant Fletcher.'

He dipped his head ever so slightly, his eyes running over her in a lazy, unreadable sweep that set her pulse rate tripping. 'Dr Courtney.'

Izzy's smile started to crack around the edges. Did he have to look at her so unwaveringly, as if he knew how much he unsettled her? Was he laughing at her behind that inscrutable cop mask? 'What can I do for you? Would you like to make an appointment for me to come out and see your father today? I could probably work something in for later this afternoon. I'm pretty solidly booked but—'

He handed her the package the delivery guy had delivered the night before, his eyes locking on hers in a way that made the base of her spine shiver and fizz. 'You left this in my car last night.'

Izzy could practically hear Margie's eyes popping out of her head behind the reception counter. 'Oh… right, thanks.' She took the package from him and held it against her chest, where her heart was doing double time.

'Aren't you going to open it?' Margie said.

'Um…not right now.'

Was that a hint of mockery glinting in Zach Fletcher's eyes? 'What time would suit you?' he asked.

'I…I think I'd rather do it when I get home.'

The glint in his eyes was unmistakable this time, so too was the slight curve at one side of his mouth. His version of a smile? It made her hungry to see a real one. Was he capable of stretching that grim mouth that far? 'I meant what time would suit you to see my father.'

Izzy's blush deepened. What was it about this man that made her feel about twelve years old? Well, maybe not twelve years old. Right now she was feeling *incredibly* adult. X-rated adult. Every particle of her flesh was shockingly aware of him. Her skin was tight, her senses alert, her pulse rate rising, her heart fluttering like a butterfly trapped in the narrow neck of a bottle. 'Oh…' She swung back to Margie. 'What time am I free?'

'Your last patient is at four forty-five. It's a twenty-minute drive out to Fletcher Downs so shall we say five-thirty, give or take a few minutes?' Margie said.

'I'll make sure I'm there to let you in,' Zach said.

'My father can be a bit grouchy meeting people for the first time. Don't let him get to you.'

Izzy raised her chin the tiniest fraction. 'I'm used to handling difficult people.'

His eyes measured hers for a pulsing moment. 'Margie will give you a map. If you pass Blake's waterhole, you've gone too far.'

'I'm sure I'll find it without any trouble,' Izzy said. 'I have satellite navigation in my car.'

He gave a brisk nod that encompassed the receptionist as well as Izzy and left the clinic.

'Are you going to tell me how you ended up in his car last night or am I going to have to guess?' Margie asked.

Izzy let out a breath as she turned back around. 'He gave me a lift home.'

Margie's eyes widened with intrigue. 'From the pub? It's like half a block by city standards.'

'Yes, well, apparently Sergeant Fletcher thinks it's terribly unsafe to walk home at night without an escort. Typical cop, they think everyone's a potential criminal. They never see the good in people, only the bad. They have power issues too. You can pick it up a mile off. I'd bet my bottom dollar Zach Fletcher is a total control freak. And a blind man could see he has a chip on his shoulder the size of a boulder.'

Margie smiled a knowing smile. 'You like him.'

'What on earth gives you that idea?' Izzy gave a scornful little laugh but even to her ears it sounded tinny. 'He's not my type.'

And I bet I'm not his either.

CHAPTER THREE

ZACH HAD BEEN at the homestead long enough to change out of his uniform, make his father a cup of tea, and take Popeye for a walk down to the dam and back when he saw Isabella Courtney coming up the driveway.

He waved a fly away from his face as he watched her handle the corrugations of the gravel driveway that was as long as some city streets. A dust cloud plumed out in her wake and a flock of sulphur-crested white cockatoos and salmon-pink corellas flew out of the gum trees that lined the driveway before settling in another copse of trees closer to the dam. The chorus of cicadas was loud in the oven-warm air and in the distance the grey kangaroo he'd rescued as a joey, and who now had a joey of her own, hopped towards a few tufts of grass that had pushed up through the parched ground around the home paddock's water trough.

Popeye gave a whine and looked up at Zach as his body did its little happy dance at the thought of a visitor. 'Cool it, buddy,' Zach said. 'She's not staying long.'

It was hard to ignore the stirring of male hormones in his body as he watched her alight from the car. She had a natural grace about her, lissom and lithe, like a ballerina or yoga enthusiast. She wasn't particularly tall, or at least not compared to him at six feet three in bare feet. She was about five-six or -seven with a waist he could probably span with his hands, and her features were classically beautiful but in a rather understated way. She wore little or no make-up and her mid-length chestnut hair was tied back in a ponytail she had wound around itself in a casual knot, giving her a fresh, youthful look.

But it was her mouth his gaze kept tracking to. It was soft and full and had an upward curve that made it look like she was always on the brink of smiling.

'Oh, what an adorable dog!' Her smile lit up her brown eyes so much that they sparkled as she bent down to greet Popeye. 'Oh, you darling little poppet. Who's a good boy? Hang on a minute—*are* you a boy? Oh, yes, you are, you sweet little thing. Yes, I love you too.' She laughed a tinkling-bell laugh and stood up again, her smile still stunningly bright as she stood and faced Zach. 'Is he yours?'

Zach had to take a moment to gather himself after being on the receiving end of that dazzling smile.

Earth to Zach. Do you read me?

He wondered if he should fob Popeye off as his father's but he had a feeling she wouldn't buy it for a moment. 'Yes.'

She angled her head at him in an appraising manner. 'Funny, I had you picked as a collie or kelpie man, or maybe a German shepherd or Doberman guy.'

He kept his expression blank. 'The station manager has working dogs. Popeye's just a pet.'

She brushed a tendril of hair away from her face that the light breeze had worked loose. 'This is a lovely property. I couldn't believe how many birds I saw coming up the driveway.'

'You're not seeing it at its best. We need rain.'

She scanned the paddocks with one of her hands shading her eyes against the sun. 'It's still beautiful— Oh, there's a kangaroo and it's got a joey! He just popped his head out. How gorgeous!'

'That's Annie,' Zach said.

She swung around to look at him again. 'Is she a pet too?'

'Not really.' He waved another fly away from his face. 'Her mother was killed on the highway. I reared her by hand and released her back into the wild a few years ago, but she hangs about a bit, mostly because of the drought.'

Her eyes widened in surprise. 'You reared her yourself?'

'Yeah.'

Her pretty little nose was wrinkled over the bridge from her small frown. 'Like with a bottle or something?'

'Yep. Six feeds a day.'

'How did you juggle that with work?'

'I took her with me in a pillowcase.'

She blinked a couple of times as if she couldn't quite imagine him playing wet-nurse. 'That's…amazing…' She looked back at the paddock where Annie was grazing. 'It must be wonderful to have all this space to yourself. To be this close to wildlife and to breathe in such fresh air instead of pollution.'

Zach saw her finely shaped nostrils widen to take in the eucalyptus scent of the bush. He picked up a faint trace of her fragrance in the air: a flowery mix that was redolent of gardenias and vanilla. The sun caught the golden highlights in her hair and he found himself wondering what it would feel like to run his fingers through those glossy, silky strands.

Get a grip.

He thrust his hands in his pockets, out of the way of temptation. She was a blow-in and would be gone before the first dust storm hit town. His track record with keeping women around wasn't flash. His mother had whinged and whined and then withdrawn into herself for ten years before she'd finally bolted and never returned. His fiancée hadn't even got as far as the Outback before the call of the city had drawn her back. Why would Isabella Courtney with her high-class upbringing have anything to offer him?

She turned back to look at him and a slight blush bloomed in her cheeks. 'I guess I should get on with why I came here. Is your father inside?'

'Yes. Come this way.'

Izzy stepped into the cool interior of the homestead but it took her eyes a moment to adjust to the dim interior after the assault of the bright sunlight outside. A man who was an older version of Zach sat in an armchair in the sitting room off the long, wide hallway; a walking frame was positioned nearby. He had steel-grey hair at his temples and his skin was weathered by long periods in the sun but he was still a fine-looking man. He had the same aura of self-containment his son possessed, and a strong uncompromising jaw, although his cheeks were hollowed by recent weight loss. His mouth had a downward turn and his blue eyes had damson-coloured shadows beneath them, as if he had trouble sleeping.

'Dad, Dr Courtney is here,' Zach said.

'Hello, Mr Fletcher.' Izzy held out her hand but dropped it back by her side when Doug Fletcher rudely ignored it.

He turned his steely gaze to his son. 'Why didn't you tell me she was a bloody Pom?'

Zach tightened his mouth. 'Because it has nothing to do with her ability as a medical practitioner.'

'I don't want any toffee-nosed Poms darkening my doorstep ever again. Do you hear me? Get her out of here.'

'Mr Fletcher, I—'

'You need to have regular check-ups and Dr Courtney is the only doctor in the region,' Zach said. 'You either see her or you see no one. I'm not driving three hundred kilometres each way to have your blood pressure checked every week.'

'My blood pressure was fine until you brought her here!' Doug snapped.

Izzy put a hand on Zach's arm. 'It's all right, Sergeant Fletcher. I'll come back some other time.'

Doug glared at her. 'You'll be trespassing if you do.'

'Well, at least the cops won't be far away to charge me, will they?' she said.

Doug's expression was as dark as thunder as he shuffled past them to exit the room. Izzy heard Zach release a long breath and turned to look at him. 'I'm sorry. I don't think I handled that very well.'

He raked a hand through his hair, leaving it sticking up at odd angles. 'You'd think after twenty-three years he'd give it a break, wouldn't you?'

'Is that how long it's been since your mother left?'

He gave her a grim look. 'Yeah. I guess you twigged she was English.'

'Peggy McLeod told me.'

He walked over to the open fireplace and kicked a gum nut back into the grate. His back and shoulders were so tense Izzy could see each muscle outlined by his close-fitting T-shirt. He rubbed the back of his neck before he turned back around to face her. 'I'm worried about him.'

'I can see that.'

'I mean *really* worried.'

Izzy saw the haunted shadows in his eyes. 'You think he's depressed?'

'Let's put it this way, I don't leave him alone for long periods. And I've taken all the guns over to a friend's place.'

She felt her heart tighten at the thought of him having to keep a step ahead of his father all the time. The pressure on the loved ones of people struggling with depression was enormous. And Zach seemed to be doing it solo. 'Has his mood dropped recently or has he been feeling low for a while?'

'It's been going down progressively since he came out of rehab.' He let out another breath as he dragged his hand over his face. 'Each day I seem to lose a little bit more of him.'

Izzy could just imagine the toll it was taking on him. He had so many responsibilities to shoulder, running his father's property as well as his career as a cop. 'Would he see someone in Sydney if I set up an appointment? I know it's a long trip but surely it would be worth it to get him the help he needs.'

'He won't go back to the city, not after spending three months in hospital. He won't even go as far as Bourke.'

'Does he have any friends who could spend time

with him?' she asked. 'It might help lift his mood to be more active socially.'

The look he threw her was derisive. 'My father is not the tea-party type.'

'What about Margie Green?'

His brows came together. 'What about her?'

'She's a close friend, isn't she? Or she was in the old days before your parents got together.'

His expression was guarded now; the drawbridge had come up again. 'You seem to have gained a lot of inside information for the short time you've been in town.'

Izzy compressed her lips. 'I can't help it if people tell me stuff. I can assure you I don't go looking for it.'

He curled his lip in a mocking manner. 'I bet you don't.'

She picked up her doctor's bag from the floor with brisk efficiency. 'I think it's time I left. I've clearly outstayed my welcome.'

Izzy had marched to the front door before he caught up with her. 'Dr Courtney.' It was a command, not a request or even an apology. She drew in a tight breath and turned to face him. His expression still had that reserved unreadable quality to it but something about his eyes made her think he was not so much angry at her as at the situation he found himself in.

'Yes?'

He held her gaze for a long moment without speaking. It was as if he was searching through a filing drawer in his brain for the right words.

'*Yes?*' Izzy prompted.

'Don't give up on him.' He did that hair-scrape thing again. 'He needs time.'

'Will four weeks be long enough, do you think?' she asked.

He gave her another measured look before he opened the screen door for her. 'Let's hope so.'

'So, what did you call your new boyfriend I sent you?' Hannah asked when she video-messaged Izzy a couple of nights later.

Izzy looked at the blow-up male doll she had propped up in one of the armchairs in the sitting room. 'I've called him Max. He's surprisingly good company for a man. He doesn't hog the remote control and he doesn't eat all the chocolate biscuits.'

Hannah giggled. 'Have you slept with him?'

Izzy rolled her eyes. 'Ha-ha. I'm enjoying having the bed to myself, thank you very much.'

'So, no hot guys out in the bush?'

She hoped the webcam wasn't picking up the colour of her warm cheeks. She hadn't told Hannah about her case of mistaken identity with Zach Fletcher. She wasn't sure why. Normally she told Hannah everything that was going on in her life...well, maybe not *everything*. She had never been the type of girl to tell all about dates and boyfriends. There were some things she liked to keep private. 'I'm supposed to be using this time to sort myself out in the love department. I don't want to complicate my recovery by diving head first into an-other relationship.'

'You weren't in love with Richard, Izzy. You know you weren't. You were just doing what your parents expected of you. He filled the hole in your life after Jamie died. I'm glad you saw sense in time. Don't get me wrong—I really like Richard but he's not the one for you.'

Izzy knew what Hannah said was true. She had let things drift along for too long, raising everyone's hopes and expectations in the process. Her parents were still a little touchy on the subject of her split with Richard, whom they saw as the ideal son-in-law. The stand-in son for the one they had lost after a long and agonising battle with sarcoma.

Her decision to come out to the Australian Outback on a working holiday had been part of her strategy to take more control over her life. It was a way to remind her family that she was serious about her career. They still thought she was just dabbling at medicine until it was time to settle down and have a couple of children to carry on the long line of Courtney blood now that her older brother Jamie wasn't around to do it.

But she loved being a doctor. She loved it that she could help people in such a powerful way. Not just healing illnesses but changing lives, even saving them on occasion.

Like Jamie might have been saved if he had been diagnosed earlier...

Thinking about her brother made her heart feel like it had been stabbed. It actually seemed to jerk in her chest every time his name was mentioned, as if it were trying to escape the lunge of the sword of memory.

'Maybe you'll meet some rich cattleman out there and fall madly in love and never come home again, other than for visits,' Hannah said.

'I don't think that's likely.' Izzy couldn't imagine leaving England permanently. Her roots went down too deep. She even loved the capricious weather.

No, this trip out here was timely but not permanent.

Besides, with Jamie gone she was her parents' only child and heir. Not going home to claim her birthright would be unthinkable. She just needed a few months to let them get used to the idea of her living her own life and following her own dreams, instead of living vicariously through theirs.

Izzy's phone buzzed where it was plugged into the charger on the kitchen bench. 'Got to go, Han. I think that's a local call coming through. I'll call you in a day or two. Bye.' She picked up her phone. 'Isabella Courtney.'

'Zach Fletcher here.' Even the way he said his name was sharp and to the point.

'Good evening, Sergeant,' Izzy said, just as crisply. 'What can I do for you?'

'I just got a call about an accident out by the Honeywells' place. It doesn't sound serious but I thought you should come out with me to check on the driver. The volunteer ambos are on their way. I can be at your place in two minutes. It will save you having to find your way out there in the dark.'

'Fine. I'll wait at the front for you.'

Izzy had her doctor's bag at the ready when Zach pulled up outside her cottage. She got into the car and clipped on her seat belt, far more conscious than she wanted to be of him sitting behind the wheel with one of those unreadable expressions on his face.

Would it hurt him to crack a smile?

Say a polite hello?

Make a comment on the weather?

'Do you know who's had the accident?' she asked.

'Damien Redbank.' He gunned the engine once he

turned onto the highway and Izzy's spine slammed back against the seat. 'His father Charles is a big property owner out here. Loads of money, short on common sense, if you get my drift.'

Izzy sent him a glance. 'The son or the father?'

The top edge of his mouth curled upwards but it wasn't anywhere near a smile. 'The kid's all right. Just needs to grow up.'

'How old is he?'

'Eighteen and a train wreck waiting to happen.'

'What about his mother?'

'His parents are divorced. Vanessa Redbank remarried a few years ago.' He waited a beat before adding, 'She has a new family now.'

Izzy glanced at him again. His mouth had tightened into its default position of grim. 'Does Damien see his mother?'

'Occasionally.'

Occasionally probably wasn't good enough, Izzy thought. 'Where does she live?'

'Melbourne.'

'At least it's not the other side of the world.' She bit her lip and wished she hadn't spoken her thoughts out loud. 'I'm sorry...I hope I didn't offend you.'

He gave her a quick glance. 'Offend me how?'

Izzy tried to read his look but the mask was firmly back in place. 'It must have been really tough on you when your mother left. England is a long way away from here. It feels like *everywhere* is a long way away from here. It would've seemed even longer to a young child.'

'I wasn't a young child. I was ten.' His voice was stripped bare of emotion; as if he was reading from a script and not speaking from personal experience. 'Plenty old enough to take care of myself.'

Izzy could imagine him watching as his mother had driven away from the property for the last time. His face blank, his spine and shoulders stoically braced, while no doubt inside him a tsunami of emotion had been roiling. Had his father comforted him or had he been too consumed by his own devastation over the breakdown of his marriage? No wonder Zach had an aura of unreachability about him. It was a circle of deep loneliness that kept him apart from others. He didn't want to need people so he kept well back from them.

Unlike her, who felt totally crushed if everyone didn't take an instant shine to her. Doing and saying the right thing—*people-pleasing*—had been the script she had been handed from the cradle. It was only now that she had stepped off the stage, so to speak, that she could see how terribly lonely and isolated she had felt.

Still felt...

When had she not felt lonely? Being sent to boarding school hadn't helped. She had wanted to go to a day school close to home but her protests had been ignored. All Courtneys went to boarding school. It was a tradition that went back generations. It was what the aristocracy did. But Izzy had been too bookish and too shy to be the most popular girl. Not athletic enough to be chosen first, let alone be appointed the captain of any of the sporting teams. Too keen to please her teachers, which hadn't won her any friends. Too frightened to do the wrong thing in case she was made a spectacle of in front of the whole school. Until she'd met Hannah a couple of years later, her life had been terrifyingly, achingly lonely.

* * *

'When I was ten I still couldn't go to sleep unless all of my Barbie dolls were lined up in bed with me in exactly the right order.' *Why are you telling him this stuff?* 'I've still got them. Not with me, of course.'

Zach's gaze touched hers briefly. It was the first time she had seen a hint of a smile dare to come anywhere near the vicinity of his mouth. But just as soon as it appeared it vanished. He turned his attention back to the grey ribbon of road in front of them where in the distance Izzy could see the shape of a car wedged at a steep angle against the bank running alongside the road. Another car had pulled up alongside, presumably the person who had called for help.

'Damien's father's not going to be too happy about this,' Zach said. 'He's only had that car a couple of weeks.'

'But surely he'll be more concerned about his son?' Izzy said. 'Cars can be replaced. People can't.'

The line of his mouth tilted in a cynical manner as he killed the engine. 'Try telling Damien's mother that.'

CHAPTER FOUR

WHEN IZZY GOT to the car the young driver was sitting on the roadside, holding his right arm against his chest. 'Damien? Hi, I'm Isabella Courtney, the new locum doctor in town. I'm going to check you over. Is that OK?'

Damien gave her a belligerent look. 'I'm fine. I don't need a doctor. And before you ask—' he sent Zach a glance '—no, I wasn't drinking.'

'I still have to do a breathalyser on you, mate,' Zach said. 'It's regulation when there's been an accident.'

'A stupid wombat was in the middle of the road,' Damien said. 'I had to swerve to miss it.'

'That arm looks pretty uncomfortable,' Izzy said. 'How about I take a look at it and if it's not too bad we can send you home.'

He rolled his eyes in that universal teenage *this sucks* manner, but he co-operated while she examined him. He had some minor abrasions on his forehead and face but the airbag had prevented any major injury. His humerus, however, was angled and swollen, indicative of a broken arm. Izzy took his pulse and found it was very weak and the forearm looked dusky due to the artery being kinked at the fracture site.

'I'm going to have to straighten that arm to restore blood flow,' she said. 'I'll give you something to take the edge off it but it still might hurt a bit.' She took out a Penthrane inhalant, which would deliver rapid analgesia. 'Take a few deep breaths on this…yes, that's right. Good job.'

While Damien was taking deep breaths on the inhalant Izzy put traction on the arm and aligned it. He gave a yowl during the process but the pulse had come back into the wrist and the hand and forearm had pinked up.

'Sorry about that,' she said. 'You did really well. I'm going to put a splint on your arm so we can get you to hospital. You're going to need an orthopaedic surgeon to have a look at that fracture.'

Damien muttered a swear word under his breath. 'My dad is going to kill me.'

'I've just called him,' Zach said. 'He's on his way. The ambos are five minutes away,' he said to Izzy.

'Good,' Izzy said, as she unpacked the inflatable splint. The boy was shivering with shock by now so she gave him an injection of morphine. She was about to ask Zach to pass her the blanket out of the kit when he handed it to her. She gave him a smile. 'Mind-reader.'

He gave a shrug. 'Been at a lot of accidents.'

Izzy hated to think of how terrible some of them might have been. Cops and ambulance personnel were always at the centre of drama and tragedy. The toll it took on them was well documented. But out in the bush, where the officers often personally knew the victims, it was particularly harrowing.

The volunteer ambulance officers were two of the people Izzy had met the other night at the pub, Ken Gordon and Roger Parker. After briefing them on the boy's condition, she supervised them as they loaded Damien onto a stretcher, supporting his arm. And then, once he was loaded, she put in an IV and set some fluids running. The Royal Flying Doctor Service would take over once the ambulance had delivered the boy to the meeting point about eighty kilometres away.

Not long after the ambulance had left, a four-wheel-drive farm vehicle pulled up. A middle-aged man got out from behind the wheel and came over to where Zach was sorting out the towing of the damaged vehicle with the local farmer who had called in the accident.

'Is it a write-off?' Charles Redbank asked.

Izzy paused in the process of stripping off her sterile gloves. Although Zach had called Charles and told him Damien was OK, she still found it strange that he would want to check on the car before he saw his son. What sort of father was he? Was a car really more important to him than his own flesh and blood?

Zach put his pen back in his top pocket as he faced Charles. His mouth looked particularly grim. 'No.'

'Bloody fool,' Charles muttered. 'Was he drinking?' 'No.'

'He's not seriously hurt.' Izzy stepped forward. 'He has a broken arm that will need to be seen by an orthopaedic surgeon. I've arranged for him to be flown to Bourke. If you hurry you can catch up with the ambulance. It's only just left. You probably passed it on the road.'

'I came in on the side road from Turner's Creek,' Charles said. 'And you can think again if you think I'm going to chase after him just because he's got a broken arm. He can deal with it. He's an adult, or he's supposed to be.'

Yes, and he's had a great role model, Izzy thought. 'Damien will need a few things if he stays in hospital for a day or two. A change of clothes, a toothbrush, toiletries—that sort of thing.'

Charles gave her the once-over. 'Are you the new doctor?'

'Yes. Isabella Courtney.'

His eyes ran over her again, lingering a little too long on her breasts. 'Bit young to be a doctor, aren't you?'

Izzy had faced similar comments for most of her medical career. She did her best to not let it get to her. Just because she had a youthful appearance, it didn't mean she wasn't good at her job. 'I can assure you I am quite old enough and have all the necessary qualifications.'

'Your left brake light isn't working,' Zach said to Charles.

Charles rocked back on his heels, his gaze running between Izzy and Zach like a ferret's. 'So that's the way it is, is it? Well, well, well. You're a fast worker. She's only been in town, what, a couple of days?'

Zach's jaw looked like it had been set in place by an invisible clamp. 'I told you three weeks ago to get it fixed.'

Charles's smile was goading. 'She's a bit too upmarket for you, Fletch. And what would your old man say if you brought a posh Pommy girl home, eh? That'd go down a treat, wouldn't it?'

Izzy marvelled at Zach's self-control for even *she* felt like punching Charles Redbank. Zach looked down from his considerable height advantage at the farmer, his strong gaze unwavering. 'I'll give you twenty-four hours to get that light seen to. Ian Cooke is going to tow the car into Joe's workshop. He's gone back to town for the truck now. I'm heading to Bourke for a court appearance tomorrow. If you pack a few things for Damien, I'll swing by and pick them up before I leave in the morning.'

'Wouldn't want to put you to any trouble,' Charles said, with a deliberate absence of sincerity.

'It's no trouble,' Zach said. 'Damien's a good kid. He just needs a little direction.'

Charles's lip curled. 'What? And you think you're the one to give it to him?'

'That's your job,' Zach said, and turned away to leave. 'Coming, Dr Courtney?'

Izzy waited until they were in the car before she said, 'Is there a special section in the police training manual on how to handle jerks?'

He gave her a look as he started the engine. 'He's a prize one, isn't he?'

'You handled that situation so well. I was impressed.' She pulled down her seat belt and clicked it into place. 'Quite frankly, I wanted to punch him.'

'Two wrongs never make a right.'

Izzy studied him for a beat or two. 'Are you really going to Bourke for a court appearance tomorrow?'

He turned the car for town before he answered. 'I have the day off. It'll be an outing for my father if I can convince him to come. Take his mind off his own troubles for a change.'

'He's very lucky to have you.'

'He's a good dad. He's always tried to do his best, even under difficult circumstances.'

The township appeared in the distance, the sprinkling of lights glittering in the warm night air.

'You did a good job out there tonight.' Zach broke the silence that had fallen between them.

Izzy glanced at him again. 'You were expecting me not to, weren't you?'

'Have you worked in a remote region before?'

'I did a short stint in South Africa last year.'

His brows moved upwards. 'So why Outback Australia this year?'

'I've always wanted to come out here,' Izzy said. 'A lot of my friends had come out and told me how amazing it is. I spent a few days in Sydney on my way here. I'm looking forward to seeing a bit more after I finish my six months of locums. Melbourne, Adelaide, Perth, maybe a quick trip up to Broome and the Kimberleys.'

Another silence fell.

Izzy felt as if he was waiting for her to tell him her real reason for coming out here. It was what cops did. They waited. They listened. They observed. She had seen him looking at her ring hand while she'd been strapping up Damien. He'd been a cop too long to miss that sort of detail. 'I also wanted to get away from home for a while. My parents weren't too happy about me breaking off my engagement a couple of months ago.'

'How long were you engaged?'

'Four years.'

'Some people don't stay married that long.'

'True.' She waited a moment before saying, 'Margie told me you'd gone through a break-up a while back.'

'Yeah, well, I can't scratch my nose in this town without everyone hearing about it.' His tone was edgy, annoyed.

Izzy pushed on regardless. 'Were you together long?'

He threw her a hard glance. 'Why are you asking

me? Surely the locals have already given you all the gory details?'

'I'd like to hear it from you.'

He drove for another two kilometres or so before he spoke. 'We'd been seeing each other a year or so. We had only been engaged for a couple of months when my father had his accident.'

'So you came back home.'

'Yeah.'

'She didn't want to pull up stumps and come with you?'

'Nope.'

'I'm sorry.'

'Don't be. I'm not.' He pulled up in front of her cottage and swivelled in his seat to look at her. 'Was your fiancé a doctor?'

'A banker.' She put her hand on the door. 'Um, I should go in. It's getting late.'

'I'll walk you to the door.'

'That's not necessary...' It was too late. He was already out of the car and coming round to her side.

Izzy stepped out of the car but she misjudged the kerb and stumbled forward. Two iron-strong hands shot out and prevented her from falling. She felt every one of his fingers around her upper arms. That wasn't all she felt. Electric heat coursed through her from the top of her head to the balls of her feet. She could smell the scent of his skin, the sweat and dust and healthy male smell that was like a tantalising potion to her overly sanitised city nostrils. Her heart gave a skittish jump as she saw the way his grey-blue gaze tracked to her mouth. The pepper of his stubble was rough along his jaw, the vigorous regrowth a heady reminder of the potent hormones that marked him as a full-blooded man.

'You OK?' His fingers loosened a mere fraction as his eyes came back to hers.

'I—I'm fine...' She felt a blush run up over her skin, the heat coming from the secret core of her body. 'I'm not normally so clumsy.'

He released her and took a step backwards, his expression as unfathomable as ever. 'The ground is pretty rough out here. You need to take extra care until you find your feet.'

'I'll be careful.' Izzy pushed a strand of hair back off her face. 'Um, would you like to come in for a coffee?' *Oh. My. God. You just asked him in for coffee! What are you doing? Are you nuts?*

His brows twitched together. 'Coffee?'

'Don't all cops drink coffee? I have tea if you'd prefer. No doughnuts, I'm afraid. I guess it's kind of a cliché, you know, cops and doughnuts. I bet you don't even eat them.' *Stop talking!*

'Thanks, but no.'

No?

No?

It was hard not to feel slighted. Was she such hideous company that a simple coffee was out of the question? 'Fine.' Izzy forced a smile. 'Some other time, then.' She lifted a hand in a fingertip wave. 'Thanks for the lift. See you around.' She turned and walked quickly and purposefully to the cottage knowing he probably wouldn't drive away until she was safely inside.

'Dr Courtney.'

Izzy turned to see him holding her doctor's bag, which she had left on the back seat of his car. Her cheeks flared all over again. What was it about him that made her brain turn to scrambled mush? 'Oh… right. Might need that.'

He brought her bag to her on the doorstep, his fingers brushing against hers as he handed it over. The shock of his touch thrilled her senses all over again and her heart gave another skip-hop-skip inside her chest. The flecks of blue in his eyes seemed even darker than ever, his pupils black, bottomless inkwells.

'Thanks.' Her voice came out like a mouse squeak.

'You're welcome.'

The crackle of the police radio in the car sounded excessively loud. Jarring.

He gave her one of his curt nods and stepped down off the veranda, walking the short distance to his car, getting behind the wheel and driving off, all within the space of a few seconds.

Izzy slowly released her breath as she watched his taillights disappear into the distance.

Stop that thought.

You did not come all this way to make your life even more complicated.

Zach found his father sitting out on the southern side of the veranda when he got back to the homestead. He let out the tight breath he felt like he'd been holding all day and let his shoulders go down with it. 'Fancy a run out to Bourke tomorrow?'

'What for?'

'Damien Redbank had an accident this evening. He's fine, apart from a broken arm. He'll be in hospital a couple of days. I thought he could do with some company.'

'What's wrong with his father?'

'Good question.' Zach took off his police hat and raked his hands through his sweat-sticky hair.

Doug gave him a probing look. 'You OK?'

Zach tossed his hat onto the nearest cane chair. 'I've never felt more like punching someone's lights out.'

'Understandable. Charles has been pressing your buttons for a while now.'

'He's incompetent as a father,' Zach said. 'He's got no idea how to be a role model for that kid. No wonder the boy is running amok. He's crying out for someone to take notice of him. To show they care about him.'

'The boy hasn't been the same since his mother remarried.'

Zach grunted. 'Yeah, I know.'

The crickets chirruped in the garden below the veranda.

'What time are you thinking of heading out of town?' Doug asked.

'Sixish.'

A stone curlew let out its mournful cry and Popeye lifted his little black head off the faded cushion on the seat beside Zach's father's chair, but seeing Zach's stay signal quickly settled back down again with a little doggy sigh and closed his eyes.

'How'd the new doctor handle things?' Doug asked.

'Better than I thought she would, but it's still early days.'

His father slanted him a glance. 'Watch your step, son.'

'I'm good.'

'Yeah, that's we all say. Next thing you know she'll have your heart in a vice.'

'Not going to happen.' Zach opened and closed his

fingers where the tingling of Izzy's touch had lingered far too long. It had taken a truckload of self-control to decline her offer of coffee. Even if she had just been being polite in asking him in, he hadn't wanted to risk stepping over the boundaries.

His body had other ideas, of course. But he was going to have to tame its urges if he was to get through this next month without giving in to temptation. A fling with her would certainly break the dogged routine he'd slipped into but how would he feel when she packed her bags and drove out of town?

He had to concentrate on his father's health right now.

That was the priority.

Distractions—even ones as delightfully refreshing and dazzling as Izzy Courtney—would have to wait.

CHAPTER FIVE

IZZY REALISED ON her fourth patient the following morning that a rumour had been circulated about her and Zach Fletcher. Ida Jensen, a seventy-five-year-old farmer's wife, had come in to have her blood pressure medication renewed, but before Izzy could put the cuff on her arm to check her current reading, the older woman launched into a tirade.

'In my day a girl wouldn't dream of sleeping with a man before she was married, especially with a man she's only just met.' She pursed her lips in a disapproving manner. 'I don't know what the world's coming to, really I don't. Everyone having casual flings as if love and commitment mean nothing. It's shameful, that's what it is.'

'I guess not everyone shares the same values these days,' Izzy said, hoping to prevent an extended moral lecture.

'I blame the Pill. Girls don't have to worry about falling pregnant so they just do what they want with whoever they want. That boy needs a wife, not a mistress.'

'That…er, boy?'

'Zach Fletcher,' Ida said. 'Don't bother trying to deny it. Everyone knows you've got your eye on him, and him not even over the last one. Mind you, they do say you should get back on the horse, don't they? Never did like that saying. It's a bit coarse, if you ask me. But I think he needs more time. What if his ex changes her mind and comes out here to see you're involved with him?'

'I beg your pardon?'

Ida shifted in her chair like a broody hen settling on a clutch of eggs. 'Not that anyone could really blame you, of course. No one's saying he isn't good looking. Got a nice gentle nature too, when you get to know him.'

Izzy frowned. 'I'm sorry but I'm not sure where you got the idea that I'm involved with Sergeant Fletcher.'

'Don't bother denying it,' Ida said. 'I heard it from a very reliable source. Everyone's talking about it.'

'Then they can stop talking about it because it's not true!' Izzy was fast becoming agitated. 'Have you asked Sergeant Fletcher about this? I suggest you do so you can hear it from him as well that nothing is going on. This is nothing more than scurrilous gossip.' *And I have a feeling I know who started it.*

'Are you sure it's not true?' Ida looked a little uncomfortable.

'I think I would know who I was or wasn't sleeping with, don't you?' Izzy picked up the blood-pressure cuff. 'Now, let's change the subject, otherwise my blood pressure is going to need medication.'

'What? Don't you fancy him?' Ida asked after a moment.

Izzy undid the cuff from the older woman's arm and wrote the figure in her notes. 'I see here you're taking anti-inflammatories for your arthritis. Any trouble with your stomach on that dosage?'

'Not if I take them with food.'

'Is there anything else I can help you with?'

The older woman folded her lips together. 'I hope I haven't upset you.'

'Not at all,' Izzy lied.

'It's just we all love Zach so much. We want him to be happy.'

'I'm sure he appreciates your concern but he's a big boy and can surely take care of himself.'

'That's half the trouble…' Ida let out a heartfelt sigh. 'He's been taking care of himself for too long.'

Izzy stood up to signal the end of the consultation. 'Make another appointment to see me in a week. I'd like to keep an eye on your blood pressure. It was slightly elevated.'

Just like mine.

'Nice work, Fletch,' Jim Collis said, when Zach came in the next morning for the paper.

Zach didn't care for the ear-to-ear grin the storekeeper was wearing. 'What?'

Jim had hooked his thumbs in his belt and tilted backwards on his heels behind the counter. 'Getting it on with the new doctor. Talk about a fast mover. You want me to stock up on condoms?'

Zach kept his expression closed as he picked up a stock magazine his father enjoyed, as well as the paper. He put them both on the counter and took out his wallet. 'You should check your sources before you start spreading rumours like that.'

'You telling me it's not true?'

'Even if it was true, I wouldn't be standing here discussing it.'

'Charles Redbank seemed pretty convinced you two

were getting it on,' Jim said. 'Not that anyone would blame you for making a move on her. Be a good way to get that Naomi chick out of your system once and for all.'

Zach ground his molars together. It got under his skin that the whole town saw him as some sort of broken-hearted dude let down by his fiancée. He was over Naomi. It had been a convenient relationship that had worked well for both of them until he'd made the decision to come back to Jerringa Ridge to help his father. Yes, he was a little pissed off she hadn't wanted to come with him but that was her loss. In time he would find someone to fill her place, but he needed to get his father sorted out first.

'Anyway, way I see it,' Jim went on, 'if you don't hit on Izzy Courtney then you can bet your bottom dollar some other fella soon will.' He cleared his throat as the screen door opened. 'Hi, Dr Courtney, I got that honey and cinnamon yogurt you wanted.'

Zach hitched his hip as he put his wallet in his back pocket before turning to look at her. 'G'day.'

'Hello…' The blush on her cheeks was like the petals of a pink rose. She looked young and fresh, like a model from a fashion magazine. Her simple flowered cotton dress was cinched in at her tiny waist, her legs were bare and her feet in ballet flats. She had a string of pearls around her neck that were a perfect foil for her milk-pure skin. And even with all the other competing smells of the general store he could still pick up her light gardenia scent. It occurred to him to wonder why anyone would wear pearls in the Outback but it was something his mother had done and he knew from experience there was no explaining it.

'So, I'll get those condoms in for you, will I, Fletch?' Jim said with a cheeky grin. 'Extra-large, wasn't it?'

The blush on Izzy Courtney's cheeks intensified. Her eyes slipped out of reach of his and her teeth snagged at her full lower lip. 'Maybe I'll come back later…' She turned and went back out the screen door so quickly it banged loudly on its hinges.

Zach scooped up the paper and the magazine, giving Jim a look that would have cut through steel. 'You're a freaking jerk, you know that?'

Izzy turned at the sound of firm footsteps to find Zach coming towards her. That fluttery sensation she always got when she saw him tickled the floor of her stomach like an ostrich feather held by someone with a tremor. His mouth was tightly set, his expression formidable this time rather than masked. Her earlier blush still hadn't completely died down but as soon as his eyes met hers she felt it heat up another few degrees.

'We need to talk.' He spoke through lips so tight they barely moved.

'We do?' She saw his dark frown and continued, 'Yes, of course we do. Look, it's fine. It's just a rumour. It'll go away when they realise there's no truth in it.'

'I'm sorry but this is what happens in small country towns.'

'I realise that,' Izzy said. 'I've already had a couple of stern lectures from some of the more conservative elders in the community. It seems that out here it's still a sin for a woman to have sex before marriage. Funny, but they didn't mention it being a sin for men. That really annoys me. Why should you men have all the fun?'

His gaze briefly touched her mouth before glancing away to look at something in the distance, his eyes squinting against the brutal sunlight. 'Not all of us are having as much fun as you think.'

Izzy moistened her suddenly dry lips. 'How is your father? Did he go with you to Bourke?'

'Yes.'

'And how was Damien?'

'Feeling a bit sorry for himself.'

'Did his father end up going to see him?' Izzy brushed a wisp of hair away from her face.

He made a sound that sounded somewhere between a grunt and a laugh. 'No.'

'I guess he was too busy spreading rumours back here.'

His brooding frown was a deep V between his brows. 'I should've punched him when I had the chance.'

She studied Zach for a moment. Even without his uniform he still maintained that aura of command and control. She wondered what it would take to get under his skin enough to make him break out of that thick veneer of reserve. There was a quiet intensity about him, as if inside he was bottling up emotions he didn't want anyone to see. 'You don't seem the type of guy to throw the first punch.'

'Yeah, well, I don't get paid to pick fights.' He drew in a breath and released it in a measured way as if he was rebalancing himself. 'I'd better let you get to work. Have a good one.'

Izzy watched as he strode back to where his car was parked outside the general store. She too let out a long breath, but any hope of rebalancing herself was as likely as a person on crutches trying to ice-skate.

Not going to happen.

* * *

Almost a week went past before Izzy saw Zach again other than from a distance. Although they worked within a half a block of each other, he was on different shifts and she spent most days inside the clinic, other than a couple of house calls she had made out of town. But each time she stepped outside the clinic or her cottage or drove out along any of the roads she mentally prepared herself for running into him.

She had seen him coming out of the general store one evening as she'd been leaving work, but he'd been on the phone and had seemed preoccupied, and hadn't noticed her at all. For some reason that rankled. It didn't seem fair that she was suffering heart skips and stomach flips at the mere mention of his name and yet he didn't even sense her looking at him. Neither did he even glance at the clinic just in case she was coming out.

Izzy still had to field the occasional comment from a patient but she decided that was the price of being part of a small community. You couldn't sneeze in a town the size of Jerringa Ridge without everyone saying you had flu.

But on Saturday night, just as she was thinking about going to bed, she got a call from Jim Collis, who was down at the pub. 'Been a bit of trouble down here, Doc,' he said. 'Thought you might want to look in on Zach if you've got a minute. I reckon he might need a couple of stitches.'

'What happened?'

'Couple of the young fellas had too much to drink and got a bit lively. Zach's down at the station, waiting for the parents to show up. I told him to call you but he said it's just a bruise. Don't look like a bruise to me. He's lucky he didn't lose an eye, if you ask me.'

'I'll head down straight away.'

Izzy turned up the station just as a middle-aged couple came out with their son. The smell of alcohol was sour in the air as they walked past to bundle him into the car. The mother looked like she had been crying and the father looked angry enough to throw something. The son looked subdued but it was hard to tell if that was the excess alcohol taking effect or whether he'd faced charges.

When she went inside the building Zach was sitting behind the desk with a folded handkerchief held up to his left eye as he wrote some notes down on a sheet of paper. He glanced up and frowned at her. 'Who called you?'

'Jim Collis.'

He let out a muffled expletive. 'He had no right to do that.' He pushed back from the desk and stood up. 'It's nothing. Just a scratch.'

'Why don't you let me be the judge of that?' She held up her doctor's bag. 'I've come prepared.'

He let out a long breath as if he couldn't be bothered arguing and led the way out to the small kitchen area out the back. 'Make it snappy. I need to get home.'

Izzy pushed one of the two chairs towards him. 'Sit.'

'Can't you do it standing up?'

'I'm not used to doing it standing up...' A hot blush stormed into her cheeks when she saw the one-eyed glinting look he gave her. 'I mean...you're way too tall for me to reach you.' *God, that sounded almost worse!*

He sat in the chair with his long legs almost cutting

the room in half. She had nowhere to stand other than between them to get close enough to inspect his eye. She was acutely aware of the erotic undertones as his muscled legs bracketed her body. They weren't touching her at all but she felt the warmth of his thighs like the bars of a radiator. Her mind went crazy with images of him holding her between those powerful thighs, his body pumping into hers, those muscled arms pinning her against the bed, a wall, or some other surface. Scorching heat flowed through her veins even as she slammed the brakes on her wickedly wanton thoughts.

Doctor face. Doctor face. Mentally chanting it was the only way she could get herself back on track. She gently took the wadded handkerchief off his eye to find it bruised and swollen with a split in the skin above his eyebrow that was still oozing blood. 'You won't need stitches but you'll have a nice shiner by morning.'

He grunted. 'Told you it was nothing.'

Izzy's leg bumped against his as she reached for some antiseptic in her bag. It was like being touched with a laser—the tingles went right to her core. She schooled her features as she turned back to tend to his cut. *Cool and clinical. Cool and clinical.* She could do that. She always did that...well; she did when it was anyone other than Zach Fletcher.

She could hear his breathing; it was slow and even, unlike hers, which was shallow and picking up pace as every second passed.

His scent teased her nostrils, making her think of sun-warmed lemons. He had a decent crop of prickly stubble on his jaw. She felt it catch on the sensitive skin on the underside of her wrist as she dabbed at his wound. 'I'm sorry if this hurts. I'm just cleaning the area before I put on a Steri-strip to hold the edges of the wound together.'

'Can't feel a thing.'

She carefully positioned the Steri-strip over the wound. 'There. Now, all we need is some ice for that eye. Do you have any in the fridge?'

'I'll put some on at home.'

He got to his feet at the same time as she reached to dab at a smear of blood on his cheek. He put his hands on her each of her forearms, presumably to stop her fussing over him, but somehow his fingers slid down to her wrists, wrapping around them like a pair of handcuffs.

Izzy felt her breath screech to a halt as his hooded gaze went to her mouth. The tip of her tongue came out and moistened the sudden dryness of her lips. He was so close she could feel the fronts of his muscle-packed thighs against hers.

He looked at her mouth and her belly did a little somersault as she saw the way his eyes zeroed in on it, as if he was memorising its contours. 'This is a really dumb idea.'

'It is? I mean, yes, *of course* it is,' Izzy said a little breathlessly. 'An absolutely crazy thing to do. What were we thinking? Hey, is that a smile? I didn't think you knew how to.'

'I'm a little out of practice.' He brought her even closer, his warm vanilla- and milk-scented breath skating over the surface of her lips. 'Isn't there some rule about doctors getting involved with their patients?'

'I'm not really your doctor. Not officially. I mean I treated you, but *I* came to see you. You didn't come to see me. It's not the same as if you'd made an appointment and paid me to see you. I just saw you as a one-off. A favour, if you like. It's not even going on the record. All I did was put a Steri-strip on your head. You could have done it yourself.' She took a much-needed breath. 'Um…you're not really going to kiss me, are you?'

His grey-blue eyes smouldered. 'What do you think?'

Izzy couldn't think, or at least not once his mouth came down and covered hers. His mouth was firm and warm and tasted of salt and something unexpectedly sinful. His tongue flickered against the seam of her mouth, a teasing come-play-with-me-if-you-dare gesture that made her insides turn to liquid. She opened her mouth and he entered it with a sexy glide of his tongue that made the hairs on her scalp stand up on tiptoe, one by one. He found her tongue with devastating expertise, toying with it, cajoling it into a dance as old as time.

He put a hand on the small of her back and pressed her closer. The feel of his hot urgent male body against her called to everything that was female in her. She had always struggled with desire in the past. She could talk herself into it eventually, but it had never been an instantaneous reaction.

Now it was like a dam had burst. Desire flowed through her like a flash flood, making her flesh cry out for skin-on-skin contact. Her hands came up to link around his neck, her body pressing even closer against his. Her breasts tingled behind the lace of her bra; she had never been more aware of her body, how it felt, what it craved, how it responded.

He gave a low, deep sound of pleasure and deepened the kiss, his hands going to both of her hips and locking her against him. She felt the hardened ridge of him against her and a wave of want coursed through her so rampantly it took her breath away.

She started on his shirt, pulling it out of his trousers and snapping open the buttons so she could glide her hands over his muscled chest. She could feel his heart beneath her palm. Thud. Thud. Thud. She could feel where his heart had pumped his blood in preparation. It throbbed against her belly with a primal beat that resonated through her body like a deep echo, making her insides quiver and reverberate with longing.

He kept kissing her, deeply and passionately, as his hands ran up under her light cotton shirt. The feel of his broad, warm, work-roughened hands on her skin made her gasp out loud. Her blood felt like it was on fire as it raced through her veins at torpedo speed.

Her inner wild woman had been released. Uncaged. Unrestrained. And the wild man in him was more than up to the task of taming her. She felt it in the way he was kissing her.

This was a kiss that meant business.

This was a kiss that said sex was next.

His hands found her breasts, pushing aside the confines of her bra to cup her skin on skin. She shivered as his thumbs rolled each of her nipples in turn; all while his mouth continued its mind-blowing assault on her senses.

The sound of the door opening at the front had Izzy springing back from him as if someone had fired a gun. She assiduously avoided Zach's gaze as she tidied her clothes with fingers that refused to co-operate.

'You there, Fletch?' Jim Collis called out.

'Yeah. Won't be a tick.' Zach redid the buttons before tucking in his shirt. Izzy envied his cool cop composure as he went out to talk to Jim. Her nerves were in shreds at almost being discovered making out like teenagers in the back room.

'Is the doc still with you?' Jim asked.

There was a moment of telling silence.

'Yes, I'm still here.' Izzy stepped out, carrying her doctor's bag and what she hoped passed for doctor-just-finished-a-consult composure. 'I'm just leaving.'

Jim's eyes twinkled knowingly. 'So you've got him all sorted?'

'Er, yes.' She pasted on a tight smile. 'No serious damage done.'

'I hope you weren't annoyed with me, Fletch, for sending her over to patch you up?' Jim said.

Zach still had his cop face on. 'Not at all. She was very…professional.'

'Did you charge Adam Foster with assault?'

'Not this time. I gave him a warning.'

'You're too soft,' Jim said. 'Don't you think so, Dr Courtney?'

Izzy blushed to the roots of her hair. 'Um, it's late. I have to get home.' She gripped the handle of her bag and swung for the door. 'Goodnight.'

CHAPTER SIX

'WHAT HAPPENED TO your eye?' Doug Fletcher asked the following morning.

'I got in the way of Adam Foster's elbow.' Zach switched on the kettle. The less he talked about last night the better. The less *he thought* about last night the better. He had barely been able to sleep for thinking about Izzy Courtney's hot little mouth clamped to his, not to mention her hot little hands winding around his neck and smoothing over his chest. Even taking into account his eighteen-month sex drought, he couldn't remember ever being so turned on before. He had always prided himself on his self-control. But as soon as his mouth had connected with hers something had short-circuited in his brain.

He gave himself a mental shake and took out a couple of cups from the shelf above the sink. 'You want tea or coffee?'

'What did the doctor say?'

He frowned as he faced his father. 'What makes you think I saw the doctor? It's just a little cut and a black eye, for pity's sake. I don't know what all the fuss is about.'

His father gave him a probing look. 'Is it true?'

'Is what true?'

'The rumour going around town that you're sleeping with her.'

'Where'd you hear that?'

'Bill Davidson dropped in last night while you were at work. Said his wife Jean saw the doctor a couple of days back. She said the doctor blushed every time your name was mentioned.'

'Oh, for God's sake.' Zach wrenched open the fridge door for the milk.

'Find yourself another woman, by all means, but make sure she's a country girl who'll stick around,' his father said.

'Dad, give it a break. I'm not going to lose my head or my heart to Dr Courtney. She's not my type.'

'Your mother wasn't my type either but that didn't stop me falling in love with her, and look how that ended up.'

Zach let out a long breath. 'You really need to let it go. Mum's never coming back. You have to accept it.'

'She hasn't even called, not once. Not even an email or a get-well card.'

'That's because you told her never to contact you again after she forgot my thirtieth birthday, remember?'

His father scowled. 'What sort of mother forgets her own son's birthday?'

A mother who has two other younger sons she loves more, Zach thought. 'What do you want for breakfast?'

'Nothing.'

'Come on. You have to have something.'

'I'm not hungry.'

'Are you in pain?' Zach asked.

His father glowered. 'Stop fussing.'

'You must be getting pretty low on painkillers. You want me to get Dr Courtney to write a prescription for you?'

'I'll manage.'

He threw his father an exasperated look. 'How'd you get to be so stubborn? No wonder Mum walked out on you.'

His father's eyes burned with bitterness. 'That may be why she walked out on me but why'd she leave you?'

It was a question Zach had asked himself a thousand times. And all these years later he still didn't have an answer other than the most obvious.

She hadn't loved him enough to stay.

'So how are you and Zach getting on?' Margie asked on Monday morning.

Izzy worked extra-hard to keep her blush at bay. 'Fine.'

'Jim told me you saw to Zach's eye on Saturday night.'

'Yes.' Izzy kept her voice businesslike and efficient. 'Do you have Mrs Patterson's file there? I have to check on something.'

Margie handed the file across the counter. 'The Shearers' Ball is on the last weekend of your locum. Did Peggy tell you about it? It's to raise money for the community centre. It's not a glamorous shindig, like you'd have in England or anything. Just a bit of a bush dance and a chance to let your hair down. Will I put you down as a yes?'

It sounded like a lot of fun. Would Zach be there? Her insides gave a funny little skip at the thought of those strong arms holding her close to him in a waltz or a barn dance. 'I'll have a think about it.'

'Oh, but you must come!' Margie insisted. 'You'll have heaps of fun. People drive in from all over the district to come to it. We have a raffle and door prizes. It's the social event of the year. Everyone will be so disappointed if you don't show up. It'll be our way of thanking you for stepping in while William Sawyer and his wife were on holiday. They come every year without fail.'

Izzy laughed in defeat. 'All right. Sign me up.'

'Fabulous.' Margie grinned. 'Now I can twist Zach's arm.'

Izzy left the clinic at lunchtime to pick up the sandwich she'd ordered at the corner store. Jim gave her a wink and a cheeky smile as she came in. 'How's the patient?'

She looked at him blankly, even though she knew exactly which patient he meant. 'Which patient?'

'You don't have to be coy with me, Izzy. I know what you two were up to out back the other night. About time Zach got himself back out there. I bet that ex-fiancée of his hasn't spent the last eighteen months pining his absence.'

She kept her features neutral. 'Is my salad sandwich ready?'

'Yep.' He handed it over the counter, his grin still in place. 'Do me a favour?' He passed over another sandwich-sized package in a brown paper bag. 'Drop that in to Zach on your way past.'

Izzy took the package with a forced smile. 'Will do.'

Zach looked up when the door opened. Izzy was standing there framed by the bright sunlight. She was wearing trousers and a cotton top today but she looked no less feminine. Her hair was in one of those up styles that somehow managed to look makeshift and elegant at the same time. There was a hint of gloss on her lips, making them look even more kissable. He wondered what flavour it was today. Strawberry? Or was it raspberry again?

'Jim sent me with your lunch.' She passed it over the counter, her cheeks going a light shade of pink. He'd never known a woman to blush so much. What was going on inside that pretty little head of hers? Was she thinking of that kiss? Had she spent the night feeling restless and edgy while her body had throbbed with unmet needs, like his had?

'Thanks.' He stood up and put the sandwich to one side. 'I was going to call you about my father.'

'Oh?' Her expression flickered with concern. 'Is he unwell?'

'He's running out of prescription painkillers.'

She chewed at her lip. 'I'd have to officially see him before I'd write a script. There can be contraindications with other medications and so on.'

'Of course. I'll see if I can get him to come to the clinic.'

She shifted her weight from foot to foot. 'I could always come out again to the homestead, if you think he'd allow it. I know what it's like to have something unexpected sprung on you. Maybe if you told him ahead of time that I was coming out, he would be more amenable to seeing me.'

'I'll see what I can do.'

The elephant in the room was stealing all the oxygen out of the air.

'What about coming out for dinner tomorrow?' Zach

could hardly believe he had spoken the words until he heard them drop into the ringing silence.

Her eyes widened a fraction. 'Dinner?'

'It won't be anything fancy. I'm not much of a chef but I can rub a couple of ingredients together.'

'What about your dad?'

'He has to eat.'

'I know, but will he agree to eat if I'm there?'

He shrugged, as if he didn't care either way. 'Let's give it a try, shall we?'

Her eyes went to the Steri-strip above his eyebrow. 'Would you like me to check that wound for you?'

Zach wanted her to check every inch of his body, preferably while both of them were naked. He had to blink away the erotic image that flashed through his brain at that thought—her limbs entangled with his, his body plunging into hers. 'It's fine.'

Her gaze narrowed as she peered at him over the bridge of the desk. 'It looks a little red around the edges.'

So do your cheeks, he thought. Her eyes were remarkably steady on his, but he had a feeling she was working hard at keeping them there. 'It's not infected. I'm keeping an eye on it.'

'Right…well, if you think it's not healing properly let me know.'

Zach couldn't figure if it was her in particular or the thought of having sex again that was making him so horny. He had tried his best to avoid thinking about sex for months. But now Izzy Courtney, with her toffee-brown eyes and soft, kissable mouth, was occupying his thoughts and he was in a constant start of arousal. He could feel it now, the pulse of his blood ticking through his veins. His heightened awareness of her sweet, fresh scent, the way his hands wanted to stroke down the length of her arms, to encircle her slim wrists, to tug her up against him so she could feel the weight and throb of his erection before his mouth closed over hers.

Her gaze flicked to his mouth, as if she had read his mind, the point of her tongue sneaking out to moisten her plump, soft lips. 'Um… What time do you want me to come?' Her cheeks went an even darker shade of red.

'Er…tonight. For dinner. To see your dad.'

'Seven or thereabouts?'

'Lovely.' She backed out of the reception area but somehow managed to bump her elbow against the door as she turned on her way out. She stepped out into the bright sunshine and walked briskly down the steps and out of sight.

Zach didn't sit down again until the fragrance of her had finally disappeared.

'What do you mean, you're going out?' Zach asked his father that evening.

His father gave him an offhand glance. 'I'm entitled to a social life, aren't I?'

'Of course.' Zach raked a distracted hand through his hair. 'But tonight of all nights? You haven't been out for months.'

'It's been a while since I caught up with Margie Green. She invited me for dinner.'

'She's been inviting you for dinner for years and you've always declined.'

'Then it's high time I said yes. You're always on about me not socialising enough. I enjoyed that run up to Bourke. It made me realise I need to have a change of scene now and again.'

Zach frowned. 'Isabella Courtney is going to think I've set this up. I asked her to come out to see you, not me.'

'She can think what she likes,' his father said. 'Anyway, I don't want to cramp your style.'

'But what about your painkillers?' Zach asked. 'You know what your rehab specialist said. You have to stay in front of the pain, not chase it.'

Doug chewed that over for a moment. 'I'll think about going to the clinic in a day or two.' A car horn tooted outside. 'That's Margie now.' He shuffled to the door on his frame. 'Don't wait up.'

Within a few minutes of his father leaving with Margie, Izzy arrived. Zach held open the door for her while Popeye danced around her like he had springs on his paws. 'My father's gone out. You probably passed him on the driveway.'

'Yes, Margie waved to me on the way past. I bet she's pleased he finally agreed to have dinner with her.' She picked Popeye up and cuddled him beneath her chin. 'Hello, sweetie pie.'

Zach was suddenly jealous of his dog, who was nestled against the gentle swell of Izzy's breasts. He gave himself a mental kick. He had to stop thinking of that kiss. It was becoming an obsession. 'Why's that?'

'I think she's been in love with him for years,' she said, and Popeye licked her face enthusiastically, as if in agreement.

'She's wasting her time,' Zach said. 'My father is still in love with my mother.'

She put the dog back down on the floor before she faced him. 'Do you really think so?'

He looked into her beautiful brown eyes, so warm

and soft, like melted caramel. The lashes like miniature fans. She seemed totally unaware of how beautiful
she was. Unlike his ex, Naomi, who hadn't been able
to walk past a mirror or a plate of glass without checking her reflection to check that her hair and make-up
were perfect.

Another mental kick.

Harder this time.

'He's never looked at anyone else since.'

'Doesn't mean he still loves her. Some men have a lot
of trouble with letting go of bitterness after a break-up.'

Zach coughed out a disparaging laugh. 'How long
does he need? Isn't a couple of decades long enough?'

She gave a little lip-shrug. 'I guess some men are
more stubborn than others.'

He wondered if she was having a little dig at his own
stubbornness. He knew he should have found someone else by now. Most men would have done. It wasn't
that he wasn't ready... He just hadn't met anyone who
made him feel like...well, like Izzy did. Hot. Bothered.
Hungry.

At this rate he was going to knock himself unconscious with all those mental kicks. 'What would you
like to drink? I have white wine, red wine or beer...or
something soft?'

'A small glass of white wine would be lovely.' She
handed him a small container she was carrying. 'Um...I
made these. I thought your father might enjoy them.'

He opened the plastic container to find home-baked
chocolate-chip cookies inside. The smell of sugar and
chocolate was like ambrosia. 'His favourite.' *And mine.*
He met her gaze again. 'How'd you guess?'

She gave him a wry smile. 'I don't know too many men who would turn their nose up at home baking.'

'The way to a man's heart and all that.'

She looked taken aback. 'I wasn't trying to—'

'He'll love you for it. Eventually.'

After he'd put the cookies aside he handed her a glass of wine. 'Have you had the hard word put on you about the Shearers' Ball yet?'

'Margie twisted my arm yesterday to sign up. You?'

'I swear every year I'm not going to go and somehow someone always manages to convince me to show up if I'm in town. I try to keep a low profile. I'm seen as the fun police even when I'm not in uniform.'

'I've never been to a bush dance before. Is it very hard to learn the steps?'

'No, there's a caller. That's usually Bill Davidson. He's been doing it for years. His father did it before him. You'll soon get the hang of it.'

'I hope so…'

He couldn't stop looking at her mouth, how softly curved it was, how it had felt beneath the firm pressure of his. Desire was already pumping through his body. Just looking at her was enough to set him off. She was dressed in one of her simple dresses, black, sleeveless and just over the knee, with nothing but the flash of a small diamond pendant around her neck. There were diamond studs in her ears and her hair was in a high ponytail that swished from side to side when she walked. She had put on the merest touch of make-up: a neutral shade of eyeshadow with a fine line of kohl pencilled on her eyelids and beneath her eyes, emphasising the dark thickness of her lashes.

Zach cleared his throat. It was time to get the elephant on its way. 'Look, about the other night when I—'

'It's fine.' She gave him another little twisted smile. 'Really. It was just a kiss.'

'I wouldn't want you to get the wrong idea about me.' He pushed a hand through his hair. 'Contrary to what you might think, I'm not the sort of guy to feel up a woman as soon as he gets her alone.'

Her gaze slipped away from his. 'It was probably my fault.'

He frowned down at her. 'How was it *your* fault? I made the first move.'

'I kissed you back.' She bit her lower lip momentarily. 'Rather enthusiastically, if I recall.'

He *did* recall.

He could recall every thrilling moment of that kiss.

The trouble was he wanted to repeat it. But a relationship with Izzy would be distracting, to say the least. He had to concentrate on getting his dad as independent as he could before he spared a thought to what *he* wanted. He hadn't been that good at balancing the demands of a relationship and work in the past. It would be even worse now with his dad's needs front and centre. He couldn't spread himself any thinner than he was already doing.

His ex had always been on at him to give more of himself but he hadn't felt comfortable with that level of emotional intimacy. He had loved Naomi…or at least he thought he had. Sometimes he wondered if he'd just loved being part of a couple. That was a large part of the reason he'd agreed to her moving in with him. Having someone there to share the sofa with while he zoned out the harrowing demands of the day in front of the television or over a meal he hadn't had to cook.

He sounded like a chauvinist, but after living alone with his dad for all those years he'd snapped up Naomi's willingness to take over the kitchen. Asking her to marry him had been the logical next step. Her refusal to move to the country with him after his father's accident had been not so much devastating as disappointing. He was disappointed in himself. Why had he thought she would follow him wherever life took him? She had her own career. It was unfair of him to demand her to drop everything and come with him. And living in the dry, dusty Outback on a sheep property with a partially disabled and disgruntled father-in-law was a big ask.

Zach blinked himself out of the past. 'Do you want to eat outside? There's a nice breeze coming in from the south. Dad and I often eat out there when a southerly is due.'

'Lovely. Can I help bring anything out?'

He handed her a pair of salad servers and a bottle of dressing.

Her fingers brushed against his as she took the bottle from him and a lightning-fast sensation went straight to his groin. He felt the stirring of his blood; the movement of primal instinctive flesh that wanted something he had denied it for too long.

Her eyes met his, wide, doe-like, the pupils enlarged. Her tongue—*the tongue he had intimately stroked and sucked and teased*—darted out over her lips in a nervous sweeping action. He caught a whiff of her fragrance, wisteria this time instead of gardenias, but just as alluring.

But then the moment passed.

She seemed to mentally gather herself, and with another one of those short on-off smiles she turned in the direction of the veranda, her ponytail swinging behind her.

Zach looked down at Popeye, who was looking up at him with a quizzical expression in those black button eyes. 'Easy for you. You've had the chop. I have to suffer the hard way. No pun intended.'

CHAPTER SEVEN

IZZY PUT THE salad servers and the dressing on the glass-topped white cane table then turned and looked at the view from the veranda. The paddocks stretched far into the distance where she could see a line of trees where the creek snaked in a sinuous curve along the boundary of the property. The air was warm with that hint of eucalyptus she was coming to love. It was such a distinctive smell, sharp and cleansing. The setting sun had painted the sky a dusky pink, signalling another fine day for tomorrow, and a flock of kookaburras sounded in the trees by the creek, their raucous call fracturing the still evening air like the laughter of a gang of madmen.

She turned when she heard the firm tread of Zach's footsteps on the floorboards of the veranda. Popeye was following faithfully, his bright little eyes twinkling in the twilight. Zach looked utterly gorgeous dressed casually in blue denim jeans and a light blue cotton shirt that was rolled up to his forearms. The colour of his shirt intensified the blue rim in his grey eyes and the deep tan of his skin.

Her stomach gave a little flutter when he sent her a quick smile. He was so devastatingly attractive when he lost that grim look. The line of his jaw was still firm, he was too masculine for it ever to be described as anything but determined, but his mouth was sensual and sensitive rather than severe, as she had earlier thought.

Her mouth tingled in memory of how those lips had felt against hers. She remembered every moment of that heart-stopping kiss. It was imprinted on her memory like an indelible brand. She wondered if she would spend the rest of her life recalling it, measuring any subsequent kisses by its standard.

He had deftly changed the subject when she had stumblingly tried to explain her actions of the other night. He had given an apology of sorts for kissing her, but he hadn't said he wasn't going to do it again. She was not by any means a vain person but she was woman enough to know when a man showed an interest in her. He might be able to keep his expression masked and his emotions under lock and key but she had still sensed it.

She had *felt* it in his touch.

She had *tasted* it in his kiss.

She sensed it now as he handed her the glass of wine she had left behind. His eyes held hers for a little longer than they needed to, something passing in the exchange that was unspoken but no less real. She tried to avoid touching his fingers this time. It was increasingly difficult to disguise the way she reacted to him. Would any other man stir her senses quite the way he did? Her body seemed to have a mind of its own when he came near. It was like stepping inside the pull of a powerful magnet. She felt the tug in her flesh, the entire surface of her skin stretching, swelling to get closer to him.

'Thanks.' She took a careful sip of wine. 'Mmm… lovely. Is that a local one?'

He showed her the label. 'It's from a boutique vineyard a couple of hundred kilometres away. I went to boarding school with the guy who owns it.'

'How old were you when you went to boarding school?'

'Eleven.' He swirled the wine in his glass, watching as it splashed around the sides with an almost fierce concentration. 'It was the year after my mother left.' He raised the glass and took a mouthful, the strong column of his throat moving as he swallowed deeply.

'Were you dreadfully homesick?'

He glanced at her briefly before looking back out over the paddocks that were bathed in a pinkish hue instead of their tired brown. 'Not for long.'

Izzy suspected he had taught himself not to feel anything rather than suffer the pain of separation. Homesickness—like love—would be another emotion he had barred from his repertoire. His iron-strong reserve had come about the hard way—a lifetime of suppressing feelings he didn't want to own. She pictured him as an eleven-year-old, probably tall for his age, broad shouldered, whipcord lean and tanned, and yet inside just a little boy who had desperately missed his mother.

She pushed herself away from the veranda rail where she had been leaning her hip. 'I went to boarding school when I was eight. I cried buckets.'

'Eight is very young.' His voice had a gravelly sound to it and his gaze looked serious and concerned, as if he too was picturing her as a child—that small, inconsolable little pigtailed girl with her collection of Barbie dolls in a little pink suitcase.

'Yes…but somehow I got through it. I haven't got any sisters so the company of the other girls was a bonus.' *Or it was when I met Hannah.*

'Any brothers?'

Izzy felt that painful stab to her heart again. It didn't matter how many years went past, it was always the same. She found the question so confronting. It was like asking a first-time mother who had just lost her baby if she was still a mother. 'Not any more...' She swallowed to clear the lump in her throat. 'My brother Jamie died five years ago of sarcoma. He was diagnosed when he was fourteen. He was in remission for twelve years and then it came back.'

'I'm sorry.' The deep gravitas in his voice was strangely soothing.

'He wasn't diagnosed early enough.' She gripped the rails of the veranda so tightly the wood creaked beneath her hands. 'He would've had a better chance if he'd gone to a doctor earlier but he was at boarding school and didn't tell anyone about his symptoms until he came home for the holidays.' She loosened her grip and turned back to look at him. 'I think that's what tortures me most. The thought that he might've been saved.'

His eyes held hers in a silent hold that communicated a depth of understanding she hadn't thought him capable of on first meeting him. His quiet calm was a counterpoint to her inner rage at the cruel punch the fist of fate had given to her family and from which they had never recovered.

'Are your parents still together?'

'Yes, but they probably shouldn't be.' Izzy saw the slight questioning lift of his brow and continued. 'My father's had numerous affairs over the years. Even before Jamie's death. In fact, I think it started soon after Jamie was diagnosed. Mum's always clung to her comfortable life and would never do or say anything to jeopardise it, which is probably why she doesn't understand why I ended things with Richard.'

'Why *did* you break it off with him?'

Izzy looked into his blue-rimmed eyes and wondered if he was one of that increasingly rare breed of men who would take his marriage vows seriously, remaining faithful, loyal and devoted over a lifetime. 'I know this probably sounds ridiculously idealistic, romantic even, but I've always wanted to feel the sort of love that stops you in your tracks. The sort that won't go stale or become boring. The sort of love you just know is your one and only chance at happiness. The sort of love you would give everything up for. I didn't feel that for Richard. It wasn't fair to him to go on any longer pretending I did.'

His top lip lifted in a cynical manner. 'So in amongst all those medical textbooks and journals you've managed to sneak in a few romance novels, have you?'

Izzy could have chosen to be offended by his mockery but instead she gave a guilty laugh. 'One or two.' She toyed with the stem of her glass. 'My friend Hannah thinks I'm a bit of a romance tragic.'

'What did you send you in that package? A stack of sentimental books?'

'If only.' She laughed again to cover her embarrassment. Just as well it was dark enough for him not to see her blush.

'What, then?'

'*Please* don't make me tell you.'

'Come on.' His smile was back and it was just as spine-melting as before. 'You've really got my attention now.'

And you've got mine. 'Promise not to laugh?'

'Promise.'

She let out a breath in a rush. 'A blow-up doll. A male one. I've called him Max.'

He threw his head back and laughed. He had a nice-sounding laugh, rich and deep and genuine, not booming and raucous like Richard's when he'd had one too many red wines.

Izzy gave him a mock glare. 'You promised not to laugh!'

'Sorry.' He didn't look sorry. His lips were still twitching and his eyes twinkled with amusement.

'Hannah thought a stand-in boyfriend would stop me from being lonely. I think I already told you she has a weird sense of humour.'

'Are you going to take him with you when you move on?'

'I'm not sure the Sawyers will appreciate him as part of the furniture.'

'Where do you head after here?' The question was casual. Polite interest. Nothing more.

'Brisbane,' Izzy said. 'I've got a job lined up in a busy GP clinic. After that I have a stint in Darwin. The locum agency is pretty flexible. There's always somewhere needing a doctor, especially out in the bush. That's why I took this post. The guy they had lined up had to pull out at the last minute due to a family crisis. I was happy to step in. I'm enjoying it. Everyone's been lovely.'

Zach absently rubbed the toe of his booted foot against one of the uneven floorboards. 'Everyone, apart from my father.'

'I haven't given up on him.'

The silence hummed as their gazes meshed again.

Izzy's breath hitched on something, like a silk sleeve catching on a prickly bush. She moistened her lips as his gaze lowered to her mouth, her stomach feeling as if a tiny fist had reached through her clothes and clutched at her insides.

Male to female attraction was almost palpable in the air. She could feel it moving through the atmosphere like sonic waves. It spoke to her flesh, calling all the pores of her skin to lift up in a soft carpet of goose-bumps, each hair on her head to stand up and tingle at the roots. A hot wire fizzed in her core, sparking a wave of restless energy unlike anything she had ever felt before. It moved through her body, making her as aware of her erogenous zones as if he had reached out and kissed and caressed each one in turn. Her neck, just below her ears, her décolletage, her breasts, the base of her spine, the backs of her knees, her inner thighs…

His eyes moved from her gaze to her mouth and back again. He seemed to be fighting an internal battle. She could see it being played out on his tightly composed features. Temptation and common sense were waging a war and it seemed he hadn't yet decided whose team he was going to side with.

'Are you still in love with your ex?' It was a question Izzy couldn't stop herself asking. Was a little shocked she had.

The night orchestra beyond the veranda filled the silence for several bars. The percussion section of insects. A chorus of frogs. A lonely solo from a stone curlew.

Izzy found herself holding her breath, hoping he wasn't still in love with his ex-fiancée. Why? She couldn't answer. Didn't want to answer. Wasn't ready to answer.

'No.' The word was final. Decisive. It was as if a line had been drawn in his head and he wasn't going back over it.

'But you were hurt when she ended things?'

He gave her a look she couldn't quite read. 'How did your ex take it when you broke things off?'

'Remarkably well.'

One of his brows lifted. 'Oh?'

'He found a replacement within a matter of days.' Izzy looked at the contents of her glass rather than meet his gaze. 'Don't get me wrong…I didn't want him to be inconsolable or anything, but it was a slap in the face when he found someone so completely the opposite of me and so quickly.'

'Why did you accept his proposal in the first place?' Was that a hint of censure in his tone?

Izzy thought back to the elaborate proposal Richard had set up. A very public proposal that had made her feel hemmed in and claustrophobic. She hadn't had the courage to turn him down and make him lose face in front of all of her friends and colleagues. The banner across the front of the hospital with *Will You Marry Me, Izzy?* emblazoned on it had come has a complete and utter shock to her on arriving at work. She could still see Richard down on bended knee, with the Remington heirloom engagement ring taken out of his family's bank vault especially for the occasion, his face beaming with pride and enthusiasm.

No had been on her tongue but hadn't made it past her embarrassed smile. She'd told herself it was the right thing to do. They'd known each other for years. They'd drifted into casual dating and then into a physical relationship. He had been one of Jamie's close friends and had stuck by him during every gruelling bout of chemo. Her parents adored him. He was part of the family. It was her way of staying connected with her lost brother. 'Lots of reasons.'

'But not love.'

'No.' Izzy let out a breath that felt like she had been holding it inside her chest for years. 'That's why I came out here, as far away from home as possible. I want to know who I am without Richard or my parents telling me what to do and how and when I should do it. My parents have expectations for me. I guess all parents do, but I've got my own life to live. They thought I was wasting my time going to medical school when I have enough money behind me to never have to work. But I want to make a difference in people's lives. I want to be the one who saves someone's brother for them, you know?'

Zach's gaze was steady on hers, his voice low and husky. 'I do know.'

Izzy bit her lip. Had she told him too much? Revealed too much? She put her glass down. 'Sorry. Two sips of wine and I'm spilling all my secret desires.' She gave a mental cringe at her choice of words. 'Maybe I should just leave before I embarrass you as well as myself.'

Zach blocked her escape by placing a hand on her arm. 'What do you think would happen if we followed through on this?'

Her skin sizzled where his hand lay on her arm. She could feel the graze of the rough callus on his fingers, reminding her he was a man in every sense of the word. 'Um…I'm not sure what you mean. Follow through on what?'

His eyes searched hers for a lengthy moment. 'So that's the way you're going to play it. Ignore it. Pretend it's not there.' He gave a little laugh that sounded very deep and very sexy. 'That could work.'

Izzy pressed her lips together, trying to summon up some willpower. Where had it gone? Had she left it behind in England? It certainly wasn't here with her now. 'I think it's for the best, don't you?'

'You reckon you've got what it takes to unlock this banged-up cynical heart of mine, Dr Courtney?' He was mocking her again. She could see it in the way the corner of his mouth was tilted and his eyes glinted at her in the darkness.

She gave him a pert look to disguise how tempted she was to take him on. 'I'm guessing I'd need a lot more than a month, that is if I could be bothered, which I can't.'

He brushed an idle fingertip underneath the base of her upraised chin. 'I would like nothing better right now than to take you inside and show you a good time.'

Izzy suppressed the shiver of longing his light touch evoked. 'What makes you think I'd be interested?'

His gaze moved between each of her eyes. 'Have you slept with anyone since your fiancé?'

'No, but I hardly see how that's got anything to do with anything.'

His fingertip moved like a feather over her lower lip. 'Might explain the fireworks the other night.'

'Just because I got a little excited about a kiss doesn't mean I'm going to jump into bed with you any time soon.' She knew she sounded a little schoolmarmish but she desperately wanted to hide how attracted she was to him. She had never felt such an intensely physical reaction to a man before. His very presence made every nerve in her body pull tight with anticipation.

His tall, firm body was not quite touching hers but was close enough for her to feel the warmth that emanated from him. He planted a hand on the veranda post just above the left side of her head. 'Thing is...' his eyes went to her mouth again '...everyone already thinks I'm doing you.'

A wave of heat coursed through her lower body as his eyes came back to burn into hers. The thought of him 'doing' her made her insides contort with lust. She could picture it in her mind, his body so much bigger and more powerfully made than her ex-fiancé's. Somehow she knew there would be nothing predictable or formulaic about any such encounter. She wouldn't be staring at the ceiling, counting the whorls on the ceiling rose to pass the time. It would be mind-blowing pleasure from start to finish.

'It's just gossip... I'm sure it'll go away once they see there's no truth in it...' If only she could get her voice to sound firm and full of conviction instead of that breathy, phone-sex voice that seemed to be coming out.

'Maybe.'

She saw his nostrils flare as he took in the fragrance of her perfume. She could smell his lemon-based aftershave and his own warm, male smell that was equally intoxicating. She could see the shadow of stubble that peppered his jaw and around his nose and mouth and remembered with another clench of lust how it had felt so sexily abrasive against her skin when he'd kissed her.

A wick of something dangerous lit his gaze. 'Ever had a one-night stand before?'

'No.' She swept her tongue over her lips. 'You?'

'Couple of times.'

'Before or after your fiancée?'

'Before.'

Izzy couldn't drag her gaze away from his mouth. She remembered how it had tasted. How it had felt. The way his firm lips had softened and hardened in turn. The way his tongue had seduced hers. Bewitching her. Giving her a hint of the thorough possession he would take of her if she allowed him. 'So…no one since?' She couldn't believe she was asking such personal questions. It was so unlike her.

'No.' He took a wisp of her hair and curled it around one of his fingers, triggering a sensual tug in her inner core. 'We could do it and get it over with. Defuse the bomb, so to speak.'

She moistened her lips again. She could feel herself wavering on a threshold she had never encountered before. Temptation lured her like a moth towards a light that would surely scorch and destroy. 'You're very confident of yourself, aren't you?'

His gaze had a satirical light as it tussled with hers. 'I recognise lust when I see it.'

Izzy felt the lust she was trying to hide crawl all over her skin, leaving it hot and flushed. She took an uneven breath, shocked at how much she wanted him. It was an ache that throbbed in her womb, prickling and swelling the flesh of her breasts until they felt twice their normal size. 'I'm not the sort of girl who jumps into bed with virtual strangers.' *Even if he was the most attractive and intriguing man she had ever met.*

His eyes held hers for a semitone of silence. 'You know my name. Where I live. What I do for a living. You've even met my father. That hardly makes me a stranger.'

'I don't know your values.'

His mouth kicked up wryly in one corner. 'I'm a cop. Can't get more value-driven than that.'

Izzy gave him an arch look. 'I've met some pretty nasty wolves in cops' clothing in my time.'

His hand was still pressed against the post of the veranda, his strongly muscled arm close enough for her cheek to feel its warmth. His warm breath with its hint of summer wine caressed her face as he spoke in that low, deep, gravel-rough voice. 'I only bat for the good guys.'

Izzy could feel herself melting. Her muscles softened, her ligaments loosened, her hands somehow came up to rest against the hard wall of his chest. His pectoral muscles flinched under the soft press of her palms as if he found her as electrifying as she found him. His eyes were locked on hers, a question burning in their grey-blue depths. An invitation. 'I don't normally do this sort of thing…' Her voice was not her own. It was barely a whisper of sound, and yet it was full of unspoken longing.

His eyes lowered to gaze at her mouth. 'Kiss men you hardly know?'

She looked at his mouth, her belly shifting like a foot stepping on a floating plank. He had a beautiful mouth, sensual and neatly sculpted, the lips neither too thick nor too thin. 'Is that all we're doing? Kissing?'

His gaze became sexily hooded. 'Let's start with that and see where it takes us.'

CHAPTER EIGHT

His mouth came down and covered hers in a kiss that tasted of wine and carefully controlled need. It was a slow kiss, with none of the hot urgency of the other night. This one was more languid, leisurely, a slow but thorough exploration of her mouth that made her pulse skyrocket all the same.

Her heart beat like a drum against her ribcage, her hands moving up his chest to link around his neck. He was much taller than her, so that she had to lift up on her toes, bringing her pelvis into intimate contact with his. The pressure of his kiss intensified, his tongue driving through the seam of her mouth in a commanding search of hers. She felt its sexy rasp, the erotic glide and thrusts that so brazenly imitated the act of human mating. Carnal needs surged like a wild beast in her blood; she felt them do the same in his. The throbbing pulse of his erection pounded against her belly; so thick, so strong, so arrantly male it made her desire race out of her control like a rabid dog slipping its leash.

She pressed herself closer, loving the feel of his chest against her breasts, the way the cotton of his shirt smelt, so clean and laundry fresh with that sexy understory of male body heat.

His tongue played with hers, light and teasing and playful at first, determined and purposeful the next. He drew her closer with a firm, warm hand in the small of her back, the other hand skimming over her right breast, the touch light but devastatingly arousing. Izzy liked it that he hadn't made a grab for her, squeezing too tightly or baring her flesh too quickly. His fainéant touch caused a sensual riot in her body, making her ache to feel his calloused palm on her soft skin. She made a murmur of assent against his mouth, reaching for his hand and bringing it back to the swell of her breast. He cupped her through her clothes; his large palm should have made her feel inadequately small but never had she felt more feminine.

His mouth moved down from hers, along the line of her jaw, lingering at the base of her ear where every sensitive nerve shrieked in delight as his tongue laved her flesh. 'You like that?' His voice came from deep within him, throaty, husky.

She sighed with pleasure. 'Hate it.'

He gave a little rumble of laughter as his lips moved to her collarbone. 'Let's see how much you hate this, then.' His hand released the zipper on the back of her dress just enough to uncover one of her shoulders. The feel of his lips and tongue on the cap of her shoulder made her spine soften like candlewax. For a man who hadn't had sex in a while he certainly hadn't lost his touch. Izzy had never been subjected to such a potent assault on her senses. Her body was a tingling matrix of over stimulated nerves, each one screaming out for assuagement.

He moved from her shoulder to the upper curve of her breast showing above her lowered dress. His lips left a quicksilver trail of fire over her flesh, causing her to whimper as the need tightened and pulled inside her.

He tugged her dress a little lower, not bothering to unclip her bra; he simply moved it out of his way and closed his mouth over her tightly budded nipple. The moist warmth of his mouth, the graze of his teeth and the salve of his tongue as he nipped and licked and sucked her in turn made her shudder with pleasure.

Izzy splayed her fingers through the thickness of his hair, holding him to her, prolonging the delicious sensations for as long as she could. His hand on the small of her back moved around her body to possess her hip. It was a strong alpha type of hold that thrilled her senses into overload. Her inner core moistened as he brought her hard against him.

He left her breast to lick the scaffold of her collarbone in one sexy sweep of his tongue. 'We should stop.'

'W-we should?' Izzy had to remind her good girl to get back inside her head and her body. 'Yes. Right. Of course we should.' She pulled her dress back up over her shoulder but she couldn't quite manage the zip with her fumbling fingers.

He turned her so her back was towards him, his fingers an electric shock against her skin as he dragged the zipper back up. His body brushed hers from behind, his hands coming to rest on the tops of her shoulders as if he couldn't quite bring himself to release her just yet. The temptation to lean back against his arousal, to feel him probe her in that sinfully erotic fashion was overwhelming. Just the thought of him there, so close, so thick and turgid with want, was enough to make her flesh hot all over.

'Um…you can let me go now.' Her voice was still that whisper-soft thread of sound.

His hands tightened for the briefest of moments before they fell away. He stepped back, the floorboards of the veranda creaking in protest as if they too felt her disappointment. 'You want a top-up of your drink before dinner?'

Izzy couldn't believe how even his tone was, so cool and calm and collected as if his senses hadn't been subjected to the biggest shake-up of all time. 'I'd better not. What I've had so far seems to have gone straight to my head.'

Even though most of his face was in shadow she caught a glimpse of a half-smile before he turned and went back to the kitchen to see to their meal.

Izzy looked at Popeye, who was looking up at her with bright button eyes. 'Don't look at me like that. I wasn't going to do it. I'm not a one-night stand sort of girl.'

Popeye barked and then jumped off the cane chair and trotted after his master.

Zach planted his hands on the kitchen bench and drew in a long, slow breath to steady himself. It had been a long time since he had let hot-blooded passion overrule common sense. That was the stuff of teenage hormones, not of a thirty-three-year-old man who had responsibilities and priorities.

But, damn it, Izzy Courtney was tempting. His body was thrumming with need, his mouth still savouring the sweetness of hers. Was he asking for trouble to indulge in a fling with her while she was here? It wasn't as if either of them would be making any promises.

She had an end point in sight. She had plans. Commitments elsewhere. He had responsibilities he couldn't leave. Wouldn't leave.

The trouble was he liked her. Not just sexual attraction. He actually *liked* her. She was intelligent, hard-working, committed to serving the community. Everyone was talking about how well she was fitting in. He hadn't heard a bad said word about her.

Zach heard the sound of a mobile phone ringing. He glanced at his phone lying on the bench but the screen was dark. He wasn't on duty tonight, Rob Heywood was.

Izzy came in from the veranda with an apologetic look on her face. 'I'm sorry, Zach. I have to leave. Caitlin Graham's little girl Skylar has fallen off a bed while playing with her older brothers and cut her forehead. It might not be much but with little kids you can never be sure. I'm going to meet them at the clinic.'

Zach snatched up his keys. 'I'll drive down with you.'

'But I've only had a couple of sips of wine.'

'It's not that. We can take both cars.' He turned off the oven on his way past. 'Caitlyn's new boyfriend, Wayne Brody, is a bit of a hot head, especially if he's been drinking.'

Izzy's eyes widened. 'Are you saying Skylar might not have fallen out of bed?'

Zach kept his expression cop neutral. 'Best we take a look at the evidence first.'

Zach and Izzy arrived at the clinic just as a young woman in her early to mid-twenties was getting out of a car that looked like it could do with a makeover. But then, Caitlyn Graham looked the same. Her skin was weathered by a combination of harsh sun and years of smoking, the tell-tale stain of nicotine on her fingers mirroring the rust on her car, her mouth downturned at the edges as if there wasn't much in her life to smile about. There was no sign of the boyfriend Zach had mentioned, which made Izzy wonder if what he had alluded to had any grounds in truth. Caitlyn carried a whimpering two-year-old girl in her arms and two little boys of about five and seven trailed in her wake, the younger one sucking his thumb, the older one carrying a toy dinosaur.

'I'm sorry to drag you out but I think she needs stitches,' Caitlin said, hitching her daughter to her other bony hip as she took the five-year-old's hand. The little girl buried her head against her mother's thin chest and gave another mewling cry.

'Let's go inside and take a look.' Izzy smiled at the boys. 'Hi, guys. Wow, that's a nice triceratops.'

The seven-year-old gave her a scornful look from beneath long spider leg eyelashes. 'It's a stegosaurus.'

'Oh, right. My mistake.' Izzy caught Zach's glinting glance as she led the way into the clinic.

On examination little Skylar had a gash on her forehead that had stopped bleeding due to the compress her mother had placed on it but still needed a couple of stitches to ensure it healed neatly. There were no other injuries that she could see and the child otherwise seemed in good health.

'I'll put some anaesthetic cream on her forehead before I inject some local,' Izzy said to Caitlyn. 'It'll still sting a bit but hopefully not too much.'

Once the stitches were in place, Izzy handed the little tot a choice of the lollipops she kept in a jar on her desk. 'What a brave little girl you've been.'

The little girl chose a red one and silently handed it to her mother to take the cellophane wrapping off.

'Can I have one too?' the five-year-old, called Eli, asked around his thumb.

'Of course. Here you go.' Izzy then passed the jar to the seven-year-old with the stegosaurus. The boy hesitated before finally burying his hand in the jar and taking out two lollipops.

'Only one, Jobe,' Caitlyn said.

The boy gave his mother a defiant look. 'I'm taking one for Dad.'

Caitlyn's lips tightened. 'It'll be stale before you see him again.'

Izzy watched as Jobe's dark eyes hardened. It was a little shocking to see such a young child exhibiting such depth of emotion. Not childlike emotion but emotion well beyond his years. 'I'd like to see Skylar in a couple of days to check those stitches,' she said to defuse the tense atmosphere. 'If it's tricky getting into town, I can always make a house call.'

'I can get here no trouble.'

Was it her imagination or had Caitlin been a little bit too insistent? Izzy shook off the thought. Zach's comments earlier had made her unnecessarily biased. Not every stepfather was a child abuser. Jobe was a tense child but that was probably because he missed his biological father, who apparently was no longer on the scene. 'Let's make an appointment now.' She reached for the computer mouse to bring up the clinic's electronic diary.

'I'll call Margie tomorrow,' Caitlin said. 'I'd better get back. My partner will wonder what's happened.'

'You can use the phone here if you like.'

Caitlyn was already at the door. 'Come on, boys. It's way past your bedtime.'

Jobe was looking at Zach with an intense look on his face. 'Do you always carry a gun?'

'Not always,' Zach said. 'Only when I'm on duty.'

'Are you on duty now?'

'No. Sergeant Heywood is.'

'What if a bad guy came to your house? Would you be allowed to shoot him if you're not on duty?'

Caitlyn came back over and grabbed Jobe by the back of his T-shirt. 'Come on. Sergeant Fletcher's got better things to do than answer your dumb questions.'

The little boy shrugged off his mother's hand and scowled. 'They're not dumb.'

'Don't answer back or I'll give you a clip across the ear.'

Zach crouched down to Jobe's level. 'Maybe you and your brother could drop into the station one day and have a look around. I can show you how the radio works and other cool stuff.' He glanced up at Caitlyn. 'That all right with you?'

Caitlyn's mouth was so tight her lips were white. 'Sure. Whatever.'

Izzy chewed at her lower lip as she began to tidy up the treatment area. Zach came back in from seeing the young family out to the car. She turned and looked at him. 'Cute kids.'

He was frowning in a distracted manner. 'Yeah.'

'You think she would hit Jobe or the other two?'

'A lot of parents do. It's called discipline.'

'There are much better ways to discipline a child than to hit them,' Izzy said. 'How can you teach a child not to hit others if you're hitting them yourself?'

'You're preaching to the choir,' he said. 'I don't agree with it either but some parents insist it's their right to use corporal punishment.'

'I didn't notice any bruises or marks on the little one but Jobe seems a very tense little boy. He doesn't seem to have a close relationship with his mother, does he?'

'He misses his dad.'

'Where is he?'

He shrugged. 'Who knows? Probably shacked up with some other woman with another brood of kids by now.'

Izzy washed her hands at the sink and then tore off a paper towel to dry them. 'Beats me why some people have kids if they're just going to abandon them when the going gets tough.'

'Tell me about it.'

She looked at him again. 'Did your mother remarry?'

'Yes. Got a couple of sons. They take up a lot of her time.'

'I'm sorry…I shouldn't have asked.'

'It was a long time ago.'

She put the used paper towel in the pedal bin. 'Do you want kids?' *Where on earth had that question come from?* 'Sorry.' She bit her lip again. 'None of my business.'

'I do, actually.' He picked up a drug company's promotional paperweight off her desk and smoothed his right thumb over its surface. 'Not right now, though.

Maybe in a couple of years or so. I have to get a few things straightened out first.'

'Your father?'

He put the paperweight down and met her gaze. 'It's a good sign he went out tonight.'

'Yes, I agree. Social isolation isn't good for someone suffering depression.'

There was a little silence.

'What about you?' he asked. 'Do you want kids or is your career your top priority?'

'I would hate to miss out on having a family. I love my career but I really want to be a mum one day.'

It was hard to tell if her answer met with his approval or not. He had his cop face on again. 'Caitlyn Graham had Jobe when she was fifteen. She was a kid with a kid.'

'It looks like she's had it tough,' Izzy said. 'Do all three kids have the same father?'

'No, Eli and Skylar are another guy's. A drifter who came into town for a couple of years before moving on again.'

'Does Caitlyn have any extended family to support her?'

'Her mother comes to visit from Nyngan now and again but she never stays long.' His mouth took on a cynical line. 'Just long enough to have a fight with Caitlyn's new boyfriend.'

'He doesn't sound like a good role model for the boys,' Izzy said.

He gave her a grim look. 'He's not. He's been inside for assault and possession and supply of illegal drugs. He's only just come off parole. Reckon it won't be long before he ends up back behind bars.'

'Once a criminal, always a criminal?'

'In my experience, most of the leopards I've met like to hang onto their spots.'

'Don't you think people can change if they're given some direction and support?' Izzy asked.

'Maybe some.'

She picked up her bag and hitched it over her shoulder. 'Were you always this cynical or has your job made you that way?'

He held the door open for her. 'I'll tell you over dinner.'

'You still want me to—?'

His look was unreadable. 'You're still hungry, aren't you?'

Izzy had a feeling he wasn't just talking about food. 'It's getting late. Maybe I should just head home. Your dad will be back soon in any case.'

'If that's what you want.' He sounded as if he didn't care either way.

It wasn't what she wanted but she wasn't quite ready to admit it. She wasn't sure how to handle someone as deep and complicated as Zach Fletcher. He was strong and principled, almost to the point of being conservative, which, funnily enough, resonated with her own homespun values. But she was only here for another three weeks. It wouldn't be fair to start something she had no intention of finishing. 'Thanks for coming down with me to see to little Skylar.'

'You'd better get Margie to give Caitlyn a call tomorrow. She's not good at following through on stuff.'

'Yes, I gathered that.'

Once she had locked the clinic and set the alarm, Zach walked her to her car. He waited until she was inside the car with her seat belt pulled down and clipped into place.

'Thanks again.'

He tapped the roof of her car with his hand. 'Drive safely.'

'Zach?'

He stopped and turned back to look at her. 'Yes?'

'Maybe I could cook dinner for you some time…to make up for tonight?'

He gave her the briefest of smiles. 'I'll get working on my appetite.'

CHAPTER NINE

'How did your evening go with Doug Fletcher?' Izzy asked Margie the next morning at the clinic.

'I was about to ask you the same question about yours with Zach.'

'It got cut short. I got called out to Caitlyn Graham's little daughter, who'd cut her forehead,' Izzy said. 'Can you call her to make a follow-up appointment? I'd like to see Skylar on Thursday. And can you check to see whether all three kids are up to date on their vaccinations?'

'Will do. Did Caitlyn's boyfriend come with her?'

'No, but Zach warned me about him. He came with me to the clinic.'

Margie's brows lifted. 'Did he, now?'

Izzy felt a blush creep over her cheeks. 'He's a bit of a stickler for safety.'

'Wayne Brody is a ticking time bomb,' Margie said. 'Wouldn't take much to set him off. Zach's got a good nose for sensing trouble.'

'Why would Caitlyn hook up with someone so unsavoury? There must be some other much nicer young man out here.'

Margie shrugged. 'Some girls would rather be with

anybody rather than nobody. Her mother's the same. Hooked up with one deadbeat after the other. I don't think Caitlyn has ever met her biological father. I'm not sure her mother even knows who it is. Caitlyn had one stepfather after the other. Now she's doing the same to her kids. It's a cycle that goes on one generation after another. It's a case of monkey see, monkey do.'

'Are there any playgroups or activities for young mums like her around here?' Izzy asked.

'Peggy McLeod tried to set one up a few years back but her arthritis set in and she had to give it up. No one's bothered to do anything since.'

'The community centre…do you think I could book it for one morning this week?' Izzy asked. 'I could re-arrange my clinic hours. I could get some toys donated or buy them myself if I have to. It'd be a place for the mums and kids to hang out and chat and play.'

'Sounds good, but who's going to take over when your time with us is up?'

'I could get one of the mums to take charge,' Izzy said. 'It might be a chance to get Caitlyn engaged in something that would build her self-esteem.'

Margie gave a snort. 'There's nothing wrong with that girl's self-esteem. It's her taste in men that's the problem.'

'But that's exactly my point,' Izzy said. 'She thinks so badly of herself that she settles for the first person who shows an interest in her. There's a saying I heard once. You get the partner in life you think you deserve.'

Margie gave her a twinkling look. 'And who do you think you deserve?'

Izzy felt that betraying blush sneak back into her

cheeks. 'Did you manage to convince Doug to book in for a check-up?'

Margie's twinkle dulled like a cloud passing over the sun. 'I'm working on it.'

'Are you going to see him again?'

'I'm working on that too,' Margie said. 'I mentioned the Shearers' Ball but he was pretty adamant he wasn't going to go.'

'I guess it's pretty hard to dance when you're on a walking frame.'

'It's not about the dancing.' Margie's eyes suddenly watered up. 'I couldn't give a toss about the dancing. I just want to be with him. I've waited so long for him but he's got this stupid idea in his head that no one could ever want him the way he is now.'

Izzy gave Margie's shoulder a gentle squeeze. 'I hope it works out for you and him. I really do.'

Margie popped a tissue out of the box on the reception counter and blew her nose. She tossed the tissue in the bin under the desk and assembled her features back into brisk receptionist mode. 'Silly fool. A woman of my age fancying herself in love. Phhfft. Ridiculous.'

'It's not ridiculous,' Izzy said. 'Falling in love isn't something you can control. It just happens—' she caught Margie's look '—or so I'm told,' she added quickly. She took the file for her first patient of the day from the counter as the front door of the clinic opened. 'Mrs Honeywell? Come this way.'

Zach was leaving the station a couple of days later when he saw Izzy coming out of the clinic and walking towards her car. It had been a brute of a day, hot and dry with a northerly wind that was gritty and relentless.

He could think of nothing better than a cool beer and a swim out at Blake's waterhole… Actually, he could think of something way better than that. Izzy Courtney lying naked underneath him while he—

She suddenly turned and looked at him as if she had felt his gaze on her. Or read his X-rated thoughts. 'Oh…hello.' She gave him a smile that looked beaten up around the edges.

'You look like you've had a tough day.'

Her mouth twisted as she scraped a few tendrils of sticky hair back behind her ear. 'Caitlyn didn't show up for Skylar's check-up. Margie confirmed it with her but she didn't come. I called her on the phone to offer to go out there but there was no answer.' She blew out a little breath of frustration. 'I can't force her to bring the child in. And I don't want to turn up at her house as if I'm suspicious of her.'

'I've got a couple of things for Jobe and Eli,' Zach said. 'Stuff I had when I was a kid. I found them in a cupboard in one of the spare rooms at home. We can drop them round now just to see if everything's OK. Better take your car, though. Might not get such a warm welcome, turning up in mine.'

Her caramel-brown eyes brightened. 'That was thoughtful of you. What sort of things? Toys?'

Zach found himself trying to disguise a sheepish look. 'I went through a dinosaur stage when I was about seven or eight. Got a bit obsessive there for a bit.'

She gave him a smile that loosened some of the tight barbed wire wrapped around his heart. 'So you can tell a stegosaurus from a triceratops?'

'Any fool can do that.'

She pursed her lips and then must have realised he

was teasing her for her sunny smile broke free again. 'You're a nice man, Sergeant Fletcher. I think I'm starting to like you after all.'

The house Caitlyn Graham was living in was on the outskirts of Jerringa Ridge. It was a stockman's cottage from the old days that looked like it hadn't had much done to it since. The rusty gate was hanging on one hinge and the once white but now grey picket fence had so many gaps it looked like a rotten-toothed smile. A dog of mixed breeding was chained near the tank stand and let out a volley of ferocious barking as Izzy pulled her car up in front of the house. 'Can he get off, do you think?' she asked, casting Zach a worried glance.

'I'll keep an eye on him.'

'Poor dog tied up like that in this heat.' She turned off the engine and unclipped her belt. 'Is anyone around? There's no car about that I can see.'

'Stay in the car and I'll have a mosey around.' Zach got out and closed the door with a snick. The dog put its ears back and brought its body low to the ground as it snarled and bared its teeth.

Izzy watched as Zach ignored the dog as he walked up the two steps of the bull-nosed veranda, opening the screen door to knock on the cracked paint of the front door. The dog was still doing its scary impersonation of an alien beast from a horror movie but Zach didn't seem the least put off by it. He left the bag of toys near the door and came back down the veranda steps. Apart from the dinosaurs, Izzy had spotted a set of toy cars and a doll that looked suspiciously new. She had seen one just like it in the corner store yesterday but it hadn't been there when she'd picked up her sandwich today at lunchtime.

Zach made a clicking sound with his tongue and the dog stopped growling and slunk down in a submissive pose. Zach picked up the dog's water dish, took it over to the tap on the base of the tank, rinsed the rusty water out of it and filled it with fresh, setting it down in a patch of shade next to the dog's kennel. The dog drank thirstily, so thirstily Zach had to refill the dish a couple of times.

He came back to the car after doing another round of the house. 'No one home.'

Izzy started the engine. 'You certainly have a way with wild animals.'

'He's not wild.' He leaned his arm along the back of her seat as she backed the car to turn around. 'He's scared. Probably had the boot kicked into his ribs a few too many times.'

Izzy could see the tightness around his jaw. That grim look was back. The look that was like a screen behind which the horrors and cruelty and brutal inhumanity he'd seen first hand were barricaded. 'How do you cope with it? The stuff you see, I mean. The bad stuff.'

'Reckon you've seen your share of bad stuff too.'

'Yes, but I'm not usually out on the coalface. Most of the stuff I see is in the controlled environment of a clinic or hospital. And mostly it's stuff I can fix.'

He didn't speak until Izzy had driven back to the road leading to town. 'It doesn't get any easier, that's for sure. Rocking up to someone's place to tell them their only kid is lying in the morgue after a high-speed accident is the kind of stuff that gets to even the toughest cops.' He paused for a beat. 'Anything to do with kids gets me. Abuse. Neglect. Murder. It's not something you can file away like the investigation report. It stays with you. For years.' He released a jagged breath. 'For ever.'

Izzy glanced at him. 'Did you think it would be as bad as it is when you first joined the force?'

He gave her a twisted smile that had nothing to do with humour. 'Most cops fresh out of the academy think they're going to be the one that changes the world. We all think we're going to make a difference. To help people. Trouble is, some people don't want to be helped.'

'I've been talking to Margie about setting up a playgroup in town,' Izzy said, 'for mums like Caitlyn and their kids. A place to hang out and chat and swap recipes and stuff. Do you think it's a good idea?'

'Who's going to run it?'

'I will, to start with.'

He flashed her an unreadable look. 'And who's going to take over when you drive off into the sunset in search of your next big adventure?'

Izzy pressed her lips together. Was he mocking her or was he thinking of the locals getting all excited about something only to have it fall flat once she left? A little flag of hope climbed up the flagpole of her heart. Was he thinking of how *he* would feel when she left? 'I'm going to be here long enough to get it up and running. After that it's up to the locals to keep things going, if that's what they want.'

He gave a noncommittal grunt, his eyes trained on the road ahead.

Izzy let a silence pass before she added, 'So what's wrong with looking for adventure?'

'Nothing, as long as you don't hurt others going in search of it.'

'I'm not planning on hurting anyone.' She found her fingers tightening on the steering-wheel and had to force herself to relax them. 'I suppose this attitude of yours is because of your mother leaving the way she did.'

She felt the razor-sharp blade of his gaze. 'You really think you've got what it takes to make a difference out here in a month? You haven't got a hope, sweetheart.'

'Don't patronise me by calling me sweetheart.'

He gave a sound midway between a laugh and a cynical snort. 'You flounce into town, sprinkling your fairy dust around, hoping some of it will stick, but you haven't got a clue. The country out here is tough and it needs tough people to work in it and survive. It's not the place for some pretty little blow-in who's looking for something to laugh about over a latte with her friends when she gets back from her big adventure with the rednecks in the antipodes.'

Izzy tried to rein in her anger but it was like trying to control a scrub fire with an eyedropper. The one thing she hated the most was people not taking her seriously. Thinking she was too much of a flake to get the job done. A silly little socialite playing at doctors and nurses. 'Thanks for the charming summation of my motives and character,' she said through tight lips.

'Pleasure.'

She pulled up outside the police station a few bristling minutes later. 'Have a nice evening, Sergeant,' she said, her voice dripping with sarcasm.

He didn't even bother replying, or at least not verbally. He shut the car door with a sharp click that could just as easily be substituted for an imprecation.

* * *

'What's got under your skin?' Doug asked Zach over dinner later that evening. 'You've been stabbing at that steak as if it's a mortal enemy.'

Zach pushed his plate away. 'It's too hot to eat.'

'Tell me about it.' Doug wiped the back of his hand over his forehead. 'Must be something wrong with the air-con. I'm sweating like a pig.'

Zach frowned as he saw his father's sickly colour. 'You all right?'

'Will be in a minute…' Doug gripped the arms of the standard chair. 'Just a funny turn. Had one earlier… just before you got home.'

'When was the last time you took a painkiller?'

'Ran out last night.'

Zach swore under his breath. 'You're not supposed to stop them cold turkey. You're supposed to wean yourself off them. You're probably having withdrawal symptoms. It can be dangerous to suddenly stop taking them.'

Doug winced as he pushed back from the table. 'Maybe you should call the doctor for me. Pain's pretty bad…' He sucked in a breath. 'Getting worse by the minute.'

Zach mentally rolled his eyes as he reached for his phone. The one time he wanted some distance from Izzy Courtney and his father springs a turnaround on him. He considered waiting it out to see if his father recovered without intervention but he knew he would never forgive himself if things took a turn for the worse. His father's health hadn't been checked since William Sawyer had left on holidays. He was supposed to be monitored weekly for his blood pressure. Severe pain could trigger heart attacks in some patients and the last thing Zach wanted was to be responsible for inaction just because of a silly little tiff with the locum doctor.

He was annoyed with himself for reacting the way he had. He didn't want Izzy thinking she had any hold over him. So what if she wanted to get a playgroup going before she left? It was a good idea—a *great* idea. It was exactly what the town needed. She was doing all she could in the short time she was here to make a difference. Once she was done waving her magic wand around he would wave her off without a flicker of emotion showing on his face.

That was one lesson he had learned and learned well.

Izzy arrived twenty-five minutes later, carrying her doctor's bag and a coolly distant manner Zach knew he probably deserved. 'He's in the bedroom, lying down,' he said.

'How long has he been feeling unwell?'

'Since before I got home. He's run out of pain meds. It's probably withdrawal.'

'Is he happy to see me?'

He inched up the corner of his mouth in a sardonic curl. 'You think I would've called you otherwise?'

Her brown eyes flashed a little arc of lightning at him. 'Lead the way.'

Zach knew he was acting like a prize jerk. He couldn't seem to help it. It was the only way to keep his distance. He was worried about complicating his life with a dalliance with her even though he could think of nothing he wanted more than to lose himself in a bit of mindless sex. He didn't have her pegged as the sort of girl who would settle for a fling. She'd been engaged to the same man for four years. That didn't sound like a girl who was eager to put out to the first guy who showed an interest in her.

And Zach was more than interested in her.

He couldn't stop thinking about her. How she'd felt in his arms, the way her mouth had met the passion of his, the softness of her breast in his mouth, the hard little pebble of her nipple against his tongue, the taste of the skin of her neck, that sweet, flowery scent of her that reminded him of an English cottage garden in spring.

'Hello, Mr Fletcher.' Izzy's voice broke through Zach's erotic reverie. 'Zach told me you're not feeling so good this evening.'

'Pain...' Doug gestured to his abdomen and his back; his breathing was ragged now, his brow sticky with sweat. 'Bad pain...'

Zach watched as she examined his father's chest and abdomen and then his back with gentle hands. He couldn't help feeling a little jealous. He would have liked those soft little hands running over his chest and abdomen and lower. His groin swelled at the thought and he had to think of something unpleasant to get control again.

She took his father's blood pressure, her forehead puckered in concentration as she listened to his account of how he had been feeling over the last few hours.

'Any history of renal colic?' she asked. 'Kidney stones?'

'A few years back,' his father said. 'Six or seven years ago, I think. Didn't need to go to hospital or anything. I passed them eventually. Hurt like the devil. None since.'

'I'll give you a shot of morphine for the pain but I think we should organise an IVP tomorrow if the pain doesn't go away overnight,' Izzy said. 'When was the last time you passed urine?'

'Not for a while, three hours ago maybe.'

'Any pain or difficulty?'

'A bit.'

'Do you think you could give me a urine sample if I leave you with a specimen bottle?' she asked as she administered the injection.

'I'll give it a try.'

'I'll wait in the kitchen to give you some privacy.' She clipped shut her bag and walked past Zach, her body brushing his in the doorway making him go hard all over again.

'Might need a hand getting to the bathroom, Zach,' his father said.

Zach blinked a couple of times to reorient himself. 'Right. Sure.'

CHAPTER TEN

IZZY WAS SITTING on one of the kitchen chairs with Pop-eye on her lap when Zach came back in, carrying a urine sample bottle inside the press-lock plastic bag she'd provided. She put the dog on the floor and stood, taking the sample from him and giving it a quick check for blood or cloudiness that would suggest infection, before putting it next to her bag on the floor.

She straightened and kept her doctor face in place, trying to ignore the way her body was so acutely aware of the proximity of Zach's. 'Your father should be feeling a little better in the next half-hour or so. Make sure he drinks plenty of clear fluids over the next twenty-four hours. If he has any trouble passing urine, don't hesitate to call. If the bladder blocks I can insert a cath-eter to drain it until we can get him to hospital. But I don't think it will come to that. It seems a pretty stan-dard case of renal colic. Being less active, he probably doesn't feel as thirsty as much as he used to. Older men often fail to keep an adequate intake of fluids.' She knew she was talking like a medical textbook but she couldn't seem to stop it. 'That's about it. I'll be on my way. Goodbye.'

'Izzy.' His hand was firm and warm on the bare skin of her arm. It sent a current of electricity to the secret heart of her.

Izzy met his gaze. It wasn't hard and cold with anger now but tired, as if he had grown weary of screening his inner turmoil from view. Her heart stepped off its high horse and nestled back down in her chest with a soft little sign. 'Are you OK?'

His mouth softened its grim line. 'Sorry about this afternoon. I was acting like a jerk.' His thumb started stroking the skin of her arm, a back-and-forth motion that was drugging her senses.

'You've got a lot on your mind right now with your dad and everything.'

'Don't make excuses for me.' His thumb moved to the back of her hand, absently moving over the tendons in a circular motion. 'I was out of line, snapping your head off like that.'

Izzy gave him a mock reproachful arch of her brow. 'Fairy dust?'

His thumb stalled on her hand and he looked down at it as if he'd only just realised he'd been stroking it. He released her and took a step backwards, using the same hand to score a crooked pathway through his hair. 'Thanks for coming out. I appreciate it. I think you've won my dad over.'

What about you? Have I won you over? Izzy studied his now closed-off expression. 'I hope he has a settled night. Call me if you're worried. I'll keep my phone on.'

He walked her out to the car but he hardly said a word. Izzy got the impression he couldn't wait for her to leave. It made her spirits plummet. She'd thought for a moment back there he'd been going to kiss her, maybe even take it a step further.

She hadn't realised how much she wanted him to until he hadn't.

Caitlyn Graham turned up at the clinic the following day with Skylar. 'Sorry about missing our appointment,' she said. 'I took the kids for a drive to see a friend of mine on a property out of town. I forgot to phone and cancel. There's no signal out there so I couldn't call even when I remembered.'

'No problem,' Izzy said. 'Just as long as Skylar's OK.' She inspected the little tot's forehead and asked casually, 'How are the boys?'

'They're at school,' Caitlyn said. 'Jobe made a fuss about going. He hates it. He has a tantrum about going just about every morning.'

'Is he being bullied?'

'What, at school? Nah, don't think so. Wayne would have a fit if he heard Jobe couldn't stand up for himself.'

'Did you get the bag of toys Zach dropped in for the kids?' Izzy asked.

Caitlyn's expression flickered with something before she got it under control. 'Wayne wasn't too happy about that. He doesn't think it's right to spoil kids, especially if they're not behaving themselves.'

'Does Wayne get on well with the kids?'

'All right, I guess.' Caitlyn brushed her daughter's fluffy blonde hair down into some semblance of order. 'They're not his. None of my kids are.'

'Do you have any contact with Jobe's father?' Izzy asked.

'No, and I don't want to.' Caitlyn's expression tightened like a fist. 'Jobe's got it in his head Connor is some sort of hero but he's just another loser. Connor caused a lot of trouble between Brad and me—that's Eli and Skylar's dad. It's what broke us up, actually.'

'What sort of trouble?'

'Picking fights. Saying things about Brad that weren't true. Punch-ups on the street. Making me look like trailer trash. I took a restraining order out on him. He can't come anywhere near me or Jobe.'

'What about Brad? Does he have contact with Eli and Skylar?'

'Now and again but Wayne's not keen on it. Thinks I might be tempted to go back to him or something. As if.' She rolled her eyes at the thought. 'Wayne's no prize but at least he brings in a bit of money.'

'What does he do?'

'He's a truck driver. He does four runs a week, sometimes more. He's the first man I've had who's held down a regular job.'

'It must get lonely out here for you with him away a lot,' Izzy said.

'It's no picnic with three kids, but, as my mum keeps saying, I made my bed so I have to lie in it.'

Izzy brought up the subject of a playgroup at the community centre. Caitlyn shrugged as if the thought held little appeal but Izzy knew apathy was a common trait amongst young women who felt the world was against them. 'I'll let you know once we get things sorted,' she said as Caitlyn left the consulting room. 'Skylar will enjoy it and we might even be able to do an after-school one if things go well so the boys can come too.'

'I'll think about it. See what Wayne says. I like to fit in with him. Causes less trouble that way.'

Izzy closed the door once Caitlyn had left. It was a shock to realise she had no right to criticise Caitlyn for accommodating her partner's unreasonable demands.

Hadn't she done more or less the same with Richard for the last four years?

Margie put the reception phone down just as Izzy came out of her room. 'That was Doug Fletcher. He passed a couple of kidney stones last night. He's feeling much better.'

'I'm glad to hear it.'

'Not only that,' Margie continued with a beaming smile, 'he asked me to go over there tonight. I'm going to make him dinner.'

'That's lovely. I'm pleased for you.'

'I have a favour to ask.'

'You want to leave early?' Izzy asked. 'Sure. I can do the filing and lock up.'

'No, not that.' Margie gave her a beseeching look. 'Would you be a honey and invite Zach to dinner at your place tonight?'

'Um…'

'Go on. He'll feel like a gooseberry hanging around with us oldies,' Margie said. 'A night out at your place will be good for him. It'll give him a break from always having to keep an eye on his dad.'

'I don't know…'

'Or ask him to join you for a counter meal at the pub if you're not much of a cook.'

'I can cook.'

'Then what's the problem?'

Izzy schooled her features into what she hoped

passed for mild enthusiasm. 'I'll give him a call. See what he's up to. He might be on duty.'

'He's not. I already checked.'

Zach was typing a follow-up email to his commander in Bourke when Izzy came into the station. He pressed 'Send' and got to his feet. 'I was going to call you. My dad's feeling a lot better.'

'Yes, Margie told me. He called the clinic earlier this morning.'

'You were spot on with your diagnosis.'

'I may not know a triceratops from a stegosaurus but I'm a whizz at picking up renal colic.'

Zach felt a smile tug at his mouth. 'You doing anything tonight?'

She gave him a wry look. 'Apparently I'm cooking dinner for you.'

'Yeah, so I heard. You OK with that?'

'Have I got a choice?'

Zach found it cute the way she arched her left eyebrow in that haughty manner. 'I wouldn't want to put you to any trouble. I can pick up a bite to eat at the pub. Mike hates it when I do, though. He says it puts his regulars off.'

'You don't have to go in uniform.'

'Wouldn't make a bit of difference if I went in stark naked.'

Her cheeks lit up like twin fires. 'Um…dinner's at seven.'

'I'll look forward to it.' She was at the door when he asked, 'Hey, will your stand-in boyfriend Max be joining us?'

She gave him a slitted look over her shoulder and then flounced out.

* * *

Izzy had cooked for numerous dinner parties for her friends when living in London and she'd never felt the slightest hint of nerves. She was an accomplished cook; she'd made it her business to learn as she'd grown up with cooks at Courtney Manor and wasn't content to sit back and watch, like her parents, while someone else did all the work. From a young age she had taken an interest in preparing food, getting to know the kitchen staff and talking to the gardeners about growing fresh vegetables and herbs.

But preparing a meal for Zach in an Outback town that had only one shop with limited fresh supplies was a challenge, so too was trying not to think about the fact she was sure that food was not the only thing they would be sharing tonight.

She put the last touches to the table, thinking wistfully of the fragrant roses of Courtney Manor as she placed an odd-looking banksia on the table in a jam jar, the only thing she could in the cottage that was close to a vase.

Izzy looked at Max sitting at the end of the table. It had taken her half an hour to blow him up manually as she didn't have a bicycle pump. He was leaning to one side, his ventriloquist dummy-like eyes staring into space. 'I hope you're going to behave yourself, Max.' *Why are you talking to a blow-up doll?* 'No talking with your mouth full or elbows on the table, OK?'

The doorbell sounded and Izzy quickly smoothed her already smooth hair as she went to answer it. Zach was standing on the porch, wearing an open-necked white shirt with tan-coloured chinos. His hair was still damp from a shower; she could see the grooves where his comb or brush had passed through it. Her first 'Hi...' came out croakily so she cleared her throat and tried again. 'Hi. Come on in.'

'Thanks.'

She could smell the clean fresh scent of fabric softener on his shirt as he came through the door, that and the hint of lemon and spice and Outback maleness that never failed to get her senses spinning.

'I brought wine.' He handed her a bottle, his eyes moving over her in a lazy sweep that made her insides feel hollow. 'Something smells good.'

Izzy took the wine, getting a little shock from his fingers as they brushed against hers. 'I hope you're hungry.'

'Ravenous.'

She swallowed and briskly turned to get the glasses, somehow managing to half fill two without spilling a drop in spite of hands that weren't too steady. 'Max decided to join us after all.' She handed Zach a glass of the white wine he had brought. 'I hope you don't mind.'

A hint of a smile played at the corners of his mouth. 'Aren't you going to introduce us?'

Izzy felt her own smile tug at her lips. 'He's not one for small talk.'

'I'm known to be a bit on the taciturn side myself.' The smile had travelled up to his eyes with a twinkle that was devastatingly attractive.

She led the way to the small eating area off the kitchen. 'Max, this is Sergeant Zach Fletcher.' She turned to Zach. 'Zach, this is Max.'

Zach rubbed at his chin thoughtfully. 'Mmm, I guess a handshake is out of the question?'

A laugh bubbled out of Izzy's mouth. 'This is ridiculous. I'm going to kill Hannah. I swear to God I will. Would you like some nibbles?' she asked as she thrust a plate of dips and crackers towards him. 'I have to check on the entrée.'

His eyes were still smiling but they had taken on a smouldering heat that made the backs of her knees feel tingly. 'Do you think Max would get jealous if I kissed you?'

Izzy's stomach hollowed out again. 'I don't know. I've never kissed anyone in front of him before.'

He put a hand to the side of her face, a gentle cupping of her cheek, the dry warmth and slight roughness of his palm making her inner core quiver like an unset jelly. 'I wouldn't want to cut in on him but I've been dying to do this since last night.' His mouth came down towards hers, his minty breath dancing over the surface of her lips in that tantalising prelude to take-off.

Izzy let out a soft sigh of delight as his mouth connected with hers, a velvet brush of dry male lips on moist, lip-gloss-coated female ones. The moment of contact made shivers flow like a river down her spine, the first electrifying sweep of his tongue over her lips parted them, inviting her to take him in. She opened to the commanding glide of his tongue, shuddering with need as he made contact with hers in a sexy tangle that drove every other thought out of her mind other than what she was feeling in her body. The stirring of her blood, the way her feminine folds pulsed and ached to be parted and filled, just like he was doing with her mouth. The way her breasts tingled and tightened, the nipples erect in arousal.

His hands grasped her by the hips, pulling her against his own arousal, the hard heat of him probing her intimately, reminding her of everything that was different between them and yet so powerfully, irresistibly attractive.

Izzy snaked her arms around his neck, stepping up on her toes so she could keep that magical connection with his mouth on hers. She kissed him with the passion that had been lying dormant inside her body, just waiting for someone like him to awaken it. She had never felt the full force of it before. She'd felt paltry imitations of it, but nothing like this.

This was fiery.

This was unstoppable.

This was inevitable.

'I want you.' Izzy couldn't believe she had said the words out loud, but even if she hadn't done so her body was saying them for her. The way she was clinging to him, draping her body over him like a second layer of skin, was surely leaving him in no doubt of her need for him. She pressed three hot little kisses, one after the other, on his mouth and repeated the words she had never said to anyone else and meant them quite the way she meant them now. 'I want you to make love to me.'

Zach brought his hands back up to cup her face. 'Sure?'

Izzy gazed into his beautiful haunted eyes. 'Don't you recognise consent when you see it?'

His thumbs stroked her cheeks, his eyes focused on her mouth as if it were the most fascinating thing he had ever seen. 'It's been a while for me.'

'I'm sure you still know the moves.'

One of his thumbs brushed over her lower lip in a caress that made the base of her spine shiver. 'Are we having a one-night stand or is this something else?'

'What do you want it to be?'

He took a while to answer, his gaze still homed in on her mouth, the pads of his thumbs doing that mesmerising stroking, one across her cheek, the other on her lower lip. 'You're only here for another couple of weeks. Neither of us is in the position to make promises.'

'I'm not asking for promises,' Izzy said. 'I had promises and they sucked.'

His mouth kicked up at the corner. 'Yeah, me too.'

She placed her fingertip on his bottom lip, caressing it the way he had done to hers. 'I've never had a fling with someone before.'

Something in his gaze smouldered. Simmered. Burned. 'Flings can be fun as long as both parties are clear on the rules.'

Izzy shivered as he took her finger in his mouth, his teeth biting down just firmly enough for her insides to flutter in anticipatory excitement. 'You're mighty big on rules, aren't you, Sergeant? I guess that's because of that gun you're wearing.'

His hands encircled her wrists like handcuffs, his pelvis carnally suggestive against hers. 'I'm not wearing my gun.'

Her brow arched in a sultry fashion. 'Could've fooled me.'

He scooped her up in his arms in an effortless lift, calling out over his shoulder as he carried her towards the bedroom, 'Start without us, Max. We've got some business to see to.'

Izzy quaked with pleasure when Zach slid her down the length of his body once he had her in the bedroom. And there was a *lot* of his body compared to hers. So tall, so lean and yet so powerfully muscled she barely came up to his shoulder once she'd kicked off her heels. His hands cupped her bottom and pulled her against him, letting her feel the weight and heft of his erection. Even through the barrier of their clothes it was the most erotic feeling to have him pulse and pound against her. He kissed her lingeringly, deeply, taking his time to build her need of him until she was whimpering, gasping, clawing at him to get him naked.

'What's the hurry?' he said against the side of her neck.

Izzy kissed his mouth, his chin, and then flicked the tip of her tongue into the dish below his Adam's apple. 'I've heard things go at a much slower pace in the Outback but I didn't realise that included sex.'

He gave a little rumble of laughter and pulled the zipper down the back of her dress in a single lightning-fast movement. 'You want speed, sweetheart?' He unclipped her bra and tossed it to the floor. 'Then let's see if we can pick up the pace a bit, shall we?'

Izzy whooshed out a breath as she landed on her back on the mattress with a little bounce. As quickly as he had removed her clothes, he got rid of his own, coming down over her, gloriously, deliciously naked.

The sexy entanglement of limbs, of long and hard and toned and tanned and hair-roughened muscles entwining with softer, smoother, shorter ones made everything that was feminine in her roll over in delight. His hands, those gorgeously manly hands, sexily grazed the soft skin of her breasts. That sizzling-hot male mouth with its surrounding stubble suckled on each one in turn, the right one first and then the left, the suction just right, the pressure and tug of his teeth perfect, the roll and sweep of his tongue mind-blowing.

Izzy had never been all that vocal during sex in the past. The occasional sigh or murmur perhaps—sometimes just to feed Richard's ego rather than from feeling anything spectacular herself—but nothing like the gasps and whimpers that were coming out of her now. It wasn't just Zach's mouth that was wreaking such havoc on her senses but the feel and shape of his body as it pinned hers to the bed. Not too heavy, not awkward or clumsy, but potent and powerful, determined and yet respectful.

He moved down from her breasts to sear a scorching pathway to her bellybutton and beyond. She automatically tensed when he came to the seam of her body, but immediately sensing her hesitation he placed his palm over her lower abdomen to calm her. 'Trust me, Izzy. I can make it good for you.'

Should she tell him she had never experienced such intimacy before? She didn't want to make Richard sound like a prude, but the truth was he had made it clear early on in their relationship that he found oral sex distasteful. In spite of her knowledge as a doctor to the contrary, his attitude had made her feel as if her body was unpleasant, unattractive and somehow defective. 'Um...I've never done it before... I mean no one's done it to me...'

He looked at her quizzically. 'Your ex didn't?'

She knew she was blushing. But rather than hide it she decided to be honest with him. 'It wasn't Richard's thing.'

He was still frowning. 'But it's one of the best ways for a woman to have an orgasm.'

Izzy was silent for just a second or two too long.

He cocked an eyebrow at her questioningly. 'You have had an orgasm, right?'

'Of course…' Majorly fiery blush this time. 'Plenty of times.'

'Izzy.' The way Zach said her name was like a parent catching a child out for lying.

'It was hard for me to get there…I always took too long to get in the mood and then Richard would pressure me and I…' Izzy gave him a helpless look '…I usually faked it.'

His frown had made a pleat between his grey eyes. 'Usually?'

'Mostly.' She bit her lip at his look. 'It was easier that way. I didn't want to hurt Richard's feelings or make him feel inadequate. Seems to me some men have such fragile egos when it comes to their sexual prowess.'

He stroked her face with his fingers. 'Being able to satisfy a partner is one of the most enjoyable aspects of sex. I want you to enjoy it, Izzy. Don't pretend with me. Be honest. Take all the time you need.'

Izzy pressed her lips against his. 'If we take too long Max might wonder what we're doing.'

He smiled against her mouth. 'I reckon he's got a pretty fair idea.' And then he kissed her.

CHAPTER ELEVEN

'THANK YOU SO much for stepping in last night,' Margie said when Izzy arrived at work the next morning. 'Doug and I had the most wonderful time. It was as if the last twenty-three years hadn't happened. We talked for hours and hours. Just as well Zach didn't get back till midnight.' Her eyes twinkled meaningfully. 'Must have been a pretty decent dinner you cooked for him. He looked very satisfied.'

Izzy had all but given up on trying to disguise her blush. Her whole body was still glowing from the passionate lovemaking she had experienced in Zach's arms last night. He had been both tender and demanding, insisting on a level of physical honesty from her that was way outside her experience. But she had loved every earth-shattering second of it.

The things she had discovered about her body had amazed her. It was capable of intense and repeated orgasms. Zach had taught her how to relax enough to embrace the powerful sensations, to let her inhibitions go, to stop over-thinking and worrying she wasn't doing things according to a schedule. He had let her choose her own timetable and his pleasure when it had come had been just as intense as hers. That the pleasure had been mutual had given their sensual encounter a depth, an almost sacred aspect she'd found strangely moving.

The only niggling worry she had was how was she going to move on after their fling was over? Falling in love with him or anyone was not part of her plan for her six months away from home. She had only just extricated herself from a long-term relationship. The last thing she wanted was to tie herself up in another one, even if Zach was the most intriguing and attractive man she had met in a long time. Strike that—had *ever* met.

'Yes, well, there's certainly nothing wrong with his appetite,' Izzy said as she popped her bag into the cupboard next to the patients' filing shelves.

'Are you going to see him again?'

'I see him practically every day.' Izzy straightened her skirt as she turned round. 'In a town this size everyone sees everyone every day.'

Margie pursed her lips in a you-can't-fool-me manner. 'You know what I mean. Are you officially a couple? I know the gossip started the moment you showed up in town but that was Charles Redbank's doing. He just wanted to make trouble. He's never forgiven Zach for booking him for speeding a couple of months back.'

'We're not officially anything.' Izzy resented even having to say that much. She wasn't used to discussing her private life with anyone other than Hannah and even then there were some things she wasn't prepared to reveal. Even to herself.

'It'd be lovely if you stayed on a bit longer,' Margie said. 'Everyone loves you. Even that old sourpuss Ida Jensen thinks you're an angel now that you've sorted out her blood-pressure medication. And Peggy McLeod's thrilled you suggested she help start up the playgroup again. She's already got a heap of toys and play equipment donated from the locals. She even got Caitlyn Graham's boyfriend, Wayne Brody, to donate some. He dropped by a bag of stuff yesterday, most of it brand new. Wasn't that nice of him?'

Izzy kept her features schooled, even though inside she was fuming. 'Unbelievably nice of him.'

Margie glanced at the diary. 'Your first patient isn't until nine-thirty. You've got time for a coffee. Want me to make you one here or shall I run up to the general store and get you a latte from Jim's new machine?'

'I'll go,' Izzy said. 'There's something I want to see Sergeant Fletcher about on the way past.'

Zach was typing up an incident report on the computer at the station when he heard the sound of footsteps coming up the path. He knew it was Izzy even before he looked up to check. His skin started to tingle; it hadn't stopped tingling since last night, but it went up a gear when he caught a whiff of summer flowers. He had gone home last night with her fragrance lingering on his skin. He had even considered skipping a shower this morning to keep it there. The way she had come apart in his arms had not only thrilled him, it had made him feel something he hadn't expected to feel.

Didn't want to feel.

He stood as she came in. 'Morning.' He knew he sounded a bit formal but he was having trouble getting that feeling he didn't want to feel back in the box where he had stashed it last night.

His manner obviously annoyed her for her brow puckered in a frown and her lips pulled tight. 'Sorry to disturb you while you're busy, but I forgot to tell you something last night.'

Would this be the bit about how she didn't want to continue their fling? He mentally prepared himself, keeping his face as blank as possible. 'Fire away.'

Her hands were balled into tight little fists by her sides, her cheeks like two bright red apples, and her toffee-brown eyes flashing. 'The toys you left for Caitlyn's kids?' She didn't give him time to say anything in response but continued; 'Wayne wouldn't let her give them to the kids.'

Zach was so relieved her tirade wasn't about ending their affair it took him a moment to respond. 'There's not much I can do about that. They were a gift and if Caitlyn didn't want to accept—'

'You're not listening to me,' she said with a little stamp of her foot. 'Caitlyn would've loved them for the kids, I know she would, she's too frightened to stand up to Wayne. But even worse than that, he passed them off as his own donation to Peggy McLeod for the community centre playgroup. He's passing off *your* gift as his own largesse. It makes my blood boil so much I want to explode!'

He came round from behind the desk and took her trembling-with-rage shoulders in his hands. 'Hey, it's not worth getting upset about it. At least the kids will have a chance to play with the toys when they go to the centre.'

Her pretty little face was scrunched up in a furious scowl. 'If that control freak lets them go. He'll probably put a stop to that too. Can't you do something? Like arrest him for making a false declaration of generosity or something?'

Zach fought back a smile as he rubbed his hands up and down her silky arms. 'My experience with guys like him is that the more you show how much they get under your skin the more they enjoy it. Best thing you can do is support Caitlyn and the kids. Helping to build up her confidence as a parent is a great start.'

She let out a sign that released her tense shoulders. 'I guess you're right…'

He tipped up her chin and meshed his gaze with her still troubled one. 'Do you have any plans for tonight?'

Her eyes lost their dullness and began to sparkle. 'I don't know. I'll have to check what Max has got planned. He might want to hang out. Watch a movie or something. He gets lonely if he's left on his own too long.'

Zach had no hope of suppressing his smile. 'Then why don't we take him on a picnic out to Blake's waterhole? I'll bring the food. I'll pick you up at six-thirty so we can catch the sunset.'

She scrunched up her face again but her eyes were dancing. 'I'm not sure Max has a pair of bathers.'

Zach gave her a glinting smile as he brought his mouth down to hers. 'Tell him he won't need them.'

Izzy spread the picnic blanket down over a patch of sunburned grass near the waterhole while Zach brought the picnic basket and their towels from the car. The sun was still high and hot enough to crisp and crackle the air with the sound of cicadas. But down by the water's edge the smell of the dusty earth was relieved by the earthy scent of cool, deep water shadowed by the overhanging craggy-armed gums. Long gold fingers of sunlight were poking between the branches to gild the water, along with a light breeze that was playfully tickling the surface.

Zach put the picnic basket down on the blanket. 'Swim first or would you like a cold drink?'

Izzy looked at him, dressed in faded blue denim jeans with their one tattered knee, his light grey body-hugging T-shirt showcasing every toned muscle of his chest and shoulders and abdomen. He looked strong and fit and capable, the sort of man you would go to in a crisis. The sort of man you could depend on, a man who was not only strong on the outside but had an inner reserve of calm deliberation. He was the sort of man who wasn't daunted by hard work or a challenging task. The way he had moved back to the bush to help his father even though it had cost him his relationship with his fiancée confirmed it. He was a man of principles, conviction. Loyalty.

It made her think of Richard, who within a couple of days of her ending their relationship had found a replacement.

Zach, on the other hand, had spent the last eighteen months quietly grieving the loss of his relationship and the future he had planned for himself, devoting his time to his father and the community. Doing whatever it took, no matter how difficult, to help his father come to terms with the limitations that had been placed on him. He didn't complain. He didn't grouse or whinge about it. He just got on with it.

Zach must have mistaken her silence for something else. 'There are no nasties in the water, if that's what's putting you off. An eel or two, a few tadpoles and frogs but nothing to be too worried about.'

A shiver of unease slithered down her spine. 'Snakes?'

'They're definitely about but more will see you than you see them.' He gave her a quick grin. 'I'll go in first and scare them away, OK?'

'Big, brave man.'

He tugged his T-shirt over his head and tossed it onto one of the sun-warmed rocks nearby. 'Yeah, well, that's more than I can say about that roommate of yours squibbing at the last minute.'

Izzy feasted her eyes on his washboard stomach and then her heart gave a little flip as he reached for the zipper on his jeans. She disguised her reaction behind humour but was sure he wasn't fooled for a second. 'It wasn't that he was scared or anything. He's got very sensitive skin. He was worried about mosquitoes. One prick and he might never recover.'

Zach's smile made her skin lift up in goose-bumps as big as the gravel they had driven over earlier. He came and stood right in front of her, dressed in nothing but his shape-hugging black underwear. He flicked the collar of her lightweight cotton blouse with two of his fingers. 'Need some help getting your gear off?'

Izzy found it hard to breathe with him so deliciously close. The smell of him, the citrus and physically active man smell of him made her insides squirm with longing. His grey-blue eyes were glinting, his mouth slanted in a sexy smile that never failed to make her feminine core contract and release in want. Her body remembered every stroke and glide and powerful thrust of his inside hers last night. Her feminine muscles tightened in feverish anticipation, the musky, silky moisture of her body automatically activated in response to his intimate proximity. 'Are you offering to do a strip search, Sergeant Fletcher?' she asked with a flirty smile.

His eyes gleamed with sensual promise as his fingers went to the buttons on her shirt. 'Let's see what you've got hidden under here, shall we?'

One by one he undid each button, somehow making it into a game of intense eroticism. His fingers scorched her skin each time he released another button from its tiny buttonhole, the action triggering yet another pulse of primal longing deep in her flesh. He peeled the shirt off her shoulders, and then tracked his finger down between her breasts, still encased in her bra. 'Beautiful.'

How one word uttered in that deep, husky tone could make her feel like a supermodel was beyond her. It wasn't just a line, a throw-away comment to get what he wanted. She knew he meant it. She could feel it in his touch, the gentle way he had of cupping her breasts once he'd released her bra, the way his thumbs stroked over her nipples with a touch that was both achingly tender and yet tantalisingly arousing.

Her cotton summer skirt was next to go, the zip going down, the little hoop of fabric circling her ankles before he took her hand and helped her step away from it like stepping out of a puddle. He put a warm, work-roughened hand to the curve of her hip just above the line of her knickers, holding her close enough to the potent heat of his body for her to feel his reaction to her closeness.

He was powerfully erect. She could feel the thrum of his blood through the lace of her knickers, the hot, urgent pressure of him stirring her senses into frantic overload.

He touched her then, a single stroke down the lace-covered seam of her body, a teasing taste of the intimate invasion to come. She whimpered as he slid her knickers aside, waiting a heart-stopping beat before he touched her again, skin on skin.

Izzy tugged his underwear down so she could do the same to him, taking him in her hands, stroking him, caressing the silky steel of him until he was breathing as raggedly as she was.

He slipped a finger inside her, swallowing her gasp as his mouth came down on hers. His kiss was passionate, thorough, and intensely erotic as his tongue tangled with hers in a cat-and-mouse caper.

Izzy's caressing of him became bolder, squeezing and releasing, smoothing up and down his length, running her fingertip over the ooze of his essence, breathing in the musky scent of mutual arousal.

There was something wildly, deeply primitive about being naked with a man in the bush. No sounds other than their hectic breathing and those of nature. The distant warble of magpies, the throaty arck-arck of a crow flying overhead, the whisper of the breeze moving through the gum leaves, sounding like thousands of finger-length strips of tinsel paper being jostled together.

Zach pressed her down on the tartan blanket, pushing the picnic things out of the way with his elbow, quickly sourcing a condom before entering her with a thrust that made her cry out with bone-deep pleasure. He set a fast rhythm that was as primal as their surroundings, the intensity of it thrilling her senses in a way she had never thought possible just a few short weeks ago. Her life in England had never felt more distant. It was like having another completely different identity that belonged back there.

Over there she was a buttoned-up girl who had spent

years of her life pretending to be happy, pleasing others rather than pleasing herself.

Out here she was a wild and wanton woman, having smoking-hot sex with a man she hadn't known a fortnight ago.

And now…now she was rocking in his arms as if her world began and ended with him. The physicality of their relationship was shocking, the blunt, almost brutal honesty of the needs of their bodies as they strove for completion was as carnal as two wild animals mating. Even the sound of her cries as she came were those of a woman she didn't know, had never encountered before. Wild, shrieking cries that spoke of a depth of passion that had never been tapped into or expressed before.

Zach's release was not as vocal but Izzy felt the power of it as he tensed, pumped and then flowed.

He didn't move for a long moment. His body rested on hers in the aftermath, his breathing slowly returning to normal as she stroked her hands up and down his back and shoulders, their bodies still intimately joined.

'I think there's a pebble sticking into my butt,' Izzy finally said.

He rolled her over so she was lying on top of him, his eyes heavily lidded, sleepy with satiation. 'Better?'

'Much.'

He circled her right breast with a lazy finger. 'Ever skinny dipped before?'

'Not with a man present.' Izzy gave him a wry smile. 'I did it with Hannah and a couple of other girlfriends when we were thirteen at my birthday party. It was a dare.'

His finger made a slow, nerve-tingling circuit of her

other breast. 'Is that how the crazy birthday stuff with her started?'

Izzy sent her own fingers on an exploration of his flat brown nipple nestled amongst his springy chest hair. 'Come to think of it, yes. She was always on about me being too worried about what other people thought. She made it her mission in life to shock me out of my "aristocratic mediocrity", as she calls it.'

He stroked his hand over the flank of her thigh. 'Somehow mediocre isn't the first word that comes to mind when I think of you.'

Izzy angled her head at him. 'So what word does?'

He gave her a slow smile that crinkled up the corners of his eyes in a devastatingly attractive manner. 'Cute. Funny. Sexy.'

She traced the outline of his smile with her fingertip. 'I never felt sexy before. Not the way I do with you.' She bit down on her lip, wondering if she'd been too honest, revealed too much.

He brushed her lower lip with his thumb. 'You do that a lot.'

'What?'

'Bite your lip.'

Izzy had to stop her teeth from doing it again. 'It's a nervous habit. Half the time I'm not even aware I'm doing it.'

His thumb caressed her lip as if soothing it from the assault of her teeth. 'Why don't you come down here and bite mine instead?'

Izzy leaned down and started nibbling at his lower lip, using her teeth to tug and tease. She used her tongue to sweep over where her teeth had been, before starting the process all over again. Nip. Tug. Nip. Tug.

He gave little grunts of approval, one of his hands splayed in her hair as he held her head close to his. 'Harder,' he commanded.

A shudder of pleasure shimmied down her spine as his hand fisted in her hair. She pulled at his lip with her teeth, stroked it with her tongue and then pushed her tongue into his mouth to meet his. Zach murmured his pleasure and took control of the kiss, his masterful tongue darting and diving around hers.

It was an exhilarating kiss, wild and abandoned and yet still with an element of tenderness that ambushed her emotionally.

She wasn't supposed to be feeling anything but lust for this man.

This was a fling.

A casual hook-up like all her girlfriends experienced from time to time. It was a chance to own her sexuality, to express it without the confining and formal bounds of a relationship.

She was only here for another couple of weeks. She was moving on to new sights and experiences, filling her six months away from home with adventure and memories to look back on in the years to come.

Falling in love would be a crazy…a totally disastrous thing to do…

Izzy eased off Zach while he dealt with the condom. She gathered her tousled hair and tied it into a makeshift knot, using the tresses as an anchor. Her body tingled with the memory of his touch as she got to her feet, tiny aftershocks of pleasure rippling through her.

She was dazed by sensational sex, that's all it was.

It wasn't love. How could it be?

Maybe it was time to cool off.

'Are you sure it's safe to swim here?'

'Not for diving but it's fine for a dip.' He took her hand and led her down to the water. 'Not quite St Barts, is it?'

Izzy glanced at him. 'You've been there?'

'Once.' He looked out over the water as if he was seeing the exclusive Caribbean holiday destination in his mind's eye, his mouth curled up in a cynical arc. 'With my mother and her new family when I was fourteen. Cost her husband a packet. I'm sure he only took us all there to make a point of how good her life was with him instead of my father. I didn't go on holidays with them after that. I got tired of having all that wealth thrust in my face.'

Izzy moved her fingers against his. 'I hated most of my family holidays. I'm sure we only went to most of the places we went to because that's where my parents thought people expected to see us. Skiing at exclusive lodges in Aspen. Sailing around the Mediterranean on yachts that cost more than most people ever see in a lifetime. I would've loved to go camping under the stars in the wilderness but, no, it was butlers and chauffeurs and five stars all the way.'

He looked at her with a wry smile tilting his mouth. 'Funny, isn't it, that you always want what you don't have?'

I have what I want right now. Izzy quickly filed away the thought. She looked down at the mud that was squelching between her toes. The water was refreshingly cool against her heated skin. She went in a little further, holding Zach's hand for balance until she was waist deep. 'Mmm, that's lovely.' She went in a bit deeper but something cold and slimy brushed against her leg and she yelped and sprang back and clung to Zach like a limpet. 'Eeek! What was that?'

He held her against him, laughing softly. 'It was just a bit of weed. Nothing to worry about. You're safe with me.'

Her arms were locked around his neck, her legs wrapped around his waist and her mouth within touching distance of his. She watched as his gaze went to her mouth, the way his lashes lowered in that sleepily hooded way a man did when he was thinking about sex. A new wave of desire rolled through her as his mouth came down and fused with hers.

You're safe with me.

Izzy wasn't safe. Not the way she wanted to be. Not the way she needed to be.

She was in very great danger indeed.

CHAPTER TWELVE

As Zach packed the picnic things back in the car Izzy looked up at the brilliant night sky with its scattering of stars like handfuls of diamonds flung across a bolt of dark blue velvet. The air was still warm and the night orchestra's chorus had recruited two extra voices: a tawny frogmouth owl and a vixen fox, looking for a mate.

That distinctive bark was a sound from home, making Izzy feel a sudden pang of homesickness. She wondered if sounds like those of a lonely feral fox had caused Zach's mother to grieve for the life she had left behind. Had the years fighting drought and dust and flies or floods and failed crops and flyblown sheep finally broken her spirit? Or had she simply fallen out of love with her husband? Leaving a husband one no longer loved was understandable, but leaving a child to travel to the other side of the world was something else again. Leaving Zach behind must have been a very difficult decision.

Izzy couldn't imagine a mother choosing her freedom over her child, but she recognised that not all mothers found the experience as satisfying and fulfilling as others.

Leaving Zach behind...

The words reverberated inside her head. That was what she would have to do in a matter of a fortnight. She would never see him again. He would move on with his life, no doubt in a year or two find a good, sensible, no-nonsense country girl to settle down with, raise a family and work the land as his father and grandfather and forebears had done before him. She imagined him sitting at the scrubbed pine kitchen table at Fletcher Downs homestead surrounded by his wife and children. He would make a wonderful father. She had seen him with Caitlyn's children, generous, gentle and calm.

Izzy heard his footfall on the gravel as he came to join her. 'Have you found the Southern Cross?' he asked.

'I think so.' She pointed to a constellation of stars in the south. 'Is that it there?'

He followed the line of her arm and nodded. 'Yep, that's it. Good work. You must've done your research.'

Izzy turned and looked at him, something in her heart contracting as if a hand had grabbed at it and squeezed. 'Would you ever consider living somewhere else?' she asked.

A frown flickered over his brow. 'You mean like back in the city?'

Izzy wasn't sure what she meant. She wasn't sure why she had even asked. 'Will you quit your work as a cop and take over Fletcher Downs once your father officially retires?'

He looked back at the dark overturned bowl of the sky, his gaze going all the way to the horizon, where a thin lip of light lingered just before the sun dipped to wake the other side of the world. 'I love my work as a cop…well, most of the time. But the land is in my blood. The Fletcher name goes back a long way in these parts, all the way back to the first European settlers. I'm my dad's only heir. I can't afford to pay a manager for ever. The property would have to be sold if I didn't take it on full time.'

'But is that what *you* want?'

He continued to focus on the distant horizon with a grim set to his features. 'What I want is my dad to get back to full health and mobility but that doesn't look like it's going to happen any time soon.'

'But at least he's becoming more socially active,' Izzy said. 'That's a great step forward. Margie's determined to get him out more. It would be so nice if they got together, don't you think?'

He looked back at her with that same grave look. 'My father will never get married again. He's been burned once. He would never go back for a second dose.'

'But that's crazy,' Izzy said. 'Margie loves him. She's loved him since she was a girl. They belong together. Anyone can see that.'

His lip curled upwards but it wasn't so much mocking as wry. 'Stick to your medical journals, Izzy. Those romance novels you read are messing with your head.'

It's not my head they're messing with, Izzy thought as she followed him back to the car.

It was her heart.

Zach brought a beer out to his father on the veranda a couple of days later. 'Here you go. But only the one. Remember what the doctor said about drinking plenty of clear fluids.'

'Thanks.' Doug took a long sip, and then let a silence slip past before asking, 'You seeing her tonight?'

Zach reached down to tickle Popeye's ears. 'Not tonight.'

'Wise of you.'

'What's that supposed to mean?'

Doug took another sip of his beer before answering. 'Better not get too used to having her around. She's going to be packing up and leaving before you know it.'

Zach tried to ignore the savage twist of his insides at the thought of Izzy driving out of town once her locum was up. He'd heard a whisper the locals were going to use the Shearers' Ball as a send-off for her. William Sawyer and his wife would be back from their trip soon and life would return to normal in Jerringa Ridge.

Normal.

What a weird word to describe his life. When had it ever been normal? Growing up since the age of ten without a mother. Years of putting up with his father's ongoing bitterness over his marriage break-up. For years he hadn't even been able to mention his mother without his father flinching as if he had landed a punch on him.

Dealing with the conflicted emotions of visiting his mother in her gracious home in Surrey, where he didn't fit in with the formal furniture or her even more formal ridiculously wealthy new husband who never seemed to wear anything but a suit and a silk cravat, even on St Barts. Those gut-wrenching where-do-I-belong feelings intensifying once her new sons Jules and Oliver had been born. Coming back home and feeling just as conflicted trying to settle back in to life at Fletcher Downs or at boarding school.

Always feeling the outsider.

'I know what I'm doing, Dad.'

His father glanced at him briefly before turning to look at the light fading over the paddocks. It was a full minute, maybe longer before he spoke. 'I'm not going to get any better than this, am I? No point pretending I am.'

Zach found the sudden shift in conversation disorienting. 'Sure you are. You're doing fine.' He was doing it again. It was his fall-back position. A pattern of the last twenty-three years he couldn't seem to get out of— playing Pollyanna to his father's woe-is-me moods. He could recall all the pep-talk phrases he'd used in the past: *Time heals everything. You'll find someone else. Take it one day at a time. Baby steps. Everything happens for a reason.*

Doug's hand tightened on his can of beer until the aluminium crackled. 'I should've married Margie. I should've done it years ago. Now it's too late.'

It's never too late was on the tip of Zach's tongue but he refrained from voicing it. 'Is that what Margie wants? Marriage?'

'It's what most women want, isn't it?' His father gave his beer can another crunch. 'A husband, a family, a home they can be proud of. Security.'

'Margie's already got a family and a house and her job is secure,' Zach said. 'Seems to me what she wants is companionship.'

His father's top lip curled in a manner so like his own it was disquieting to witness. 'And what sort of companion am I? I can't even get on a stepladder and change a bloody light bulb.'

'There's more to a relationship than who puts out the garbage or takes the dog for a walk,' Zach said.

His father didn't seem to be listening. He was still looking out over the paddocks with a frown between his eyes. 'I didn't see it at the time…all those years ago I didn't see Margie for who she was. She was always just one of the local girls, fun to be around but didn't stand out. Then I met your mother.' He made a self-deprecating sound. 'What a fool I was to think I could make someone like her happy. I tried for ten years to keep her. Ten years of living with the dread she would one day pack up and leave. And then she did.' He clicked his fingers. *Snap.* 'She was gone.'

Zach remembered it all too well. He could still remember exactly where he had been standing on the veranda as he'd watched his mother drive away. He had gripped the veranda rail so tightly his hands had ached for days. He had watched with his heart feeling as heavy as a headstone in his chest. His mouth had been as dry as the red dust his mother's car had stirred up as she'd wheeled away.

For weeks, months, even years every time he heard a car come up the long driveway he would feel his heart leap in hope that she was coming back.

She never did.

Doug looked at Zach. 'It wasn't her fault. Not all of it. I was fighting to keep this place going after your grandfather died and then your grandmother so soon after. I didn't give her the attention she needed. You can't take an orchid out of an English conservatory and expect it to survive in the Outback. You have to nurture it, protect it.'

'Do you still love her?'

Doug's mouth twisted. 'There's a part of me that will always love your mother. Maybe not the same way

I did. It's like keeping that old pair of work boots near the back door. I'm not quite ready to part with them yet.'

'I'm not sure Mum would appreciate being compared to a pair of your old smelly work boots,' Zach said wryly, thinking of his mother's penchant for cashmere and pearls and designer shoes.

A small sad smile skirted around the edges of Doug's mouth. 'No…probably not.'

A silence passed.

'Why's it too late for you and Margie?' Zach asked. 'You're only fifty-eight. She's, what? Fifty-two or -three? You could have a good thirty or forty years together.'

'Look at me, Zach.' His father's eyes glittered with tightly held-back emotion. 'Take a good look. I'm like this now, shuffling about like a man in his eighties. What am I going to be like in five or even ten years' time? You heard what the specialist said. I was lucky to get this far. I can't do it to Margie. I can't turn her into a carer instead of a wife and lover. It'd make her hate me.' His chin quivered as he fought to keep his voice under control. 'I couldn't bear to have another woman I love end up hating me.'

'I think you're underestimating Margie,' Zach said. 'She's not like Mum. She's strong and dependable and loyal.'

'And you're such a big expert on women, aren't you, Zach? You've got one broken engagement on the leader board already. How soon before there's another?'

'There's not going to be another.'

'Why?' His father's lip was still up in that nasty little curl. 'Because you won't risk asking her, will you?'

Zach could barely get the words out through his clenched teeth. 'Ask who?'

His father pushed himself to his feet, nailing Zach with his gaze. 'That toffee-nosed little doctor you spend every spare moment of your time with.'

'I'm not in love with Isabella Courtney.'

'No, of course you're not.' Doug gave a scornful grunt of laughter. 'Keep on telling yourself that, son. If nothing else, it'll make the day she leaves a little easier on you.'

Izzy knew it was cowardly of her to pretend to be busy with catching up on emails and work-related stuff two nights in a row but spending all her spare time with Zach was making it increasingly difficult for her to keep her emotions separate from the physical side of their relationship. No wonder sex was called making love. Every look, every touch, every kiss, every spine-tingling orgasm seemed to up the ante until she wasn't sure what she felt any more. Was it love or was it lust?

Had it been a mistake to indulge in an affair with him? She had spent four years making love—*having sex*—with Richard and had never felt anything like the depth of feeling she did with Zach, and she had only known him three weeks.

And there was only one to go.

Margie looked very downcast when Izzy got to the clinic the next morning. She was sitting behind the reception desk with red-rimmed eyes and her shoulders slumped. 'Don't ask.'

'Doug?'

Margie reached for a tissue from the box on her desk. 'He said it's best if we don't see each other any more, only as friends. I've been friends with him for most of my life but it's not enough. I want more.'

'Oh, Margie, I'm so sorry. I thought things were going so well.'

Margie dabbed at her eyes. 'It's my fault for thinking I could change his mind. I should have left well alone. Now he knows how I feel about him it makes me feel so stupid. Like a lovesick schoolgirl or something.'

'Is there anything I can do?'

'Not unless you can make him fall out of love with his ex-wife.'

Izzy frowned. 'Do you really think that's what it's about?'

'What else could it be? Olivia was his grand passion.' Margie plucked another tissue out of the box and blew her nose.

'What if it's more to do with his limitations? He's a proud man. Having to rely on others for help must be really tough on someone like him.'

'But I love him. I don't care if he can't get around the way he used to. Why can't he just accept that I love him no matter what?'

Izzy gave her a sympathetic look. 'Maybe he needs more time. From what I've read of his notes, his injuries were pretty severe. And this latest bout of renal colic has probably freaked him out a bit. It's very common for every ache or pain in someone who's suffered a major illness or trauma to get magnified in their head.'

Margie gave a sound of agreement. 'Well, enough about me and my troubles. How are you and Zach getting on?'

'Fine.'

'Just fine?'

Izzy picked off a yellowed leaf from the pot plant on

the counter. 'There's nothing serious going on between us. We both know and understand that.'

'Would you like it to be more?'

'I'm leaving at the end of next week.'

'That's not the answer I was looking for,' Margie said.

'It's the only one I'm prepared to give.'

Margie looked at her thoughtfully for a lengthy moment. 'Don't make the same mistake I made, Izzy. I should've told Doug years ago what I felt for him. Now it's too late.'

'I spent four years with a man and then realised I didn't love him enough to marry him,' Izzy said. 'What makes you think I would be so confident about my feelings after less than four weeks?'

Margie gave her a sage look. 'Because when you know you just know.'

CHAPTER THIRTEEN

Izzy WALKED DOWN to the community centre during her lunch break. She had arranged to meet Peggy McLeod there as well as Caitlyn Graham, who had finally agreed to work with Peggy in a mentor and mentee role. Peggy as a mother and grandmother with years of wisdom and experience working in the community was just what Caitlyn needed as a role model. Peggy had even offered to babysit Skylar occasionally when the boys were at school so Caitlyn could get a bit of a break. But when Izzy arrived at the centre Peggy was on her own.

'Where's Caitlyn?'

Peggy gave Izzy a miffed look over her shoulder as she placed a box of building blocks on the shelves one of the local farmers had made specially. 'Decided she had better things to do.'

'But I confirmed it with her yesterday,' Izzy said. 'She said she was looking forward to it. It was the first time I'd ever seen her excited about something.'

'Yes, well, she called me not five minutes ago and told me she's changed her mind.'

Changed her mind or had it changed for her? Izzy wondered. 'I think I'd better go and check on her. Maybe one of the kids is sick or something.'

'The boys are at school,' Peggy said. 'I waved to them in the playground when I drove past.'

'Maybe Skylar's sick.'

'Then why didn't she just say so?'

Izzy frowned. 'What *did* she say?'

Peggy pursed her lips. 'Just that she'd changed her mind. Told me she didn't want me babysitting for her either. I've brought up five kids and I'm a grandmother twelve times over. What does she think I am? An axe murderer or something?'

'Don't take it personally,' Izzy said. 'She's not used to having anyone step in and help her. I'll duck out there now and see if I can get her to change her mind.'

Izzy thought about calling Zach to come with her but changed her mind at the last minute. His car wasn't at the station in any case and she didn't want to make a big issue out of what could just be a case of Caitlyn's lack of self-esteem kicking in. She'd tried calling her a couple of times but the phone had gone to message bank.

Caitlyn's old car was parked near the house but apart from the frenzied barking of the dog near the tank stand there was no sign of life. Izzy walked tentatively to the front door, saying, 'Nice doggy, good doggy,' with as much sincerity as she could muster. She put her hand up to knock but the door suddenly opened and she found herself face to face with a thick-set man in his late twenties, who was even scarier than the dog lunging on its chain to her left.

'What do you want?' the man snarled.

'Um… Hello, is Caitlyn home? I'm Isabella Courtney, the locum filling in for—'

'Did she call you?'

'No, I just thought I'd drop past and—'

'She don't need no doctor so you can get back in your fancy car and get the hell out of here.'

The sound of Skylar crying piteously in one of the back rooms of the house made Izzy's heart lurch. 'Is Skylar OK? She sounds terribly upset. Is she—?'

'You want me to let the dog off?' His cold eyes glared at her through the tattered mesh of the screen door.

Izzy garnered what was left of her courage. She straightened her shoulders and looked him in the eye with what she hoped looked like steely determination. 'I'd like to talk to Caitlyn before I leave.'

Wayne suddenly shoved the screen door wide open, which forced her to take a couple of rapid steps backwards that sent her backwards off the veranda to land in an ungainly heap on her bottom in the dust. 'I said clear off,' he said.

Izzy scrambled to her feet, feeling a fool and a coward and so angry and utterly powerless she wanted to scream. But she knew the best thing to do was to leave and call Zach as soon as she was out of danger. She dusted off the back of her skirt and walked back to her car with as much dignity as she could muster. Her hand trembled uncontrollably as she tried to get her car key in the ignition slot to start the engine. It took her five tries to do it. Her heart was hammering in her chest and terrified sobs were choking out of her throat as she drove out of the driveway.

Zach was on the road when he got a distressed call from Izzy. 'Hey, slow down, sweetheart. I can't understand a word you're saying.'

She was crying and gasping, her breathing so erratic

it sounded like she was choking. 'I think Wayne's hurt Caitlyn. She didn't turn up at the playgroup. I heard Skylar screaming in the background. I think he'd been drinking. I could smell it. You have to do something. You have to hurry.'

'Where are you?'

'I—I'm on the road just past the t-turnoff.'

'Stop driving. Pull over. Do it right now.' He didn't let out his breath until he heard her do as he'd commanded. 'Good girl. Now wait for me. I'm only a few minutes away. I'll call Rob for back-up. Just stay put, OK?'

'OK…'

Zach called his colleague and quickly filled him in. He drove as fast as he could to where Izzy was parked on the side of the road. She was as white as a stick of chalk and tumbled out of the car even before he had pulled to a halt.

He gathered her close, reassuring himself she was all right before he put her from him. 'I'm going to check things out. I've called the volunteer ambulance and put them on standby. I want you to stay here until I see what the go is. I'll call you if we need you. It might not be as serious as you think.'

Her eyes looked as big as a Shetland pony's. 'You won't get hurt, will you?'

'Course not.' He quickly kissed her on the forehead. 'I've got a gun, remember?'

Izzy took a steadying breath as she waited for Zach to contact her. It seemed like ten hours but it was only ten minutes before he called her to inform her Caitlyn and Skylar were fine. 'Brody was his usual charming self,' he said. 'But Caitlyn insisted he hadn't hurt her or the child. She didn't appear to have any marks or bruises and the child seemed settled enough. She was sound asleep when I looked in on her. Apparently Brody was insisting she take a nap and wouldn't let Caitlyn go in to comfort her.'

'And you believed him?'

'I can't arrest him without evidence and Caitlyn swears he didn't do anything.'

Izzy blew out a breath of frustration. 'If he didn't hurt her today he will do sooner or later. I just know it.'

'Welcome to the world of tricky relationships.'

They can't get any trickier than the one I'm in, Izzy thought. 'Can I see you after work?'

'Not too busy with emails and video calls to your friends?'

'Not tonight.'

'Good,' he said. 'I happen to be free too.'

Izzy got back to the clinic in time to see her list of afternoon patients but just as she was about to finish for the day Margie popped her head into her consulting room. 'You got a minute?'

'Sure.' Izzy put down the pen she had been using to write up her last patient's details, mentally preparing herself for another emotional outpouring of Margie's unrequited love story. It wasn't that she didn't want to listen or support her. It was just too close to what she was feeling about Zach. How could it be possible to fall in love with someone so quickly? Did that sort of thing really happen or was that just in Hollywood movies? Was she imagining how she felt? Was it just this crazy lust fest she had going on with him that was colouring her judgement?

Margie rolled her lips together, looking awkward and embarrassed as she came into the room. 'It's not about Doug or anything like that… It's a personal thing. A health thing.'

'What's the problem?'

'I found a lump.'

'In your breast?'

Margie nodded, and then gave her lower lip a little chew. 'I've been a bit slack about doing my own checks but when you ordered that mammogram for Kathleen Fisher earlier today it got me thinking. I went to the bathroom just then. I found a lump.'

Izzy got up from her chair and came from behind the desk. 'Hop on the examination table and I'll have a feel of it for you. Try not to worry too much. Breast tissue can go through lots of changes for any number of reasons.'

Margie lay back on the table and unbuttoned her blouse and unclipped her bra. 'I can't believe I've been so stupid not to check my own breasts. I haven't done it for months, maybe even a couple of years.'

Izzy palpated Margie's left breast where, high in the upper part, there was a definite firm nodule, about the size of a walnut. 'You're right, there is a lump there. Is it tender at all?'

'No, it's not sore at all. It's cancer, isn't it?'

'Hang on, Margie. It could be any of several things. It could be a cyst, some hormonal thickening, maybe a benign tumour. It could possibly be cancer, but we have to do some tests in Bourke to tell what it is.'

'What do we do now?' Margie's expression was stricken. 'I'm worried. What am I going to tell the kids?'

'We'll do what we always do—we'll go step by step, figure out what the lump is and then fix it,' Izzy said. 'First we get a mammogram and ultrasound. Then, at the same time, we'll get the mammogram people to take a needle sample of the lump. That should give us the diagnosis. If it's a cyst, we just aspirate the fluid with a needle and that's usually the end of it. If the biopsy shows cancer cells, we get a surgeon to deal with it.'

'If it's cancer, will I have to have a mastectomy?'

'Mastectomies are very uncommon these days. Usually just the lump plus one lymph gland is removed, and then the breast gets some radiotherapy. If the lymph node was positive, possibly some more surgery to the armpit and maybe some chemo or hormonal therapies.'

Margie swung her legs off the examination table, her expression contorted with anguish as her fingers fumbled with the buttons on her blouse. 'I don't want to die. I have so much I want to do. I want to see my grandkids grow up. I want Doug to—' She suddenly looked at Izzy. 'Oh, God, what am I going to say to Doug? He'll never want me now, not if I've got cancer.'

Izzy took Margie's hand and gave it a comforting squeeze. 'No one's talking about dying. These days breast cancer is a very treatable disease when it's caught early. Let's take this one step at a time.'

'But who will run the clinic while I go to Bourke for the biopsy?'

'I'm sure I'll manage for a day without you,' Izzy said. 'I can divert the phone to mine, or maybe I could ask Peggy to sit by the phone. I'm sure she wouldn't mind.'

Margie sank her teeth into her lip. 'You know…the scary thing is if you hadn't been here filling in for William Sawyer I might not have bothered asking him to check me. I've known him so long it's kind of embarrassing, you know?'

'A lot of women feel the same way you do about seeing a male doctor for anything gynaecological or for breast issues, but all doctors, male or female, are trained to assess both male and female conditions.' Izzy wrote out the biopsy order form and a referral letter. 'I'll phone the surgeon and see if I can get you in this week. The sooner we know what we're dealing with the better.'

'Thanks, Izzy.' Margie clutched the letter to her chest. 'I don't mind if you tell Zach about this. I think Doug would want to know.'

'Why don't you call Doug yourself?'

Margie's eyes watered up. 'Because I'll just howl and blubber like a baby. I think it's better if he hears it from Zach. Will you be seeing him tonight?'

'He's dropping in after work.'

Margie's hand stalled on the doorknob as she looked back at Izzy over her shoulder. 'William is going to retire in a year or so. Maybe if you stayed you could job-share or something.'

'I can't stay. My home is in England.' She said it like a mantra. Like a creed. 'It's where I belong.'

'Is that where your heart is?'

'Of course.' Izzy kept her expression under such tight control it was painful. 'Where else would it be?'

Izzy opened the door to Zach a couple of hours later. 'Hi.'

He ran a finger down the length of her cheek in a touch as light as a brushstroke. 'You OK?'

She blew out a long exhausted-sounding breath. 'What a day.'

He closed the door behind him and reached for her, cupping her face in his hands and kissing her gently on the mouth. A soft, comforting kiss that was somehow far more meaningful and moving than if he'd let loose with a storm of passion. It was his sensitivity that made her heart contract. It wasn't because she was in love with him. That thought was off limits. Her brain was barricaded like a crime scene. Cordoned off. *Do Not Enter.*

He pulled back to look at her, still holding her hands in his. 'I've got some good news.'

Izzy gave him a weary look. 'I could certainly do with some. What is it?'

'Caitlyn Graham filed a domestic assault complaint an hour ago. That's why I'm late. Rob's taking Wayne Brody to Bourke to formally charge him.'

Izzy clutched at his hands. 'Is she all right? Should I go and see her?'

'She's gone to Peggy McLeod's place with the kids. I thought you'd had enough drama for one day.'

'What happened? I thought you were certain he hadn't hurt her when you went out there?'

'He hadn't at that stage,' Zach said. 'He'd verbally threatened her. Refused to let her leave the house, that sort of thing. But a couple of hours after we left, when the boys got home from school on the bus he started trying to lay into her. Apparently he's done it before but never in front of the boys. Jobe called triple zero.'

'Are you sure Caitlyn's not hurt? Are the kids OK?'

'Brody was too tanked to do much after the first swing, which Caitlyn luckily managed to dodge. She barricaded herself and the kids in the bathroom and waited for Rob and me to arrive.'

Izzy shuddered at the thought of the terror Caitlyn and the kids must have felt. 'I'm so glad she's finally out of danger. I felt sure it would only be a matter of time before he did something to her or one of the kids. He was so threatening to me. I thought he was going to assault me for sure.'

'If he had, he would've had me to answer to.' A quiver went through her at the implacability in his tone and his grey-blue eyes had a hard, self-satisfied glitter to them as he added, 'As it was, I already had a little score to settle with him.'

Izzy ran a gentle fingertip over the angry graze marks on the backs of the knuckles on his right hand. 'You wouldn't do anything outside the law, would you, Sergeant?' she asked.

He gave her an inscrutable smile. 'I'm one of the good guys, remember?'

She stepped up on tiptoe and pressed a kiss to his lips. 'I didn't realise they still made men like you any more.'

He threaded his fingers through her hair, gently massaging her scalp. 'You sure you're OK?'

Sensitive. Thoughtful. Gallant. What's not to love?

Izzy stepped back behind the yellow and black tape in her head. 'Margie has a lump in her breast.'

His brows snapped together in shock. 'Cancer?'

'I don't know yet. She has to have a mammogram and ultrasound and possibly a fine needle biopsy. I've managed to get her an appointment the day after tomorrow.' Izzy let out a breath. 'She wanted me to tell you so you could tell your dad.'

'Why doesn't she want to tell him herself?'

'I asked her the same thing but she's worried about getting too upset.'

He dropped his hands from her head and raked one through his own hair. 'Poor Margie. This town would be lost without her. My dad would be lost without her.'

'What a pity he hasn't told her that,' Izzy said on another sigh.

He gave her a thoughtful look. 'He will when he realises it.'

CHAPTER FOURTEEN

'CANCER?' DOUG'S FACE blanched. 'Why on earth didn't she tell me herself?'

Zach mentally rolled his eyes. 'You're the one who blew her off because she was getting too close.'

His father looked the colour of grey chalk. 'Is it serious? Is she going to die?'

'I don't know the answer to that. No one does yet. Izzy's organised a biopsy for her in Bourke. We'll know more after the results of that come through.'

'I need to see her. Will you drive me there now? I just want to see her to make sure she's all right.'

'What, *now?*'

'Why not now?' Doug said. 'She shouldn't be on her own at a time like this. Better still, I'll pack a bag and stay with her. I'll go with her to the appointment. She'll want someone with her. Might as well be me.'

Zach felt a warm spill of hope spread through his chest. 'You sure about this? You haven't stayed anywhere overnight other than hospital or rehab since the accident.'

Doug gave him a glowering look. 'I'm not a complete invalid, you know. I might not be able to do some of the things I used to do but I can still support a friend when they need me. Margie was the first person other than you to come to see me after the accident. She sat for days by my bedside. It's only right that I support her through this.'

Three days later Izzy opened the letter from the surgeon with trembling hands. Margie and Doug were sitting together in her consulting room, holding hands like teenagers on their first date.

'I want you to know I'm going to marry Margie, no matter what that letter says,' Doug said. 'I've already talked to Reverend Taylor.'

Izzy acknowledged that with a smile. Zach had already told her the good news. Now it was time for the bad news. She looked at the typed words on the single sheet of paper with the pathology report attached. She breathed out a sigh of relief. Not such bad news after all. 'It's not as bad as it could be. It's a DCIS—'

'What's that?' Doug asked, before Izzy could explain.

'DCIS is duct cancer in situ. It's not cancer but a step before you to get to cancer. It's like catching the horse just before it bolts.'

'So I don't have cancer? But you said duct cancer. I don't understand. Do I have it or not?' Margie asked.

'I'll try and explain it the best I can,' Izzy said. 'Think of it like this. Our body is made up of trillions of cells. Each cell has a computer program in it, telling it what to do. The computer program becomes damaged in some cell and the cell doesn't do what it's supposed to do. The worst-case scenario is when a whole lot of damage occurs, the cell goes out of control, starts multiplying too many copies of itself and won't stop. The copies spread throughout the body. That's cancer. But DCIS is where only a little bit of damage has occurred so far—the cell is a bit iffy when it comes to taking orders, but isn't yet out of control. If the lump is fully removed the problem has been cured.'

'Cured? Just by removing the lump? You mean surgery will fix this?' Doug asked.

'Yes, but the surgeon is still recommending radiotherapy afterwards because although the palpable lump of DCIS will be removed, there could be other unstable cells in the breast about to do the same thing. You'll need regular follow-up but it's certainly a lot better news than it could have been.'

Doug hugged Margie so tightly it looked like he was going to snap her in two. 'I can't believe what a fool I've been for all these years. We'll get married as soon as it can be arranged and go on a fancy cruise for our honeymoon once you've got the all-clear.'

Margie laughed and hugged him back. 'I feel like I've won the lottery. I'm not going to die and I've got the man of my dreams wanting to marry me.' She turned to Izzy. 'How can I thank you?'

'Nothing to thank me for,' Izzy said. 'I'm just doing my job.'

Which will end in two days' time.

Zach had been dreading the Shearers' Ball. Not just because too many of the locals had too much to drink and he had to be the fun police, but because it was the last night Izzy was going to be in town. Neither of them had mentioned that fact over the last couple of days. The drama with Margie and then the relief of his father finally getting his act together had pushed the elephant out of the room.

Now it was back…but Zach was painfully aware its bags were packed.

As soon as Zach arrived at the community centre where the country-style ball was being held he saw Izzy. She was wearing a fifties-style dress with a circle skirt in a bright shade of red that made her look like a poppy in a field of dandelions. He had never seen her look more beautiful. He had never seen *anyone* look more beautiful. Her hair was up in that half casual, half formal style, her creamy skin was highlighted with the lightest touch of make-up and those gorgeous kissable lips shimmered with lip-gloss.

The locals surrounded her, each one wanting to have their share of her. Caitlyn Graham was there with the kids, looking relaxed and happy for the first time in years. Peggy McLeod was cuddling Skylar and smiling at something Caitlyn had said to Izzy.

Jim Collis wandered over with a beer in his hand. 'She's something else, isn't she?'

Zach kept his expression masked. 'I see you got your tyres fixed.'

'Cost me a fortune.' Jim took another swig of his beer. 'Hey, good news about Margie and your old man. About bloody time. Look at them over there. Anyone would think they were sixteen again.'

Zach looked towards the back of the community hall where his father was seated next to Margie on a hay bale, their hands joined, his father's walking frame proving a rather useful receptacle for Margie's hand-bag as well as a place to put their drinks and a plate of the delicious food Peggy and her team had organised. 'Yeah. I'm happy for him. For both of them.'

'So…' Jim gave Zach a nudge with his elbow. 'What about you and the doc?'

'She's leaving tomorrow.' Zach said it as if the words weren't gnawing a giant hole in his chest. 'Got a new locum position in Brisbane. Starting on Monday.'

'Brisbane's not so far away. Maybe you could—'

'What would be the point?' Zach said. 'She's going back to England in July. It's where she belongs. Excuse me.' He gave Jim a dismissive look. 'I'm going to get something to drink.'

Izzy saw Zach standing to the left of the entrance of the community centre with a can of lemonade in his hand. He had his cop face on, acknowledging the locals who greeted him with a stiff movement of his lips as if it physically pained him to crack a full smile. She knew events like these were often quite stressful for country police officers. There were always a couple of locals who liked to drink a little too much and things could turn from a fun-loving party into an out of control mêlée in less time than it took to shake a cocktail. Friends could become enemies in a matter of minutes and the cop on duty had to be ready to control things and keep order.

Izzy had spent a few hours last night with Zach but the topic of her leaving had been carefully skirted around. She'd told him she was looking forward to the Brisbane locum but even as she'd said the words she'd felt a sinkhole of sadness open up inside her. It was like her mouth was saying one thing while her heart was saying another. *Feeling* another. But it wasn't like she could tell him how she felt. What woman in her right mind would tell a man she had only known a month that she loved him? He'd think she was mad.

It was a fling. A casual hook-up that had suited both of them. They had both needed to get over their broken engagements. Their short-term relationship had been a healing process, an exercise in closure so now they were both free to move on with their lives.

The trouble was it didn't feel like a fling. It had never felt like a fling.

Izzy went over to him with a plate of savoury nibbles Peggy had thrust in her hand on her way past. 'Having fun over here all by yourself?'

He gave her a dry look. 'You know that word "wall-flower"? I'm more of a wall tree.'

She smiled. 'I'm pretty good on a city nightclub dance floor but out here among the hay bales I'm not sure what might happen.'

'Are you asking me to dance with you?'

Izzy was asking much more than that and wondered if he could see it in her eyes. His expression, however, was much harder to read. He had that invisible wall around him but whether it was because he was on duty or because he was holding back from her for other reasons she couldn't quite tell. 'Not if you don't want to.'

He put his can of lemonade on a nearby trestle table. 'Come on.' He took her hand as the music started. 'One dance then I'm back on duty.'

As soon as his arms went around her Izzy felt as if everyone else in the community centre had faded into the background. It was just Zach and her on the hay-strewn dance floor, their bodies moving as one in a waltz to a poignant country music ballad.

Zach's breath stirred her hair as he turned her round in a manoeuvre that would have got a ten out of ten on a reality dance show. 'You know what happens if you play country music backwards?'

Izzy looked up at him with a quizzical smile. 'No, what?'

'You get your job back, your dead dog comes back to life and your girlfriend stops sleeping with your best mate.'

It was a funny joke and it should have made her laugh out loud but instead she felt like crying. She blinked a couple of times and forced a smile. 'I'm really going to miss Popeye. Do you think I could—?' She looked at his shirt collar instead. 'No, maybe not. I'm not very good at goodbyes.'

'What time do you leave?' The question was as casual as *What do you think of the weather?*

'Early. It's a long drive.' Izzy was still focusing her gaze on his collar but it had become blurry. 'I don't want to rush it.'

'Izzy…' His throat moved up and down as if he had taken a bigger than normal swallow.

She looked into his grey-blue eyes, her heart feeling like it had moved out of her chest and was now beating in her oesophagus. 'Yes?'

His eyes moved back and forth between each of hers as if he was searching for something hidden there. 'Thank you for what you did for my father.'

Izzy wondered if that was what he had really intended to say. There was something about his tone and his manner that didn't seem quite right. 'I didn't do anything.'

He stopped dancing and stood with his arms still

around her, his eyes locked on hers. It was as if he had completely forgotten they were in the middle of the community centre dance floor, with the whole town watching on the sidelines. 'You didn't give up on him.'

Izzy gave him another wry smile. 'I like to give everyone a decent chance.'

He looked about to say something else but the jostling of the other dancers seemed to jolt him back into the present. A shutter came down on his face and he spoke in a flat monotone. 'We're holding up traffic.' He dropped his hands from her and stepped back. 'I'll let you mingle. I'll catch you later.'

'Zach...?' Izzy's voice was so husky it didn't stand a chance over the loud floor-stomping music Bill Davidson had exchanged for the ballad. She watched as Zach walked out of the community centre without even acknowledging Damien Redbank, who spoke to him on the way past.

It was another hour before Izzy could get anywhere near Zach again. She got caught up in a progressive barn dance and then a vigorous Scottish dance that left one of the older locals a little short of breath. She had to make sure the man was not having a cardiac arrest before she could go in search of Zach. She found him talking on his mobile out by the tank stand. He acknowledged her with a brief flicker of his lips as he slipped his phone away. 'All danced out?'

Izzy grimaced as she tucked a damp strand of hair behind her ear. 'I've been swung about so energetically I think both my shoulders have popped out of their sockets.'

'The Gay Gordons not your thing, then?' It was difficult to tell if he was smiling or not as his face was now in shadow.

'I loved it. It's the best workout I've had since…well, since last night.'

He stepped out of the cloaking shadow of the community centre but didn't look at her; instead, he was looking out into the sprawling endless darkness beyond town. 'That was my mother on the phone.'

'Does she call you often?'

'Not often.' Izzy heard him scrape the gravel with the toe of his boot. 'That's probably as much my fault as hers.'

'Would you ever consider going over to see her again some time?'

He lifted a shoulder and then let it drop. 'Maybe.'

'Maybe you could look me up if you do.' As soon as she'd said the words she wished she hadn't. They made her sound as if she was content to be nothing more than a booty call. She wanted more. *So much more.*

'What would be the point?'

Izzy rolled her lips together. 'It would be nice to catch up.'

'To do what?' His eyes looked as hard as diamond chips now. 'To pick up where we left off?'

She let out a slow, measured breath. 'I just thought—'

'What did you think, Izzy?' His tone hardened, along with his gaze. 'That I'd ask you to hang around so we could pretend a little longer this is going to last for ever? This was never about for ever. We've had our fun. Now it's time for you to leave as planned.'

Izzy swallowed a knot of pain. 'Is that what you want?'

His expression went back to its fall-back position. Distant. Aloof. Closed off. 'Of course it is.'

'I don't believe you.' She held his strong gaze with indomitable force. 'You're lying. You want me to stay. I know you do. You *want* me, Zach. I feel it in every fibre of my being. How can you stand there and pretend you don't?'

His mouth flattened. 'Don't make this ugly, Izzy.'

'You're the one making it ugly,' she said. 'You're making out that what we've shared has been nothing more than some tawdry little affair. How can you do that?'

A pulse beat like a hammer in his jaw. 'It was good sex. But I can have that with anyone. So can you.'

Izzy looked at him in wounded shock. This was not how things were supposed to be. The flag of hope in her chest was slipping back down the flagpole in despair. It was strangling her. Choking her. He was supposed to tell her he wanted more time with her. That he wanted her to stay. That he loved her. Not tell her she was replaceable.

Somehow she garnered her pride. 'Fine. Let's do it your way, then.' She stuck out her hand. 'Goodbye, Zach.'

He ignored her hand. He stood looking down at her with a stony expression on his face as if everything inside him had turned to marble. He didn't even speak. Not one word. Even the ticking pulse in his jaw had stopped.

Izzy returned her hand to her side. She would not let him see how much she was hurting. She straightened her shoulders and put one foot in front of the other as she walked back to the lights and music of the community centre.

When she got to the door and glanced back he was nowhere to be seen.

'All packed?' Margie asked, her smile sad and her eyes watery, as Izzy was about to head off the next morning.

'All packed.' Izzy had covered the track marks of her tears with the clever use of make-up but she wasn't sure the camouflage was going to last too long. Fresh tears were pricking like needles at the backs of her eyes and her heart felt like it was cracking into pieces. She'd lain awake most of the night, hoping Zach would come to her and tell her he'd made a terrible mistake, that he wanted her to stay, that he loved her with a for-ever love. But he hadn't turned up. He hadn't even sent a text. But that was his way. She had only known him four weeks but she knew that much about him. Once his mind was made up that was it. Over and out. No going back.

Doug shuffled forward to envelop her in a hug. 'Thanks.'

Izzy knew how much emotion was in that one simple word. She felt it vibrating in his body as she hugged him back as if he too was trying not to cry. 'Take care of yourself.'

'Where's Zach?' Margie asked Doug. 'I thought he'd be here to say goodbye.'

Doug's expression showed his frustration. 'I haven't seen him since daylight. Didn't say a word to me other than grunting something about taking Popeye for a walk. Haven't seen him since.'

'But I thought—' Margie began.

'He said all that needed to be said last night,' Izzy said, keeping her expression masked.

'Should've been here to see you off,' Doug said, frowning. 'What's got into him?'

Margie gave him a cautioning look before reaching to hug Izzy. 'I'm going to miss you *so* much.'

'I'll miss you too.'

With one last hug apiece Izzy got into her car and drove out of town. She had to blink to clear her vision as an overwhelming tide of emotion welled up inside her; it felt like she was leaving a part of herself behind.

She was.

Her heart.

Zach skimmed a stone across the surface of Blake's waterhole, watching as it skipped across the water six times before sinking. His record was fourteen skips but he wasn't getting anywhere near that today. He had been out here since dawn, trying to make sense of his feelings after his decision last night to end things with Izzy.

He kept reminding himself it was better this way. A clean cut healed faster than a festering sore.

But it didn't feel better. It felt worse. It hurt to think of Izzy driving away to her next post, finding some other guy to spend the rest of her life with while he tried to get on with his life out here.

He had never been a big believer in love at first sight. He had shied away from it because of what had happened between his parents. They'd married after a whirlwind courtship and his mother had spent the next decade being miserable and taking it out on everyone around her.

He didn't want to do that to Izzy. She hadn't had

enough time to get to know herself outside a relationship. He had no right to ask her to stay. What if she ended up hating him for it after a few weeks, months or years down the track?

He skimmed another stone but it only managed four skips before sinking. It felt like his heart, plummeting to the depths where it would never find the light of day again.

He thought of Izzy's smile, the way it lit up her face, the way it had beamed upon the dark sadness he had buried inside himself all those years ago. Would anyone else make him feel that spreading warmth inside his chest? Would anyone else make him feel alive and hopeful in spite of all the sickness and depravity of humanity he had to deal with in his work?

Izzy was not just a ray of sunshine.

She was *his* light.

He'd wanted to tell her last night. He'd *ached* to tell her. The words had been there but he'd kept swallowing them back down with common sense.

She was young and idealistic, full of romantic notions that didn't always play out in the real world. He was cynical and older in years, not to mention experience.

How could they make it work? How did any relationship work? *Could* they make theirs work?

How could he let her leave without telling her what he felt about her? If she didn't feel the same, he would have to bear that. At least he would be honest with her. He owed her that.

He owed himself that.

Zach drove out to the highway with Popeye on the seat beside him. 'I can't believe I'm doing this.' Popeye gave an excited yap. 'I mean it's crazy. I never do things like this. We've only known each other a month. It's not like she said she loved me. Not outright. What if I've got this wrong? What if she says no?' His fingers gripped the steering-wheel so tightly he was reminded of his grip on the veranda rail all those years ago.

What would have happened if he'd called out to his mother that day? Would it have changed anything? If nothing else, at least it would have assured his mother he loved her, even if she'd still felt the need to leave. He had never told his mother he loved her. Not since he was a little kid. That was something he would have to fix.

But not right now.

Miraculously, he suddenly saw Izzy's car ahead. He forced himself to slow down and watched her for a while, mentally rehearsing what he was going to say. He wasn't good at expressing emotion. He had spent his childhood locking away what he'd felt. His job had reinforced that pattern, demanding he kept his emotions under control at all times and in all places. What if he couldn't say what he wanted to say? Should he just blurt it out or lead in to it? His stomach was in knots. His heart felt as if it was in danger of splitting right down the middle.

He loved her.

He *really* loved her.

Not the pedestrian feelings he'd felt for Naomi.

His love for Izzy was a once-in-a-lifetime love. An all-or-nothing love.

A grand passion.

A for-ever love.

He suddenly realised her car was gathering speed. He checked his radar monitor. She was going twenty kilometres per hour over the limit! Acting on autopilot, he reached for his siren and lights switch, all the bells and whistles blaring as he put his foot down on the throttle.

Izzy was reaching for another tissue when she heard a police siren behind her. She glanced in the rear-view mirror, her heart flipping like a pancake flung by a master chef when she saw Zach behind the wheel, bearing down on her. She put her foot on the brake and pulled over to the gravel verge, trying to wipe the smeared mascara away from beneath her eyes. If he wanted a cold, clean break then that's what she would give him. Cold and clinical.

His tall, commanding figure appeared at her driver's window. The rim of his police hat shadowed his eyes and his voice was all business. 'Want to tell me why you were going twenty over the limit?'

She pressed her lips together. So that was going to be his parting gift, was it? *A speeding ticket!* 'I'm sorry, Officer, but I was reaching for a tissue.'

'Why are you crying?'

'I'm *not* crying.'

'Get out of the car.'

Izzy glowered at him. 'What *is* this?'

'I said get out of the car.'

She blew her cheeks out on a breath and stepped out, throwing him a defiant look. 'See? I'm not crying.'

His gaze held hers with his inscrutable one. 'Either you've been crying or you put your make-up on in the dark.'

Izzy put her hands on her hips and stared him down. 'Is it a crime to feel a little sad about leaving a town

I've grown to love? Is it, Sergeant show-no-emotion Fletcher? If so, go ahead and book me.'

A tiny glint came into his eyes. 'You love Jerringa Ridge?'

She folded her arms across her chest, still keeping her defiant glare in place. 'Yes.'

'What do you love about it?'

She was starting to feel a flutter of hope inside her chest, like a butterfly coming out of a chrysalis. 'I love the way it made me feel like I was the most beautiful person in the world. I love the way it made me feel passion I've never felt before. I love the way it opened its arms to me and held me close and made me feel safe.'

'That all?'

'That about covers it.'

He gave a slow nod. 'So...Brisbane, huh?'

She kept her chin up. 'Yes.'

He took off his hat and put it on the roof of her car, his movements slow, measured. 'You looking forward to that?'

'Not particularly.'

'Why not?'

Izzy looked into his now twinkling eyes. 'Because I'd much rather be here with you.'

He put his arms around her then, holding her so tightly against him she felt every button on his shirt pressing into her skin. 'I love you,' he said. 'I should've told you last night. I almost did...but I didn't want to put any pressure on you to stay. A public proposal seemed... I don't know...kind of tacky. Kind of manipulative.'

She looked up into his face with a wide-eyed look. 'A proposal?'

His expression was suddenly serious again. 'Izzy,

darling, I know we've only known each other a month. I know you have a life back in England, family and friends and roots that go deep. I would never ask you to give any of that up. All I'm asking is for you to give us a chance. We can make our home wherever you want to be. I can employ a manager for Fletcher Downs. Dad and Margie will be able to keep an eye on things. We can have the best of both worlds.' He cupped her face in his hands. '*You* are my world, darling girl. Marry me?'

Izzy smiled the widest smile she had ever smiled. 'Yes.'

He looked shocked. Taken aback. '*Yes?*'

'Yes, Zach.' She gave a little laugh at his expression. 'I will marry you. Why are you looking so surprised?'

'Because I didn't think it was possible to find someone like you.' He stroked her hair back from her face, his expression tender. 'Someone who would make me feel like this. I didn't know it could happen so fast and so completely. I want to spend the rest of my life with you. I think a part of me realised that the first time we kissed. It scared the hell out of me, to tell you the truth.'

'I felt that way too,' Izzy said. 'I was so miserable last night. I couldn't believe you were just going to leave it at that after all we'd shared. Our relationship was supposed to be a fling but nothing about it felt like a fling to me.'

He hugged her tightly again. 'I was trying to do the right thing by you by letting you go. But I couldn't believe how the right thing felt so incredibly painful. I decided I had to tell you how I felt, otherwise I'd spend the rest of my life regretting it.'

Her eyes twinkled as she looked up to hold his gaze. 'Promise me something?'

'Anything.'

'No five-star destinations for our honeymoon, OK?'

His eyes glinted again. 'You want to go camping?'

'Yes, and I want to swim naked and make love under the stars.' She hugged him close. 'I don't even mind if Max comes along as long as he has his own tent.'

'No way, baby girl,' Zach said. 'Max will have to find another place to stay while we're on our honeymoon. I'm not sharing you with anyone. Where is he, by the way?'

She gave him a sheepish look. 'He's in the boot. He wasn't too happy about being stashed in there but your dad and Margie came to say goodbye and I didn't have time to let him down properly.'

Zach grinned at her and pulled her close again. 'Maybe if I kiss you right now I won't think I'm dreaming this is happening. What do you reckon?'

She smiled as his mouth came down towards hers. 'I think that's an excellent idea.'

* * * * *